War

THE
MAHARAJAH'S
GENERAL

By Paul Fraser Collard

The Scarlet Thief
The Maharajah's General

Paul Fraser Collard

THE MAHARAJAH'S GENERAL

headline

First published in Great Britain in 2013 by
HEADLINE PUBLISHING GROUP

1

Cataloguing in Publication Data is available from the British Library

ISBN 978 1 4722 0027 3 (Hardback)
ISBN 978 1 4722 0029 7 (Trade Paperback)

Typeset in Sabon by Avon DataSet Ltd, Bidford-on-Avon, Warwickshire

Printed and bound in Great Britain by Clays Ltd, St Ives plc

Headline's policy is to use papers that are natural, renewable and
recyclable products and made from wood grown in sustainable
forests. The logging and manufacturing processes are expected
to conform to the environmental regulations of the country of origin.

HEADLINE PUBLISHING GROUP
An Hachette UK Company
338 Euston Road
London NW1 3BH

www.headline.co.uk
www.hachette.co.uk

To Mum and Dad

Glossary

———◦●◦———

bandook	slang for a rifle or musket
caravanserai	travellers' resting place
Chillianwala	Battle of Chillianwala, 13 January 1849
chummery	officers living together sharing living expenses
dacoit	bandit/thief
dak gharry	post cart/small carriage pulled by horses
doli	covered litter, sedan chair
durbar	royal court, public audience held by a native ruler
fakeer (fakir)	monk, holy man
firangi	derogatory term for a European
havildar	native sergeant
howdah	a covered seat usually with a canopy and railings positioned on the back of an elephant
huzoor	sir, lord
ikrarnama	written bond of allegiance to the British Crown
jezzail (jezail)	type of native flintlock rifle
khansama	housekeeper/steward
khoob! khoob!	fine! fine!
khus-khus tatties	grass screens used to cover windows

kurta	long shirt or tunic
langoti	loincloth
maidan	open space in or near a town
nabob	corruption of 'nawab' (Muslim term for senior official or governor), used by the British to describe wealthy European merchants or retired officials who had made their fortune in India
nautch girl	dancing girl
palki (palanquin)	box-litter for travelling in, carried by servants
pandit (pundit)	Hindu scholar, teacher
pagdi	turban, cloth or scarf wrapped around a hat
pankha-wala	servant operating a large cooling fan
prantara-durga	a fortress built on the summit of a hill or mountain
rajkumar	Son of the Maharajah
rajkumari	Daughter of the Maharajah
rissaldar	native cavalry officer equivalent to a captain
sahib	master, lord, sir
sarkar (sirkar)	Persian term for government – used to mean the British
sepoy	native soldier serving in the East India Company's army
shikari	lead hunter
Stoczek	Battle of Stoczek, 14 February 1830
syce	groom
subedar	native infantry officer equivalent to a captain
talwar	curved native sword, similar to 1796 light cavalry sabre
thug	follower of a religious sect, renowned for carrying out ritualistic murders (thuggee)
tiffin	light meal or snack served at lunchtime

Chapter One

———◆●◆———

The British officer gripped the window frame tightly as the dak gharry lurched and scrabbled its way closer to the city of Bhundapur. He held fast until the wild pitching ceased, the action instinctive after so long incarcerated in a seemingly never-ending procession of carriages, palkis and dolis. His exhausting journey had taken weeks, and now, as he finally neared his destination, the officer felt the stirring of unease deep in his gut.

He tugged nervously on the hem of his scarlet shell jacket with the green facings of his new regiment before running his hand over his unfashionably short hair. He had dressed at the caravanserai where he had spent the night. Unlike so many of the British officers he eschewed any form of facial hair and that morning he had shaved closely, meticulous in his preparation, the ritual of preparing for the day ahead deeply ingrained. Now he was anxious that he looked travel-worn and unkempt, so he brushed at his uniform, doing his best to straighten out the inevitable creases and remove the most obvious specks of dirt.

He was reaching the end of the last leg of a journey that had started far away on the Crimean peninsula. Months of travel had led to this moment, to the last hours before he caught up with his fate. He patted the pocket of his scarlet coat, checking for the umpteenth time that his documents were still in place. They had brought him this far. The next few hours would tell if they would see him safely ensconced in his new home and in his place as a commissioned officer in one Her Majesty's regiments.

The precious papers, now creased and worn, named the officer as Captain James Danbury of Her Majesty's 24th Regiment of Foot. A captain was a man of station and importance. One who would be expected to take his place in the British establishment that ruled a land so far from home.

The 24th's newest officer sat back amidst the cushions and pillows of the dak and thought on what he knew of his new command. The 24th was a regular army regiment. It was stationed in India to bolster the forces of the East India Company, the mercantile company that administered and ruled the country in the name of the Queen. The East India Company ostensibly borrowed, and paid for, the regular troops who were spread amongst the three presidencies into which the country was divided.

Each presidency boasted its own army. The bulk of each force was made up of native infantry regiments composed of locally recruited soldiers, led by British officers. Alongside these native regiments were a number of European infantry battalions, whose ranks were filled by British and Irish recruits. The officers of both held commissions granted by the East India Company, rather than by the Queen. It led to a social distinction between the Queen's officers in the regular army regiments, and those only holding a commission granted by the EIC. The officer had only been in the country for a few short weeks, but already he had learnt that snobbery was rife, the intricate layers of society guarded with a diligence and a jealousy that would shock even the snootiest London matriarch.

The man possessing the papers of Captain Danbury would take his place in the 24th's hierarchy, assuming command of a company of redcoats. It was a precious responsibility, but not one with which he was unfamiliar. He had commanded a company in the Crimea, at the tumultuous battle at the Alma River. There he had learnt what it truly meant to lead men, the responsibility that came with the shiny gold buttons and being called 'sir'. Being an officer was a position that few deserved and even fewer earned. Yet the man in the dak gharry had travelled thousands of miles for the opportunity to once again command the men so cruelly titled 'the scum of the earth', risking his life for the sake of a tattered parchment and the power it ordained. For Captain James Danbury was dead. His name, identity and uniform now belonged to Jack Lark, an impostor, who sat in the lurching dak gharry, his guts screwed tight with tension as he anxiously waited to discover if his newest identity would pass muster, or if he was simply being transported to denunciation and a cold, lonely dawn on the scaffold.

Jack cursed as the dak lurched, forcing him to grab at the seat opposite to avoid being thrown into an undignified heap on the floor. As he recovered his poise, he saw a small, dark-faced child capering in the scrubby field beside the road, clearly entranced by an imaginary game. Jack smiled as he watched the boy at play, envying him his freedom.

He looked past the boy, his attention taken by a forbidding tower on the skyline. It dominated the small village that clustered around its skirts, casting a long shadow across the sorry collection of drab mud and thatch houses. The tower was battered, a relic of a distant past. Yet there was a dignity to it, a grace that belied the pockmarked walls and broken stone. It had endured through the centuries, its lonely vigil immune to the machinations of men. It was a symbol of what had been, and Jack shivered as an uneasy chill ran down his spine. He hid his own past away, refusing to dwell on the dark memories that lurked in the corners of his mind, and forced himself to think of what was to come. He had journeyed far, chasing a future that was not his own. He was fast approaching the time when he would confront it and discover his fate.

Sujan saw the tiger, yet he felt no fear. The huge beast crept through the thick grass and would have passed by unnoticed were it not for the warrior who guarded his family's goats so diligently.

Only the bravest could take up their spear and move silently towards the mighty hunter, whose power terrified lesser men, men who would run screaming in fear at the merest glimpse of his shadow. Sujan hefted his weapon, feeling the balance in its beautifully crafted shaft. The weight was reassuring in his hand, and his fingers curled around the lovingly polished wood, his fingertips caressing the intricate carvings that had taken the best craftsmen in the village days of toil to create. Slowly, patiently, he eased his way to where the huge animal had stopped, its mouth open as it tasted the air. He took no chances as he manoeuvred stealthily to free up a clean shot for his spear, taking his time, his eyes never leaving his target.

Then the tiger saw him, and roared.

A weaker man would have fled, his precious goats left for the beast to devour. Yet Sujan rose fearlessly from his haunches, his muscles stretched tight as he pulled back his arm. With every ounce of his strength he flung his spear at the huge animal, an involuntary grunt forced from his lips. Driven by a skill only the mightiest of warriors possessed, the spear exploded through the grasses, the razor-sharp tip at its point tearing through the tiger's powerful body, embedding itself in the animal's heart, killing the fearful beast in an instant.

Seeing his foe struck down, Sujan leapt to his feet, his arms flung wide in celebration, his face creased in a triumphant scowl, his voice screeching in delight. The high-pitched wail scared an ancient vulture into reluctant flight from where it had watched the contest from a nearby rock, the sudden movement silencing the hero's wild roars of victory.

Sujan walked forward, bending low to retrieve the thin, splintered stick, the only weapon his grandfather trusted him with to guard the ten flea-bitten goats in the family herd. With his hand scratching busily under his langoti, Sujan turned his back on the boulder he had slain. The fearsome tiger was nothing more dangerous than a moss-covered rock that had taken the small boy's fancy as he idled away the long afternoon waiting for his grandfather to appear to help him drive the meagre herd back to their home on the far side of the village. At seven, Sujan was left alone for most of the day with just the sinewy goats for company and his eager imagination for enter-tainment.

The small boy pulled aside his loincloth, carelessly emptying his bladder into a thorny bush as he tried to conjure up another game to while away the lonely tedium of another hour. He looked around sharply as he heard the sound of a dak, his thin stream of urine meandering across the dusty soil as he turned.

His face twisted with hatred as he saw the dak gharry bouncing its way along the trunk road to Bhundapur. He caught a glimpse of a white face staring in his direction – another firangi officer on his way to join the foreigners' camp outside the city. The officer lifted a hand in greeting, his cold grey stare disconcerting even from a distance.

Sujan turned away, spitting into the dust, just as his grandfather did whenever he talked of the pale firangi who had come from the cold lands to rule over them. Sujan did not understand why men like his grandfather had allowed the foreigners to take control of their country, but he had learnt not to ask. He was cuffed around the head too often enough already. At least the white men and their fat women were good for the village. They came in small parties to stare at the tower, the loud, red-faced men and their shrieking, brazen woman gazing in wonder at the place where the villagers had taken the bodies of their dead relatives since time immemorial. The firangi were easy prey for the sharp-minded locals, who charged an extortionate fee for their meagre offering of hospitality and grew fat on the money. No other village in the valley could hope to match their wealth.

Sujan finished pissing and went back to his goats, yelling at one that was drifting too far on its tireless quest to find food. He looked at the sky and saw that it would be hours yet until his grandfather returned, so he closed his eyes and tried to conjure the image of a wandering vagabond, an interesting challenge for the warrior who was charged with defending his family's precious herd.

He opened his eyes as he heard the sound of movement. He expected to see another dak on its long journey to the British cantonment at Bhundapur, but his eyes widened in horror as instead he saw his imagination given life, though he had never conceived of a horde such as the one that had appeared over the crest of the ridge to the south of the village. Forgetting his goats and the duty his grandfather had beaten into him since he had first learnt to walk, the boy ran.

For the wild men had come down from the hills. The bandits, the dacoits and the thugs. The landless men. The bitter and the disappointed. The unloved and the unwanted.

They came in a mob, a wave of hatred that washed across the dusty ground, smothering the sun-bleached soil with fear. The villagers watched in horror as the end of their precious existence arrived, their wealth and pride the bait that had lured the monster from out of the darkness. The silent tower now set to bear witness to the bandits' desire for vengeance on those who had condemned them to the bitter life of the banished.

They were led by the one they called the Tiger. Some said he was not a man at all, but a god, or a prince of the darkness that shrouded the godless. No mortal man could stand against him. Those that tried were killed. Struck down by his merciless hand or by his word, a curse from the lips of the Tiger certain to bring only lingering agony followed by death.

Yet men flocked to his banner, intent on theft, on rape and on revenge on the world that had forgotten them. The Tiger offered them all a home. A sanctuary. Uniting them in hatred against the Maharajah of Sawadh, who had condemned them to their loveless fate and who ruled their land with an iron rod. Men found guilty of any crime were sentenced to mutilation, death or banishment, the living death that was so much more painful than a swift beheading or precise strangulation.

Now the Maharajah had learnt of their band. He had pledged their annihilation, his honour stained by their very being. So the bandits lived a life of fear, always moving on, never staying in one place for too long as they tried to outrun the retribution that was sure to find them. The village and its precious tower would offer them rich pickings, providing food and shelter for a week, perhaps two. They would strip it bare, using its people and feeding on its abundant supplies before they moved on to the next place. They did not fear the tower or its white-robed priests. The Tiger and his men had long left behind the superstitious world of religion and its many and various gods.

Their souls were already lost, and they swept through the village like a plague.

Chapter Two

———•◆•———

'Captain Danbury, what a delightful surprise.'

Jack Lark did his best to look composed as he was led into the office of his new commanding officer. He nodded his thanks to the khansama who had ushered him into the spacious room. The shuffling figure bowed obsequiously, his hand fluttering across his face, his discomfort at being thanked obvious.

'No need to thank the damn steward. You quite made his day by not cuffing him around the ears.' The officer seated behind the monstrous mahogany desk rose to his feet, his wide-backed chair scraping noisily across the highly polished wooden floor.

'Proudfoot.' He thrust his hand forward forcefully.

'Danbury.' Jack did his best to hide his amusement at the curt introduction, giving his assumed name with as much confidence as he could summon. He took the hand offered to him, shaking it firmly whilst wondering at the strange figure welcoming him to his new post.

Proudfoot was close to a foot shorter than Jack. Behind the bushy beard and thick moustache his face bore the evidence of a long time spent in the East, a craggy network of creases, folds and wrinkles that made him appear older than his forty-one years.

Yet it was not his premature age alone that made him fascinating. Jack studied with growing amusement the strange attire his new commander wore, the contrast to his own regimental uniform stark. Proudfoot chose to dress as a nabob, with a flowing, richly decorated tunic over baggy pantaloons. A fine web of coloured thread spread over the cream linen, creating intricate patterns that rippled and moved as he returned to his seat behind the slab of mahogany that was more comparable to a dining table than the humble working desk of an official in the East India Company.

A slight grimace of distaste on his face made it clear he had noticed the wry scrutiny of his choice of clothes.

'Take a seat.' Proudfoot indicated a fine leather chair opposite his own. He followed the invitation by bellowing at the pankha-wala, a young boy of no more than ten who sat in the corner of the room, pulling on a thick cord that moved the large sail attached to the ceiling back and forth, wafting a gentle breeze down on to the official and his guest. Chastened by his master's rebuke, the boy bent his head so that his forehead was an inch away from the floor, whilst his wiry arms increased the tempo of the fan's motion.

'Now, to business.' Proudfoot gathered up the documents he had been working on and shuffled them into an ordered pile before placing them neatly to one side. He took a moment to line them up so they were perfectly perpendicular to a small stack of similar thick cream papers waiting for his attention. 'So, Danbury. Why aren't you dead?'

The question was delivered deadpan, without a trace of humour or warmth.

Jack's face remained collected while he thought about the odd question, even though his heart was racing ten to the dozen as he felt the strings of his new life unravelling before it had even begun. 'Would you care to explain that remark, sir?'

'What I mean, my dear fellow,' Proudfoot smiled, but with little evidence of good humour, 'is that I received a letter just a few days ago regretfully informing me that the recent purchaser of the vacant commission in the 24th had died in the Crimea, and that I was to expect notice of a new purchaser within the month. You are meant to be dead, Danbury. Quite dead.'

'I'm sorry to disappoint you, sir, but as you can see, I'm very much alive.'

'Indeed. So I see. The paperwork will be quite incorrect now, damn it,' Proudfoot cursed, his irritation obvious. 'Well, I suppose it cannot be helped. I shall be forced to write a letter to the Governor's office to let them know of the change of circumstances. It really would've been simpler if you were dead.'

Jack smiled. 'Not for me.'

Proudfoot stared hard, his eyes searching Jack's face for a sign of insubordination. He scowled, clearly displeased with whatever he saw there, then turned his attention to his steel pen, fastidiously wiping clean the nib, meticulously removing every vestige of ink. When he was quite satisfied, he placed the pen on the top of the closest pile of documents, his hand immediately returning to it to fussily ensure that it was lined up at right angles to the top of the papers.

'Welcome.' Proudfoot delivered the belated greeting with gusto, as if he had resolved to start the conversation afresh and put Jack's inconvenient health to one side. 'Welcome to Bhundapur.'

'Thank you. I'm pleased to be here at last. It has been a long journey.' Jack hid his relief. He felt his unease begin to fade. It was unsettling to hear that Proudfoot had not been expecting Danbury's arrival, but he had a feeling the wheels of government would run slowly on the frontier of the Empire. He could only hope that Proudfoot's letter would create enough confusion to make sure he was safe, for the time being at least. Once settled at Bhundapur, he could do his best to make sure that confusion continued, and hope that no one would look to find a replacement for an officer who had already arrived.

'Indeed. We are glad to have you with us.' Proudfoot eased back in his chair, more comfortable now the conversation had turned towards less irregular matters. 'We are a small band but we all rub along quite nicely. As I'm sure you are aware, I'm the only political officer here. I report directly to the Governor, but other than that, I am pretty much left to my own devices.' He shrugged his shoulders in a theatrical gesture of modesty, before shaking his head as if unable to comprehend quite how he managed to cope with such a challenging remit. 'When you think that this area is the size of half a dozen English counties put together, you will begin to understand the task at hand. As you will know, I run the affairs of the Company in Sawadh. I am the commander of all the forces here, both military and police. I am both magistrate and superintendent of law and I am even in charge of the jail itself. I run the treasury and am responsible for all our accounts whilst also being both the assessor and collector of taxes. For all public works I am executive engineer as well as superintendent. I am postmaster, commissioner of the ordinance and I even supervise the mule train and the company bullocks. In short, Danbury, I am king, general, judge and jury.'

Jack did his best to seem impressed. 'It sounds interesting.'

Proudfoot's face creased into a frown at the mild response. He shook his head again before resolving to carry on. 'Let me show you the lie of the land.' He disappeared momentarily from view as he rummaged in the bottom right-hand drawer of his enormous desk. When he re-emerged, he unrolled a creased and well-used map covered with a network of pencilled comments and a web of different-coloured lines and circles.

'Here we are.' He thrust his ink-stained thumb into the dead centre of the unrolled map. 'Just north of the region we know now as the Bundelkhand Agency, an area ruled by a menagerie of misfits and despots until we finally forced them to cede power to us back in '02. We now run the place but we allow most of the damn maharajahs to keep their titles so long as they give us free rein and sign their ikrarnama.' Proudfoot paused as he looked up to check that Jack was paying full attention. He was pleased to see him staring hard at the map, his face creased in concentration.

'We are here in Bhundapur,' Proudfoot continued, 'slap bang in the centre of Sawadh. To the north is Oudh, the only other state that is still nominally independent. Over here to the west is Jhansi, the biggest of the local states, with a bitch of a rani called Lakshmibai on the throne. We have at least been able to annex the damn place, and it now falls under the control of the Central India Agency, which also runs the states in the Bundelkhand. The old rajah died without an heir, so we were able to apply Lord Dalhousie's doctrine, taking the place properly under British rule. It is so much simpler that way, although allowing the rani stay on is a mistake in my opinion. The little strumpet is bound to cause trouble sooner or later. I have written to the Governor, but for the moment that is how things stand. Otherwise I find myself very much in agreement with Dalhousie's policy. The management of the country will be safer and more efficient if we can reduce the number of these damn feudal states by annexing as many as we can. Do you agree, Danbury?'

Jack was beginning to feel out of his depth. He had learnt a little of the politics of the country during his journey, but there were still wide gaps in his knowledge. He would have to learn fast. 'I believe we must do what we can to improve the lot of the poorer classes, sir. I would say that is our duty, and if annexation allows us to achieve it, then I believe that is the path we must follow. I understand these maharajahs are a whimsical bunch. Under their rule the people have no protection, and that cannot be a happy state of affairs.'

'Whimsical!' Proudfoot found Jack's choice of word amusing. 'I have never known a more decadent, lazy, conceited and callow collection of creatures than these maharajahs. We must take them all firmly under our control. We have already been successful by annexing Jhansi, Satara and Nagpur, and I see no reason why we should not do the same here.' He sat back in his chair. 'Have you heard much of the Maharajah of Sawadh?'

'Only a little. I understand that he rules here under your supervision as resident.'

'Well, you are correct on that point.' Proudfoot smiled in recognition of his own status before his face quickly creased into another scowl. 'Sawadh became one of our princely states after the fall of the last of the Marathas. The previous Maharajah saw sense and signed his treaty with barely a quibble when he saw what happened to anyone foolish enough to stand against us. The agreement allows his family to continue to rule here, but under my supervision. I won't bore you with the details, but in short it allows us to make a great deal of money through loans from the Maharajah to our treasury, and by charging for the presence of our forces here.'

Jack did not have to feign his interest. The complicated network of treaties, agencies, annexation and agents was still foreign to him and he was keen to learn more. 'So it sounds like we have what we want here?'

'Not at all!' Proudfoot revealed what he thought of Jack's naïve observation with a theatrical wave of his hand. 'We do well enough financially, but we lack full control. Added to that, the Maharajah is a damn pest. Not that I'm granted more than a moment in the great man's presence. Never more than once a month anyway, and that's only if he leaves his citadel out in the middle of nowhere and actually deigns to come to Bhundapur. When we do meet, he nods and smiles and says all the right things. Yet he is constantly pushing against my authority, making appointments without my approval, building up the defences at that palace of his or sending his army here, there and yonder without my permission. The damned man is a thorn in my side.'

'So what are you going to do about it?'

'A good question, Danbury.' For the first time Proudfoot smiled with genuine warmth. 'I rather think Dalhousie's doctrine can also be applied here. That will make things,' he paused before smiling wolfishly, 'neater.'

'Does the Maharajah have no heir? I rather thought that was a requirement for us to be able to annex a state upon the death of its ruler.' Jack was doing his best to show what little he knew of the doctrine named after Lord Dalhousie, the governor general who had first introduced it. He had listened carefully to the conversations of the other officers on the steamship that had brought him to Calcutta. If he recalled correctly, Dalhousie had decreed that when a ruler died without an heir, his state would be annexed and placed under direct British rule. It was a controversial policy that ignored the tradition of childless rulers adopting an heir. But men like Proudfoot and Dalhousie were not ones to let such a trivial matter stand in the way of ensuring the efficient government of the country.

'Oh, he claims to have an heir.' Proudfoot flapped his hand to wave away Jack's observation. 'These princes breed like damn rabbits, whelping brats on any of the thousand harlots they have at their command. But I cannot believe for one moment that he is legitimate. The Maharajah knows the rules as well as anyone. He has concocted a cock-and-bull story about his wife dying in childbirth, which is all very tragic I am sure, but that doesn't mean I have to believe it. He would be a fool not to claim some bastard as his heir and ensure the line of succession. But he did not count on dealing with someone like me. I shall not be fooled!'

Jack scowled. 'That would seem a little harsh, sir. What if this boy truly is the Maharajah's son?'

'Well, what of it! I am not here to mollycoddle some brat just because a damn fool tells me to. It will be neater for us all if the state of Sawadh is annexed. Then it too can fall under the control of the Bundelkhand Agency and this circus can end. The Crown will rule here unfettered, Danbury. It really is better for us all.'

'So we are intent on the annexation?'

'Of course.'

'No matter if we have a legitimate right to do so or not.'

'I understand, Danbury. I am an Englishman too. But this isn't some damn game of cricket. We have to leave our sense of fair play back at home.' Proudfoot looked suitably grave, as if the notion of unsportsmanlike conduct caused him pain. 'They don't play by the rules out here and so neither can we. If we turn our backs for an instant then we leave ourselves open to revolt and anarchy. I will not allow that.'

'I understand, sir.' Jack did his best to keep his voice level, hiding his true feelings.

'Good fellow. It takes a while to become acclimatised to our ways out here on the frontier of the Empire. It is not the simple soldiering you have been used to. It requires a more subtle understanding of the people.'

'I'm sure it does.' Jack's expression was neutral, but there was a trace of scorn in his tone. It was not lost on Proudfoot.

'These things are rarely straightforward, Danbury. It's something you must learn to accept if you are to prosper here. The locals outnumber us by thousands to our every one. We must be strong in our purpose. If they sense we are weak, then we are doomed. To maintain order, all I have is a company of the 24th, supported by three companies of the 12th Bengal Native Infantry, both stationed here in Bhundapur, and a single squadron of the 1st Bengal Cavalry over at Fort St John, a day's ride from here. Barely five hundred men when the damn Maharajah has an army at least twenty times the size. Your men are the only British troops for hundreds of miles and I rely on them to be the backbone of my forces. Lieutenant Fenris has been running things in your absence, and I commend him to you. He is a fine officer and I expect you will be gratified to have him.'

'I look forward to making up my own mind on that count.'

Proudfoot looked up sharply. He opened his mouth as if about to disagree before thinking better of it, contenting himself with a gentle shake of his head at his new subordinate's belligerence.

'Major Dutton commands our contingent from the 12th. He has fashioned them into a fine body of men. Although I expect you'll wish to make your own mind up about that too.' Proudfoot sneered, enjoying his own barbed rebuke.

Jack smiled, unconcerned by the comment. 'Indeed. I look forward to being able to inspect them.'

Proudfoot puffed his cheeks out. 'That is not quite what I meant. Look here, Danbury. I am very aware that many Queen's officers look down on those commissioned by the Company, but I will not tolerate such arrogance here. We are united in our purpose and I will not allow any prejudice to divert us.'

'You are quite right, sir. I merely meant that I am keenly anticipating having the opportunity to see the 12th in the flesh.' Jack's reply was polite, but there was little indication of apology in his expression.

'Well, I suspect you'll get that opportunity shortly. I am sure we will all be very gratified to have the opinion of an experienced soldier.' Proudfoot's voice was icy. 'Did you see any action in the Crimea?'

'A little.' A shiver ran down Jack's spine as he involuntarily recalled the storming of the great redoubt on the slopes overlooking the Alma River. The Russian gunners had mercilessly shredded the redcoats' ranks, in a desperate bid to turn back the tide of men that marched so steadily towards them. The redcoats had ignored their fearsome casualties, advancing though the dreadful fire to take the redoubt. Jack had been in the front rank of the assault.

'Good fellow.' Proudfoot nodded his approval. 'We need men of action here. Men who are not frightened of taking the opportunities presented to them. Men like us, Danbury. Men like us.'

He had leant forward as he had spoken, his passion obvious. Now he eased back in his chair as if the discussion had been exhausting.

'Well, I am very pleased to find we are to have an experienced soldier with us. I sincerely hope we will not have need of your particular skills, but I shall not shrink from a fight if one is forced upon me. Now we must look to get you settled in. I think it will help you if you share a bungalow with Fenris at the start. He has more than enough space. You can form a chummery until you get settled.'

Proudfoot plucked a small silver bell from the corner of his desk, ringing it with a single casual flick of the wrist. The door to the office was whipped open before the gentle sound had quite finished, the official's khansama marching smartly into the room and snapping to attention.

'Show Captain Danbury to Lieutenant Fenris' bungalow.'

The two officers got to their feet and Proudfoot walked quickly around the desk to shake Danbury by the hand, signalling the close of their meeting.

'I shall send my steward to collect you for dinner.' Proudfoot smiled, once more showing real warmth. 'It is good you are here, Danbury. I have a feeling you will fit in nicely. We have need of men of good breeding and experience.'

Jack returned the smile, the irony of Proudfoot's words amusing. He might have had as much right to be there as a maharajah's bastard had to claim a throne, but he was determined to make good his ambition and once again secure the life he craved. He had to, no matter what difficulties he faced. He had nothing else.

Chapter Three

⸺•⬥•⸺

*J*ack sat alone in the darkened room his eyes closed as he savoured the peace of solitude, his body enjoying the cool air that filtered through the wetted grass screens that covered the windows. His heavy scarlet uniform coat lay discarded on the simple iron bedstead that took up most of the space in the bungalow's single guest room to which he had been shown. He had arrived after the hour for tiffin, and so, much to his relief, the bungalow's other occupant, Lieutenant Fenris, was with his men, carrying out his afternoon duties now that luncheon, and the worst of the day's heat, was out of the way. With the cantonment's other officers and civilian officials working until late in the afternoon, Jack would be spared the strain of the necessary introductions until later. Proudfoot's dinner loomed large on the immediate horizon, yet for the moment, at least, he could shed the outer shell of the Queen's officer, revealing the man who dwelt beneath its protective folds.

It was only at moments such as this that he allowed his thoughts to venture into the recesses of his mind that he kept closed off and secured when in company. He had been not lying when he told Major Proudfoot that it had been a long journey to Bhundapur, but the official could not begin to imagine just how far he had come. His journey had begun in a hospital in Scutari. It was a hellish place, a disgrace that the British people were only just now becoming aware of, thanks to the candid eyewitness accounts arriving from William Russell of *The Times*. The newspapers Jack had been able to buy in Calcutta were full of Russell's reports, shocking tales of the suffering being endured by the wounded and sick soldiers left to rot in the fetid and squalid conditions found in the allied hospital.

In such an appalling environment soldiers were dying at a terrifying rate, and there in a quiet back room, James Danbury became one of them, his dreams of a future in India and a new life in the Queen's most striking colony dying with him. His only legacy had been an identity for a man becoming accustomed to a life of loneliness and guilt. For former orderly Jack Lark, Danbury's death had opened a path to a new future, a life as a captain in the 24th Regiment of Foot, an escape from a bitter past.

Jack flapped his hand ineffectually at a fly that was buzzing around his face, and poked into the murkiest corners of his mind, picking at the memories that festered in the darkness. Remembering the past.

He had once been rebuked for his lack of gumption, for failing to seize the opportunities life presented. He had loved the young woman who had delivered the reprimand, but she had died, and he had been left alone and without direction. In the awful hours following her death, Jack had been forced to leave the regiment that had been his home since he had joined the redcoats, as he journeyed to war at the side of his master, Captain Arthur Sloames.

But fate would not let him escape so easily. Sloames sickened and died, leaving Jack alone once more. Abandoned and bereft of any ties, he had embarked on his first charade, becoming the officer he had always dreamt of being; assuming the name and station of Captain Arthur Sloames, the commander of the Light Company in the King's Royal Fusiliers. He had been determined to prove that the product of London's poorest rookeries could be the equal of those born with the money and influence to purchase their rank, their place in society guaranteed by a respectable family and backed by three per cent government stock. He had done it to prove to the girl who had loved him that she not been wrong to choose him.

As Sloames, Jack had led his men into the terrifying cauldron of battle, the vicious fight at the Alma River a proving ground for his ability as an officer. The harsh reality had made a mockery of his naïve aspirations, the carnage of the battle washing away in a cascade of blood and horror any ambition he had once nurtured.

Now, as he sat alone in the bungalow, Jack contemplated his future, seeking a way forward that would allow him to shrug off the shackles of his former life and carry the burden of guilt that had crushed his soul since the Alma.

The setting sun lit the darkening sky with a fabulous display of red and ochre, the day's final, vibrant celebration before the onrushing darkness laid claim to the baked land. The silent streets awoke as the burning heat faded, the inhabitants of the cantonment emerging from their sanctuaries. The town sprang back into life, the bustle and commotion of the early evening breathing life back into the sun-bleached streets.

The British cantonment was separated from the city of Bhundapur by a wide maidan, a broad sweep of ground that kept the adminitrators and enforcers of Her Majesty's will wholly apart from the town over which they held jurisdiction, the cultural divide manifest in half a mile of dusty scrub and parched soil.

Facing the maidan was the row of officers' bungalows. Broadly spaced and immaculate in a coat of bright whitewash, the homes of the leaders of the British forces and the highest-ranked civil appointees enjoyed a breathtaking view over the city. Neatly trimmed hedges and pristine rose gardens provided natural partitions between the houses, the complex web of irrigation channels that fed their gardens snaking backwards like umbilical cords linking the elegant greenery to the series of wells and bullock-powered pumps that drew the precious water from deep underground.

Large dusty parade grounds provided plenty of space to drill the four companies of infantry under Proudfoot's command. A firing ground on the side of the cantonment furthest from the town allowed the red-coated infantry to train away from the prying eyes of the ever-watchful sentries standing guard on the high stone wall that had protected Bhundapur from attack for centuries.

Behind the row of officers' bungalows were the barracks for the British redcoats. Wide, airy rooms with high ceilings and tall windows, surrounded by a broad veranda, allowed the Queen's soldiers to live in comfort, even in the blistering heat. The smaller, darker barracks of the native troops were pushed well to the western edge of the cantonment, the sepoys kept apart even from the lowliest of British redcoats.

The cantonment was an ordered, very English haven for the men stationed in this distant corner of the British Empire. It allowed them to live a life apart from the population they governed, immune to the precarious nature of their situation. For they were surrounded and alone, outnumbered by thousands to their every one, yet they carried on with their lives as if they were in the peaceful English countryside and not close to the wild frontier of the Empire; self-satisfied and complacent even as the storm clouds gathered on the horizon.

Jack tugged hard at the hem of his scarlet jacket, straightening the creases that had formed as he walked the short distance to Major Proudfoot's bungalow. Even in the cooler evening air he was sweating, the cotton handkerchief he had brought with him already sodden from constant wiping across his face. The thick uniform was wholly unsuited to the Indian climate, yet the army made no allowances, so the Queen's officers sweated their way through their duties, their cotton shirts needing to be changed many times a day lest the stench offend the noses of any who ventured near.

Gentle laughter reached Jack's ears, the clink of the cut crystal clearly audible over the constant clicking and calling of the vast multitude of insects that prowled and fluttered through the darkness. He closed his eyes as he tried to summon the willpower to face the company that had assembled to greet the newly arrived officer.

The polite cough of the khansama forced him to open his eyes. Jack smiled as he saw the discreet servant looking back at him. As much as he would wish it differently, it was time to play the part he had chosen. So, like an actor striding from the wings, he nodded to the patient servant and walked towards the gathering with as much determination as he could muster.

* * *

'Danbury! Welcome.' Proudfoot stood at the top of the steps that led up to the porch at the front of his large bungalow. As cordial as his words were, Jack detected a trace of annoyance in his commander's voice, as if he had been waiting with growing impatience for his new captain to belatedly appear.

'Do come in. I have a number of people anxious to meet you.'

The major held out an arm, ushering Jack inside the brightly lit bungalow. Proudfoot had once again eschewed military attire, favouring a close-fitting dinner jacket of the deepest red with an intricate web of gold thread swirling over the breast. A thick white cravat was wrapped tightly around his neck, forcing his chin upwards so that he peered down his nose as Jack strode quickly up the steps and into the light.

'Welcome, Danbury, welcome,' repeated Proudfoot, shaking Jack warmly by the hand, his grip dry and cool despite the heat. He held the handshake and leant forward to speak softly into Jack's ear. 'The regimentals are all well and good in Calcutta, Danbury old man, but out here you really must look to adapt. I'll set you up with my tailor. He's a fine chap, for a local. We'll have you kitted out properly in a jiffy. Now,' he pulled back and smiled, all trace of his former irritation gone, 'let's get on with it, shall we?'

The sea of faces turned in unison as Jack was led into the bungalow's generously proportioned drawing room. With its high ceiling, the room felt airy and cool, an effect enhanced by the tint of green added to the whitewash that had been meticulously applied to the walls. The windows had been covered by the sort of thin wire-mesh screens more usually seen in a butcher's shop back in England, a defence against the multitude of insects drawn by the room's bright lights. Jack was surprised to see no grass tatties at the windows, yet the room felt surprisingly cool, although the air was ripe with the pungent perfume of the few ladies present, the heady aromas vying for dominance with all the vigour of a Russian skirmish line.

A pair of strange contraptions had been built around two of the drawing room's windows; Jack supposed these were a pair of the new-fangled thermantidotes that were all the rage for cooling the air in the more fashionable homes in Calcutta. The clever combination of air funnels, fans and water-soaked screens did not come cheap. Proudfoot was clearly a man of means.

Jack did his best to hide his nerves as he looked around the small congregation, bobbing his head in acknowledgement of the attention directed towards him. Disappointingly, the strangers were just as he had expected. The flushed and rounded faces of the officials, their chins bulging over starched collars that constricted their wide necks and forced their spare chins into thick ribbons of flesh under their jaws. The confident appraisal of the junior officers as they sized up the new arrival and wondered what competition they faced. The guarded eyes of the women as they surreptitiously inspected his lean body, any desire hidden behind a dignified facade of insouciant respectability.

He let himself be led into the throng, his heart beating faster. He knew that the challenge of maintaining his deception would be at its greatest with people born into the world into which he had intruded. He had declined the invitations he had received whilst waiting for his transport to be arranged for precisely that reason, unwilling to test his ability to carry off his assumed identity, even in the transient society of Calcutta. Now that he was in Bhundapur, such situations could not be avoided, and he did his best to look composed even as his bowels twisted with apprehension. He might be able to convince officers on campaign, or passengers on a Peninsular and Oriental steamer, that he knew what he was about, but this was the first time he had encountered such a social gathering. He would rather face a column of Russian infantry than converse with a middle-aged spinster, who would seize upon any lack of social grace with relish. A drawing room of ageing Englishmen and women was as much of a threat to his continued survival as a battlefield, and twice as complicated.

He pushed the fears away and fixed his expression into what he hoped was a friendly smile, doing his best to acknowledge the greetings directed towards him. The faces passed in a blur, the nods and smiles merging into one. Among the surging throng he caught a glimpse of a younger face, belonging to a blonde girl who stood out like an eagle in a pigeon coop. A pair of green eyes matched his appraisal with a confident, mocking stare before she was hidden from view by the meaty shoulders of the matronly figure being ushered towards him on the arm of a portly, grey-bearded gentleman dressed in full regimentals.

'Danbury, let me introduce you to Major Dutton.' Proudfoot took Jack by the elbow, propelling him towards the commander of the contingent from the 12th Bengal Native Infantry.

'Dutton.' The major's handshake was as curt and abrupt as his introduction of his wife. 'Hilary.'

'Danbury. I am pleased to meet you both.' Jack hoped his words conveyed an enthusiasm he did not feel. The major's wife had an ample bosom, artlessly displayed by a shoulderless dress of vivid scarlet that clung precariously to her many folds and creases. Jack had enough time to notice Proudfoot slipping away as the introductions were made before he was forced to cock an ear in what he hoped was a sign of encouragement as Mrs Dutton started to speak.

'How was your journey, Captain Danbury? It is such a long way from Calcutta.' Dutton's wife smiled as she spoke, but there was no hiding the salacious appraisal she gave or the sparkle in her eyes as she savoured what she saw.

'Enough of your mothering, my dear.' Dutton interrupted his wife, saving Jack from a meaningless reply about heat, bullock carts and interminable delays. He took an immediate liking to the blunt officer. 'The man will have had his fill of damned travelling, is that not so, Danbury?'

'Indeed,' Jack replied politely, doing his best to smile reassuringly at Mrs Dutton as she shrank away from the conversation, her husband's authority clear.

'Ready for some real soldiering, I expect.' Dutton smiled wolfishly at the notion, revealing an array of discoloured teeth. 'All this shilly-shallying around takes its toll on a man, what?'

'Quite true.'

Dutton leant forward to speak in a confiding whisper. 'I could see you were a man of action as soon as I clapped eyes on you. How was the Crimea? Did you see much action?'

'A little.'

'Say no more. I can see it in your eyes. I have not had the occasion myself. Not been that lucky.' Dutton failed to hide his obvious disappointment at having been denied the opportunity to hear the guns roar in anger on a battlefield.

Jack did not know how to reply. Was the major unlucky not to have fought a battle, or simply fortunate? The horror he himself had experienced at the Alma should have made that an easy question to answer. Yet he could well remember his own desire to fight, to experience the hardest challenge a soldier could face. He might wish with all his soul that the battle had not happened, but he could not deny the pride he felt at having taken part.

Dutton watched him closely, nodding as if in approval at the distant look that came over the new captain. 'There is unlikely to be any fighting here, more's the damn pity.'

Jack forced his mind away from his memories. 'Truly? What of this maharajah?'

'The Maharajah is a fool. He surrounds himself with his fancy lancers and thinks of himself as a great warrior chief. But I tell you this, Danbury. If he were ever to be foolish enough to challenge us, we would tear his ragtag little army to pieces in a heartbeat. No, there will be no battles here. At least none that Mr Russell of *The Times* would find of note.'

Jack nodded in agreement. He had read Russell's accounts of the fighting in the Crimea. The papers he had been able to find on the journey were always long out of date, but he believed Russell was giving a fair account of the campaign. The reporter was certainly no fool or lickspittle, offering his share of criticism of General Raglan and the army's leadership, much of which Jack fully agreed with. It was hard to imagine anything happening in the forgotten kingdom of Sawadh that would catch any journalist's attention. However, he was intrigued to hear the major write off the Maharajah's army with such certainty. 'I was led to understand we were heavily outnumbered here,' he said. 'Surely that would count for something?'

'Outnumbered we are, that is true. And it is enough to keep all these damn peacocks pissing in their breeches at the very thought.' Dutton could not hide his look of distaste as he used his drink to gesture around the room. Of all the officers present, only he and Jack were in their regimental uniforms, the rest preferring an array of vibrantly coloured costumes, as if there was a silent competition to wear the most garish or the most outlandish garb. 'But I would back my three hundred against three thousand of the Maharajah's,' he continued, fixing Jack with a hard stare as he dared the Queen's officer to gainsay him.

Jack kept his expression neutral, even if there was something concerning in the major's blind confidence. He was saved from any further reply as Proudfoot reappeared at his elbow.

'Come, Danbury. More people to meet.' He was keen to steer Jack onwards, towards the next stop on his tour of introductions.

'Come and visit us when you are settled, Danbury. I would like you to run your eyes over my men,' Dutton proposed as Proudfoot led Jack away. 'They are good boys. They would give a solid account of themselves if ever the need arose. They would fight hard. Damned hard.'

Jack heard the longing in Dutton's voice. The man was clearly desperate for a fight. With Proudfoot so keen to annex the Maharajah's lands, it made for a dangerous combination. If the Maharajah didn't back down, then a fight was inevitable. Political machinations would give way to violence and men like Dutton would be handed the authority to force home the Queen's will.

Chapter Four

———⋅◆⋅———

'Reverend, our new captain.'

Proudfoot's introductions had got shorter as he promenaded his new subordinate around the room, his sentences eroding as rapidly as his enthusiasm. For Jack, the procession of introductions had passed by in a blur of names, firm handshakes and meaningless nothings. The station at Bhundapur was small, little more than an outpost of the British Empire, yet it still boasted half a dozen commissioned officers from the Honourable East India Company, with at least that number again of civil appointees, along with their associated wives and relations.

Jack had now gained some knowledge of the people with whom he would live in the coming months. It would take much longer to understand and follow the complex web of power that would govern life in the cantonment. His short time in India had taught him that social standing was guarded as jealously as a maharajah's treasure. To commit a social faux pas, however unintentional, was to court disgrace. Not for the first time he wondered at the sanity of his decision to force himself into a world in which he did not belong.

'I am delighted to meet you, Captain. Now tell me. Are you bass, baritone or has the good Lord finally delivered me a tenor?'

'Don't start bothering Danbury with your choir already, Reverend. The poor fellow has only just arrived.' Proudfoot's disdain for the portly chaplain was painfully obvious in his icy manner. 'Now, Danbury. I'll leave you with Reverend Youngsummers.' The major was keen to be away and Jack was glad to see him go. Being paraded around the room like a prize heifer had been uncomfortable enough, and he did not think he would have been able to stand Proudfoot's tugging on his elbow for another minute without his temper snapping.

Reverend Youngsummers gently patted his ample stomach as Proudfoot made his excuses, a soft belch escaping a wide, fleshy mouth that gave him an unfavourable comparison with a toad. The clergyman's aged black jacket strained at the buttons as it struggled to encompass his bulk, its thick shoulders and wide collar liberally covered with flakes of fallen scurf.

'You've no drink.' Youngsummers' disapproval was clear. 'Let me remedy that tragedy.'

He lifted his left hand, clicking his fingers towards one of the many serving staff standing like statues against the walls, then pointed to his own empty glass and raised two fingers. In the time it took him to turn back to face Jack, two fresh glasses of brandy and soda arrived in the hands of the servant charged with supplying this corner of the room with a ready supply of alcohol.

'There you go, a quick peg before dinner. Proudfoot may lack taste, but he keeps a good table and a tolerable cellar. You will find, Danbury, that one needs a good diet in this infernal heat. It is the only way to survive.' Youngsummers' eyes narrowed in anticipation at the thought of food. From his sizeable girth it was clear that the chaplain enthusiastically followed his own advice.

'I shall do my best,' Jack replied, trying not to smile at the odd creature in front of him.

Youngsummers raised his glass to his mouth and drained it in two huge gulps. 'I should introduce you to my daughter.' He turned to bring a slight, blonde-haired girl into the conversation, careless of the trickle of brandy that crept from the corner of his mouth to stain the once white dog collar that was fighting to remain fixed round his bulbous neck.

'Isabel, this is Danbury, the 24th's new captain.'

The girl who had caught Jack's eye when he first entered the room now stood in front of him, offering a brief curtsy before fixing him with the same mocking, mischievous green eyes. Jack's weariness left him in a heartbeat.

'Captain Danbury.' Isabel had to lift her chin high to maintain eye contact. She was slimmer than Jack had imaged from his single glimpse of her. The simple green dress she wore shimmered in the candlelight, matching both the colour and the sparkle in her eyes. She was captivating.

'Isabel has come to visit me before going to live with her aunt in Truro. I selfishly wanted her all to myself one last time.' Reverend Youngsummers looked at his daughter fondly, reaching out to pat her gloved hand with affection.

'Now, Papa. You know full well that we have not yet fixed my plans.'

Jack watched as he saw the full weight of Isabel's charm brought to bear on her father. If Reverend Youngsummers had the willpower to send his daughter back to England, then he was a better man than Jack was.

'We shall see, my dear. We shall see. Do you have family, Danbury?'

'No, sir. I am quite alone in the world.' Jack was doing his best not to stare. Isabel was beautiful. He could see now that her hair was redder than he had first thought, a touch of ginger amidst the blonde curls that were artfully styled in what he supposed was the latest fashion.

'Then you cannot know a father's pain.' Youngsummers frowned as he saw that the new captain was clearly charmed by his daughter. 'You desire nothing more than for your precious child to remain with you always, yet you know you must let them go if they are to live the life you desire for them.' He spoke wistfully, careless of revealing his emotions to a stranger.

'Perhaps Captain Danbury will know that one day, Papa.' Isabel ignored her father, focusing all her charm on the new officer, who blushed at her attention. 'He is much too young to be thinking of making a family.' She gave Jack a teasing smile, making the most oblique reference to procreation sound like an invitation to dive into the nearest bedroom.

'I am not so young.' Isabel was so vibrant that Jack could not resist studying her face as he addressed her. It was a delight, her features slim and elegant, yet it was her hair that charmed him the most, with its unruly curls that fanned around her face. She had tried to tame the wildest sections with narrow metal clips, each decorated with a single glass bead that encompassed every hue in the rainbow. In the gentle light of the room they flickered as her head moved, a vivid kaleidoscope of vibrant colour.

'Nonsense. Why, you cannot be more than two and twenty,' Isabel mocked, her eyes narrowing provocatively as she estimated his age.

Isabel's beauty had transported Jack into his past, his mind returning to the memory of another young woman. It had been many months, but the pain of her death was still fresh.

Isabel pouted at his lack of reaction. 'There, I have offended you by speaking of age.'

'Now, my dear. I very much doubt if Captain Danbury would be so easily put out. Is that not so, Danbury?'

Jack had to force his mind back to the present. 'Indeed.' He heard the coldness in his own voice and saw Isabel purse her lips as though considering something.

'Perhaps Captain Danbury would like to join us on our expedition the day after tomorrow, Papa. It would allow us to get to know him better, before Major Proudfoot buries him in work.'

'A capital notion.' Youngsummers signalled for another drink as he approved his daughter's suggestion. 'Danbury, we have a long-awaited opportunity to visit a local wonder. Isabel likes nothing better than a chance to explore some of the crumbling, dusty edifices that seem to appeal to the local peasants. She has a rum idea of it being a fitting occupation for a young woman. I expect she gets that from her mother, my late wife.' His mouth turned down at the corners, as if he tasted something sour. He gulped at his fresh drink, which had been brought by the willing servant, using the brandy and soda to scour the bitterness from his mouth.

'I believe I noticed the tower you speak of on my way here.' Jack tried to sound gracious as he attempted to make good his escape. As pleasing as it would be to have a day out with the delightful Isabel, he would rather rub his arse with a brick before he spent time with her father. 'I would dearly like the chance to explore it, but I am not sure that will be possible for the moment. I must attend to my new command.'

'I'm sure Proudfoot would see the benefit.' Youngsummers used his hand to stifle another deep belch. 'And as you will discover, Danbury, my daughter tends to get what she desires. I doubt even Proudfoot has the wherewithal to gainsay her.'

Isabel's eyes flushed with triumph. 'There. It is settled. You shall come.'

'Who will go where?' Their conversation was interrupted by the urbane tones of an English officer. 'Am I missing out on the social outing of the season?'

'Arthur! We are merely inviting Captain Danbury to join us on our excursion to the mysterious tower of silence that I have told you about countless times.'

'Lucky fellow.' The officer turned so that he was face to face with Jack. 'So you're Danbury. I'm pleased to meet you. I'm Arthur Fenris.'

Jack looked into the face of his subordinate, taking in the cool, mocking stare. Fenris was far too comfortable for a lieutenant meeting his captain for the first time, and Jack wondered what licence the man had been given as he awaited his new commander.

Believing his introduction to be complete, Fenris turned his charisma back on Isabel. 'So when was I to be invited?' His playful tone made it clear there was no censure intended by the rebuke. As he spoke, Fenris angled his body, subtly but effectively pushing Jack to the fringe of the conversation.

'Don't be a ninny, Arthur. Of course you're invited.'

'Well I'm not certain I wish to accompany you now,' Fenris teased. 'You will have no need of two heroes to guard you.'

'A lady can never have enough heroes,' Isabel lifted her chin in what Jack believed was a gesture of defiance. It was clear the Reverend's daughter was used to getting her own way.

Isolated on the periphery of the conversation, Jack had a moment to study his new subaltern. Lieutenant Fenris had the build and stature of a hunter. He was taller than Jack, with the broad shoulders and narrow waist of someone who valued their appearance and took measures to maintain it. With an unruly mop of black hair and a pair of thick mutton-chop whiskers, it was easy to understand why Isabel was so clearly entranced.

If his physique were not enough, then Fenris' choice of dress would turn many a maiden's head. He wore a long jacket of cream linen that hung to his thighs, coupled with a pair of tight-cut trousers in the same fabric. The plainness of the suit contrasted with his bright blue waistcoat, decorated with fabulous swirls and stitching picked out in bronze thread. Around the neck of his white linen shirt he wore a cravat of plain gold, held in place with a single pin topped with a fat pearl. Every cantonment had its dandy, and it was clear that Jack's subaltern relished the role at Bhundapur.

'So what of it, Danbury? Shall we both squire Miss Youngsummers?' Fenris spoke in jocular tones, yet it did not endear him to Jack. He was not alone in finding the presence of the young lieutenant grating, and Reverend Youngsummers politely excused himself from the conversation as he continued his pursuit of exhausting Proudfoot's supply of brandy.

'I shall go but you shall stay here,' said Jack, irritated by Fenris' peremptory manner. 'I would not want to leave the men without either of their officers.'

'I beg your pardon?' There was a flash of anger in the younger officer's eyes as his new captain pulled rank.

'If we are to get along, I suggest you see the surgeon and get your ears cleaned out. Tomorrow I plan to inspect the men before we conduct a morning of drill followed by an afternoon at musket practice. I want to see how well they can shoot. I would be grateful if you could make the necessary arrangements.'

Fenris looked as if he had swallowed a turd. 'Are those your orders, sir?' He appeared to gag on the title, as if speaking the word caused him physical pain. Isabel inched closer, her eyes sparkling with enjoyment at the tension between the two men.

'They are. What is the name of the senior sergeant?'

'That would be Colour Sergeant Hughes, sir,' Fenris replied with a healthy dollop of sarcasm.

'Please let him know I shall want to see him first thing in the morning.'

'Have you cleared this with Major Proudfoot?' Fenris sneered as he spoke, his anger at being so openly treated as a subordinate obvious.

Jack felt his own anger flare. 'I do not need the permission of the major to run my command as I see fit. Do not presume to question me again, is that clear?'

Fenris opened his mouth as if to argue further. He controlled himself with some difficulty. 'Abundantly clear, sir.'

Jack felt the need for fresh air. Despite Proudfoot's thermantidotes the room felt stuffy, and the perfume-rich air caught in his throat. With the briefest of nods, he excused himself and made for the door.

The smirk he glimpsed on Isabel's face did nothing to improve his mood. He had not given Fenris a dressing-down for her benefit. Jack would get his command into shape, and if that required upsetting his callow prig of a lieutenant, then that was a small price to pay.

Jack jogged down the steps of the bungalow, sucking in a huge lungful of the clean night air. It was a relief to be free. The long evening spent standing in the confines of Proudfoot's drawing room had awakened the recurring pain in his back, and he needed to find somewhere to sit in peace so that he could try to knead the ache away.

'Danbury!'

His spine stiffened as he recognised the drawled tones calling for his attention.

'Stop there, I say.'

Jack forced his tiredness away and turned to face a red-faced Fenris, who was galloping down the steps behind him.

'Damn you, Danbury. What makes you think you can talk to me like that?' Fenris opened his tirade whilst still several paces away from where Jack had stopped.

'You will call me "sir" when you address me.' Jack spoke in calm, measured tones, as if addressing a recalcitrant child.

His captain's sangfroid did nothing to calm Fenris down. 'I shall not, you damn blackguard. How dare you? Speaking to me in such a way in front of Miss Youngsummers was disgraceful. I should bloody well call you out.'

Jack's temper started to fray. 'You will address me correctly at all times and you will be dressed in your regulation uniform when you do so. I will not tolerate an officer in my company going around dressed as some damn nabob.'

'Go to hell. When Major Proudfoot hears of this—'

'I don't give a damn what Proudfoot says,' Jack interrupted, with real venom in his voice. 'You are under my command, not his. You will conduct yourself as I see fit.'

'Damn your eyes, Danbury.'

Jack reached forward and grabbed Fenris around the arm, pulling the officer forward so his face was inches from his own. 'Listen to me, Lieutenant. I have no intention of letting a mewling turd under my command tell me what I should or should not do.'

Fenris sneered, despite the naked threat in Jack's eyes. 'Now look here, Danbury . . .' He tried to pull out of Jack's grip, but couldn't break free from the vice-like hold.

'I have fought and killed until my arm felt like lead, and then I fought and killed some more.' Jack snarled his words into Fenris' face. 'I have watched the horror on a man's face when he realises he is going to die. If you choose to fight me, then I will strike you down.'

He released his hold on the lieutenant's arm, throwing it away abruptly so that Fenris staggered backwards. The younger officer's face twisted into a snarl and he took a pace forward. Jack saw the violence in his subaltern's eyes, the shame and the anger burning brightly in his face. He braced himself for a wild rush, his muscles tensing as his body took control, an icy calm flowing through him as he prepared to fight.

Then Fenris turned, his attention taken by the sounds of a hushed and appalled audience. Jack looked past his shaken lieutenant and saw for the first time the large crowd that had gathered at the top of the steps. The look of delighted horror on the fascinated faces made it clear that they had been watching the two officers the whole time as they bawled at each other like a pair of feuding costermongers.

Standing at the front of the group, Major Proudfoot caught Jack's eye. Then with a slow shake of his head he ushered his guests back inside.

Jack turned and walked away, heedless of the eyes boring into his spine. He did not care if he caused a scandal that would be the talk of the cantonment. Soldiers deserved the best officers, and Jack would not allow them to be commanded by some upper-class popinjay who simply fancied the gold braid and being called 'sir'. Fenris would have to learn that lesson, no matter how painful it might prove.

Chapter Five

———◆◆◆———

*J*ack was dressed and out of the chummery before he even heard Fenris begin to stir. He had no intention of repeating the previous night's conversation. He did not regret anything he had said, but he wanted to start his first day in the cantonment without the bitter tang of acrimony in the air.

'Good morning, sir, can I help you?' A young corporal greeted him as he approached the 24th's lines.

'Good morning, Corporal, I'm looking for Colour Sergeant Hughes.'

The corporal looked anxious, despite the politely worded request. 'I'll go and fetch him for you, sir. If you'll just wait there . . .'

Jack sensed he was being treated with caution. The young corporal was clearly nervous at being faced by his new company commander, and keen to hold him off until the company's senior non-commissioned officer could be summoned to deal with him.

'What's your name, Corporal?'

The corporal looked twice as worried. 'Jones, sir.'

Jack nodded and tried to smile in what he hoped was a reassuring way. 'I can hear from your voice that you are from Wales. Which part?'

'Brecon, sir.' Corporal Jones had been trying to move away, but now hovered in an awkward position, half at attention. 'I'll get Colour Sergeant Hughes now, shall I, sir?'

Jack nodded firmly as he realised he was torturing the younger man. 'Carry on, Corporal Jones.'

The young corporal scampered away. Jack used the time to look around the company lines. The pathways between the barracks and the rest of the cantonment were well cared for, the gravel neatly raked and the stones that marked them out recently whitewashed. It spoke well of the company's non-commissioned officers, and he hoped that the rest of the company was as well turned out.

'Good morning, sir. You must be Captain Danbury.'

The calm voice interrupted Jack's quiet inspection and he turned to see a tall, barrel-chested redcoat marching towards him. The crowned Union Jack and crossed swords above the chevrons of a sergeant identified the man wearing them as Colour Sergeant Hughes. Jack instinctively felt a prickle of unease. He had been an ordinary redcoat for too long not too feel troubled coming face-to-face with the company's senior sergeant.

'Good morning, Colour Sergeant.'

'I must apologise for not being here to greet you. You're early, if you don't mind my saying so, sir. Mr Fenris told me to expect you this morning, but he didn't say it would be this early.'

Jack's brow furrowed at the statement, even though it was delivered in a friendly enough tone. 'I think this is quite late enough. We have a lot to do this morning. We will start with morning parade, then I want to watch the men at their drill. Did Lieutenant Fenris explain that they are to attend a firing practice at the range later?'

'He did indeed, sir. Everything has been prepared and the men are ready to be inspected at your convenience.'

Jack smiled. He had the feeling he would get on well with this businesslike colour sergeant. The relationship was an important one. It was a foolish or naïve officer who did not understand that he needed the full support of his NCOs. Officers might wear the scarlet and lace, but it was the experienced sergeants and corporals who were the real leaders of the company; without them, no officer could ever hope to be an effective commander.

'I am looking forward to seeing the men.' Jack spoke briskly as he began to take charge. He was revelling in being back at the head of a company. He had missed it more than he had believed possible. 'I hope they can shoot as well as they paint.' He nodded to the whitewashed stones by his feet.

'The boys can shoot all right, sir. We haven't seen neither hide nor hair of the new Enfield, but I would wager we will meet your expectations with our muskets.'

'Very good.' Jack was intrigued. He had heard some talk of the army's new rifle. In the Crimea, his men had used the Minié rifle. Against the Russian conscripts it had proved itself to be a dreadfully effective weapon, the heavy bullets capable of tearing through successive ranks in the dense enemy formations. The cleverly designed bullets deformed when they were fired, allowing them to grip the grooves in the rifle's barrel as well as ensuring that little of the explosive power of the cartridge was lost. If the new Enfield was a superior weapon, then it was going to give the redcoats a huge advantage. His new command still used the percussion-cap musket. It was an old-fashioned weapon, and his men would have to excel at their drill if they were to make up for its lack of range and power.

'I saw the effect of the Minié in the Crimea.' Jack was enjoying being back amongst fellow redcoats. It was a relief to talk about the merits of rifles, rather than endure the polite yet trivial small talk of society. 'It certainly proved its worth there.'

'I am sure it's a good weapon, sir. But the men aren't so sure. They like their muskets. They don't see the need for change. If it was good enough for them boys at Waterloo, then it's good enough for us.'

'Well,' Jack did his best to ignore the traditional inertia of the redcoats, 'I shall certainly enjoy seeing them shoot. For now, please order them on parade.'

Hughes stamped to attention and flashed Jack a solid salute. 'Yes, sir.'

Jack felt a rush of emotion as he acknowledged the salute. It had been too long since he had given orders. He felt the shackles falling away. He was back where he belonged, doing a job he loved. He was home.

* * *

Jack heard the heavy tramp of feet on the wooden veranda outside the office. He lifted his head from the company's books as he listened to the raised voice berating an unfortunate Corporal Jones. He recognised it at once.

He held back the flash of temper he felt flare inside. The morning had gone well. The men of his new company had impressed him, both with their turnout and with their drill. He had left them to prepare for the day ahead and burrowed his way into the books, trying to commit to memory the names and histories of the men now under his command. It had been slow going. He was not a fast reader and it had been difficult to decipher the company clerk's tight script, but he had been enjoying himself as he started the vital process of getting to know the men. Now Lieutenant Fenris had deigned to appear, and Jack knew he would not be left in peace for much longer.

Sure enough, a flushed face appeared at the door to the company office. 'May I ask what the deuce is going on here?' Fenris stalked into the small room and stood in front of the desk where Jack sat carefully closing the thick ledger he had been studying.

'Good morning, Lieutenant. Please shut the door and take a seat.'

Fenris turned and slammed the door. He did not sit, but stood at Jack's desk, his hands held petulantly on his hips. 'Now look here, Danbury—'

Jack did not let him continue. 'Sit down!' He gave the order with all the force of a man who had commanded in battle.

Fenris' mouth snapped shut with an audible click. Jack thought he would ignore the order, but with a visible effort at controlling himself, he managed to pull up a chair and take a seat, vibrating with barely suppressed anger.

'Captain Danbury.' Fenris' voice was icy. 'Might I remind you that I have been in charge of this company for the past six months. I appreciate your wish to assume command' – he choked on the word but managed to carry on – 'but I must ask that you give me the respect I am due and allow me to continue to run the company until you are in a position to understand how things are done here.'

Jack was battling his temper. It would be easy to unleash the tirade he felt building inside him. But he was the senior officer. He had to think of the men first. It would harm the company if its two officers were at loggerheads. As much as he would enjoy tearing another strip off his lieutenant, he had to give the younger man a way back.

'Lieutenant Fenris, I rather think we have got off on the wrong foot. Major Proudfoot has told me that you are to be commended for your time in command of the company. From what I have seen, he is quite correct.'

Fenris preened at the praise. 'Then more reason to let me run things until you are settled.'

Jack swallowed hard. It was becoming clear that Fenris possessed neither the wit nor the intelligence to seize the olive branch he was offering. 'I am quite capable of getting to work right away. I would like to think you would assist me in that.'

'I think you are wrong. You seek to undermine me. As you showed in front of Miss Youngsummers.'

Jack understood that they had reached the heart of the problem. Fenris did not care about the command of the company. He cared about his image, about the loss of face in front of the most beautiful girl in the cantonment. 'Your behaviour was at fault, Lieutenant. I do not apologise for what I said, but perhaps I should have let it wait until this morning.'

'Damn right. You made me look a fool.'

'That was not my intention.'

'Then you should be more bloody careful what you say.'

Jack sat back in his chair. He suddenly felt weary. 'I think we have said enough on this matter. I will consider it closed.'

Fenris scowled. 'Very well. As you have apologised, I shall be a gentleman and look to forget the matter.' He stood quickly, tossing his head with clear disdain. 'I shall order Hughes to parade the men.'

'There is no need.' Jack opened the ledger, using the lines of names as a balm to his temper. 'I have paraded the men already. They are getting ready for the firing range.'

Fenris glowered. 'Did you not think to wait for me to arrive? Good God, this is too much, Danbury, too much indeed.' His face was colouring as he began to rage. 'I was willing to overlook your behaviour last evening, but now it appears you are determined to cut me out of the company. I shall not stand for such treatment. You may outrank me, but I think you will see differently once I have spoken to Proudfoot. I do not know who you think you are, swanking in here as if you own the place. But let me tell you, I shall not be easily brushed aside. My father—'

Jack slammed his hand on to the desk, cutting his subaltern off in mid-sentence before he rose to his feet, his face like thunder.

'Enough!' He roared the single word, his attempts to curb his temper failing. 'You forget who you are talking to, *Lieutenant*.' His voice was scornful as he emphasised the rank. 'I suggest you return to your quarters and calm yourself down.'

Fenris looked stunned. 'You are dismissing me?'

'You leave me no choice.' Jack sat back down heavily and turned his attention back to the company ledger, doing his best to calm the tremble in his hands.

Fenris was speechless. He managed a snort of contempt before he spun on his heel and stomped from the room.

Jack tried to concentrate on the list of names of the men under his command, but his heart was pounding and he couldn't see anything other than a blur. He got to his feet, suddenly needing to move, and stalked to the window. A grass screen covered it, and he stood in the gentle breeze wafting through the tightly woven fibres.

'Excuse me, sir. A visitor for you.' Jack turned as Corporal Jones tentatively stuck his head around the door to the office. From the Welshman's expression it was clear he had heard every word of the altercation.

Jack sighed. He was in no mood to be civil. He knew he was expected to call on all the officers and senior officials and their wives in his first days in the cantonment. He hated obeying such expectations but he had thought he would be given a few days to get settled before he would have to start receiving visitors and planning his own social engagements.

'Very well, show him in.'

Jones blushed. 'Um, it's a her, sir. I rather fancy you'll be pleased.' The corporal retreated quickly, giving his new captain no time to reply.

Isabel Youngsummers appeared in the doorway. 'I do hope I am not disturbing you, Captain?'

Jack felt his temper disappear in a waft of French perfume. 'Not at all.' He rushed around the desk, kicking against its side as his haste made him clumsy. 'Please take a seat.' He pulled out the chair recently vacated by Fenris.

'No thank you. I must not stay. I have no chaperone.'

Jack coloured. 'Of course.'

'I simply wished to enquire whether you have any particular requests for tomorrow's picnic.'

Jack was left standing uncomfortably close to Isabel, holding the chair awkwardly, as if using it as a shield to keep them apart. He let go and retreated to his own side of the desk.

'No thank you. I eat anything,' he blurted, then kicked himself. He sounded like a greedy schoolboy.

Isabel simply smiled. 'That is easy, then. My father insists on taking enough food to feed the five thousand. Just in case, as it were.'

For the first time Jack sensed the young woman's own awkwardness. He realised she was here on a pretence, her question of no consequence whatsoever. The idea that she had come just to see him pleased him enormously.

'It is kind of you to think of me.'

Isabel blushed. The flush spread up from the nape of her neck and Jack had to fight the urge to stare.

'Until tomorrow, then.' He couldn't think of anything to say, so he ended the conversation with regret.

Isabel said nothing as she turned and left him alone once more. But the smell of her perfume lingered, the delicate fragrance reminding Jack of her presence. Perhaps he would look forward to the next day's exploration after all.

Chapter Six

'There it is!'
Isabel squealed in delight as she pointed ahead.
Silhouetted against the skyline the rough-hewn stone tower stood like a beacon, calling to the hot and dusty party that was struggling to climb the rocky pathway leading to the crest of the rough, craggy slope, just as it had called to the thousands before them.

A dozen birds of prey circled around the tower's summit, drifting and soaring on eddies of warm air that swirled around the hilltop on which it had been built. Its sides were pitted and scarred, the cracks and fissures evidence of the trial of standing through the centuries, buffeted by storms and lashed by the monsoon rains. Most of the slopes around it showed the signs of attempts at cultivation, generations of farmers working tirelessly to grow a meagre crop in the thin soil. Yet none encroached near the tower and a wide band of desolate scrub surrounded the tall spire as if it had sucked all the goodness from the ground, like a leech sucking the blood from an open wound.

The slopes below the tower were blanketed with the simple mud and thatch houses of the people who tried to eke out an existence far from the main towns. Herds of goats wandered the hillside, their pitiful bleats and cries the only sound disturbing the peace of the high ground. The local people relied on their herds for food; the arid, dusty soil was of little use to any inclined to farm. The animals' tireless search for nourishment made the surrounding hills all the more desolate, the few shrubs that clung to life little more than thorny twigs, any trace of greenery stripped away by the goats' relentless foraging.

Jack tried to find some enthusiasm now that the tower was finally in sight. It was something of a relief to have escaped his difficult subaltern for the day. He had not spoken to Lieutenant Fenris since the previous morning, any further unpleasantness avoided at least for the moment. His body was less relieved. His backside was sore after hours spent in the saddle, the constant motion of the horse waking the pain in his back that sent spasms racing up and down his spine. He was not an accomplished rider, the skill only recently acquired since arriving in India as a necessity for his journey up from Calcutta. His proficiency had been sorely tested by the long ride into the hills, and now his aching, cramping muscles were threatening to give up completely.

Despite the discomfort, he had to admit that riding the horse borrowed from Proudfoot's extensive stables was preferable to the strength-sapping march the men of his escort had endured. Proudfoot had insisted that the Youngsummers should have protection from the bandits and dacoits that plagued the more remote corners of his domain. The ten men from Dutton's native infantry contingent had marched in silence; the only words Jack had heard from any of them were the commands issued by the havildar who led them.

The sepoys wore a uniform similar to that of their British counterparts. The famous red jacket was the same, the five rows of braid across the front and around the cuffs as smart as anything seen in the barracks of England. In their working dress, the native infantrymen wore baggy white knee-length breeches in place of the more usual dark blue trousers, and whilst the British infantry still wore the traditional shako that had been a hallmark of the redcoat for centuries, the native troops wore a soft white Kilmarnock cap, much more suited to the heat of the relentless Indian sun. Instead of the

thick leather stock worn around the neck to force the wearer to
adopt a soldierly bearing, the native soldiers wore beads or went
bare-necked, much to the frustration of the British redcoats, whose
uniforms bore no adaptation for the harsh climate they were forced
to endure.

Jack nodded at the havildar as the escort marched past. Major
Dutton had been right to be proud of his men, and Jack found
himself hoping that those of his own company would conduct
themselves in the same professional and soldierly manner.

'Slow down, my dear. This is no time for a race.' Reverend
Youngsummers admonished his daughter for her fast pace as he
brought up the rear of the party, his exhausted horse lathered in
sweat from carrying its hefty burden.

'Come now, Papa. We are nearly there.' Isabel fairly shone with
delight, her joy at being away from the confines of cantonment life
obvious. 'Then we can rest and enjoy the picnic I have prepared.'

The idea of a rest and food had the desired effect, and
Youngsummers spurred his horse hard so that he could catch
up with his daughter. 'Tell me, did you bring some of those devilled
eggs that Mrs Dutton has been promising me for the last month?'

'I brought a dozen, Papa. Enough even for you.' Isabel laughed as
she teased her father, throwing her head back so that the soft pale
blue scarf she had wrapped over her hair fell back. She laughed
again, revelling in her freedom. Jack did his best not to stare as she
released her glorious curls from the shackles of their clips and ties.

The small party ground its way up the hill, entering a narrow
defile. On either side the ground rose sharply, the dusty, scree slope
too steep for easy passage, and Jack felt a flicker of unease as he saw
his small command compressed into the narrow space.

He shook off the disquiet. It was too much of a relief to be
stationary to spoil the moment with doubts, and he took a minute to
enjoy simply sitting still. He had heard tales of picnic parties, of
well-to-do people taking a dozen servants and moving the contents
of a small house into the depths of the English countryside to enjoy
a view or to sit by a river and read poetry. He had never imagined
attending one himself, least of all on a dusty, scorching hillside
thousands of miles from home.

He waited patiently for the last of the five porters who laboured to carry the myriad items Isabel had deemed essential to the success of her simple expedition, before reluctantly urging his horse back into motion, grimacing as the movement jarred his aching back.

A single shot rang out, the sharp retort echoing around the hillside. The bullet struck a rock no more than two yards away from the sepoys' right-hand file. A dozen more followed, the air filled with the bowel-loosening snap of bullets whipping past.

Any thoughts of a quiet picnic disappeared in a flash of musket fire. They were under attack.

Isabel screamed.

Jack slipped from the saddle, trying to make sense out of the confusion. There was another fusillade of bullets, sharp puffs of dust flung high into the air as the deadly missiles struck the ground all around the terrified party.

'Form skirmish line!' Jack's voice cracked as he shouted the first order, his mouth dry. He flinched as a bullet scored past his head, the first spasm of fear coursing through his veins.

More shots rang out, yet already they were becoming ragged, the sporadic rate of fire betraying a lack of discipline. Jack had no idea who was firing on them, but at least it was clear that the ambushers were not trained soldiers. Yet the desultory fire had stopped the party in its tracks, pinning them in place.

The sound of a bullet striking flesh caught Jack's attention. It was a horrible sound, like a butcher slamming a carcass on to his chopping block, and one he had heard too many times in the Crimea not to recognise.

He saw at once where the sound had come from. Isabel's horse was twisting on the spot as blood poured from a deep wound to its shoulder, blackening its mottled brown coat. Before she could free her feet from the stirrups, the maddened beast jerked hard to the left, flinging its rider off as the pain of the wound drove it wild.

Isabel's slight frame was thrown to the ground, the jarring impact clearly audible from where Jack slipped and skidded towards her. More shots crashed down around them as he threw himself to his knees, instinctively screening her prone body where she lay face down in the dust. He reached out his hand, clasping the stunned girl around the shoulder. He could feel her muscles quiver under his touch, the softness of her flesh beneath his fingers sending a sudden, violent surge of lust through his body. He was shocked by the power of the unexpected rush of emotions, feelings he had believed scoured from his soul.

Isabel looked up, her eyes glazed. She lifted her head from the ground, trying to push herself up. A thin trickle of blood flowed down her cheek, the bright trail of red a vivid contrast against the ghostly pallor of her face.

'Stay down.' Jack snarled the command through gritted teeth, angry at himself for sensing something in the contact with Isabel's young body that had no place when his small party was in danger. He felt her go limp as she submitted to his control. He waited, counting off the seconds, anticipating a lull in the firing. A number of shots rang out together, the haphazard volley giving him enough of an opportunity to move. He took a firm hold of Isabel's arm, tugging her to her feet before dragging her into cover behind a moss-covered boulder that was big enough to shelter her from the enemy's fire.

'Damn you, Danbury!' Isabel's anger was obvious. As soon as Jack let go of her arm, her hands scrabbled at the buckles of the bag that hung around her neck. Her eyes flashed with triumph as she pulled out a compact revolver. 'I can fight.'

'You will stay here and do such thing.'

'Don't you dare give me orders.' Isabel matched Jack's angry tone. 'Now sort this mess out and don't concern yourself with protecting me. I have all the protection I need.' She brandished the small revolver, and from the look in her eyes, there was no doubt she would not be afraid to use it.

'You will stay here and damn well do as I say, or I shall have one of the men keep you here at gunpoint,' Jack snapped. 'Is that clear, Miss Youngsummers?'

He saw the hurt on her face, the pout on her lips that was becoming so familiar. He turned his back on her, hoping he had cowed her into obeying him for the moment, burying the feelings that she stirred inside him. There would be a time to wonder at the emotions she had awoken, but only if the two of them survived.

The red-coated native soldiers had reacted quickly and efficiently. The havildar had followed Jack's order, aligning the ranks calmly so that they formed an extended line, facing the direction of the gunfire. The porters had gone to ground, hiding away, trusting to the escort to keep them safe.

The small party was held up on the long slope that led to the village and the tower. The fire was coming from the raised ground on their right flank. Jack took in the situation quickly, his eyes never still as he assessed the threat, his mind already racing as he planned how to get his charges, and his men, out of danger. It was time to bring order out of the chaos. It was time to fight back.

'Havildar. Load!'

Jack strode away from Isabel, bellowing orders, taking charge, whilst doing his best to ignore the flickering bullets that stung the air around him. The ambush had come from above where the party had been labouring up the slope. Shooting downhill made aiming difficult, and to Jack's relief most of the shots were whispering past well over their heads. The cough that followed each shot told Jack that they were being fired on by muskets, and he offered a silent prayer of thanks that whoever was attacking did not have access to the powerful rifles the British soldiers had used to such deadly effect in the Crimea. If the enemy had hoped to flay the party with musket fire, then they were going to be disappointed.

Jack turned around, assessing the situation, listening to the measured tones of the havildar as he took his men through the drill of loading their pieces. Just like Jack's men in the 24th, Dutton's soldiers were still using a percussion-cap musket that had been in issue for over a decade and differed little from the weapon used at Waterloo forty years previously. It did not have anything like the range, or the power of the Minié rifle, and Jack knew he would have to make sure he did not overestimate the power of his men's volley.

The sepoys finished loading, the extended ranks shuffling as the men flinched at the bullets snapping past their ears or stinging the ground around their feet.

Jack nodded at the havildar.

'Front rank. Front rank, prepare to fire!'

'Aim at the smoke.' Jack called out the extra command before nodding again.

'Fire!'

The volley crashed out; the five muskets of the front rank firing in unison. They immediately began to reload as the second rank lifted their muskets to their shoulders. The crisp commands of the havildar marked their movements, the men carrying out their drill as they had been trained, the countless hours of practice paying dividends now they were under fire.

The red-coated machine roared into life, fighting back with the calm professionalism of the trained soldier.

Reverend Youngsummers kicked hard as he urged his tired mount up the scree slope that led towards the tower. His heart pounded in his chest, his breath as laboured as if he had run up the slope himself. He had not known fear before that day. Nothing had prepared him for the churning pit of horror deep in his belly that screwed his guts into a knot of terror. He twisted in the saddle, searching for a glimpse of his daughter, his lips moving in a constant silent prayer, his bowels clenching and threatening to void as his fear bubbled inside him.

He hesitated as he watched his daughter thrown from the saddle. His hands pulled on his horse's reins, momentarily slowing its headlong progress, his father's love making him pause. As he prepared to turn, he spotted the 24th's new captain scrabble his way towards his daughter's crumpled body. He saw Isabel move, her head lifting from the ground, the confirmation that she lived sending a surge of relief flooding through him.

Another round of gunfire rang out, the flurry of shots sending bullets crashing around the ears of the small party. Youngsummers felt his terror rebuilding, his stomach twisting as if the devil himself was inside, squirming in his guts, cruelly injecting the fear that consumed his soul.

He abandoned his precious daughter to the care of a stranger and sought escape.

'Get on, damn you. Get on!' He heard the fear in his own voice as he kicked his heels callously against his horse's sides, careless of his cruelty, desperate to get away from the bullets that had torn through the sunburnt air.

He could not die. He could not carry out God's work as a corpse. The Reverend Youngsummers ran from the danger, reassuring himself that he did God's will by saving his own skin.

'Oh dear Lord, save me.' He pushed himself up in the saddle, leaning his weight forward to urge the tiring horse on, his bowels exploding and farting the moment his backside lifted from the saddle.

The scabby hillside suddenly fell away in front of him, revealing a patch of dead ground he had not seen as he charged up the slope. A hundred yards of barren scrub still separated him from the edge of the village. All that remained between danger and safety.

Yet it might as well have been a thousand.

'No! Dear God, no.'

Youngsummers had abandoned his only daughter in a desperate bid for safety. Yet his coward's flight had not secured him the security he craved.

Instead, Reverend Archibald Youngsummers had found the Tiger.

Chapter Seven

———◆———

The second British volley crashed out, the sound rippling and echoing down the valley.

'Rear rank. Reload.'

'Front rank! Front rank, prepare to fire!'

The havildar strode behind the rear rank, his watchful glare roving over his charges as they reloaded.

Jack flinched as a bullet scored past his head, reacting to the high-pitched sound as it punched through the air despite his best efforts to remain composed in front of his men. He knew the volume of fire was nothing compared to the barrage into which the British had marched with such stoic calm at the Alma. Yet despite all he had experienced, his body still reacted with fear, his trembling hands all the evidence he needed to know that he had not become immune to the proximity of death.

A red-coated sepoy took a glancing wound to his upper arm. The slight, dark-skinned soldier surprised Jack with a stream of foul infective straight from the dockside at Chatham as he staunched the flow of blood, before retaking his place in the line.

The sepoys' volleys were having the effect Jack had intended. The enemy fire had slackened considerably, the ambushers driven into cover by the British response. Their return fire was sporadic, and Jack counted the puffs of smoke on the hillside, anxious to be able to get his small command away.

He had just opened his mouth to order a final volley when a cheer erupted from in front of where the redcoats stood. It was a visceral snarl, the sound warriors made when released to fight, and was followed by the noise of dozens of armed men moving at once. The scrape of metal on metal as weapons were drawn and readied for use.

Jack looked up the slope and cursed. He realised at once that the gunmen on the hillside had been given one role: to pin the party in place and divert their attention whilst the main force of the ambush manoeuvred into position into the dead ground in front of the stalled column. It was a simple plan, but it was effective.

'Fix bayonets!' He did his best to sound calm. The ten redcoats heard the order and reached for the scabbards in their belts that held the long steel bayonets. They were vicious weapons, deadly tools in the hands of a trained redcoat. For centuries, British soldiers had closed with their enemies, using the sharpened steel to win the famous victories of which they were so very proud.

The sepoys clicked the bayonets on to the locking points at the tip of their muskets before wheeling in line so that their two-man-deep formation faced the crest of the slope. It was a pitiful defence, about as formidable as a child's sandcastle trying to hold back the tide. Yet the redcoats stood their ground, pointing their wicked bayonets forward. Ready for the enemy to appear.

'Aim low when they come. Hit the bastards in the belly.' Jack offered the advice through gritted teeth. 'Aim low.'

He reached down and tugged his regulation sabre from its scabbard. It felt horribly light in his hand. It was a cheap blade, the Calcutta dealer's assurance that it was made from true English steel now looking as paper-thin as the sword itself. With his other hand he drew his Adams revolver, the sturdy weapon primed and loaded. At least he had one weapon he knew he could rely on.

'Prepare to charge.'

Ten dark faces turned to face him at once, the same look of horror and shock in each set of eyes. Only the havildar kept his expression neutral. He held Jack's gaze for a long moment, his eyes betraying nothing.

'Prepare to charge.' The native sergeant echoed Jack's order before taking his place behind the thin red line.

Jack glanced quickly over his shoulder to check that Isabel had stayed where he had left her. There was no time for her to do anything but trust to her escort. The only hope for them all lay in fighting hard and driving off the ambush.

Jack would not wait for the enemy to arrive. He would gamble everything on a single volley followed by a madcap charge. Ten native soldiers, one havildar and one impostor would risk a wild assault against the enemy. Eleven bayonets and a suspect sword against a horde.

The slope stretched away in front of them, the distant tower standing proud against the palest blue sky. A single thin smear of cloud crept leisurely across the view like a steam-powered barge on a gentle afternoon's cruise. The enemy's musket fire had died away, so that only the noise of armed men on the move marred the tranquillity.

The redcoats stood silent and steady, waiting for the enemy to appear. The men gripped their muskets tightly, holding them at the ready, the white of their knuckles evidence of the tension that surged through them.

The first figure appeared, silhouetted against the skyline. The single bandit stood alone, his sword lifted high as he contemplated the thin line that barred his path. Then the rest of the mob appeared, surging past the lone figure, their blades raised as they charged the red-coated soldiers who had dared to enter their domain.

There were many more than Jack had imagined. Some were naked save for a langoti around the groin. Their skin glistened with a thick layer of grease, their hands holding anything that could be used to cudgel or hack a man to death. Others were dressed like knights of old, the fierce sunlight reflecting from their polished armour, their gleaming sabres bared and ready to kill. There were flashes of red in the throng, the vivid scarlet of a deserter's coat bright in the packed ranks. But mainly Jack just saw disaster, his small command no match for the multitude that thundered towards them.

The enemy leader appeared. He was a giant of a man mounted on an enormous warhorse, and he loomed over his men like a vengeful god. He was dressed as finely as a prince, with thick, swirling black robes, his bearing as regal as that of an English duke. His thickly bearded face was creased in a ferocious scowl, his mouth stretched wide as he urged his men up and over the crest, calling for them to kill, to slay those who had strayed near to his lair.

'Prepare to fire!'

Ten bayonet-tipped muskets were brought to the shoulder at the curt command, the redcoats taking up the slack in the trigger as they readied for the order to fire.

Jack held back the final command. He saw the muzzles waver as the men struggled to hold the unwieldy weapons steady, the seventeen inches of steel making them unbalanced and clumsy. There would be time for a single volley. One chance for the muskets to spit out death before the men would be unleashed and ordered to charge. Jack could not afford to waste it, and he forced himself to stand calm, waiting until the enemy was close enough so that every shot would find a target.

The disordered mob surged forward. Still Jack delayed the order to fire, even though the ambushers were so close that he could see every detail on the faces rushing towards him.

The mob was no more than fifty yards away, just moments from reaching the thin red line that stood with such stoic defiance in their path.

'Fire!' Jack bellowed the order, releasing the tension that had gripped him since the first bandit had appeared.

The sepoys obeyed immediately, the sudden thunderclap of sound shocking in its violence as the muskets fired as one.

He had deliberately left the volley late, the front of the mob barely twenty-five yards from the frail British line. At such close range every bullet smacked into an enemy body, flensing those who had rushed to the fore.

'Charge! Charge!'

Jack felt his fear released. Nothing mattered now. Nothing except the need to fight, to take his sword and hack at the enemy.

This was the intoxicating madness that he had half forgotten. The soul-searing surge of hate and anger that combined with his fear to drive him willingly into the dreadful cauldron of battle.

He tore out of the cloud of smoke created by the discharging muskets. The ambush had been bludgeoned to a halt. Bloodied, crumpled bodies formed a grotesque barrier and tangled around the feet of those nearest to them, the impetus of the bandits' charge broken by the brutal volley.

He heard a roar behind him as the sepoys followed his lead, their sudden scream a horrific contrast to the stoic silence with which they had watched the enemy close on them. The men in red coats were unleashed to do what they had been trained to do.

It was time to kill.

Jack rushed at the stalled mob, the last few yards disappearing in a blur of movement as he led his men forward. He ducked under a farmer's sickle wielded by a man dressed in nothing more than a simple loincloth. The curving blade flashed past, missing his neck by no more than an inch. He was on the man in a heartbeat, the narrow escape meaning nothing as the madness of battle surged through him. There was time to see terror ripple through the man's greased body before Jack rammed his sword into his throat.

As he tore his blade from the gruesome wound, his victim fell to the ground, his hands clasped around the dreadful ruin of his neck. Jack was forced to step swiftly to his left to avoid a spear-thrust aimed at his side, the speed of the melee leaving no time for thought. He back-swung his sword, using the sharpened rear edge to gouge across the face of the white-robed man who had just attempted to kill him. Another spear-thrust from the mass that swirled around him tore through his red coat, missing his flesh by inches. Jack spun as he felt the impact, slashing upwards, releasing a howl of frustration as it bounced off the heavy robes of his assailant, the thin edge of the cheap sword already too dull to cut through the thickly bound cloth. But the blow drove the attacker back, giving Jack enough time to raise his revolver.

The barrel of the weapon was no more than six inches from the nearest attacker in the press of bodies. He pulled the trigger, aiming at the snarling face of a heavily armoured man who was lifting a thick talwar above his head, readying himself for a blow that would shatter Jack's skull with a single strike. The bullet punched into the man's face, blood and scraps of flesh flung wide as it smashed through skin and bone. The man fell and Jack felt nothing, already searching for his next target, his soul emptied of all emotion save the need to kill.

He aimed into the whirl of bodies, pulling the trigger again and again, each shot knocking another one of the enemy from their feet, the pistol deadly in the bloody close-quarters fight. His fusillade drove the ambushers away from him as he cut a dreadful swathe of death through their ranks. It gave his sepoys an opening, and they threw themselves into the gap he had created, their bayonets reaching for the enemy, their shrill banshee cries the last sound many of the ambushers would ever hear. They thrust into the mass of bodies, wielding their bayonets in the short, professional jabs they had learnt on the drill square. The ground under their feet was littered with the dead and the dying, the hideous stench of blood and opened bowels filling their nostrils as they surged forward, seeking the next victim for their blades. It would have taken a brave man or a fool to stand in their way, and the disparate horde recoiled from the disciplined charge.

Jack let his men push past him. His blood thundered with the need to throw himself back into the melee, but he forced himself to still the urge, his need for knowledge overriding the visceral instinct to fight. The sepoys' thrust into the enemy's ranks gave him a few precious seconds to try to make sense of the desperate struggle. Seconds he could not afford to waste if he was to defy the gods and snatch a bloody victory from the gaping jaws of defeat.

The ambushers were giving ground, melting away from the horror of the sepoys' volley and their merciless bayonets. Yet despite their bravery and brutal efficiency, the red-coated soldiers were still outnumbered. The mob might have been giving ground in front of the assault, but more and more were moving to the flanks, swarming around the handful of British soldiers.

When they rediscovered their courage, Jack's command would be overwhelmed.

Chapter Eight

———◆•◆•◆———

Isabel crouched behind the boulder, transfixed by the gory spectacle going on no more than two dozen yards from where she hid. For as long as she could remember she had read about battle, captivated by the dry, urbane accounts of campaigns and set-piece war written by generals and commanders. She had devoured every book she could find, from Livy to Wellington, yet she had never before contemplated the brutality that she saw unfurling before her. The dusty, emotionless words did nothing to convey the dreadful struggle in which men hacked and gouged in a desperate fight to kill or be killed. There was no glory in war, and the sordid, squalid sight she was witnessing left her struggling to control the waves of nausea that lurched through her body.

The black-robed leader of the enemy horde detached himself from the fighting. Even across the yards of scrub she felt his eyes bore into her. Her throat constricted in fear as he eased his charger round, turning its head to face where she hid, before kicking the mount into motion, riding straight for her. He never once let his eyes leave her, staring into her terrified gaze as he rode down the slope.

'Danbury!' The scream tore from her throat as the heavily armoured figure slid from his horse a few yards in front of her. The man was huge, a figure from a nightmare, his robes the colour of night, his black eyes pitiless. He was a vision of hell manifest on earth.

Agile despite his bulk, the huge warrior landed gently on his feet. Isabel saw the purpose in his action. Fear surged through her, a visceral wave of animal terror more powerful than anything she had ever known. It burst out of her like a river in flood breaching its banks.

'Danbury! Danbury!' She shrieked his name in panic, her voice shrill.

The black-robed figure was unmoved, no trace of emotion visible behind the beard that smothered his face. He lifted a single gauntleted hand, holding it towards her as if inviting her to dance. Her fear reasserting itself, she stood mute, powerless to resist.

'Come.' The man's voice was soft, barely above a whisper, and Isabel struggled to hear the single command over the cacophony of the fight that carried on regardless of her plight. The fingers encased in thick black leather gloves flexed, beckoning her to him.

She felt her body jerk into motion as if tugged forward by an invisible chain. She thought nothing of the silver revolver she still held in her left hand, the idea of resisting never once entering her mind. Her movements felt ponderous, as if the ground was cloying mud rather than dusty soil. Her eyes fixed on the face that observed her progress with serenity and she reached out her free hand, demurely offering it as if she were shyly accepting a suitor's request for a dance at a dowager's ball.

She laid her small hand in the centre of the leather gauntlet and surrendered.

The ambushers swarmed forward, surrounding the small group of sepoys, forcing Jack back into the fight. He flicked his sword out, deflecting a richly jewelled talwar that reached for his eyes, then brought his own blade around in a glittering arc to parry an ancient bayonet-tipped musket that was thrust at his stomach. More blades reached forward, the enemy's courage growing with every second as the wild horde sensed the weakness in the tiring sepoys.

The first of Jack's men went down, a pig-sticking spear finding its way past his jabbing bayonet. The leaf-shaped head slid through the thick scarlet coat and into the sepoy's flesh, the fiendish shriek of triumph emitted by its owner the last sound the dying soldier would ever hear. The sight of the first red-coated devil falling to the ground galvanised the rest of the mob. Those too cunning, or too fearful, to have been at the forefront of the attack sensed the change, belatedly pushing forward, their desire to fight kindled now that victory seemed certain.

As one the mob closed on the small band of soldiers that had fought with such courage. Like a pack of wild dogs they flung themselves into the fight, each keen to wet their blade in the sepoys' blood, eager for the gory proof of their valour.

The surviving members of the escort did not stand a chance. The enemy swarmed around them, countless blades whirling, attacks coming from all sides. Yet still the sepoys fought on, stamping their feet forward, thrusting their bayonets at the bodies that pressed against them, their leaden arms and aching muscles forced to continue the fight, the soldiers of the foreign Queen refusing to submit meekly to their fate.

Above the cacophony of the fight, Jack heard Isabel scream his assumed name. He shoved a naked fanatic backwards with his shoulder, using the point of his sword to tear a fist-sized hole in the man's grease-covered stomach, then forced his way out of the vicious melee, his blunted sword bludgeoning those of the ambushers seeking to attack the rear of the sepoys' fragile formation. He had no concept of how long they had fought, the passage of time meaningless in the grotesque struggle where a single heartbeat could pass between life and death. All he knew was that Isabel's terrified scream was a call for help he had to heed.

Free of the fight, Jack ran hard, ignoring the spasm of pain in the pit of his spine and the dreadful ache in his sword arm, focusing his attention on the tall figure that loomed over Isabel's tiny frame. At any second he expected the man to turn, to react to the single foolish redcoat charging towards him. But the black-robed giant stayed facing Isabel, his back left undefended and exposed. It gave Jack an opportunity, and he strained every tired sinew as he strove to reach Isabel and somehow drag her to safety.

The ground passed slowly under his boots, the uneven surface twisting each footfall. He was certain his legs would give way at any moment, buckling under the strain of racing down the slope to send him tumbling and falling to the floor. Yet somehow he kept his footing, and he counted off the seconds as he hurtled towards the black-robed figure. Yard by yard, step by step he closed the gap between them, no longer hearing the attackers' shouts of victory or the thunder of his own heartbeat in his ears.

He screamed as he charged, the final few yards disappearing in a sudden rush as he flung himself at the huge man, releasing his tension into a blow aimed at the back of the bandit's neck. It was a vicious attack, driven by all of Jack's anger at the futility of the desperate fight. His sword vibrated in his hand as it sliced through the air, the aching muscles in his forearm already bracing for the moment of impact, for the shock of the blade ripping into the enemy leader's flesh.

The talwar came out of nowhere. The black-robed figure spun round, his richly decorated blade whispering upwards with the speed of a striking cobra, the huge two-handed sword blocking the blow that had been a heartbeat away from ending his life.

The counterattack smashed Jack's sword to one side, violently deflecting his blade away. Jack was immediately thrown completely off balance and he tumbled to the floor, hitting the stony ground with a bone-jarring thump. As he fell, the talwar flickered through the air, missing his head by a fraction of an inch.

Jack threw himself to one side as soon as he hit the ground, using the momentum of his fall to roll away from his enemy, ignoring the stabs of agony as his body scraped across the rocky soil. Once, twice the talwar stabbed downwards, missing him by no more than a hair's breadth, the attacks coming at him so fast that he could do nothing but throw himself down the slope and hope that he could avoid the deadly blade.

His wild tumble gained momentum, the incline of the slope adding speed to his movement. He sensed another attack, the flash of the talwar slicing through the air inches from his nose. The blade went wide; it gave Jack the slightest of openings and he pushed with his legs, scrabbling for purchase. He scrambled to his feet with as much speed as he could muster, and with a dull clang his notched and pitted sword met the dreadful talwar. His desperate parry battered the blade to one side, saving him moments before his enemy's sword would have been thrust into his guts.

The fierce surge of elation at once again being able to fight was short-lived. The black-robed figure stepped forward, unleashing a flurry of attacks that had Jack sliding backwards as he struggled to counter the pace of his enemy's movements. The talwar sliced through the air, each slash followed within a heartbeat by another, a relentless salvo that drove him back down the slope, his sword arm ringing as he blocked each blow as best he could.

'For pity's sake, shoot him,' he screamed at Isabel.

She gave no sign of having heard him. The small silver revolver was still clutched in her left hand, but it hung uselessly by her side, the terrified girl giving no thought to the weapon that she had brandished with such defiance only a short time before.

Jack twisted to one side, his attempt to get Isabel's attention momentarily distracting him and nearly letting the black-robed swordsman's blade slip past his faltering defence. Again and again he parried the fast-moving talwar. He was forced to forget Isabel as he fought for his life, every ounce of his strength needed to counter the terrifying rain of blows that came at him one after another, each driven by a strength he could barely match.

The black-robed figure started to chant as he fought. Underscored by the metallic clash of swords, the deep voice rumbled in a hypnotic rhythm. Jack did his best to pay no heed to the words, but they unsettled him nonetheless, the menace in the foreign phrases clear.

With a loud cry the chant stopped. The black-robed figure paused for no more than a single heartbeat before his sword whirled through the air, slashing towards Jack in a blow of immense power.

Jack thrust his battered sabre forward. His speed saved him, the two blades coming together a fraction of a second before the talwar would have crashed into his unprotected head. Yet the noise of the impact was wrong. With a dull thud, Jack's sabre shattered, the cheap steel cleaved in half by the power of the bandit leader's attack. He could only stare in horror as the top half of his weapon spun away, leaving only the shattered stump in his hand.

Jack's stubborn defence was ended, leaving him unarmed and defenceless. He felt the shadow of death loom over him as the black-robed figure pulled back his sword arm, preparing the thrust that Jack could no longer counter. He looked into his enemy's face and knew he was about to die.

Chapter Nine

Isabel had watched as if paralysed as the black-robed figure flayed mercilessly at the British officer. At any moment she expected the fast-moving talwar to break through Danbury's desperate defence, his faltering defiance certain to be no match for the power of his assailant's wild assault.

Somehow, though, Danbury stayed alive, his sabre meeting every blow. Isabel had never seen such ferocity. The two men fought at a frightening pace, their blades moving with such speed that she could barely even see the dreadful steel as it flashed through the air. She did not hear Danbury call to her. It was only when the dark-robed figure started to chant that she felt herself return to her senses. She felt Danbury begin to waver, the sinister incantation unsettling the British captain.

'Danbury!' She screamed his name as the chant came to its terrifying conclusion, but her voice was lost in the black-robed figure's cry and she could only watch in horror as his sword slashed towards Danbury with a speed and power that seemed impossible to counter.

The sound of the British officer's sword snapping reached her in the moments after the dreadful chant came to an end. She saw the appalled look on Danbury's face as he realised he was about to die.

She ran forward, careless of the enemy horde that had begun to swarm down the slope. Her only thought was to help, to try to save the red-coated officer before he was struck down in front of her eyes.

'Danbury! Catch!' She drew back her arm, tossing the beleaguered captain a lifeline, praying that she had acted in time to save him.

The silver metal of the revolver flashed once in the sun as Isabel's throw sent it spinning through the air. Jack flung the stump of his broken sword towards the black-robed figure, freeing his hands of the now useless weapon. He snatched at the tiny revolver, snapping it from the air, the sharp metal stinging his hand. Without pause he brought his arm around, pointing the gun straight at the face of the man about to kill him. His thumb slid over the back of the finely crafted weapon, cocking the hammer, readying it to fire.

The heavily bearded face loomed over the simple sight at the end of the revolver's barrel. At such close range Jack knew he could not miss, and he felt a surge of savage joy as he pulled the trigger.

Instead of the crash of gunpowder igniting, there was nothing but an impotent click. Isabel's precious revolver had failed to fire.

The black-robed figure sheathed his sword. He took a pace backwards before disdainfully turning away from the man who had come so close to killing him.

Jack dropped the useless pistol, letting it fall from his hand as he felt defeat swamp him. He stood mute, watching the savage mob race down the slope towards him. The bandits circled around, their blades threatening, but none was willing to be the first to strike. Their leader flicked a gauntleted hand in Jack's direction, a curt word of command putting an end to the impasse. A swarthy figure took a pace forward, hefting a heavy club. Without a word he slammed it into the back of Jack's head, bludgeoning him to the ground.

The darkness swallowed his soul. Jack felt its cold embrace, its touch as delicate and as jealous as a lover's. He did not fight it as once he had. Instead he welcomed it, submitting to it with the grace of a maiden bride on her marriage bed. There was no fear in giving in. Just relief. He faced the blackness and willed it to take him.

But the darkness rejected him, thrusting him away, throwing him towards the distant light. Jack screamed inwardly with frustration as he felt the icy tendrils release him, forcing him to return to the place that terrified him most.

Jack opened his eyes. At first it was hard to tell if they were truly open or not. He could feel a hard stone floor under his body, its dampness soaking into his clothes. He could smell mould and decay, the stench of unwashed bodies and animal waste thick in his nostrils. He tasted the staleness of the air, the cold, dead flavour of the dark.

'Danbury?'

The voice startled him. His name was spoken in no more than a whisper but there was no mistaking its owner. Isabel Youngsummers had sensed him stirring and called to him, summoning him back to the world he had so dearly wished to leave.

'Danbury, are you awake?'

Jack's cramped and aching muscles protested as he started to move. He forced himself to sit, finally coming truly alive, belatedly starting to take stock of his surroundings.

There was little for his eyes to focus on. The room had been hacked into rock, the walls still bearing the marks of the simple tools that had been used to gouge and scrape the space from the hard ground. A single door was shut tight, the small window in its centre barred with thick metal columns, each crusted with rust. The window was the only source of light, a single torch that burnt just outside the door casting forbidding shadows into the depths of the fetid space.

'Danbury! Thank God.' Isabel's relief was clear. 'We thought you might be dead.'

'You may soon wish that were the case.'

Jack heard the second voice and turned his head, his neck complaining as it jarred with the movement. The Reverend Youngsummers sat slumped against the wall to his right.

'It is good to see you, Danbury, but I fear you may have preferred it were you not to have woken.' Youngsummers sobbed as he finished speaking, an anguished wail escaping his thick lips. 'We are doomed.'

'Papa!' Isabel's hands lifted to her face, hiding the sight of her father's distress.

'Dear God, why are you doing this to me?' Youngsummers pushed himself forward and on to his knees. He raised his arms to the ceiling as he beseeched his God, lamenting his bitter fate. 'Why submit me to this torture? Why have you forsaken your loyal servant? Why?' He fell silent, his head bowed so that his thick chin rested on his chest, his corpulent frame rocking with the motion of his sobs.

'What happened?' Jack spoke for the first time, his voice thick with phlegm. He spat hard, careless of the look of disgust on the Reverend's tear-streaked face.

Youngsummers slumped back into his former position, exhausted by his pitiful plea.

'They've kept us alive because of the colour of our skin.' The clergyman spoke in the exhausted voice of a dying man. 'So that they can torture us.'

'Don't be such a fool, Papa,' Isabel snapped. Her eyes flashed with the same look of defiance Jack had seen when they were first ambushed. 'They've kept us alive because they believe we have value. They will think to ransom us. We cannot lose hope.'

'Hope!' Youngsummers wailed the word. 'Do you not see, daughter? God has forsaken me. He has given me up to the godless. He has abandoned me.'

'Papa! Do not speak like that. We are alive.'

'Isabel is right.' Jack spoke, silencing father and daughter. They both turned to face him, looking to him for guidance. 'They have kept us alive because we have value to them. What happened to the men?'

'Dead. All dead. They butchered them.' Youngsummers relished the words, finding strength in the suffering of others.

'They died fighting,' Isabel corrected her father. 'They fought hard. As did you, Danbury.'

Jack took no pleasure in hearing Isabel's praise. 'We lost. We should have fought harder.'

'That is a foolish thing to say. Against so many there was nothing more you could do.'

Jack's brow furrowed as he looked at Isabel. 'I am not so sure.'

'So what will happen to us?' asked Isabel, her voice timid. She sounded very much like the frightened little girl she really was.

'They will kill us!' Youngsummers interrupted. 'These black-guards have no qualms. They are godless scum and they will slaughter us without a thought.'

'That's enough.' Jack injected some snap into his tone. It was the voice of an officer, one that was used to being obeyed.

Youngsummers opened his mouth to object before a look at the hard eyes of the British captain silenced him.

'We are alive,' Jack continued. 'If they wanted us dead they would have killed us on the spot. I doubt these fellows know much of patience. Isabel is right. They will try to ransom us.'

Isabel nodded as she listened intently to his words. Her father was not so calm.

'You know nothing of these people, least of all what they will do to us.' Youngsummers looked at his daughter, licking his lips nervously before leaning closer to Jack. 'I fear for my daughter's chastity.' The words were said in a whisper, a furtive look on the Reverend's face.

'They will have to kill me first.'

Youngsummers snorted his derision at Jack's bold claim. 'I am sure they would not find that so difficult, Danbury. How can you speak of fighting?'

Jack grinned. 'Because I'm redcoat. It's what we do.'

'Spoken like a fool.' Youngsummers' jowls creased in irritation.

'Be careful who you call a fool, Reverend.'

Youngsummers raised a trembling finger and pointed it towards Jack's heart. 'You, sir, you are a fool if you think your precious pride matters one bit. I call you a fool, for you speak foolish words.'

Jack felt a spark of temper but he bit his tongue. He had learnt to curb his emotion when confronted by bombastic buffoons.

The Reverend Youngsummers knew no such forbearance. 'You are the reason we are here! It is you who is to blame for our incarceration at the hands of those godless barbarians.' His fear added fuel to his tongue. 'You were ordered to protect us. And you failed, Danbury. You failed! I face a martyr's death because you could not obey that simple instruction! It is your fault. Yours! You are a disgrace!'

Youngsummers fell silent, his rage spent. His pudgy hands smothered his face as the tears came, his body rocking back and forth, his distress overwhelming him.

Isabel had sat in shocked silence as her father broke down. Her whey-coloured face revealed her anguish, her self-control eroding when she heard the horror in her father's voice, his certainty that they faced death taking a grip on her heart.

Jack smiled as he looked at her, yet she simply stared back at him, her eyes wide with terror.

'Your father is right. I am a disgrace.' He spoke in the even tones of a father reading a night-time story to calm his child's fear of the darkness, his words intended to calm and soothe. 'But I meant what I said. I shall die trying to protect you. I promise.'

He offered the promise willingly and he meant every word. He did not fear death. It was life that terrified him.

Chapter Ten

———◆———

'For the love of heaven. It has begun. They are coming for me!' Reverend Youngsummers greeted the sudden burst of noise with horror.

'Be quiet.' Jack snapped the command as his ears strained to hear. It had been a long night, the silence that had lapsed over the prisoners wearing at Jack's patience. He guessed that it was not yet dawn, but trapped in the gloomy prison he had no real notion of the passage of time. Now something had awoken to shatter the quiet, and Jack was in no mood to be gentle on the pessimistic doomsayer.

He moved quickly so he could peer out of the door's single window. His order had silenced Youngsummers, who fell back into morose silence, slumping against the wall in resignation.

'What is it?' Isabel had risen lithely to her feet and now she pressed against Jack's shoulder as she tried to see movement outside their dank prison.

The noise came again. It sounded like a child running a stick down a line of metal railings. It came in bursts, each louder than the previous, before dying out, the silence pressing back so that they felt they had surely been mistaken, that nothing stirred to disturb the black nothingness of the night.

Then the shouting started, the frightened bellows of men waking to chaos, and the silence disappeared under a bewildering hubbub of sound as the rabble that had defeated the small band of British sepoys arose to confusion. The crackle of gunfire underscored the panic, its staccato rhythm increasing in tempo to match the bedlam it had created.

Jack could feel Isabel's breath on the nape of his neck, the warmth at once soothing and stimulating. He could sense her body trembling, her breathing quicker as she too heard the sudden bursts of gunfire, her fear and her hope rising in equal measure.

'What is it?' She raised her hand, placing it on Jack's shoulder as she sought reassurance. 'Is it a rescue?'

Jack's breath caught in his throat as he felt Isabel's fingers press into the muscles of his shoulder. 'It's gunfire. But it's not ours.' Her hand felt as if it was on fire, her flesh burning into his skin even through the thick layers of his uniform.

'How can you tell?'

'There are no regular volleys, and the firing is too erratic even for skirmishers.' Jack turned his head so he could look at Isabel. He could smell the faded perfume she had applied the previous morning, the sweet aroma still intoxicating. 'I don't know who it is.'

A sudden scrabble of footsteps saved Jack from further questioning. There were enough blazing torches rammed into ancient wall brackets to allow him to make out what has happening in the corridor outside. It bent to the right, so he could see no more than a few feet, but the noise was unmistakable. Someone was rushing towards the damp cell that had become their prison.

He was certain that the sudden gunfire meant that the bandits' camp was under attack. He was equally sure that someone would remember the hostages, even in the midst of the sudden melee. It would take but a quick word of command to dispatch a few men to quickly dispose of the three English prisoners, and he felt his heart lurch as he realised the danger that was surely hurtling towards them.

He pushed Isabel to one side, thinking to shield her from the assault, taking up a position to block any intruder's entrance to the room. The footsteps sounded loud in the corridor. More than one man was heading their way.

Jack caught a glimpse of shadowy figures rushing down the corridor before the door was thumped hard. The sharp scrape of metal was loud in the small room, a rusty iron lock grating as it was wrenched open. He was tensing himself to fight when a desperate notion came to him. He spun on the spot, pushing Isabel in front of him and throwing himself towards the murkiest corner of the room, into what he hoped were the darkest of the shadows.

Youngsummers lurched to his feet as he saw his daughter propelled towards mortal danger.

'You blackguard!' The protest burst out as the door was thrown open to crash back on its hinges.

Isabel screamed at the sight of two armed men, their drawn swords flickering in the dull light that had belatedly reached the darkened room. Youngsummers blundered forward, reaching for his daughter's arm, the rush of courage pitching him directly into the path of the men sent to kill them.

The first man's eyes darted around the room, searching for danger. He saw the thin young girl who shrieked as if the devil himself were arriving to claim her soul. He saw too the fat man who staggered into his path, his foreign words echoing loudly in the confined space. He did not see the third prisoner, the white-faced officer who had fought with such ferocity that afternoon.

The second man held back, reluctant to enter the darkened room, using his companion's body as a shield.

Jack launched himself from the darkness, screaming like a banshee as he lashed out at the leading bandit. He smashed his fist into the centre of the man's face before driving his left hand into the side of his head, cracking his fist against the hard skull.

His victim crumpled, bludgeoned by the unexpected assault, his sword clattering to the ground as it fell from his nerveless grip. Jack bent and snatched up the fallen weapon, whipping the blade through the air, turning to face the second man.

Isabel screamed at the sudden, shocking violence. Jack ignored her terror and slashed his stolen sword forward, forcing the second would-be killer to parry. He struck again, punching an opening in his opponent's defence, a visceral shout of anger escaping his lips. As he prepared to thrust his blade home, Youngsummers rushed past, bellowing in fear and knocking against Jack's arm, spoiling the killing stroke. The clumsy clergyman stumbled away, heedless of his actions, thinking of nothing more than reaching the darkest corner of the room.

The bandit seized on the sudden reprieve and counterattacked, coming at Jack with a quick series of blows that drove him backwards. In the darkness it was hard to see the fast-moving blade, and Jack was reduced to a desperate defence as he tried to keep the enemy's sword at bay.

'Lord, save me!' Youngsummers shrieked as the pair came close to his sanctuary. In his terror he lashed out with his feet, catching the bandit on the calf. The blow was no more powerful than a child's but it made the would-be killer stumble. Jack saw the talwar drop and launched himself forward. His sword took the bandit in the throat. The blade drove deep, tearing away the man's life in a rush of blood, killing him in a heartbeat.

'Danbury, look out!' Isabel screamed the warning as the first attacker stumbled to his feet, snatching a thin dagger from within the folds of his black robes.

Jack threw himself around to face the new threat, ripping his sword free so that blood and scraps of flesh were torn from the wound and flung far into the room.

The surviving bandit was slow. Jack's ferocious assault had left him dazed and hurting. Yet he saw the attack coming and lurched backwards so that Jack's blade whirled past, the tip of the sword whispering no more than a hair's breadth from his bloodied face. With an incoherent shriek he bounded forward, his wrist locked so that he could drive his dagger deep into his enemy.

Jack saw the razor-sharp blade reaching for him. In desperation he flung his left hand forward, locking it tight on to the other man's wrist. He could feel the muscles pulsing under his grasping fingers, the sinews in the flesh twisting as his opponent tried to free himself.

The bandit slammed his free hand forward, smacking Jack hard on the side of the head, trying to knock him backwards. Jack's head rang from the blow but somehow he held on, his fingers digging into the other man's wrist. His sword arm was trapped between their two bodies, so he let his blade go and pulled his right hand free, bracing himself to strike back.

He saw the man's lip curl in a snarl of animal anger, his teeth stained red with his own blood. The bandit spat at Jack and used both hands to try to wrestle the dagger away from the man he had been sent to kill, cursing the firangi officer who refused to die.

Jack felt the strength in the man's arms as they fought for control of the blade. He knew he had only moments before he lost his hold on the dagger. But his right hand was now free and he thrust it forward and grabbed his attacker by the balls. The man screamed in agony as Jack took hold, twisting his hand, his fingers digging in like claws, the flesh tearing under his grip. The bandit let out an inhuman shriek and let go of the dagger, both his hands scrabbling to free himself from the agony.

Jack snatched the dagger from the air. He had a moment to register the look of horror in his enemy's eyes before he buried the sharpened blade deep into the man's heart.

The bandit looked down in astonishment to see his own knife sticking out of his chest, blood coursing down its length. His fingers clutched at the weapon, his face set in a look of astonishment and bitter reproach.

Jack twisted his wrist and tugged the dagger from the bandit's chest, ignoring the blood that poured down the blade to fall hot and sticky on to his hand. He stepped back and let the corpse fall to the floor, the look of terrified anguish now locked on the man's features for ever. Then he threw the bloody dagger to one side and bent to retrieve the fallen sabre.

'Isabel. It's time to go.' He spoke firmly. He saw the fear in her eyes, but there was no time to dwell on whether she was afraid of the closeness of death or of the man who had fought to save her.

'I'm ready.' To her credit, Isabel rallied fast. 'Papa, come.'

Youngsummers did not move. He sat slumped against the wall, his face covered with scraps of flesh and flecks of blood that had been flung from the tip of Jack's sword as he fought. His eyes were open, but they were glazed and staring straight ahead.

'Papa. We are safe now. We need to go.' Isabel reached forward and gently stroked her father's cheek.

Youngsummers lifted a hand in front of his face, flapping Isabel's away. 'The devil has come for me. I am in hell.'

'Papa!' Isabel snapped the word and reached for her father again, only for her hand to be pushed away once more.

'Do you not see?' Youngsummers locked his staring eyes on to his daughter. 'The devil wants me. He wants me!'

Isabel stamped her foot and turned to Jack. 'He won't come. You'll have to carry him.'

Jack paid her no heed. He had checked the bodies of both bandits to make sure they were truly dead before moving out of their tiny prison to peer anxiously around the corner of the corridor that led towards the outside.

'Captain Danbury.' Isabel demanded his attention. 'You will have to carry my father to safety.'

Jack took one last long look around the corner before turning to face Isabel. She stood, hands on hips, in the centre of the room, the bodies of the two dead men forgotten as she issued her orders. Jack could only marvel at her spirit. She had been moments from death, yet now her anger rose like that of a spoiled child as she sought to get her own way.

'We must go.' He kept his voice calm, despite knowing they had to hurry before more killers were sent after them. 'He can stay here. He'll be safe enough for now.'

'Leave him here? Never!' Isabel's eyes widened in anger.

'In that case, get him up and he can come with us.'

'He won't move. He's having an attack of the vapours.'

'Then he stays here.'

'He will not. You must carry him.'

Jack felt his mouth crease into a grin at the absurd notion. He detected the fury on Isabel's face as she saw his reaction, so he smiled wider.

'I don't think so. Perhaps it would be better for you both to stay here. I'll come back for you when it is safe to do so.'

'You shall do no such thing,' Isabel's voice rose in anger. She stepped forward, decorously skirting the lifeless hand of one of the men sent to kill her so she could wag her finger in Jack's face. 'You will do as I tell you.'

Jack caught her hand, holding the finger tight in his bloody grasp, and bent his head low so that it was only an inch or so from Isabel's face. The temptation to kiss her was almost overpowering.

'Can you really see me carrying him? Who is being the fool now?' His desire made him harsh, and he saw his hard words crush the anger from the young girl's face just as he crushed her finger in his hand.

Isabel pulled away and he let her go, turning his back on her lest she see the lust that he was sure was written into every pore of his face.

'Very well. He will stay here but I am coming with you.' She spoke the words in the icy tones of a dowager giving instructions to her butler.

Jack turned and bowed at the waist. 'Yes, milady.'

He did not wait to see how Isabel would react. Instead, he walked out of the room.

It was time to see what stirred in the darkness.

Chapter Eleven

The sounds of battle echoed down the narrow passageway. Jack kept his sword to the fore, muttering a silent prayer as he crept forward. The wall on his right blocked the free movement of his sword arm, so he was forced to walk with his arm bent awkwardly as he tried to keep his stolen blade at the ready.

The sounds of fighting grew louder with every step. Jack slowed his pace as the floor levelled out, certain he had to be close to reaching the end of the passage. He pushed himself hard against the left side of the tunnel, giving his sword arm as much room as he could, and inched his way forward. He turned quickly, gesturing for Isabel to stay back, fearful of striking her should he be forced to fight. She shrank back instantly, any notion of disobedience driven away by the tension of tiptoeing along the dark corridor.

The loud crash of a musket being fired assaulted his eardrums, the thunderclap of sound amplified by the thick walls. A thin cloud of pungent smoke billowed towards him, the familiar smell of rotten eggs sticking in his throat. He paused for a moment, tensing his muscles, before throwing himself round the corner, trusting to his speed to overcome any danger waiting after the final bend.

A turbaned figure knelt behind a makeshift barricade that blocked the exit from the passageway. The bandit had just pulled an aged Brown Bess musket back over the barricade, a thin trail of smoke snaking from its bayonet-tipped barrel. He looked behind him in astonishment, his jaw hanging in amazement, as a red-coated British officer appeared from the depths of the tunnel.

Jack gave the shocked musketeer no time to recover. He smashed his sword's hilt on to the top of the man's head, bludgeoning him to the ground with the single blow. Then he dragged the fallen man out of the way and crouched down behind the rough barricade, trying to make sense of the confusion that swirled in the darkness beyond the passageway.

A scene of chaos greeted his eyes. It was still night, but the scene was lit by half a dozen watch-fires, the flickering light casting disorientating shadows amongst the shapes of fast-moving bodies. Men ran in every direction, some brandishing weapons, others with arms full of plunder. Crumpled bodies lay scattered across the ground, proof of the effectiveness of the gunfire the prisoners had heard. As Jack watched, he saw a mounted figure ride past no more than ten yards from where he crouched. A loud voice called out, and Jack recognised the calm orders of a commander. The black-robed leader of the mob had arrived to take charge.

Another volley of gunshots rang out. More bodies slumped to the ground as bullets found their mark. The bandit leader roared at his men, bellowing orders, and the mob started to form a crude line facing the gunfire, ignoring their brethren who had been struck down.

More men were summoned from the darkness to join the defensive position. Those with firearms squatted down, aiming their pieces into the darkness. At a fierce word of command they opened fire, delivering a volley that tore out into the night. It was nothing like the volley a British battalion could deliver; instead of barking out in unison, the bandits' fusillade dragged out, many seconds passing between the first shot and the last. Yet the black-robed leader had got his men fighting back, aiming at the flashes of light that revealed the presence of their enemy.

The incoming fire stopped. The silence stretched out, the powder smoke from the volley drifting away on the light breeze that flitted across the open ground.

The enemy had disappeared.

The bandits looked at each other, their anxiety obvious. The silence pulled at their nerves, the sudden calm as threatening as the shots that had thundered round them. Their black-robed leader walked his horse forward, peering into the darkness, trying to sense where the danger had gone.

Then came a new sound. It was barely audible at first, nothing more than a gentle murmur from far in the distance. But it grew, slowly and steadily, building in intensity, the tempo increasing into a regular staccato rhythm.

The bandits shrank back as the noise increased, their thin line contracting in fear, the frightened men seeking the comfort of being close to one another. The drumming was relentless, the vibration reverberating through the ground so it felt as though the soil trembled under their feet.

Jack peered out into the darkness, his eyes searching for the source of the ominous noise. He could see nothing but shadows, menacing shapes that flittered across his vision.

'What is it?'

He felt Isabel's breath on his cheek as she whispered the question. He had not heard her approach, the subtle sounds of her movement lost in the constant drumming that continued to build, hammering into their eardrums, the vibration jarring their bodies.

Jack was given no time to answer. From the depths of the darkness a mass of horsemen charged forward. They emerged in one long line, the riders stirrup to stirrup. With a sudden roar they gouged their spurs into their horses' flanks, urging them on, the final yards to be covered as quickly as possible as the riders committed their mounts to the all-consuming madness of the charge.

Jack was aware of a sense of order as the cavalry burst from the night, the controlled ranks evidence of countless hours of training. The riders wore sky-blue tunics with tight white breeches and a single pouch-belt from right shoulder to left hip. On their heads each wore a square-topped helmet with a single thick white plume that stood proud on the peak. They made a fine sight as they galloped out of the darkness, the splendour of the cavalry charge revealed in all of its dreadful glory.

In the white-gloved hand of each horseman was a lance, its long shaft braced under the right arm. The razor-sharp points moved lower as the riders tensed for the point of impact, the deadly blades keening for the blood of the enemy. The unstoppable wall of death hurtled forward, the lancers' faces twisted into snarls of hatred as they picked the first targets for their dreadful weapons.

The terrified bandits broke. The gunfire had brought them together, but now they scattered in every direction, throwing their weapons to the floor in their desperate haste to escape. Yet there was nowhere for them to run, no sanctuary to be found on the barren hillside.

From his hidden viewpoint Jack saw confusion tear through their ranks. He was close enough to see the panic on their faces, their despair and terror as they ran to escape the terrifying charge.

The lancers rode on to the hilltop, their line still steady and straight.

And the killing began.

Lances were pulled back as the cavalrymen picked their targets, their tension released as they thrust their weapons forward. They speared their first victims, the sharpened points exploding into the flesh of the men who were trying to escape.

The precise line broke up as the first bandits fell to the ground, their bodies torn by the dreadful weapons. The lancers raced on, overrunning and cutting down the enemy without mercy. Some turned to fight, lifting sabres or talwars to try to counter the dreadful combination of man and beast that thundered towards them. These men at least died with a weapon in their hands, yet not one lancer was unseated, not one horse cut or speared by their desperate acts of defiance, those brave enough to stand their ground pierced by the deadly reach of the lance before they could strike back.

The lancers ruthlessly pursued the fleeing bandits, determined that none would escape. Jack watched in morbid fascination as the fight descended into a hunt and the lancers spurred after their foe, breaking ranks to ride down any bandit still alive.

In front of the barricade, the black-robed leader stood motionless. For a moment, Jack was certain the bandits' leader would charge the lancers, but instead he gathered his reins in one black-gauntleted hand and whirled his horse round, ramming his heels into the animal's sides as he made his own bid for safety. A handful of his men followed their chief, throwing away their weapons in their desperate flight.

It was only as the black-robed leader galloped clear that Jack realised where he was. The bandits had conducted their doomed defence on the top of a hill that dominated the surrounding area. It was clear of any building, the closest peasant hovel a good two hundred yards away down the slope. Jack thrust his head past the barricade, looking round to confirm that his first suspicion had been correct. The tower rose away above him, its aged stone sides stretching up into the night.

The tower that Isabel had been so keen to visit.

With nowhere else to run to, many of the fleeing men were making for the tower. None would reach it. They were slaughtered to a man, stuck down by the lancers, who callously butchered them as they tried to escape.

Jack and Isabel watched the orgy of death that was happening a matter of yards from where they hid. The corridor to their prison was slightly to one side of the tower, screened from view by a thick clump of thorny bushes. Jack could only guess that their improvised prison provided some sort of storage for the main tower, the simple room hacked from the ground to shelter precious supplies or valuable animals from the torrid weather that would besiege the area for so much of the year.

Yet they were not totally hidden. Two bandits fleeing from the lancers' charge must have seen the glow from the entrance as they ran from the slaughter, and they changed direction, heading straight for the barricade.

'Danbury!' Isabel saw the danger first, her fingers clutching at Jack's arm as she called out in alarm.

'Get back! Now, damn it. Move!' Jack pushed her back down the corridor and away from the barricade. His haste made him rough, and she tripped as she tried to obey, clattering painfully to the ground so that she lay sprawled directly behind where Jack would have to fight.

'Stay down!' Jack cursed under his breath as he failed to get

Isabel out of sight. Yet there was no time for any further action, the two desperate bandits now only a few yards away from the barricade.

Jack glanced around and noticed the musket that had been dropped by the turbaned defender. Without hesitation he threw down his stolen talwar and snatched the firearm up, his hands curling round the familiar shape. It felt warm to his touch and he savoured the comforting weight. It had been a long time since he had last handled a musket, yet he felt the confidence surge through him.

The leading bandit reached the barricade. He slashed his sabre in an arc to drive Jack away from the simple obstruction. Jack eased his weight back, letting the sword whisper past inches in front of his face. It was almost too easy. He saw the look of astonishment on the bandit's face as his blow missed its target, the dreadful realisation that he had left himself wide open and defenceless.

'One.' Jack stamped his foot down, throwing his weight forward as he thrust the bayonet into the bandit's body.

'Two.' He twisted the weapon as the bayonet ripped into the man's stomach, turning the blade to stop it becoming stuck in the dying man's flesh.

'Three.' He recovered his weapon, pulling it back with as much force as he had driven it forward, carelessly slicing the blade through the desperate fingers that grasped it in despair.

'Four.' He stamped his foot forward again, aiming the blade at the stomach of the second bandit, who had been revealed as the body of the first slid screaming to the floor. The bayonet reached over the top of the barricade as Jack thrust with all his strength. In desperation, the second bandit tried to parry the blow, swiping his sword sideways in a frantic attempt to beat the weapon aside.

'Five.' Jack pulled the musket back as soon as he felt the bandit's sword batter against it. He saw the man's eyes flash white as he tried to recover from the desperate counter, his wild defence unbalancing him and leaving him wide open.

'Six.' Again Jack stamped forward, ramming his blade into the centre of the second bandit's body, paying no heed to the sabre that carved a thick slice of wood from the weapon's barrel as the man's parry arrived a heartbeat too late to save him.

'Seven.' He pulled the musket back, ignoring the thick pulse of blood that gushed over the bayonet to run through the thick groove in its top that was designed for that very purpose. The second bandit slumped to the ground, collapsing over the body of the first, both men victims of Jack's ruthless skill.

Jack paused, his muscles tensed. He had felt nothing as he fought, every movement instinctive. It was the drill that was hammered into every raw recruit, the drill masters relentless in their pursuit of perfection as they instilled in the redcoats the ability to use the vicious bayonet with ruthless precision. It was the training that made every one of them a killer.

Past the barricade, the fight was over. The bodies of the bandits were scattered across the ground, some lying in heaps where half a dozen men had been slain in a huddle, some sprawled singly, their torn corpses left to pour their life blood into the dusty soil alone.

The bandits had been massacred, barely a handful escaping the ruthlessly executed attack. The Tiger's band of misfits and renegades had been broken.

Chapter Twelve

─────◆─────

'Is it over?'

Isabel's voice was timid. She still lay on the floor and her hands lifted to cover her face as she saw the British officer turn, his face still twisted in the awful snarl of a killer, blood dripping from the tip of the bayonet that he had wielded with such dreadful purpose. He was a figure from a nightmare, and Isabel felt fear flutter in her heart. The presence of death was so close that she could smell the sour tang of spilt blood and the sickly-sweet aroma of torn flesh. He had killed the men in a matter of seconds, dispatching their souls in front of her terrified gaze. Now he came towards her, and for a moment she thought the dreadful gore-smeared blade would reach for her.

Then she saw his face change. The tension left his expression, a trace of the familiar rueful smile returning.

'My apologies. I didn't mean to push you so hard.'

He offered her his hand to help her to his feet. The change in his manner was sudden; from killer to civilised gentleman in a single heartbeat. Yet Isabel hesitated, her heart still pounding as she contemplated the strong hand reaching down to her. She saw the blood that was already turning black on his skin, the spilt blood of his enemies staining his flesh. She could only wonder at what stain such a fight would leave on his soul.

She saw the flicker of annoyance flitter across his face when she did not immediately respond to his command. Ignoring the fear that squirmed inside her, she obeyed, placing her much smaller hand into his and allowing herself to be pulled to her feet. As she stood, she looked into his dark grey eyes. They met her scrutiny calmly as they stood within inches of each other. She saw then the life in his soul, the burning spark that belied the suffering and the burden she sensed he carried. She had watched him kill and he had terrified her with his merciless skill. Yet she was drawn to him like no other man she had known.

He pulled back, as if suddenly awkward to be so close to her.

'Go back to your father. Tell him we are safe.' He gave the order brusquely, yet she heard his breath catch in his throat. She knew then that she wanted him. She wanted the British captain to be hers.

Jack slid over the barricade, keeping the musket with its bloody bayonet in his right hand. He stepped carefully over the bodies of his fallen enemies before striding forward with a confidence that belied the dread settling deep in his gut.

A cry of alarm greeted his sudden appearance. The nearest blue-coated lancer spied him and immediately wrenched at the reins of his horse that were bundled into his left hand. Jack saw the lance blade twitch as the cavalryman brought the point up before he jabbed his spurs into his mount's sides, urging it into a quick walk.

More lancers turned to stare at the white-faced redcoat who had emerged unannounced into their midst. Many had already dismounted and were going through the laborious task of checking that the many fallen bodies were indeed dead. Those that were not were quickly dispatched with a blade across the throat. There was to be no mercy that day.

Jack's mouth went dry as the lancer increased his speed. The razor-sharp tip of the lance was aimed directly at his heart. It never wavered, even as the horse's gait changed from a trot to a canter. Jack knew then what terror the bandits must have experienced as the lancers burst from the night. He had felt it once before, and the memory of a gloomy Crimean field surged into his mind. The lancers that day had been Russian Cossacks, but his fear of the wicked weapon was the same.

He stood tall, letting his confidence show in his bearing. He would not betray fear. He was a British officer and he faced the lancer with all the dignity that his assumed rank bestowed. He threw the musket to one side and lifted both hands, holding them palms facing forward, showing the lancer that he presented no threat.

The lancer gave no sign of recognising the gesture. Jack saw his body tense as the horse increased speed, the rider bending slightly at the waist as he lifted his weight from the saddle.

'Stop!' Jack shouted the command. More heads turned at the foreign word, yet the lancer plunged on regardless. The horse's hooves drummed into the ground, the rhythm that Jack had heard earlier now reserved for him alone. His body trembled as he saw the lance point rushing towards him, his flesh twitching in expectation, as though he could already feel the icy blade sinking in. Yet he refused to turn, to throw himself to safety. He stood in the rider's path, as still as a training-ground mannequin, his pride his only defence.

The rhythmic pounding of the horse's hooves stopped abruptly in a harsh jangle of tackle as the lancer reined in hard, bringing his mount to a noisy, breathless halt.

The two men stared at each other.

'You are a brave man, Englishman.'

The voice was full of obvious humour, the words reverberating as the lancer chuckled.

Jack pulled hard at the flanks of his scarlet coat, straightening the thickly woven cloth that had ridden up as he had clambered over the barricade. It dawned on him that the lancer's charge had been a test of his courage. He hoped he had passed. The point of the lance was no more than six inches away from his breast, the deadly blade held completely still. With heart still pounding, he looked up into the grinning face of the lancer.

'And you are a fair rider. I commend your skill.' He spoke the words as calmly as he could, ignoring the vicious point that trembled as its owner laughed aloud at Jack's sangfroid.

The horseman pulled back the lance, turning to toss the long weapon to a bearer who had rushed up the moment he had stopped. For the first time Jack noticed that the man who had come so close to killing him was dressed differently from the rest of the blue-coated lancers. The white pouch-belt was missing, replaced instead with golden frogging that covered the front panel of the lancer's blue coat. His shoulder boards carried thick bullion epaulets and his helmet was missing the thick white plume that Jack had noticed all the other lancers wearing.

'Good morning, Englishman. I am the Maharajah of Sawadh, and you owe me your life.'

'Did you see the bastard escape?'

'I did.'

'Damn it. Damn it all to hell!' The Maharajah cursed as Jack gave him the news that the black-robed leader of the bandits had given him the slip. The ruler of Sawadh spoke fluent English without a trace of an accent, and he clearly relished the opportunity to converse with a British officer. The two men sat perched on the barricade that Jack had hidden behind, whilst the lancers went around the bloody business of clearing the hilltop of its gruesome debris.

The Maharajah pulled off his heavy helmet, wiping a hand across his forehead to slick away a thick band of sweat. To Jack's surprise, he was completely hairless, his bald crown criss-crossed with a network of scars, a map of a life of hard-earned experience. The rest of his body was compact and powerful. He was clearly not the kind of ruler to live the decadent lifestyle of popular imagination. He was a warrior, and he carried himself with the calm poise of a man assured of his own power.

Jack sensed the Maharajah looking at him. He was finding it easy to like the foreign ruler, whose brown eyes twinkled with hidden mirth, as if he was party to a special joke that only he found amusing. He was an engaging man, and Jack had to remind himself to stay on his guard. The Maharajah could well soon be an enemy of the Crown, something Jack would do well to remember.

'So what is your name, Englishman?' The Maharajah's gaze never left Jack's as he spoke, as if he was searching the Englishman's soul.

'La— Danbury.' The words stuck in Jack's throat. For reasons he did not truly understand, he had been about to reveal his given name. The Maharajah's scrutiny was unsettling, and even telling the habitual lie was made hard. Jack swallowed his anxiety and forced himself to concentrate. As intimate as the situation was, he had a notion that his life was still in danger.

His hesitation was not lost on the Maharajah. The warm smile faded as the ruler of Sawadh contemplated Jack's stumble.

'Well met, Captain Danbury.' The smile returned with all its former force. 'I had heard you had arrived. But I didn't expect to meet you so soon. Welcome to Sawadh.'

'Do you greet all your visitors so?' The memory of the bitter fight with the bandits was still very real in Jack's mind.

'I'm truly sorry you were attacked. The Tiger and his filthy band have been a thorn in my side for too long.'

'Not any more.'

'We shall see. I'll not rest until that bastard is dead.' The Maharajah spat as he cursed the bandit leader.

'I've a feeling he'll be a hard man to run down.'

The Maharajah looked at Jack sharply. 'Did you fight him?'

Jack met the unrelenting stare. 'I did.' He paused before continuing. 'I lost.'

The Maharajah nodded in understanding. 'He fights hard. The local people will tell you that he is invincible. That he is a prince of darkness that no mortal man can slay. Oh, how I look forward to proving them wrong. If he ever stays around long enough to fight me, he will die with my bloody lance rammed up his damned arse.'

Jack remembered the power in the black-robed leader's blows, the speed with which he had thrust and parried. Mortal or not, he was a deadly adversary. 'I wish you luck.'

'Luck! I don't need luck. Give me my lance and my horse and I'll see him dead.'

The smile was gone, replaced instead with a look of iron determination. Jack shuddered involuntarily as he remembered facing the Maharajah's charge. It would be a rare spectacle indeed if the two warriors ever did meet in combat.

'So why today?' Jack asked the question that had been in his mind ever since he had first spotted the organised attack on the bandits.

'Because of you, of course.' The Maharajah leant forward to clap his hand on Jack's thigh. 'I have been chasing the Tiger and his cursed band for weeks now. I would not have found him had he not attacked you. One of my patrols heard the gunfire and happily I was close enough to get here before the bastards disappeared again. It was good fortune for us both, I think. Besides, I couldn't let some bloody bandits kill three British subjects. That damned man Proudfoot would've made too much of it.'

'Then I must thank you.'

'Yes, you must!' The Maharajah laughed aloud at the notion. 'You must sing my praises and tell that bloody man that he would do well to leave me alone. I suffer his presence, as I must. I have my father to thank for that. But he grows too puffed up with importance for his own good and for the good of you all. He works here. He does not rule.'

'You should tell him that yourself. You are more than eloquent enough. You speak English as well as any of us.'

'Well that's the benefit of an English education, old man.' The Maharajah was relaxed. If he found it odd to be sitting chatting whilst only a matter of yards away his troops were gathering up the remains of men who just an hour before had been living and breathing, it did not show in his bonhomie and easy manner. 'My father insisted. He'd been forced to sign away some of his power to you damn British, so he wanted to make sure I was educated in your ways and in your language. Knowing your enemy, he called it, and I thank him daily for his foresight.'

The Maharajah turned away as two of his lancers approached. He slid off the barricade and issued a series of firm commands before turning back to face Jack once more.

'We have captured more of the Tiger's men, but there is no sign of the bastard himself. He has flown the coop.' He smiled, relishing his use of English idiom.

More lancers appeared, dragging a motley collection of bed-raggled bandits with them. The unfortunate souls had been well beaten, none able to hold their heads up or take much notice of their surroundings. The Maharajah issued further commands, his orders delivered with crisp authority. His men hurried to obey, immediately starting to strip the clothes from their bloodied captives.

'What will happen to them?' Jack asked as he slid from his perch, walking forward to stand at the Maharajah's side. The two men watched in silence as the lancers quickly stripped the surviving bandits naked before dragging them off towards the village.

'They will die.' The Maharajah fixed Jack with a firm glare, daring him to disapprove.

'How will they die?' Jack was not easily cowed. Even by a king.

'They will be taken to the village so that those poor wretches who survived their attentions can witness their fate. They will be tied to the ground and left as food for the wild dogs, but only after we have removed their manhood.' The Maharajah searched Jack's face for reaction.

Jack wrestled with his emotions, doing his best to keep his expression neutral. The transformation in the Maharajah was sudden and shocking. One moment he was a civilised gentleman, talking with all the ease of a member of a London club. The next he was a savage warrior king who could crook a single finger and order a man's death in a heartbeat.

'Do you disapprove, Danbury? Do you find my orders barbaric?' The Maharajah dared Jack to speak out.

Jack did not disappoint him. 'I do.' He took a deep breath before speaking his mind, unable to stay silent. 'If they deserve to die, then why submit them to such foul torture? I understand the need for death. But I don't see the need for suffering.'

The Maharajah acknowledged his words with a nod. 'It takes courage to gainsay a king, Danbury. You, at least, are not all powder and no balls, unlike so many of your damned countrymen.' He sighed. 'You know nothing of our ways, you damned English. You think you can apply your customs and your laws even though you are thousands of miles from home. I admire that. Your conceit and arrogance is something to respect. But it also makes you dangerous.'

'We want what is best. For you and for your people.'

'What is best? And who are you to say what is best? Who appointed the English as the arbitrator of what is right and what is wrong? Do we not know what is best for ourselves? Do I not know what is best for my people?'

The Maharajah shook his head to compose himself. His passion had risen as he had spoken, and it took a moment for him to bring his rising temper back under control.

'These men are punished as an example to their kind and as a warning to their bastard leader. He will know what manner of man I am.'

'He didn't strike me as the kind of man who would be easily frightened.' Jack dared to respond forcefully. 'Not even by that.'

But the Maharajah did not seem the least bit offended. He smiled at Jack's forthright opinion. 'I will rid the world of the Tiger, Danbury. This is my land. It is my people who suffer at his hands. I will find him, I will kill him, and I will drag his carcass through every town and every village so that my people may know that I killed the man who could not be killed. They will see that their ruler still protects them and that my army still guards their future. They will see that it is I who rule here and not some white-faced strangers who think they can buy my kingdom and bind me up in all those bits of paper that they set such stock by. These are my people. You English would do well to remember that.'

Jack saw the passion on the Maharajah's face as he spoke. He thought of Proudfoot and his plans to annex the state of Sawadh regardless of his legal right to do so. He knew then that any such plan would result in conflict; the Maharajah would never surrender the future of his kingdom without a fight. Dutton would get his wish.

If Proudfoot were intent on annexation, then there would surely be war in Sawadh.

Chapter Thirteen

'Captain Danbury! Assist me this instant.'

Reverend Youngsummers stood leaning against the barricade, his chest heaving with the exertion of walking up the sloping corridor that led from their temporary prison. Any reluctance the clergyman had felt about leaving his sanctuary had clearly disappeared now that the danger was gone.

'Excuse me a moment, sir.' Jack nodded as he left the Maharajah's side and walked over to the barricade. He heaved a bullet-scarred wooden crate to one side, leaving an opening big enough for even Youngsummers to squeeze through. He spotted Isabel trailing behind but there was no opportunity to catch her eye before her father's bulk screened her from his view.

'I cannot fathom why you left me in that infernal place, Danbury. You should've brought me with you,' Youngsummers admonished Jack as he pushed past the barricade, easing his hefty buttocks through the narrow passage that now looked a lot smaller than when Jack had first tugged the crate away. 'It really was badly done, Danbury. Badly done indeed.'

'You were indisposed.' Jack tried to sound pleasant in the face of the underserved rebuke, well aware that the Maharajah was listening to every word. 'I didn't want to risk causing you any further harm.'

Like a stubborn cork finally wrenched from a bottle, Youngsummers forced his way out through the barricade. 'Nonsense, man.' He was clearly not appeased by Jack's words. 'You left me to fend for myself when you had been sworn to protect me. But enough of that for the moment; there will be plenty of time for an inquest at a more suitable juncture. For the moment, please do me the honour of telling me just who these fellows are.' He had apparently regained some of his usual bombastic style. 'I cannot say I recognise them.' The clergyman peered down his thick nose as he tried to identify the uniform of the men who had saved him.

'Truly?' Jack was surprised. He understood that Youngsummers had been in Bhundapur for nearly a year; surely he must have some idea as to the identity of the lancers and their leader.

'Do not be impertinent. I never ask a question if I already know its answer.' Youngsummers was growing in confidence again as he sensed a number of the lancers looking in his direction. 'Pray tell me who these blackguards are so that I may decide what course of action is best. It will fall to me, as the senior official here, to negotiate with these ruffians.' He seemed to puff up with the importance of his own words, relishing playing to the audience.

Holding out a hand, he summoned Isabel to his side, taking her arm and wrapping it protectively around his own. It was an indication of her distress that she obeyed meekly, and Jack felt an immediate concern for her well-being after all she had witnessed in the past day and night.

'If you would be so kind as to introduce me to their leader, Danbury.' Youngsummers continued to sneer as he spoke, clearly unimpressed at being faced by the lancers. 'The damned savage won't likely understand a word we say, but we must show willing.'

'Certainly, Reverend. It'll be my pleasure.' Jack heard the sarcasm in his own voice. He stepped back a few paces so that he could usher the Maharajah into the conversation.

'Reverend Youngsummers, may I introduce the Maharajah of Sawadh.' Jack turned to the Maharajah, delighted at the look of utter astonishment on the clergyman's face. 'Sir, may I introduce

Reverend Youngsummers, the chaplain at Bhundapur, and his daughter, Isabel.'

The Maharajah greeted the introduction with a huge guffaw. He stepped forward, clapping his hand forcefully on Jack's arm as he did so.

'You are a scoundrel, Danbury.' The comment was muttered and solely for Jack's benefit as the Maharajah moved towards Youngsummers, who was visibly shaking as the foreign ruler approached.

'Delighted to meet you at long last, my dear Reverend. I've heard much about you.' The Maharajah reached forward and shook Youngsummers by the hand. If he was put off by the clergyman's limp and unenthusiastic grip, he did not let it show. A wide smile crept across his face.

'Good Lord.' Youngsummers stammered as he spoke.

The Maharajah paid him no heed, his attention now focused fully on Isabel, who curtsied demurely, lowering her eyes before looking up at him through her thick lashes.

'Isabel Youngsummers.' The Maharajah rolled the name on his tongue as if tasting it. 'I had been told you were a rare beauty, but those reports did not do you justice.' He bowed at the waist as he offered both hands to Isabel, gently lifting her back to her feet.

Isabel blushed at the flattery, the flush of colour spreading from her neck to her pale cheeks. 'You are too kind, sir.'

'No need for modesty, my dear. I merely speak as I find. It is one of the privileges of being a king.'

'My liege, if I could have a moment.' Youngsummers cleared his throat noisily before carrying on, clearly unsure how to address the Maharajah. 'May I enquire what you intend to do with us?'

A trace of annoyance flared on the Maharajah's face as the Reverend interrupted his study of Isabel. 'Do with you? I have no notion what I shall do with you.'

'Well, um, sire, in that case, I must insist you return us to the nearest British establishment with all due haste.' Youngsummers frowned as he saw that his daughter remained the subject of the Maharajah's intense scrutiny. He ploughed on, trying to speak in a suitably grave tone. 'Otherwise I cannot be held accountable for what may occur.'

The Maharajah tore his eyes from Isabel and placed his hands on his hips as he pondered Youngsummers' bold choice of words. 'Do you presume to give me orders, Reverend?'

'Not at all, Your Highness, not in the slightest.' Youngsummers was clearly flustered. The Maharajah stood uncomfortably close, the force of his personality making the clergyman regret ever having opened his mouth. 'I merely wish to point out that the authorities will not be pleased should they learn that you did not permit us to return to our rightful place as soon as possible.'

'The authorities? What authorities? Am I not the only authority that matters here?' The Maharajah stamped his foot in obvious irritation.

'Yes, Your Majesty. Of course.' Youngsummers fluttered his hands in front of his wide stomach, as if to shoo the Maharajah away. He looked around for support, but Jack was in no mood to assist. 'I meant no insult. I merely wish to ensure the safe return of my daughter to the station at Bhundapur.'

'Good. I hope we understand each other, Reverend. I would hate there to be any confusion. For the moment, I must ask you to be patient. It is nearly dawn, so I suggest that you rest as best you can. I will have one of my men bring you some food.'

Youngsummers nodded in mute acceptance, clearly relieved that the Maharajah was bringing the conversation to a close, the promise of food enough to buy his silence.

The Maharajah turned and stalked away. More blue-coated lancers were arriving on the bloodstained hilltop, the carbines on their saddles revealing the identity of the gunmen who had succeeded in forcing the bandits to gather together. The Maharajah welcomed them with loud praise, leaving the three former prisoners to themselves.

Jack did his best to compose himself. They had been saved from the Tiger, but they were still not yet safe.

The country was on the brink of war. When it came, there would be no refuge for anyone with a white face. Not until the Maharajah and his army had been destroyed.

* * *

Dawn crept across the far horizon, reds, oranges and ochres rushing to paint the sky with warmth, banishing the forbidding colours of the night. The first grazes of blue followed quickly, heralding the azure vastness that would fill the heavens until dusk.

The world came to life. The animals that had survived the bandits' ransacking of the village started to voice their protest at being confined, a cacophony of bleats, grunts, barks and hisses greeting the dawn. The lancers' horses added their own noise, urging their masters into activity. As the last grey shadows of the night crept stealthily away, the cavalrymen bustled into life, beginning the long list of chores that had to be done to prepare themselves and their horses for the day ahead.

The three former prisoners sat in silence around a simple fire that the lancer charged with their care had coaxed to life. They had broken their fast on some of the rations the cavalrymen carried in their saddlebags, none of which had managed to meet Reverend Youngsummers' high expectations.

'If only they had been able to locate our provisions. Then we would not be forced to eat this muck.' For the umpteenth time Youngsummers lamented the loss of his picnic, as he stared sorrowfully at the dried mutton and hard bread he was continuing to eat at a healthy rate, despite his misgivings.

Jack forced himself to his feet, urging his aching joints into action. He watched the Maharajah's lancers as they went about their duties, running a professional eye over the troops he might one day have to fight. He was impressed by what he saw. The blue-coated cavalry worked with the industry of trained soldiers, their movements practised and efficient. Everything he saw told him that Major Dutton had been too complacent in his judgement of the Maharajah's army. The British contingent at Proudfoot's disposal was beginning to look woefully inadequate.

A series of loud shouts interrupted his casual inspection of the lancers. Like any good commander, the Maharajah had established a number of vedettes, and now a single rider was spurring hard up the slope to the top of the hill where the bulk of the lancers had made their bivouac.

Jack brushed away the dust that covered his uniform. He turned to face the direction the rider had come from, kneading the small of his back to work away some of the nagging pain that the hours on the hard ground had awoken.

His hands froze in place.

A column of soldiers had marched into view. Even from a distance there was no mistaking the red coats that had been made famous on countless battlefields in the four corners of the globe.

The British army had arrived.

Jack stood to one side as the column of redcoats marched up the hillside. The sun was still low in the sky, but already the heat of the day was starting to build. He felt the first prickles of sweat emerge as he did up the last of the brass buttons on his heavy scarlet coat, forcing the stiff collar into place and setting his shako straight on his head. He might have been missing his weapons, but he did his best to look as presentable as possible as he prepared to greet his new command.

The Maharajah ordered his own men to form up in column as he readied them to meet the arrival of the British forces. He stationed himself at the front of his troops, lolling easily in the saddle as he waited for the foreign soldiers whose presence in his land so grated on his pride.

Jack watched the redcoats closely. The tight column lost some of its order as the men struggled to maintain their spacing on the slippery loose soil and rock of the scree slope, which continually gave way under their feet. He savoured the opportunity of leading a company again, eagerly anticipating the coming months and weeks when he would get to know every facet of his new command. It was the privilege that he coveted most, the one that meant so much more than all the gaudy trinkets that bedecked an officer's life. Despite all he had experienced since he had first stolen James Danbury's identity, he still felt pride as his red-coated soldiers marched resolutely on.

Reverend Youngsummers strode forward to greet the column, arms spread wide in greeting. As Jack listened to the clergyman's sonorous voice delivering a loud prayer of thanks for his deliverance, he continued to watch his new command carefully, assessing their bearing after what must have been a long and draining night march. He was pleased with what he saw, the men marching with elan as they showed off their skills in front of the Maharajah and his lancers. He read the expressions on many of the faces, recognising the mix of anxiety and distrust of infantrymen parading in front of cavalry. He smiled, understanding the feeling well. The smile faded as he noticed the presence of Lieutenant Fenris. His dashing subaltern sat his fine white horse well, riding with grace and composure despite what had been a long ride from the British cantonment.

Jack was about to move forward and offer his own greeting when he noticed that there was a second officer present with his company. He froze, staring at the man in confusion. He could not comprehend why there should be another officer wearing the uniform of a captain in the 24th Foot; a uniform identical to the one Jack himself wore.

He closed his eyes as it all began to make sense. He had thought the army would be slow; that the long, protracted negotiations that followed the death of an officer on campaign would give him months before the real Captain Danbury's commission could be sold. He had been utterly wrong. The presence of the second mounted officer proved his assumptions to be nothing more than hopeful folly, condemning him to a bitter future, one that would likely lead to a cold dawn on the scaffold.

The new owner of the late Captain Danbury's commission had arrived. Jack's charade was over before it had barely begun.

Chapter Fourteen

———◆———

'There's the damned impostor! Arrest him!' Lieutenant Fenris bellowed the accusation as soon as he clapped eyes on Jack, his voice rising in excitement.

'What on earth?' Youngsummers' prayer was quickly forgotten as Fenris bounded from the saddle and rushed past the astonished clergyman.

Jack had always known this moment could come, but he had believed he would be safe for longer than the few days he had spent at Bhundapur. He cursed his fortune but straightened his spine and resolved to meet his denunciation with as much dignity as he could muster. He had often wondered how he would face it. He had imagined every reaction – anger, fear, denial – but had never conceived that he would feel so little. His heartbeat had barely increased in the time since Fenris had shouted his crime aloud, despite the look of shock and horror he saw appear on Isabel's face.

'You damned blackguard.' Fenris' lips pulled back in anger as he snarled the words.

Jack could see the younger officer's body vibrating with barely controlled rage. The intention to strike was obvious, his right hand already balled tightly into a fist and moving upwards, the blow driven by all his pent-up anger. But Jack was quicker. He grasped

Fenris tightly by the forearm before it had travelled more than a few inches. There was time enough to register the shock on the young officer's face before Jack snapped his forehead forward, smashing it into the centre of Fenris' face.

The leading rank of redcoats dashed forward at the double as their officer hit the ground. Led by a corporal whose name Jack could not place, they hefted their muskets, ready to use them against the man they had been ordered to arrest the moment they arrived.

Jack lifted his hands in surrender. His forehead might have throbbed from the blow but there was satisfaction in seeing Fenris on the floor, cupping his hands over his broken nose in a futile attempt to staunch the flow of blood that gushed from the wound.

'No rumpus, all right?' The corporal asked the question hopefully, clearly not relishing the unpleasant task of arresting the man he had believed was his commanding officer.

'I'll not cause you a problem, Corporal.' Jack kept his eyes on Fenris as he spoke, wary of a sudden attack.

But the sight of his own blood had dampened the lieutenant's urge to fight. 'You'll hang, you bastard,' Fenris gasped, the effort of speaking jarring his battered face.

'Hang? Who will hang? Would someone please tell me what is going on?'

Isabel Youngsummers had rushed over as soon as Fenris had hit the ground. She now demanded an answer to her question, her wavering voice betraying her shock. Her father had chosen to ignore the confrontation and was instead engaging the new captain of the 24th with a barrage of questions, accusations and commands. The Maharajah and his lancers stood immobile, content to remain spectators so long as the British chose to fight amongst themselves.

Isabel squatted to the ground, deftly extracting Fenris' handkerchief from his pocket. She pressed it to the centre of the lieutenant's face whilst using her free hand to tilt his head backwards so that he looked to the sky.

'That man is a damned impostor and he'll hang for his crime.' It was hard to make out the words as Fenris tried to speak and breathe through his mouth at the same time, but Isabel understood enough to offer a shocked gasp.

'An impostor! I don't believe it. Danbury, tell me what is going on here this instant.'

'He's quite correct.' Jack fixed his eyes on Isabel's. 'I am an impostor. I'm not Danbury. I'm not even an officer.'

'Isabel, that bloody hurts!' Fenris tried to push away Isabel's hand, which gripped his nose tightly as she tried to make sense of Jack's revelation.

The protest brought her out of her silence. 'You are not Captain Danbury?'

'No. My name's Jack.'

'And you are a fraud and a blackguard and I shall piss on your grave.' Some of the fire was returning to Fenris' belly as Isabel's presence urged him to show more courage.

'Arthur!' Isabel released Fenris' bloodied nose, causing him to curse as the action sent a bolt of pain through the centre of his brain.

'He is correct. I may well hang.' Jack leant down and offered Isabel his hand.

'Why? Why must you hang?' She took his hand, rising to her feet so that she stood barely a foot from him.

Jack wanted nothing more than to reach out and run his hand through her hair. She had done her best to assert some order to its appearance, clipping it with the hairpins that had so caught his attention when he had first seen her at Proudfoot's soirée. But her work had been temporary at best, and more than one errant lock had escaped her hastily constructed arrangement and now whispered across her face.

'I must hang as an example to others. I have broken Queen's Regulations and so I will be punished.'

'But why did you do it?' Isabel gripped his hand hard as she questioned his motives. 'You must have known it would end like this one day.'

'Because I had nothing else.'

Isabel opened her mouth to speak, but thought better of it and instead stood in silence, her hand in Jack's, trying to understand the sudden revelation.

'You did it because you are a knave and a thief and you'll hang, you bastard, because you damn well deserve it.' Fenris staggered to his feet, using the green cuff of his scarlet jacket to mop up the last of the blood still trickling from his nostrils. 'Corporal, put this man in manacles and guard him well.' He took firm hold of Isabel's arm, propelling her forcefully out of Jack's grip and leading her back towards her father. 'And strip him of his uniform,' he added as he walked away, disdainfully turning his back on Jack, refusing even to look at him. 'That bastard has no right to wear it.'

Jack submitted to the rough hands as they tugged his scarlet coat from his back. He retreated to the nothingness of his emotions, even as the manacles took him in their cold, remorseless grasp. He kept his eyes down, focusing them on a pile of dirt that was stained with Fenris' blood. He no longer had a part to play in this early-morning scene, so like any good actor he tried to merge into the background lest the audience be drawn to him rather than those on the main stage. It was time to submit to his fate.

Jack marched in the centre of the small column, the corporal and his guard surrounding him with their bared bayonets in case he lost his mind and tried to mount a desperate escape. His shoulders ached from the unnatural position they were forced to adopt now that his hands were manacled behind his back, and the pit of his spine ached dreadfully, dogging his every step. He focused on the pain, examining the way it surged around his body, using the hurt to dispel the despair in his soul.

He had been given no opportunity to plead his case. The Maharajah had kept at a distance, treating the handover of the former prisoners as if it were not of sufficient concern to trouble the attention of a king. Jack would have enjoyed a final conversation with the foreign ruler; he had sensed a kindred spirit, despite the huge gulf in their status. Yet just as it had been when he was nothing more than a common redcoat, such familiarity was now denied him. The new captain of the 24th, whose name he had learnt was Kingsley, had avoided all contact with him, as if he would somehow become contaminated should he acknowledge the presence of the man who had dared to assume his commission. Jack was left to the care of the corporal of the guard, who treated him as well as the situation allowed.

To Jack's dismay, he had not found an opportunity to speak to Isabel, who remained close to her father's side, as if tethered by some invisible rope. He was certain that any feelings she might have started to develop towards him would now have twisted into dark disgust as his deception was revealed in all its sordid glory. It was hard not to regret missing out on what might have been. But if he closed his eyes, he could still summon an image of the first girl he had truly loved. Remembering what he had lost made losing what might have been easier to bear.

Kingsley, Fenris and the men of the 24th had been forced to spend many uncomfortable hours in the remains of the village, waiting for the heat of the day to diminish before they could begin the long march back to Bhundapur. Their return was further delayed by Reverend Youngsummers, who insisted on being allowed to sleep through the greater portion of the day, his claim of nervous exhaustion made with such conviction that neither Kingsley nor Fenris had been able to convince him to rouse himself until he was good and ready.

With departure delayed so long, it would have been pragmatic to wait until the early hours of the following morning to set off, but the British officers were awkward in front of the Maharajah and his men, and so had ordered their small column to march late in the afternoon, even though there was no hope of reaching their destination before nightfall. Lieutenant Fenris argued long and loud for them to continue through the night; he was keen to reach Bhundapur, anticipating the laurels he would win for carrying out the orders they had been given. The young officer had spoken loudly enough for Jack to learn that the column had been dispatched with the twin objectives of discovering what had happened to Youngsummers and his daughter, and also apprehending the impostor who had dared to arrive in their midst.

Captain Kingsley, however, had been forced to listen to Reverend Youngsummers' tales of bandits and deadly ambushes, the clergyman's fears of a night march described with biblical vigour. Kingsley was not a man to take risks, his natural caution giving credence to the dangers outlined by Youngsummers, so the redcoats were ordered to make a bivouac in the darkness.

When the column stopped for the night, Jack was left to find what rest he could, his hands still bound by the heavy manacles, but now at least in front of his body. The redcoats hastily built fires; they were grateful to sink to the ground with their mates, wholly unconcerned about a night spent away from the confines of their barrack rooms. Once the final orders of the day had been issued, the two British officers left the men to their own devices, the divide between the two groups as rigidly enforced in the field as it was in the cantonment. Jack was simply abandoned between them, ignored and alone, the addition of a set of ankle fetters securing him in place.

'Jack?'

Isabel used the name tentatively, and at first Jack didn't hear her. He had been lost in another world, reliving his life as an orderly, remembering the days of serving his first officer as if it had been just a few weeks previously and not so many months ago.

'Jack?' She spoke with more force, refusing to be ignored.

'What?' Jack's voice came out as a croak. His mouth and throat were parched and it felt as if he had to physically tear his tongue from the roof of his mouth to be able to speak.

'It's Isabel.' She spoke in the careful tone of the young to the old and decrepit.

Jack squinted through a single eye as Isabel crouched beside him. He could smell her, the subtle scent of a woman's sweat underscored with that lingering trace of perfume. She looked downcast at his silence. She removed the stopper to a full canteen of water and offered it; Jack took it gratefully in both hands, relishing the opportunity to slake his thirst, his body trembling with desire the moment he felt the first precious drops moisten his tongue.

'Thank you.' He handed back the canteen awkwardly, the heavy iron manacles making his movements laboured.

Isabel placed the canteen to one side and sat cross-legged on the ground beside him, looking every inch the schoolgirl she had so recently been.

'No more lies.' She spoke quietly, guarding her emotions. 'I just want the truth.' She searched Jack's eyes to see if he understood.

'Was everything just an act?'

'No. Not all of it.' Jack closed his eyes as he remembered the desperate struggle in the prison they had shared. When he opened them again he saw her watching his face closely. 'I cannot pretend to fight.'

'You fought to save me. Just as you promised.'

'I did. I figured you were worth the effort.'

'I have never thanked you.'

'There was no need. You were only threatened because I failed to protect you properly. I should've seen the danger the moment those bloody bandits opened fire. I should've got you away.' He did not try to contain his bitterness. He had thought he had found a place in life, his ability in the searing cauldron of battle the one thing he had believed he could rely upon. The failure rankled, stinging his stubborn pride.

'You were not to know.' Isabel shuddered as she remembered the dreadful fight.

'I fought. But I lost. It's not the first time.'

'Why? When did you lose before?'

Jack looked at Isabel, wondering if he should open the darkest recesses of his soul. The desire to share his past was strong, but he could not burden the young girl with his bitter memories. It would not be fair. And soon, none of it would matter anyway.

'I loved somebody once. It didn't work out as I planned.' Jack contented himself with revealing the half-truth.

'You must have loved her very much.'

The words astonished him. Isabel did not avert her eyes as he looked at her in amazement. 'How can you tell?'

'How?' Isabel smiled for the first time. 'It's easy. You carry your sorrow in your eyes.' She reached out her hand, placing it gently on top of Jack's. 'I think you have suffered enough.'

'I don't think Fenris would agree.'

'Arthur acts like a spoiled child. You dared to offend his precious dignity and so he hates you.'

'But he likes you.' Jack felt a sudden rush of jealousy at the notion. Isabel would have to have been made of stone not to find the dashing young officer attractive. Fenris must have turned her head.

He most certainly would have tried.

'I know.' She acknowledged Jack's observation.

'He could be a fine man.'

She smiled at his choice of words. 'He could be. But he is not. He is not for me.'

'I cannot say I'm not pleased.' Jack matched her smile, turning his hand to squeeze her own.

'You saved my life. I shall not forget that, Jack. No matter what happens.'

Jack slowly shook his head. 'No.' He spoke firmly, letting go of her hand. 'You owe me nothing. Consider it my final gallant act, my parting gift to the world.'

'Isabel! Come here this instant.' Reverend Youngsummers shouted across to his errant daughter as if he had spotted her conversing with the devil himself.

Isabel's head turned as her father shouted for her; the anger in his voice was clear. She sighed, and Jack felt her breath kiss against his cheek. Then she uncrossed her legs and got to her feet, her hands brushing her dress flat and knocking off any bits of dirt that had stuck to it as she sat on the ground.

She looked down at Jack. 'I will not forget what you did, Jack. Whatever you say.'

Without another word she turned and walked away, her head bowed as she obediently returned to her father's side. She did not want him to see the desire on her face, or the spark of excitement in her eyes as she dared to consider doing something that would scandalise the tight-knit society in which she was forced to live. If only she could summon the courage.

Chapter Fifteen

ack lay on his back, looking up at the stars. He had never paid them much heed before. Indeed, he did not think he had truly noticed them until he left his mother's gin palace in Whitechapel to join the redcoats. There was little sky to be seen in the stinking rookery in which he had been brought up. In the enclosed confines of the city, it was hard to even make out the sky in the narrow gaps between the tops of the buildings, or through the near-impenetrable smog that filled the air no matter what the season. In the rookeries, staring up at the heavens was asking for trouble. Letting your guard down, even for a single heartbeat, was a quick route to an early grave, a final trip down to the Thames, the last resting place for so many of the denizens of the foul places where no one sane or sober chose to go.

Now he gazed at a sky with more stars than he could count. He liked their serenity. Whatever happened, they continued to look down, unperturbed by sorrow or by war. They did not care if someone lived, or if they died. If someone stole a scarlet coat or dreamt of a future far removed from the one allotted to them. The stars were always the same.

He heard a noise, a scrabble of feet not far from where he lay. He closed his eyes, shutting off his view of the heavens as he concentrated his hearing on the sound. It could have been an animal; a whole menagerie of beasts stirred when the darkness arrived, to scuttle and hurry about their business through the cold night hours before the sun rose. Yet he could hear breathing, the subtle sound of someone trying very carefully to be completely quiet.

'Jack?'

The icy whisper still took him by surprise. His body jolted at the sudden call, a rush of blood surging through his veins to hammer noisily in his ears. Gingerly he eased himself into a sitting position, scanning the darkness. As he did so, his manacles and fetters clattered noisily.

'Hush.' The voice urged him to silence.

Jack did his best to obey, moving with infinite slowness as he manoeuvred round so that he could face the soft voice that had murmured from the darkness. He could just make out a thin silhouette bending towards him.

'Hush yourself.' He spoke quietly. He knew who had come to disturb his peace. 'You shouldn't be here.'

'Be quiet.' The voice delivered the rebuke with a little more force, its owner clearly annoyed that Jack was treating the situation in such a glib manner. 'I've come to rescue you.'

Jack did his best not to laugh aloud at the bold announcement. 'And how do you propose to do that, Isabel?'

Isabel Youngsummers crept forward and gently slid to her knees beside him. Even in the dim light Jack could see her flushed cheeks, the exhilaration at her escapade clear. She had bound her hair into a dark blue headscarf and swathed her body in a thick brown cloak, both for warmth and to deaden the brightness of her dress.

'If you are going to speak to me in that tone, then perhaps I'll not bother.'

'You shouldn't be here, Isabel. Your father will have a fit if he finds out.'

'He won't know.' Isabel spoke quickly and quietly.

She was right to be confident. It was unlikely anyone would hear her. The bivouac was never completely quiet, the sounds of men snoring, farting and fidgeting loud enough to cover any whispered conversation. The real danger came from a sentry spotting the extra silhouette near where Jack should have been sitting in isolation. Yet the sentries' job was to face outwards, scanning the ominous shadows for danger, so the risk of discovery was small. But that did not stop Jack fretting. Isabel would be severely rebuked for her exploits if she were discovered, and he did not want her to be punished for his sake.

'You should go back.'

'Never,' Isabel replied firmly. 'I shall never go back.'

'Never?'

'He wants to send me home.' There was real pain in her voice. 'He has vowed to book me on the next available steamship. He will send to me my aunt's, where I will sit and do nothing until I am married off. I would rather die.'

'He'll likely kill you himself if he discovers you talking to me.'

'I'm not here to talk to you, you ninny. I said I have come to rescue you, and so I shall.'

Jack lifted his arms, showing her the heavy manacles that bound his hands, grimacing at the pain the gesture provoked. The skin around the clasps had been rubbed raw, chafed by the unyielding metal so that it was bloody and weeping. 'And what about these?'

Isabel smiled with devilment, her eyes alive with her own daring. 'Oh. I hadn't thought about that. Why, if only I had the key.'

Her hand fished beneath her cloak and she produced a pair of heavy iron keys with all the panache of a music hall magician.

Jack looked at her in admiration. 'Blow me. How did you get those?'

Isabel chuckled at the look of surprise on his face. 'Oh, now you're interested. You still want me to go back?'

Jack grinned. 'I do. But give me the damn keys first.'

Isabel pulled back her hand, removing the keys from his reach. 'Oh no you don't. If I give you these, you must promise to take me with you.'

'Take you with me? Take you where, exactly? If I make a run for it, I will be hunted like a damn fox. You would not want that.'

'You're right. I don't. But we won't be on the run.'

'Really? Perhaps you are an angel then, using your godly powers to spirit us away. For there is nowhere to hide here.'

Isabel looked nervously over her shoulder as Jack took the Lord's name in vain. It would take a long time for her father's shadow to leave her side.

'There is.' She spoke firmly and with obvious confidence. 'I've thought it all through. I know exactly where we shall go. And once we are there, no one will be able to reach us.'

'My God, Isabel, are you corned? Did you steal some of your father's brandy?'

Isabel flickered her free hand forward, deftly delivering a gentle slap to his arm. 'Of course not.'

'Then what's your plan? Where is this wonderful sanctuary? Where can we hide where no one will find us?' Jack fired the questions at her, a trace of annoyance in his voice. He would be happy to risk an escape, for he truly had nothing left to lose. But he did not have high hopes of success; the local people would certainly not be willing to offer shelter to a white-faced stranger. But it was worth a try, if only to irk Lieutenant Fenris.

'We shall go to the Maharajah. He'll save us. We will join his court.' She smiled the sweet smile of victory, for she was quite correct. She had thought of the one place where they would be safe.

Only the Maharajah could save them now.

Jack took Isabel's hand as they crept through the bivouac. He could see the sentries at their posts, the two pairs of redcoats staring dutifully into the darkness as they willed away the long hours of their sentry duty. He kept a close eye on them as he led Isabel through the sleeping camp, hoping that no one could hear the pounding of his heart, which seemed loud enough to wake the dead.

He kept well away from the slumbering redcoats, guiding Isabel in a wide circle as he aimed for the small group of horses that had been tethered together a short distance from where the officers had chosen to rest for the night. The camp was still in the dead hours after midnight, the last wakeful redcoats settling down for some rest before the next day's march, which would begin before the daylight crept back to scour the darkness away.

Isabel let out a gasp of distaste as they moved out of the last light of the fires. 'What on earth is that?' She raised a hand to her face, trying to protect her mouth and nose from the foul aroma.

Jack turned and saw the look on her face. He grinned. 'The latrine. Try not to step in anything.'

'That's horrid.'

Isabel's disgust was evident, but he had chosen the route with care. Anyone seeing movement heading towards the temporary latrine would think nothing of it; many of the redcoats stumbled into the darkness to relieve themselves during the night. Once past the reeking pits they would be able to move rapidly towards the horses that offered their best chance of escape.

Jack risked a glimpse back over his shoulder as he led Isabel into the night. He had used her cloak to improvise the slumped shape of a sleeping figure, arranging it so that anyone checking on him would see what looked like a slumbering form. It would not fool his captors for long when the company prepared to march, but by then he hoped he and Isabel would be far away.

He rubbed at the sores on his wrists, relishing the freedom of movement. He had learnt from bitter experience that even the worst pain did not last for ever, even the most vicious of wounds healing with time. At least, that was true for wounds to the body. Wounds to the soul were different, only ever scabbing over, the tears and fissures left to fester beneath. But he had learnt not to pick at those, letting them rot in the depths of his mind, the pain dulled by familiarity yet never completely going away.

It did not take long to reach the horses. He let Isabel go first; she was more experienced with the animals then he was. She moved forward quickly, murmuring sweet nothings as she approached the horse she had ridden that day. It gave a quiet whinny of recognition and blew loudly through its nostrils as it smelt the open hand Isabel held to its nose.

Jack looked around, anxiously scanning the slumbering bivouac for signs of alarm. All was still, the redcoats blissfully unaware that the impostor they had been sent to arrest was making off. He saw the sleeping form of Lieutenant Fenris, the young officer enjoying the peaceful rest of the victorious. Jack only wished he could be there when Fenris realised that his prisoner had escaped.

He smiled at the notion. He knew there was unfinished business between the two of them. The kind of business that could only be settled sword in hand. As Isabel deftly saddled two of the horses, he wondered when that encounter would come. For he knew Fenris would not rest until he had been brought low, the lieutenant's hatred sure to be fanned by his disappearance with Isabel. He relished the idea. He would not shirk from the fight, whenever it came.

Chapter Sixteen

───◦•◦───

'Isabel. It's time to get up.'

Jack gingerly nudged the sleeping form with the toe of his boot. He could make little sense of where her body lay under the thick wrappings of blanket, and he hoped he had not inadvertently poked a sensitive area with his unsubtle alarm call.

'Isabel.' He spoke again, raising his voice to make sure it penetrated the cloth that swaddled her head. To his satisfaction he saw her start to stir, and almost certain that she would heed his call to rise, he returned to the fire that he had tended during the long, lonely hours of the night.

They had ridden through the dawn, then on throughout the long, hot day until after night had fallen. He had seen Isabel swaying in the saddle, her exhaustion obvious. As much as he would have liked to keep going, he had sensed that she was at the end of her strength. They had unsaddled the horses, and created a meagre sanctuary on a lonely, windswept hillside, sheltering as best they could amongst a group of large boulders.

He picked up a stick and stabbed the fire back into life. It had been a tedious night. He had chosen to sit and keep watch despite his tiredness, nervous that they would be discovered despite the distance they had covered. The anxiety had gnawed at him but he did his best to keep it contained, forcing himself to sit still whilst Isabel slept. She would need her full strength should they be forced to avoid any persistent pursuit during the coming day.

He kept his eyes low, concentrating on the flickering flames that danced into life in front of him. He craved a decent drink, sorely missing the reviving effects of some tart green coffee or the thick, tarry soldiers' tea that was made wherever British redcoats rose to face the day. He wondered if there would be tea at the Maharajah's court, and he walked over to search through the saddlebags on Lieutenant Fenris' horse to see if the British officer had possessed enough sense to carry some with him.

The image of Lieutenant Fenris rising the previous morning to see that his prisoner had not only escaped but had also taken the young officer's horse with him crept into Jack's mind. It was a notion to savour, and he found himself chuckling softly as he pictured the rage that must have surely followed.

'And what is amusing you this morning?' Isabel tiptoed across to sit in front of the fire, still swaddled in the thick army blanket that had kept her warm through the chill hours of the night.

'Fenris. I was imagining how he must have reacted when he discovered I had stolen his horse.' Jack gave up his search, muttering a curse under his breath at the lieutenant's feckless decision not to carry any of the precious leaves. He walked back to the warmth of the fire, contemplating a day without tea.

'Poor Arthur.' Isabel looked wistful as she carefully took a seat next to Jack.

'Poor Arthur, my eye.' He felt not a single ounce of sympathy for his former lieutenant. 'It's no more than he deserves.'

Isabel grinned mischievously. 'And Father will be furious.' She relished the statement, her satisfaction at her father's distress obvious.

Jack looked hard at the young girl sitting opposite him. He could only marvel at her spirit. She had left her family behind, gambling her future and potentially her life on a wild adventure with only a proven criminal for a companion. Yet she did not seem the least bit perturbed at her actions; even a night spent with only rocks for a bed had done nothing to dampen her ardour for the escapade.

'Will they still come after us?' she asked, wrapping the blanket tightly around herself to ward off the morning's chill.

'They might. They'll want to, that's for certain. But I reckon they'll have no choice but to go back to Bhundapur and report what has happened. Proudfoot will have to be told, so I imagine we are safe for the moment.'

'Proudfoot will be cross.'

Jack shook his head at the childish turn of phrase. 'He won't be cross. He will be apoplectic. I almost wish I was there to see him give those bastards a tongue-lashing.'

'Poor Arthur, and poor Captain Kingsley. He has only just arrived, and now he will be in trouble with his commander.'

'Save your pity for us.' Jack poked the fire with force, causing it to flare up. 'We still don't know where we are bloody going.'

Isabel pouted at Jack's obvious irritation. 'There's no need to look like you are sucking on a lemon. I didn't hear you mention that when I rescued you.'

'I had other things on my mind.'

'Well more fool you. I cannot be expected to think of everything. I got you free, didn't I?'

Jack reached out and pressed his hand on to Isabel's. 'I am grateful. Truly. I just wish I knew which way to go. It is up to me to keep you safe.'

Isabel looked down at his hand but made no move to remove it from her own. It was the first intimate contact they had shared since they had ridden off into the night, and it promised much.

'Will you tell me your name?' She asked the question quietly.

'Does it matter?' Jack matched her tone. He could feel the warmth of her hand underneath his. He concentrated on how it felt as his fingertips moved gently to tease out a pattern on her skin.

'I would like to know who you are.'

'You will not find that in my name.' He smiled at his own pomposity. 'It's Lark. Jack Lark.'

She did not speak again, satisfied by the revelation. They sat together, staring out into the wild, barren landscape, sharing the moment.

'I suppose I had better get ready.' Isabel sighed as she broke the spell between them. 'I expect you will want me to ride all day again?'

Jack took his hand back, immediately missing the feeling of Isabel's warm skin. 'I expect so. But we need to find out where to go.'

'Perhaps we can ask?'

Jack chuckled at the notion. 'I'm not sure I speak enough of the local language to ask for directions. Do you?'

'No.' Isabel smiled at her own foolishness. 'The servants all spoke English. I do speak French, though. And a little Latin.'

Jack laughed aloud. 'Well, that should prove useful.' He enjoyed watching the expression on Isabel's face, savouring the sight of her fresh beauty. 'I knew a fellow who spoke Latin once. He went quite mad.'

Isabel laughed along with him. They continued to sit together, enjoying each other's company, comfortable in the silence.

'Jack,' Isabel was serious when she spoke again, 'are we in danger?'

He opened his mouth, his first thought to scotch the idea immediately. But he had spent too long living with lies to begin this new life with more of the same.

'Yes.' He watched her closely, looking for a flicker of fear in her emerald eyes. 'Our best hope is to come across some of the Maharajah's men. Then at least we have a chance, though I suspect they will do nothing more than escort us back to Bhundapur. If we encounter anyone else, then there is not a lot I can do. I don't even have a weapon.' He smiled ruefully at the admission. 'If it comes to that, we will have to ride for it. At least you will. I suspect I will simply fall off.' He tried to make light of the situation, yet there was little he could do to disguise the peril into which they had plunged so willingly.

'I know you will keep me safe, Jack. I've seen you fight, remember. I know how vicious you are.' Isabel shook off her fear, choosing instead to copy Jack and do her best to lighten the mood.

Jack laughed at her choice of words. 'Vicious? I thought I was rather heroic.'

He was pleased to see her smile back. 'My hero!' She fluttered her eyelids in a theatrical gesture of adoration before quickly rising to her feet. 'Now I must ask you to turn your back so I can get ready.'

'Yes, milady.' Jack knuckled his forehead in a gesture of obedience. 'Unless I can be of some assistance? I was once an officer's orderly, you know.'

'No thank you,' Isabel said firmly. 'I shall manage quite well on my own. You must promise not to peek.'

'I promise.' He made a show of inching round so that he faced the opposite direction. 'I shall not dare to watch. Who knows what I would see.'

'You'd better not. I'll be keeping an eye on you.' Isabel wagged her finger at Jack's back. She had thought she would feel awkward in his company; after all, she had never been left alone with a man before. She walked back to where she had abandoned her few belongings, all that she now possessed in the world. She tried to feel concern for her future, summoning up the image of her father to elicit some feelings of sorrow or of guilt. But she felt nothing save excitement. They might not know where they were going, but she would not turn back. Not now. Not ever.

Jack and Isabel rode on to the higher ground. Mountains rose around them like battlemented towers, their soaring pinnacles and spires reaching far up into the dark blue vastness of the sky. They saw little sign of life. Nothing but the birds of prey that soared on the eddies of hot air swirling far above. They had hoped to find a village, or at least some form of habitation, but few of the locals were foolish enough to try to eke out an existence in this barren region, and they saw no evidence of settlement other than some abandoned forts perched high on distant hilltops.

Yet not all was bare and lifeless. Occasional folds or dips in the ground supported lush patches of vibrant growth, a rare treat for eyes that otherwise saw nothing but the dusty grey of the scree slopes around them. These pools of life boasted vivid colours, the bright reds, blues, purples and oranges of the mountain flowers offering a stark contrast to their dull surroundings.

Occasionally the sound of moving water interrupted the lonely quiet, the gentle trickle of a mountain stream or the subtler noise of a thin smear of water sliding across the rocks. Otherwise it was silent, the only noise their horses' hooves as their iron-shod feet clattered heavily on the rocky soil.

They rode on, surrounded by the vastness of the highlands, the far-reaching views of ravines, sharp peaks, towering mountains, leaping waterfalls and never-ending sloping hillsides only adding to the feeling of isolation.

They spied the dust cloud long before the horsemen came into view. The open ground gave them no place to hide, the barren slope they were on bereft of all living things save for a scattering of thorny bushes and scrubby plants. It was tempting to immediately gouge their spurs into the sides of their tired horses, forcing them into a reluctant gallop in a bid to be far away before the unknown riders came close. But the long morning in the saddle had dampened the desire for more time spent meandering around the bare hills with no clear idea of where they were headed. So instead of flight, they stopped and waited to see who else was journeying through the high ground far to the east of Bhundapur.

'Be ready to gallop.' Jack pulled his horse to a halt as he prepared Isabel to flee. His lack of skill on horseback left him standing impotently a good yard and a half behind Isabel, who shook her head in mock despair as she saw what he had been trying to do. With a deft flick of her reins she edged her own horse backwards and to the side so that she could stand next to him, her skills instinctive.

'You really do need some lessons in how to ride, don't you, Jack?' she teased.

'It was never high on my list of priorities.' Jack squinted hard, trying to identify the approaching riders. 'We didn't have an awful lot of horses where I grew up.' He thought of the area around his mother's gin palace. The only animals he had ever seen were the many mangy dogs that managed to exist on the rubbish and noxious offal that littered the streets. His former self could never have imagined even being close to a horse, let alone riding one.

'How remiss.' Isabel seemed genuinely baffled at the notion of not being able to ride. 'I cannot imagine my childhood without my ponies. What is life without a good ride?'

Jack smiled at the innocent naïvety of her remark but kept his eyes fixed on the party of horsemen that was now making directly for them. It was clear they had been spotted and were now firmly in the other riders' sights.

'There are four of them,' Isabel announced suddenly, breaking the silence that had fallen over them as they both squinted into the bright light.

'Your eyes are better than mine.' Jack relaxed his face, giving up the effort of trying to identify the approaching horsemen. 'Are they in uniform?'

It was hard to sit and wait for Isabel to answer the question. His worst fear was that they were being approached by a group of bandits. He had tried to convince himself that it was unlikely the local dacoits paraded around on horseback, but he knew he would have little chance of fighting off even an unarmed schoolboy. Isabel was right to chide him for his incompetence; at anything other than a gentle walk, it was all he could do to stay in the saddle. Quite how anyone could fight and ride at the same time was beyond him.

'They are dressed all in blue.'

Jack tensed as Isabel gave him the vital information he needed. 'Lancers.' There was little comfort in knowing who they faced; the vivid memory of nearly being run through by the Maharajah's lance was still fresh.

'What shall we do?' Isabel turned to face Jack as she posed the question. They had discussed the chances of meeting some of the Maharajah's forces. At the time it had seemed the best thing that could happen to them, but now that four of the Maharajah's elite lancers were bearing down on them, the idea that they could meekly request safe passage to their leader's citadel suddenly seemed incredibly naïve.

'We wait. Let's hope they are feeling friendly.'

'And if not?' Isabel reached across, resting her hand on Jack's leg as she sought reassurance.

Jack barely felt her touch. He sensed his body tensing as it did in the moments before battle. This time he was unarmed and completely unable to fight. He had never felt so impotent.

'Then you turn the head of that damn horse around and gallop like the fiends of hell are chasing you.'

'You won't be able to keep up.' Isabel's voice was mocking, despite the danger.

'I'll not even try.' Jack reached down and took her hand in a firm grip. 'But you must.' He squeezed hard to emphasise the seriousness of his words. 'I will delay them and you will ride back to Bhundapur and beg for your father's forgiveness.'

Isabel opened her mouth to protest, but Jack let go of her hand, silencing her with a raised finger. 'You will do as I say, Isabel.'

He gave her no time to reply. Touching his heels to the sides of his horse, he eased it into a walk. He would not sit and wait meekly for his fate to arrive.

He gathered his reins into one hand, doing his best to adjust his weight to cover the slight tremor that threatened to topple him from the saddle. Then he lifted his free hand and rode to meet the Maharajah's lancers.

Chapter Seventeen

The fortress rose sharply from the plain. It dominated the skyline, demanding attention. It was a prantara-durga, a hilltop fortress, and it had been the home of the maharajahs of Sawadh for centuries.

The walls were immense. Made from huge blocks of stone, they rose from the sheer sides of the hillside as if they had been carved from the very rock on which they stood. At their top, the battlements looked down on the wide plain with arrogance, the wide embrasures and merlons arrayed in tight, calculated patterns that would allow the defenders to pour a merciless fire on anyone foolish enough to try to assault the mighty fortress. Huge bastions had been built along the walls, bolstering the strength of the defences. This complex arrangement of wall and tower followed the contours of the hillside, forming five angled sides with a solitary gate at the very centre of the southernmost wall. The natural shape gave the fortress its name. It was the Taragarh, the star fort, and it was impregnable.

The wide stone walls of the fortress had been built as far out as the hillside allowed to create a wide area between them and the citadel that sat serenely in the very centre of the defences. Part palace and part stronghold, the Taragarh was the final bastion of the Maharajah's power. It had been attacked many times in the five hundred years since it had first been built. Many local chiefs and rulers had cast envious glances at its imposing defences. None had come close to making good on their ambition, not a single assault breaching the walls, their hopes left to rot and fester amidst the corpses of their soldiers.

The fortress had not been left to idle complacently through the centuries. Successive maharajahs had sought to improve the defences, seeking to secure their advantage as the years passed and warfare changed beyond all recognition. Pragmatically-minded engineers had been summoned to the distant site, their knowledge used to apply the latest stratagems of warfare, adapting the stronghold to better counter the many advances in the art of war.

The power of gunpowder had brought about the most radical changes, to prevent the Taragarh becoming nothing more than a relic of the past, an easy target for the cannons and siege trains that could destroy the proudest and longest-standing fortress in a matter of days. The height of the massive walls had been reduced, whilst their base was thickened and strengthened. The pattern of crenellations and merlons had been altered to create wide embrasures for dozens of cannon to be aimed outwards, their overlapping fields of fire calculated with meticulous care. The ancient citadel was given all the power of the modern world.

Lest the cold application of mathematics and science leave the Taragarh barren and ugly, the maharajahs also summoned the finest architects and artists and employed the best craftsmen and painters to make sure that the palace hidden within rivalled the splendour of any other. Artworks, carvings and mosaics created a place of beauty within the steadfast fortress, a haven of luxurious tranquillity and charm wrapped in all the brutal trappings of war.

Jack's neck ached from looking upwards for so long. He had stared in fascination at the fortress that loomed above them, its high walls and bastions towering over the small party that had made its way down from the high ground. The sheer sides of the hillside rose dramatically from the floor of the wide plain that surrounded it, the smooth rocky surface soaring upwards for a hundred feet even before the walls themselves began. It was an impressive sight, and he could easily understand why the first maharajahs had selected this location for their citadel.

The ground began to incline under the feet of the horses as they started on to a broad ramp that began hundreds of yards from the main gate, turning sharply left and right at least a dozen times to make the approach to the single entrance long and slow. The breeze that had cooled them for much of the ride picked up as they mounted the exposed slope, the blue and white pennants near the tips of the lancers' weapons fluttering madly in the fast-moving air.

Jack turned in the saddle, grimacing as the movement scraped at the sore flesh of his thighs, rubbed raw by the long ride into the depths of the Maharajah's kingdom. He looked across at Isabel, catching her eye and sharing a tired, fleeting smile as the end of their journey came into sight.

They had barely spoken since they had spied the Maharajah's men. To their relief, the four lancers had been part of the force that had destroyed the Tiger's stronghold. Their leader, a burly, heavily bearded fellow with thick gold bands on his sleeve, had recognised the couple as being the same white-faced foreigners they had rescued a few days previously. It had taken a great deal of gesturing and hand-waving to convince him that they were trying to return to the Maharajah, and Jack was still not sure if they now journeyed as guests or prisoners. Yet the lancers had escorted them in safety and now led them up the long ramp to the entrance into the beautiful but cruel Taragarh.

The gateway to the citadel dominated the top of the ramp. The enormous timber gates were covered in hundreds of spikes arrayed in an ordered pattern so that not one inch was left uncovered, a defence against the might of the elephants that could be used by an attacker to try to batter a passage into the fortress. Each of the two massive gates had been pushed open to admit the long line of carts and wagons that was making the laborious climb up to the fortress. The lancers were forced to dawdle behind the bullock-pulled carts bringing fresh produce to the garrison, the narrow ramp leaving no space for them to force a way past.

The delay gave Jack time to think and to prepare for meeting the Maharajah for a second time. As he studied the seat of the man's immense power, he started to doubt the wisdom of their choice. He no longer thought of the Maharajah as the kindred spirit to whom he had been able to speak so freely. The man who commanded such a mighty fortress could never be a friend, an equal. Their decision to throw themselves on the mercy of the ruler of this strange, very foreign land suddenly seemed utterly foolish.

By the time they neared the top of the long ramp, he had convinced himself that the most likely outcome was a period of incarceration before they were swiftly sent back to the British authorities. That would be the pragmatic thing for the Maharajah to do. After all, it was the British who now administered his land, and the return of the pair of escapees would certainly garner him favour. With a heavy heart Jack resigned himself to facing the last moments of his temporary respite with as much grace as he could muster.

The cool of the gatehouse was unexpected. Once past the thick gates, the small group of horsemen entered a narrow passageway that first turned sharply to the right, before almost immediately turning to the left. Curious as ever, Jack craned his neck as they passed through the dark space, trying to count the vast number of chutes and arrow slits that covered its walls and ceilings. Any attacking force that somehow managed to force the gates would find themselves in this murderous place, their movements confined by the walls, under constant attack through the multitude of openings that would allow the defenders to bring down a dreadful storm of missiles on their heads, with God knew what horrors poured through the wide chutes in the ceiling. The thought sent an involuntary shudder through him, and he felt as much of an interloper as any attacking soldier.

As they reached the end of the passage, the small party was halted at the back of the queue of wagons that waited patiently for the guards to inspect each and every delivery. The guards were as neatly uniformed as the blue-coated lancers. Their livery was dark blue, with thick red seams running down their trousers. Their short coatees were decorated with red cuffs and collars with three rows of gold frogging across the front. On their heads were Kilmarnock caps, similar to those worn by Dutton's native troops, with red piping decorating the dark blue cloth that matched their coats. Jack noticed that several sported bright red sashes; these, along with thick white stripes on their sleeves, presumably denoted their higher rank. They were as smart a group of soldiers as he had ever seen. Even their full black beards were neat and uniform. It was as if the Maharajah had been able to replicate a single perfect specimen over and over again, creating an army from one faultless mould.

Their uniforms may have been as fine as any seen on the parade squares of the British cantonments, but their weapons showed that these were not merely ceremonial soldiers. Each guardsman wore a curving sabre at his hip that hung from a thick blue sash belted tightly around his waist, with a vicious-looking curving knife held in a separate scabbard in the small of the back. Jack could not fail to be impressed, and he once again wondered why Dutton had been so dismissive of the Maharajah's forces.

'You!'

The single barked word took Jack by surprise. They had been slowly inching towards the guards. There was still one cart in front of them when one of the Maharajah's men lifted a finger and pointed in Jack's direction.

'You there! I'm speaking to you.'

To Jack's astonishment, the words were delivered in a thick Scottish brogue.

'Are you deaf, man? I asked you a damn question.'

The cart in front of them pulled away, the driver turning to look fearfully over his shoulder as he heard the raised voices around him. Jack watched him go with envy, wishing his own passage into the fortress could be so swift.

The officer with the astonishing accent strode purposefully to stand at Jack's stirrup. 'Listen, laddie, I'll try to make this easy for you. Start by telling me your name.'

'Danbury. James Danbury.' Jack used the name he had given the Maharajah when they had first met.

'See! That wasn't so hard, now was it? I am Subedar Khan.' The guardsman introduced himself before turning away, issuing a rapid series of commands in a language Jack did not recognise.

The lancers who had brought them to the fortress were clearly being dismissed, and they seemed more than happy to abandon Jack and Isabel to Khan's men, riding away without a backward glance. Jack wondered if they were relieved to have passed on the responsibility for the two foreigners.

'If you and your lady friend could please dismount.' Khan stood back as he spoke, clearly expecting Jack to obey immediately and looking up in obvious disappointment as he failed to do so. 'Now.' The subedar pointed at the ground, in case Jack was having trouble understanding the request.

Jack heard the tone in Khan's voice. As a redcoat, he had become well used to unquestioningly obeying his superiors. They might have hailed from very different armies, but it was clear that the subedar was used to a similar level of instant obedience.

He looked across to Isabel and saw the same look of incredulity he was sure was on his own face. He shrugged and slid from the saddle, confident that Isabel would follow suit.

'That's better.' Subedar Khan towered over Jack as they finally stood face to face. 'You're going to come with me. If you try any funny business, I'll rip your head off and shit in the hole. You understand that?'

Jack nodded, doing his best not to smile at the subedar's turn of phrase.

Khan grunted in disapproval and turned to lead Jack and Isabel out of the entranceway and into the fortress proper.

The antechamber was as comfortable as any room Jack had ever seen. Even the officers' mess back in Aldershot, where he had served as an orderly, compared badly to the opulent chamber that spoke of wealth and luxury on an almost unimaginable scale. Slim silk-lined couches sat neatly on three sides of the room, each the deep purple of ripe plums and covered with a liberal layer of plump cushions decorated with intricate patterns of golden thread. The white marble floor was nearly completely covered with the deep reds and yellows of a Persian rug, whilst the walls were decorated with silk hangings that matched the colour of the couches. A series of richly coloured paintings ran around the room. They told the story of a hunt, a finely dressed rider depicted chasing down an enormous boar until, in the final picture, he stood astride the beast, his thick-shafted spear buried deep in the animal's heart. Jack had a feeling that he would shortly know precisely how the boar felt. Isabel stood in front of this last painting, her fingers gently tracing the intricate carving on its frame, entranced by the detail of the work.

Yet for all its finery, the room had been chosen as a secure place to hold unwanted guests. There were no windows and the single door was shut tight; Jack had heard the sound of a heavy bolt being thrown when they were left alone. It was a room of charm and elegance, but it was still a prison, for all its opulence. Their cage might have been gilded, but they were as much prisoners now as they had been when captured by the Tiger and his bandits.

Jack rose swiftly to his feet the moment he heard loud footsteps outside the door to the antechamber. He had been perched on the edge of one of the couches, unwilling to lounge back into the luxurious seat lest he fall asleep the moment he relaxed.

The door was thrown back and Subedar Khan strode purposefully into the room, his face creased in a scowl. A thin-framed man followed him, trying to screen himself behind the guardsman's robust body. He was dressed in a simple white kurta with a sky-blue pagdi wrapped tightly around his head and a matching sash tied around his bony waist. In his hands he carried a thick red ledger on which he had carefully balanced a fine white quill and an ornate china inkwell.

'Sit there.' Khan spoke curtly as he turned to wave his colleague to a free couch at one side of the room. The man hurried to obey the command, bending at the waist as he moved, as if trying to bow at the same time.

'I need some information from you both.' Khan turned his attention back to Jack and Isabel. 'Why don't you sit yourself down, laddie? This'll take a while.'

'I'll stand.' Jack stood foursquare in front of the native subedar. He was not daunted by the officer's size.

'As you like.' The corners of Khan's mouth twitched as if he were amused by Jack's belligerence.

'Are you not going to introduce us?' Jack indicated the

white-robed man, who immediately looked down at the floor in horror at being the subject of such attention.

Khan looked disapprovingly at Jack. 'No. Now, what are you doing here, laddie?'

'We want to see the Maharajah.'

Khan gave a short bark of a laugh. 'Oh really. I'll just tell him you're here, shall I?'

'Very good. We'll wait.'

'Funny, laddie, very funny. So you are from the 24th? A deserter and his bint, is it? You'll not be the first nor, I suspect, the last.'

Jack took a deliberate step forward. 'Be careful who you call bint, Subedar Khan.' He spoke slowly and carefully. He had played the part of an officer for long enough to know how to demonstrate authority, and for the first time he saw a shred of doubt on Khan's proud face.

'My name is James Danbury and I am a captain in Her Majesty's 24th Regiment of Foot. The Maharajah knows me. I was speaking with him just a few days ago. He nearly killed me, but I found it in my heart to forgive him for being so damn rude. My companion is Isabel Youngsummers, and the Maharajah knows her too. Not as well as he would like, but he knows her nonetheless.' Jack spoke calmly, all the while keeping his eyes fixed on Khan's face. He could sense Isabel's growing impatience at being excluded from the conversation and he just hoped she had enough sense to keep mum.

Out of the corner of his eye he could see the white-robed clerk writing furiously to keep up, his eyes wide in horror as the white-faced foreigner spoke to the subedar in such a forthright manner.

'Now,' Jack continued without pause, giving the native officer no time to interrupt, 'I suggest you stop trying to frighten us and have someone tell the Maharajah we are here. I'm certain he is a busy man, but I believe he will make time to see us.' Jack turned to face the anxious scribe, who was scribbling away for all his worth. 'Did you get all that?'

Subedar Khan said nothing. He stared at Jack for what seemed a long time. The silence stretched out, uncomfortable and awkward.

'You are a bold fellow, laddie.' Khan finally spoke, breaking the silence with a gentle chuckle. 'Why should I believe all that horseshit?'

Jack took a step forward, his face impassive. 'If you call me laddie again, I'll rip off your balls and shove them down your damn throat.'

This time Khan laughed out loud. 'I truly believe you would try. So it is to be Captain Danbury, is it?'

'My name is Captain James Danbury and I am here to see the Maharajah.' Jack felt his face flicker into a smile. It was hard not to like the straight-talking subedar.

Khan made a show of looking Jack up and down, his mouth puckering in distaste at the unkempt appearance of the man claiming to be a British officer. 'Very well, huzoor. I have never seen a mighty captain of the sarkar who dresses as you do, but you are a strange folk, so I should suppose anything is possible.'

'Like finding an English-speaking officer in the service of the Maharajah?'

Khan chuckled. 'A Scottish missionary lived in my village when I was a boy. He taught me to speak English before my father saw sense and cut his throat. Life is odd, is it not?'

Without another word he turned and marched from the room. The scribe immediately leapt to his feet to follow, dropping his quill in his haste. Jack bent and retrieved it, calmly handing it back to the terrified man, who scuttled from the room as if he had been just seen the devil himself.

Jack had done his best. They had flung themselves on the mercy of the Maharajah. Only time would tell if they had made the worst mistake of their lives.

Chapter Eighteen

Their footsteps echoed loudly on the marble floors as they were led through the corridors of the palace, the sound only partially muffled when they crossed one of the many carpets and rugs that were artfully displayed in the beautifully decorated spaces. Jack doubted he had ever felt more out of place; a clumsy beast granted admittance to a world of shimmering and delicate beauty.

He had never seen so much wealth. The walls were smothered with fabulous paintings, some small enough to fit into the pocket of his breeches, others big enough to cover an entire wall. Every few paces revealed another treasure, a bewildering array of jade, ivory, gold and silver statues and ornaments displayed on a series of exquisitely carved stone plinths. Each doorway was a work of art, the teak columns covered with a fine tracery of carvings and decorations. Glass chandeliers appeared one after another, their crystal beads and droplets glistening in the sunlight that streamed through the huge windows running down one side of every room.

Isabel was entranced, her head turning quickly from side to side to catch every detail as they hurried after the blue-robed chamberlain who had appeared to lead them from their anteroom into the depths of the palace. The chamberlain's soft white slippers whispered

across the marble floors, his movements controlled and subtle so
that it was as if he glided along, his elegant progress standing in
stark contrast to Jack's bullish gait.

Jack's discomfort made him feel belligerent, and he deliberately
walked as loudly as he could. To his satisfaction, the chamberlain
turned to look over his shoulder, the silent rebuke clear on his
disdainful features. Even Isabel scowled at him, her warning look
imploring him to behave.

They walked through a dozen rooms, each as splendid as the one
before. Their senses were assaulted with colour. Every room boasted
a different shade of decoration, a subtle but noticeable contrast to its
neighbour. Every object they passed was worth more than Jack
could hope to earn in a lifetime as a redcoat. The maharajahs were
clearly not coy about ostentatious display.

The chamberlain stopped in front of a pair of closed doors that
were guarded by two sentries wearing the same uniform as Subedar
Khan and his men. Each was armed with a fearsome-looking spear
that was almost as thick as Jack's arm, and from the look in their
eyes, he was certain that they were more than ready to use them
should anyone try to force their way past.

'You will enter the chamber in silence. His Royal Highness is in
durbar and you must do nothing to draw attention to yourselves.'
The chamberlain spoke fast, but in a hushed, reverential tone, the
same kind of voice the orderlies used in the officers' mess when their
masters were enjoying a post-lunch nap. He looked only at Jack; it
was clear he expected Isabel to say and do nothing. 'You will not
look directly at His Majesty, you will not speak, you will not call out
and you will not walk like an elephant.' His face puckered in distaste
before he continued with his staccato list of instructions. 'If His
Royal Highness deigns to speak to you, then I shall call you forward.
You must keep your eyes on the ground at all times and you will
prostrate yourself on the floor when I give the signal. You must
remain there until His Royal Highness has finished speaking. Then
you will get up and leave the room immediately. You must walk
backwards, again looking at nothing but the ground.'

The chamberlain finished his speech with a badly contained sniff
of disgust. Jack had struggled to understand the man's instructions,

his thick accent making the words close to unintelligible. But the message was clear, and he felt a flutter of nerves in the pit of his belly.

'Excuse me.' Isabel spoke for the first time, only to be roundly ignored by the chamberlain. 'What about me?' This time she reached out and touched the man's arm, determined to get his attention.

The chamberlain's mouth twisted in obvious distaste at her touch. 'You will be permitted to enter the room, but you will remain where I place you.'

'Am I not to be allowed to speak to the Maharajah?'

Jack saw Isabel's left foot tapping a fast rhythm on the floor and wisely took a pace back.

The chamberlain's eyes bulged at the very idea. 'You are a woman. You will not be allowed to speak in durbar.'

A pink flush was spreading up from the nape of Isabel's neck to colour her cheeks. 'And why is that?'

'You are a woman,' repeated the chamberlain, turning away. Clearly he considered the matter closed.

Isabel, however, did not. She reached forward, taking firm hold of his thin shoulder and pulling hard so that he spun around to face her once again. She was several inches taller than the sparsely framed man and she loomed over him as she finally released the pent-up emotion she had kept contained ever since they had arrived at the fortress.

'How dare you! I am a subject of the Queen and I shall not be kept quiet. Nor will I allow myself to be treated like some piece of unwanted baggage. I have spoken to the Maharajah before and I fully intend to do so again now.'

The chamberlain waved his hands in front of him to ward off the enraged young woman, who looked ready to commit violence. 'It is tradition.'

'Tradition, my eye. How I pity the women who have the misfortune to be born in your misbegotten country. Why, do you not know that a woman rules Great Britain? Would the Maharajah not deign to speak to her? Would he force the greatest queen this world has ever seen to remain silent?'

'No, no, no,' the chamberlain whined in reply, his voice wheedling and imploring. 'It is the way.'

'Isabel, leave the poor man alone.' Jack decided to intervene lest their chance of seeing the Maharajah disappear. 'He's only doing his job.'

Isabel turned on him, her eyes flashing in fury. 'So you think I should remain silent too! How dare you! After all I have done for you!'

'Yes. Yes, I do think you should remain silent if that is how things are done here. We cannot waltz in and expect them to lay out the red carpet for us.'

'I expect to be heard.'

'Oh, I am sure the Maharajah will want to do more than just hear you. But you must wait.'

Isabel crossed her arms in front of her. 'So I have to do as I am told?'

'Yes.' Jack smiled at the pouting face. 'This time you do as you are bloody well told, unless you want us to be clapped in irons and shipped back to Bhundapur.'

Isabel sighed in resignation. 'Very well. But don't you dare mess this up. If you do, I shall never forgive you.'

'I won't. Now stand still and look pretty. I don't imagine the Maharajah will ignore you for long. It cannot be often that he has a beautiful English rose in his court.'

Jack turned and nodded to the chamberlain, signalling that they were finally ready to enter the durbar room.

With a final haughty sniff, the chamberlain signalled the guards to open the ornate double doors.

The durbar room was hushed. With its high vaulted ceiling it felt like a grand library, and the sombre silence pressed around Jack as soon as he followed the chamberlain into the room. On one side, wide windows had been thrown open, and the air felt fresh, cooled by the breeze that rushed into the vast space. Everything in the chamber was white, with dramatic silk hangings around the windows that billowed theatrically in the breeze. After so many examples of dazzling colour and ostentatious display, the contrast was stark; the durbar room was a haven of peace and tranquillity.

Yet it was not completely silent. The sound of quiet conversation could be heard from the far end, where a crowd of onlookers were gathered, all listening with intense concentration. Jack was too far away to make out any individual words as he walked as quietly as he could in the wake of the chamberlain. As they approached the small gathering, the chamberlain turned and gestured curtly for Isabel to wait to one side, a sarcastic smile stretched across his pale lips. The solemnity of the durbar had done wonders to quell Isabel's temper, and she simply bobbed her head in acknowledgement of the command, meekly moving to the place the chamberlain indicated.

Jack did his best to place his boots with care as he once again followed the chamberlain forward. His heavy tread still echoed loudly, and more than one face turned in annoyance as his entrance disturbed those straining to hear the murmuring voices at the room's end. One by one the heads of the spectators turned to look at the firangi who had entered their midst.

The majority of the room's finely dressed occupants were pressed to the flanks, leaving the end of the enormous space as a stage for the durbar's prime participants. These were the figures that looked up last of all, their earnest conversation coming to a faltering close as Jack approached.

He did his best to stand up straight as he became the focus of the room's attention. He wished he was dressed in uniform, the outer shell of a British army captain a fine prop to a man's confidence. Instead he faced the gathering of nobles wearing nothing more than a stained shirt and a pair of filthy trousers. There was no sign of the Maharajah, and for that Jack was grateful, as he felt his confidence wane in the face of such intense scrutiny.

'Who are you?' The question was posed by one of the two men who had been engaged in the important conversation. The man took one long look at Jack and shuddered in obvious revulsion at his filthy attire.

Jack decided to ignore the chamberlain, who was flapping his hand in a desperate attempt to get Jack to prostrate himself now that he was being addressed.

'My name is Captain James Danbury.' He hoped his voice conveyed the right balance of respect and confidence.

'Danbury.' The man stumbled over the foreign pronunciation. He was finely dressed in thick red robes that did little to hide his round belly. His head was swathed in a golden turban that had a pair of ostrich feathers attached to the front by a huge gold and diamond clasp. Each of his thick, stubby fingers was covered with gold rings, and around his neck was the biggest ruby Jack had ever seen. 'I do not know a Danbury.'

'I am with the 24th Foot stationed at Bhundapur, sir.' Jack did his best to sound respectful.

'No. I do not know you.' The man's whole face wobbled as he shook his head. It was clear that he had heard all he needed to, and he turned his back on Jack, once again facing away from the rest of the room's occupants.

The second figure laughed aloud at such posturing. He was the only man in the room dressed in uniform. Now he took a step forward and clicked his heels together before offering Jack a short, clipped bow from the waist.

'Count Piotr Wysocki, once of the Régiment de Chevau-Légers Lanciers de la Garde Impériale.'

Jack did not fully understand the count's formal introduction, but there was something familiar in his choice of uniform. He had a hazy recollection of a painting in the officers' mess in Aldershot that depicted the charge of the famous Polish lancers at Waterloo. Count Piotr sported the same dark blue uniform with a crimson front panel to the jacket and a thick crimson stripe running down the seam of the snug pantaloons.

Jack quickly understood the impact of the count's presence in the Maharajah's court. 'You must be responsible for the blue-coated lancers.'

Count Piotr bobbed his head enthusiastically. 'Yes. They are my creation. Have you seen them?'

Jack shivered involuntarily at the image of the Maharajah thundering towards him with his deadly steel-tipped lance aimed squarely at his heart. 'I may have caught a glimpse of them.'

The count's eyes twinkled at the reply. 'Then you have seen how well I have trained them! They only had a rabble here before I came. Now they have a full squadron of lancers that even the

Emperor would have been proud to have in his service.'

Jack presumed that Wysocki was referring to Napoleon Bonaparte. The count did not look old enough to have served the fabled French leader; Jack would have judged him to be in his mid forties. If he had been at Waterloo, then that would have placed him firmly in his sixties. With a trim, athletic build and a lancer's uniform that fitted like a kidskin glove, it was hard to believe that that was the case.

'I am sure the Maharajah is delighted to have a man of such experience as you in his service.'

Count Piotr laughed. 'You will have to ask him. I am not so sure he fully appreciates my talents.'

'I hope I get the chance.'

'Why not ask him now?' The count moved gracefully to one side, revealing the final occupant of the room.

For the first time, Jack saw the simple wooden chair that had been placed strategically at the very end of the room. It was not the throne he had expected; in place of precious stones and exquisite carvings, there were simply the signs of long use and careful preservation.

He found himself looking into the same eyes that had stared at him from behind the eight-foot reach of a lance. He was finally once again face to face with the Maharajah.

Chapter Nineteen

———◆———

'We meet again, Captain Danbury. Or are you going to tell me your true name this time? I must confess I am finding this all rather confusing.'

The Maharajah lounged with his right leg draped over one arm of the simple wooden chair, completely at ease with his surroundings. He was dressed very simply in a loose-fitting white shirt and snug white breeches. A pair of blood-red Cossack boots reached to just below his knees, his sole concession to vanity. The fat man who had treated Jack with such disdain wore more jewellery on one pudgy finger than Jack could see on the whole of the Maharajah's body. It was becoming clear, from both his appearance and the style of the durbar room itself, that the ruler of Sawadh paid little attention to the opulent finery that so embellished the rest of his palace.

Jack saw the smile on the Maharajah's face as he spoke. He hoped it was a good sign.

'My name is Jack Lark, sir. I am afraid the rest of it was just a pretence.' Jack had no real idea how he should address the Maharajah. He had first met him dressed as an officer and so it seemed natural to continue with that approach.

'I am glad you finally feel able to tell me your name.' The Maharajah rubbed his hand vigorously against the bald dome of his head, as if physically clearing his mind. 'So tell me, Jack Lark, why would you lie about who you are?' His face showed intense interest, his eyes piercing into Jack's own as if studying the very depths of his soul.

'I was born poor. I could never hope to be an officer any other way.'

'But you wanted it? You wanted the place in life that was denied to you?'

'Yes, sir. I did.'

'So you took it?'

'Yes.'

'And then you enjoyed living the high life of an officer?'

'No. I went to war.'

The Maharajah seemed to approve of the reply, and for the first time Jack began to believe he might have a chance of convincing the ruler of Sawadh to let them stay.

'So you freely admit you are a charlatan. Must I also assume you are a thief?'

'Yes, sir.' Jack felt his eyes drift to a spot six inches above the Maharajah's head. It was easier than staring into the man's uncompromising eyes.

'And a deserter?'

'Yes, sir.'

'And a coward?'

Jack's gaze snapped downwards. He looked hard into the Maharajah's brown eyes. 'No. I have never shirked from a fight.'

The Maharajah nodded slowly. 'I accept your answer.'

With a lithe bound he got to his feet and walked to stand in front of Jack. They were of the same height, and the Maharajah came to a halt so close to him that Jack could feel the wash of his breath on his face.

'So, Jack Lark. You are an impostor, a thief and a deserter. Why have you come to me?'

'Because I had nowhere else to go.'

The Maharajah threw his head back and laughed. 'Since when did it become known amongst the mighty sahibs that I take in any waif and stray who happens to pass by?'

'I am not an ordinary waif. I came to offer you my service.'

'Your Highness.' The finely dressed fat man had moved forward to stand at his master's side and now chose to intervene. 'He is clearly a spy. He should be killed and his body thrown from the battlements.' He stumbled over the words, obviously ill at ease speaking in English. But there was no mistaking the relish with which he called for Jack to be put to death.

The Maharajah never once took his eyes off Jack. 'The vizier is quite correct. You are a spy and I will have you killed.'

Jack didn't flinch despite the icy flush that hurtled down his spine. 'So be it. But that would be a bit of a waste, don't you think?'

'A waste! Why would having you killed be a waste?' The Maharajah threw the question back at him, a few flecks of his spittle landing on Jack's face, such was the force of his words.

'Because I may be a thief and an impostor, and a deserter come to that. But I was also a British officer. I fought the Russians in the Crimea and I have commanded a company of British soldiers. I would have thought a man in your position could have use of my service.'

'A man in my position?' The Maharajah seemed genuinely intrigued.

'A king who chafes at being under the authority of a foreign power. A man who does everything he can to push against those put in charge of his kingdom but who stops short of open rebellion for fear of inciting a response stronger than he can bear. A ruler who fears for the future and for the rights of his descendants to rule in his place when he is dead and buried. I think a man like that would want to surround himself with those who know his enemy. Men who can help him.'

'You presume a lot.' There was ice in the Maharajah's voice now.

'I say what I see. I think you need me.'

'Need you! I do not need you. And you are wrong, Mr Lark. I am not afraid.'

'Perhaps you should be.'

Jack thought the Maharajah would lash out. His face was full of tension and Jack was certain he had gone too far.

The look of anger passed. 'Perhaps I should be.' The Maharajah turned on his heel and flopped heavily back into his chair. 'Where is Miss Youngsummers?'

Jack turned and looked over his shoulder. 'She is waiting dutifully at the rear of this room.'

'So you stole her too?'

'She rescued me.'

The Maharajah arched an eyebrow. 'She must be an astonishing woman. I think I will find the time to get to know her better.'

'I think I shall have to make sure that never happens, sir.'

The Maharajah gave a short laugh. 'I suggest you never try to impersonate a diplomat. You really do not have enough oil on your tongue.'

'I'll take that as a compliment.'

For a second time the vizier intervened, impatient with a conversation he could barely understand.

'He is a spy. Kill him and his woman. You have wasted enough of your time on him.'

The Maharajah took no offence at the interruption. It was clear he valued his vizier's opinion.

'So. What should I do with you? If I truly thought you a spy I would have you killed this very moment.' The Maharajah drummed his fingers on his leg. 'Count, what do you think?'

The Polish count did not reply immediately. After a moment's thought he turned to face Jack.

'Did you truly fight in the Crimea?'

'I did.'

'Where exactly?'

'At the Alma. I commanded the Light Company of the King's Royal Fusiliers. We were in the Light Division and we captured the great redoubt on our own.'

'Did you kill many Russians?'

'Yes.'

'Were you a hero?'

'No. My men were the heroes. I was simply fortunate enough to be with them.'

The count turned back to the Maharajah. 'That is good enough for me, sire. I believe him.'

The Maharajah snorted. 'You believe him because he claims to have killed a few Russian conscripts. He admits he is an impostor. Is he not lying now?'

'I can see it in his eyes. He has fought in battle. He knows what it is to lead men. I believe him, sire.'

'The count hates the Russians.' The Maharajah offered the explanation to Jack. 'He fought against them back in the thirties and he would fight against them now if he had half the chance.'

The count shrugged. 'Of course, sire. We beat them at Stoczek and I would happily give my life to face them again. Yet I have a feeling I am more likely to have to fight these damn British first.'

The Maharajah nodded at the wise comment before smiling wolfishly at Jack. 'How does that sound, Jack? Are you ready to go to war against your own countrymen?'

'No.' Jack had not even considered the idea. Yet here he was throwing himself on the mercy of the ruler of a land he knew the British authorities were planning to annex as soon as they got half a chance. If the Maharajah resisted, Jack could well find himself stuck on the wrong side. The redcoats could become his enemy.

'Your honesty is refreshing. Perhaps you are the one who should be afraid,' the Maharajah replied evenly.

'Do you plan to fight?'

'No. No sane man seeks to fight. No father wants his children to go to war.'

'Whatever happens?'

The Maharajah's eyes were suddenly moist. 'I do not know the answer to that question.' He turned to look out of the windows that gave a view on to a beautiful courtyard at the very heart of the fortress. 'You may stay, Jack Lark. As may Miss Youngsummers. You can both stay here in safety.'

He turned back and fixed Jack with the intense stare that Jack found so unsettling. 'But we must both think of the future. Of what might be. A man should know what lies in his heart so that when he must choose he is ready. For I fear we will both have to choose where our future will take us.'

He lolled back into his chair and closed his eyes.

'Durbar is finished. Count, take Mr Lark and Miss Youngsummers to that Scottish fool who let them in here. Tell him that we have a new recruit for my lancers. He is to find them whatever they need and have this one ready to join us on our hunt tomorrow. He is charged with their safety until then. Now leave me. I have need of rest.'

The room was filled with sudden bustle and energy as it was quickly cleared of the members of the Maharajah's court. The vizier shot Jack a hate-filled glare as he waddled past. Jack did his best to ignore the hostility that radiated from the pugnacious little man. By rights he should have felt nothing other than elation. After all, he had succeeded in securing a safe place for both himself and Isabel. Yet the Maharajah's words had left him with a nagging sense of unease. The threat of war was suddenly very real.

Jack stood back and looked at himself in the long mirror. The sky-blue tunic was cut close, fitting him better than any uniform he had ever owned. Yet it had still not met the exacting standards of the sprightly old tailor whom Subedar Khan had brought to his room, and who had left promising to return later to work on the fit. The white breeches were tight around his thighs and he had self-consciously assessed the way they clung around his backside. He had no idea what rank the thick white epaulettes denoted, but he could not help the prick of vanity that arose unbidden as he studied his new appearance as a lancer in the service of the Maharajah.

'You look most fine.' Isabel walked into the room, the subtle waft of her perfume preceding her. She too had been able to change her soiled, grimy clothes. The gold sari she wore shimmered in the sunlight that poured through the enormous window overlooking a courtyard with a wonderful marble fountain at its centre. She looked radiant.

'You're not so bad yourself.' Jack held out his hand and brought Isabel to his side so they could both look in the mirror at the same time. 'It's nice to see you looking like a lady again.'

Isabel blushed at the compliment. 'Thank you. So, how does it feel to wear the uniform of the enemy?' She posed the question to Jack's reflection, noticing the grimace it caused on his face.

'They are not the enemy.'

'Not yet. But they might be tomorrow, or the next day. Or the day after.'

'Let's hope it doesn't come to that.'

'But it might, Jack. And what then?'

'Then?' Jack looked down at his new, brightly polished riding boots. 'Then I don't know.'

'You cannot fight against us. That would be wrong.' Isabel spoke with the earnest zeal of a young girl. For her, the world was black and white. Despite her desire to escape her father and the suffocating future he had planned for her, it was still unthinkable that she would ever turn traitor.

Jack lived in a world of grey and shadows. He did not have her certainty.

'Let us hope it does not come to that,' he repeated.

He let his hand fall to the new sword that hung at his left hip. It was a talwar, the native version of a British cavalry sabre. It hung lower than he was used to, the longer slings of the cavalry scabbard nudging against his thigh. He had been interested to discover that the scabbard was fashioned from leather rather than the metal favoured by the British officers. Subedar Khan had explained that the softer material would lessen damage to the blade; the harsh metal scabbards blunted the edges of the swords they were supposed to protect. Jack was pleased to have been trusted with a weapon, and it felt good to have a sword hanging at his hip once more.

'You look lovely, Isabel.' He did his best to change the subject. 'You could well start a new fashion amongst the ladies of Bhundapur. They will all be green with envy the moment they see how fine you look.'

Isabel turned to one side and admired her profile in the mirror. 'Do you truly think this thing suits me? Do you not think it makes me look rather . . .' she paused as she summoned the courage to address the issue that had concerned her since she had first been wrapped in the folds of the wonderful silk, 'large in the nether regions?'

Jack laughed at her vanity. 'No, Isabel. Your nether regions look just fine to me.'

She brought the fan she held in her hand sharply down on Jack's forearm as he made a great pretence of checking the area of her new attire that had so worried her. He yelped in pain and the look in his eyes made her laugh aloud.

Then he reached for her and she sank into his arms.

Jack held her tight, smelling her perfume, bending his head so that his face was resting against her hair.

She was right to question him. The Maharajah had been quite correct. Jack was an impostor, a deserter and a thief. But was he also a turncoat? He had certainly swapped his scarlet coat for one of blue. But did that make him a traitor?

He glanced down and saw Isabel looking back at him. He closed his eyes and leant forward to kiss her for the first time, losing himself in the taste of her lips. Yet a part of him remained detached, even as he felt her body pressing against his.

The winds of change had begun to blow. Soon they would stop, and when they did, he would have to decide which way he would turn.

Chapter Twenty

The horse pawed at the ground beneath its feet. Jack could feel its muscles tensing underneath him, a shudder of excitement that left the huge beast trembling. Its jet-black coat was already streaked white with sweat after the first headlong gallop down from the fortress. He had clung on for dear life and somehow managed to remain in the saddle. It was more by luck than any latent ability, and he was relieved to have survived so far. But the day was young and he was horribly aware that there were plenty more challenges lying ahead.

They had left the fortress long before dawn, the Maharajah determined to have the first leg of the hunt completed before the sun had awoken to baste the earth in its stupefying heat. The hunters had gathered in the coolness of early morning, the low murmur of whispered conversation cut short as the first haunting call of the hunting horn, a legacy of the Maharajah's time in England, summoned them to action.

A second column had left the fortress shortly after the hunters. Half a dozen elephants, twice as many bullock-pulled carts and hundreds of servants had been dispatched to construct the resting place where the hunters would shelter through the hottest hours of the day. More guests would arrive for the noon feast before the hunters went back out when the worst of the day's heat had begun to dissipate.

Despite her polite request to take part in the day's sport, Isabel had only been given permission to join the secondary party with the rest of the guests. Jack smiled as he recalled her fury at being excluded from the hunt, when he, without half her ability to ride, had been expected to join the other men, who would spend the day enjoying the Maharajah's favourite sport of pig-sticking.

Thinking of Isabel led his thoughts to the previous evening. He had been unable to stop the kiss. And it had changed things. Isabel had been his responsibility since the moment they had stolen away from Fenris and the others, but now their growing closeness would complicate his options. He had prided himself on being able to cope alone, with no one to care for but himself. Now he would have to think of them both, a responsibility that was as daunting as preparing to lead men into battle.

Jack forced the thoughts of his future away as he contemplated the challenge of the day ahead. He would have to face the trial of keeping pace with the rest of the hunters without any of Isabel's moral support or hasty lectures on how to ride the huge stallion that he had been lent for the day.

The bustle of the other riders jostling around him posed as much danger as the wild, careering gallop. His horse's unpredictable movements forced him to make repeated anxious grabs for the edge of the saddle lest he slip in an ignominious heap to the ground. He felt like a fool. The hunters milling around him rode with dignified ease, languidly taking the refreshments offered by the many servants and syces whilst engaging their fellows in quiet conversation. The looks of pity and disdain on their faces as they gave Jack a wide berth left him in doubt that his incompetence was obvious to all.

The sound of the hunting horn rang out and the bearers sprang away from the horses, lest they be trampled in the rush. Jack leant forward and grabbed a fistful of his horse's mane as the group of riders started to move out, the next stage in the long ride about to begin. One finely dressed young man looked icily at him, his mouth puckered in distaste, then suddenly pulled on his horse's reins, using the motion to barge Jack's mount in the flank. The sudden jerk caused Jack to cling desperately to the pommel of the saddle. He might not have understood the words, but his ears still picked up the snickers and badly hidden guffaws of his fellow hunters as they relished the foreigner's shaming.

There was no time to offer any kind of response for the injury to his pride. The horse lurched into motion beneath him, following the rest of the mounts rather than in response to any urging from its rider. Jack took a firm hold and did his best to grip with his knees as Isabel had told him, determined he would not endure the shame of falling from the saddle.

The next stage of the hunt had begun.

A dense tangle of foliage stretched as far as Jack could see. Bamboo and forest trees fought to break free from the clinging embrace of the thick, thorny undergrowth, striving to reach for the sky, which was hidden behind a canopy of matted boughs. The sight of the interwoven greenery was overpowering after so long spent in the rocky high ground, and he savoured the new environment, his eyes roving over the spectacular growth as he tried to take in the wonderful kaleidoscope of colour, teeming with the promise of life

The noise of the jungle was as much of a contrast, the stillness of the mountains replaced by a cacophony of sound. The loud chirrups and clicks of a thousand types of insect jarred in his ears after so long in the silence of the higher ground. The calls of the brightly coloured birds and the gleeful whoops and shouts of a thousand monkeys provided a wonderful symphony that only emphasised how alien this new place felt to a man who hailed from the man-made rookeries of London.

The heat had built steadily throughout the morning, the humidity in the air now stifling. Jack sweated freely under his tight blue lancer's uniform, and around him the very air felt damp. It was an oppressive feeling and one that was only made worse as they pushed on to a wide trail that led deep into the dark jungle. The sudden heavy shade pressed down around him and left his eyes struggling to adjust from the bright sunshine. It was a threatening place, and his joy at such vibrant display was replaced with equal measures of unease and discomfort.

The slower going at least meant he made it to the next halt without falling off his horse. But the pit of his spine was beginning to hurt, the backache that dogged his life already adding a fresh misery to the day. The sweat had soaked through his shirt, staining the cloth of his new jacket dark blue and leaving him sodden and drained. The other riders seemed as crisp and polished as when they had started, the long, hard ride merely a precursor to the main event, whereas he was already coming close to the end of his powers of endurance.

'Sahib?' Within moments of the party coming to a halt, a syce appeared as if from nowhere to stand patiently at Jack's saddle and offer up a crystal glass full of lemon-flavoured sherbet.

Jack took the drink gratefully, downing it in several huge gulps, careless of the drops of precious liquid that escaped from the corners of his mouth. He wiped the excess from his lips with the sleeve of his coat before reaching for another glass. He was aware of a rider approaching, and he quickly drained the second drink before turning and looking into the smiling face of Count Piotr.

The count removed his square-topped lancer's helmet and used a finger to clean the remains of his own drink from his pencil-thin moustache.

'It is wonderful, is it not? I have often thought I could make my fortune by having the stuff shipped back home.'

The cool sherbet had gone some way to revitalising Jack's flagging morale, and he summoned the energy to engage the count in conversation.

'Is Poland hot, then? I had always imagined it to be cold.' He did his best to sit straight in his saddle, ignoring the spasms in his back.

'Sometimes it is cold enough to freeze your balls to your saddle.' Count Piotr clearly enjoyed his own choice of words. 'But I would be happy to drink this nectar whatever the damn weather.' His English was accented, but it was clear he spoke the language well.

Jack dipped his head in acknowledgement. 'You might well be correct.' He bent carefully and retrieved a third glass. 'It truly is just the ticket.'

His horse chose that moment to move to one side, and Jack lurched forward, distracted by the conversation, spilling a large amount of the precious liquid on to his breeches.

'You are not a horseman, Lark.' The count offered the judgement, a thin, humourless chuckle following Jack's grimace as he struggled to control his wayward mount.

'I am not.' Jack did his best to wipe away the puddle of liquid from his thigh, but only succeeded in smearing it so that the white of his new breeches was now stained a dirty yellow.

'I thought as much. If you stay here long enough, it would be my pleasure to give you some lessons.'

Jack did not like the count's choice of words. 'If?'

'The Maharajah gave you leave to stay. I do not believe he specified for how long.'

'So I have only been given a temporary reprieve? That fat bugger may still get his wish and see me dead?'

The count laughed at Jack's lack of civility. 'That fat bugger, as you call him, is the Maharajah's most trusted adviser. The vizier is not a man to be crossed. You must tread warily around him. He is as vicious as a cobra and twice as deadly.'

Jack managed to steady his horse for long enough to accept a fourth glass of the wonderfully refreshing lemon sherbet, warily keeping his free hand ready to make a quick grab for the pommel if the ill-mannered beast attempted to move once more.

'He may not have to worry about me after today. I reckon I'll be lucky if I finish this damned hunt without falling off and breaking my neck.'

'I hope not. That would be a sad end for a warrior.'

'A warrior? I don't think I have ever been called that before.'

'You have the eyes.' The count moved his horse without any obvious command, easing it alongside Jack's so he could talk more quietly. 'You have seen war. It is obvious to me, though not, I suspect, to many in the Maharajah's court.' He looked around, suddenly furtive. When he spoke again, it was in a hoarse whisper, pitched so quietly that Jack could barely hear his words. 'You will have to watch your back. This place is a damned vipers' nest. I have been here six long years and I have seen men poisoned, murdered and executed in a thousand foul ways. It is not a safe place, Jack. Not for you. Not even for me. Not for anyone.'

Jack took a careful look at his recently drained glass. 'Poisoned, you say?'

The count roared with laughter at Jack's anxious expression and clapped him hard on the arm. 'Enjoy the hunt, Jack Lark.'

Jack tossed the heavy crystal glass back to the waiting syce, the cold liquid he had so avidly consumed suddenly heavy in his stomach. The count's warning had made a mockery of his relief at having secured a refuge in the Maharajah's court. Despite the intense heat, he shivered, as if someone had just walked across his grave.

The lead shikari crashed his elephant through the undergrowth. His team of beaters thrashed and shouted around him, their long line spread wide as they sought to drive the precious boars towards the gathering of mounted hunters. Their enthusiastic din reached Jack where he sat uneasily on his horse. His hands gripped and re-gripped the thick bamboo spear he had been given when the hunters had been organised into their heats, the small groups that would be allocated a boar by the umpires who ran the hunt. Nerves fluttered in his belly, the sour taste of fear mixed with the pungent sherbet to produce a noxious cocktail that made him feel quite sick.

Count Piotr had given him a rapid run-through of the rules of the hunt. The garbled instructions had been confusing, to say the least, and Jack still had only a vague understanding of what was supposed to happen. The word and judgement of the umpires was final. When the boars, driven forward by the shikari and his men, thundered out from the thick undergrowth, it was the umpires' duty to verify that the beasts were big enough to be hunted. Only the largest would be selected and allocated to the heats. It would then be up to the riders – or spears, as the count had styled them – to ride down the enraged animals, charging through the jungle until they could close and thrust their vicious weapons into the boars' flesh. The count had explained a long list of other rules, though his advice on not crossing riding lines and impeding the other riders had made little sense to Jack, who knew it would be a miracle if he managed to stay on his horse long enough to even see the animal he was supposed to chase.

He did his best not to fidget as he waited with the other three spears of his heat. Thousands of small insects had appeared and seemed determined to feast on his flesh or to wallow in the moisture in his nose, mouth and eyes. He passed most of the long wait flapping his hand around his head in an ineffectual attempt to avoid breathing in or accidentally consuming dozens of the irritating and persistent plague.

The other riders ignored the foreigner in their midst, their quiet conversation conducted in their own language. Occasionally they would look in his direction, their guarded eyes and veiled gestures making it clear that he was the subject of their discussion. One of the spears was the same thin-faced noble who had deliberately tried to unseat Jack earlier in the day. He was clearly the leader of the group, the other pair careful to laugh loudly at his remarks, their obsequious behaviour revealing the younger man's status as eloquently as any badge of rank.

The thin-faced young man caught Jack's eye. There was no trace of humour in his deep brown eyes, no sense of shared camaraderie. There was simply disdain and dislike.

'Englishman.' His English was flawless as he called for Jack's attention.

Jack did his best to seem unfazed at being suddenly addressed in his own language, sitting as calmly and confidently as his poor posture would allow.

'You stink.'

The comment brought about a peal of laughter from the young man's cronies, as if it were the funniest thing they had ever heard. The thin-faced noble smiled with smug satisfaction, turning his horse around scornfully.

Jack ignored the barb. The boy could not have been older than fifteen or sixteen, the age when image meant everything. He himself could well remember the urge to impress.

'*Suuar aa rahe hain!*' He heard the voice of the umpire shout out the warning to the heat to prepare to begin their chase.

It was the phrase Count Piotr had told Jack to listen for; he had translated it as 'the pigs are coming'. It was time to hunt.

* * *

The horse's hooves drummed hard into the muddy floor of the jungle, thick clods of earth flung up into Jack's face as he clung on for dear life. The motion of the horse pitched him around wildly as it galloped through the thick grasses, twisting this way and that with a speed that he could not hope to control. He had given the animal its head and let it choose its own way through the dense foliage, sensing it was his only chance of keeping pace with the other riders. Twice he had nearly been decapitated by a low branch, and his fine blue lancer's coat was snagged and torn by the dozens of wait-a-bit thorn bushes that flew past before he even became aware of their presence.

Despite his best efforts, the other spears had quickly left him behind, outstripping him within moments of the umpire sending them after an enormous boar that was at least the size of a table. Jack had caught a glimpse of the mighty animal as it thundered past in a blur, a snatched glance at its wickedly sharp tusks and flared nostrils making him doubt the wisdom of trying to tackle the beast with nothing other than an unfamiliar spear.

He could hear the animal up ahead as it crashed through the scrub, but after that first brief glimpse he had seen nothing more than a fleeting shadow. His fellow riders flew after the beast, their loud shouts and whoops of delight spurring each other on. They rode hard, bent low over their saddles, all deference forgotten now the race was on. He could only marvel at their horsemanship as they charged through the jungle, twisting and leaping through the matted branches and dense undergrowth. He felt quite the old man as he brought up the rear, the distance between him and the rest of the heat opening quickly and widening steadily despite his best efforts to keep up.

He jabbed his spurs hard into his horse's flanks, a flare of annoyance at being left behind goading him on. The horse bounded forward, the raking pain in its sides pushing it to greater speed, its hooves drumming into the ground in a fast staccato. The sudden increase in pace caught Jack unawares. His spear fell from his grasp as he clutched desperately at the saddle, his balance thrown by the violent pitch and fall. He never saw the low-lying bough that jutted from a tangled patch of bamboo, stretching across his path.

The collision was sudden and violent, the speed of the horse driving Jack's body into the hardened limb with a sickening crunch. The impact snapped his jaws together, the sound echoing loudly in his head as he was catapulted backwards. He had the briefest sensation of flying through the air before he smacked into the ground, all breath driven from his body.

He lay motionless, the pain flaring white-hot across his vision. He had hit the branch with his right arm and now it felt as if he had surely broken the bone. He tried to sit up, but the pain was too intense, so he simply lay where he had fallen, staring up at the thick canopy above his head, the bright sunlight flickering down through the few gaps in the highest branches of the tall trees.

Carefully he reached across with his left hand, anxiously touching his damaged right arm, feeling for the grate and the agony of a broken bone. The pain caused him to curse aloud, but to his relief he found nothing that indicated anything worse than bad bruising.

'Sahib?'

Jack looked up and saw a smiling brown face staring down at him, the young boy making a valiant attempt at subduing a fit of the giggles.

'Sahib, shall I send for the doctor?'

Jack forced himself to sit up. The motion made him feel sick. He twisted his head and vomited into the undergrowth, spewing up a liberal amount of the lemon sherbet he had consumed. Guts emptied, he spat out a thick wad of phlegm before wiping his face on the sleeve of his blue lancer's coat, careless of the dark stain he streaked across it.

'Help me up,' he snarled at the young boy, removing the smirk from the youngster's face in an instant.

As he staggered to his feet, Jack heard a roar of victory from deep in the jungle. He might have fallen at the first hurdle, but it seemed his fellow spears had been more successful. His first taste of pig-sticking was over, his only reward a near-broken arm and dented pride.

He nodded to the young groom and started on the long walk to the midday meal. He would have a few precious hours to rest and recuperate until the cooler air of the afternoon allowed the pig-sticking to resume. The hunt was set to continue until late into the evening and he knew he would have to find the strength to rejoin the chase, the notion of giving in quite unthinkable. His ragged stubborn pride would force him to ride again.

Chapter Twenty-one

———◆———

'Goodness me, Jack. You look truly terrible. Should I presume you fell?'

'Presume what you damn well please.'

Jack was in no mood for Isabel's teasing. He had followed the young syce to an enormous canvas pavilion that had been erected in a large clearing in the jungle. His horse had been recaptured, but he had no intention of getting back in the saddle until the pain in his right arm had subsided to a more bearable level. He had stalked into the midst of the gathering, glaring at anyone who caught his eye and doing his best to ignore the looks of amusement and sneers of condescension sent his way.

He had found Isabel reclining on a chaise longue that looked as if it had been imported from the finest salon in Paris. She clearly felt comfortable in these luxurious surroundings. She had been deep in conversation with a young girl, who had made a hasty exit as soon as she saw Jack approaching. He caught a glimpse of a strikingly beautiful face and a slim, lithe figure wrapped in a white silk sari, before she disappeared into the crowd that thronged inside the open-sided pavilion. Despite his exhaustion, he felt his interest rise, and he made a note to ask Isabel who she was.

Had he not been in such a foul humour, he would have been

impressed by the Maharajah's thoughtful organisation. His servants had transformed the barren grassland into an oasis for the tired and sweaty riders. Huge fans covered the inside of the pavilion's roof with teams of pankha-walas seated around its edge pulling on the thick cords that swept enormous squares of fabric back and forth to create a wonderful breeze within the tent. All four sides had been left open, with thin gauze draped artfully to hide the dozens of sturdy wooden poles that supported the heavy frame. Inside, the pavilion was a place of refinement and comfort. The servants had arranged a whole palace's worth of furniture, an eclectic mix of chairs, sofas, tables and loungers brought into the depths of the jungle to allow the riders to sit or eat in any way they wished. Beautiful Persian rugs covered the floor, their fine, intricate weave carelessly trodden under the muddy boots of the riders, their delicate beauty sacrificed in the name of temporary elegance. One corner of the pavilion was clearly reserved for the Maharajah and his personal guests, the most dignified personages entertained in a splendour Jack doubted existed in many English country houses, let alone in the middle of a jungle. Elegant crystal and fine bone china had been brought, along with enough food and drink to serve a thousand guests, and everywhere he looked, patient servants waited to offer the riders any refreshment they desired.

'My poor Jack.' Isabel held her hand in front of her face to hide her smile. She could see the stains and the muck encrusted on Jack's new uniform, and from his growled reply to her greeting she could tell he was in no mood to be teased. 'You must have had a simply awful morning. Let me get you some of this delightful lemon sherbet. It really is quite revitalising. It is just what you need.'

'No. Thank you. I do not have the taste for it.' Jack waved away Isabel's offering. He had no desire for more of the pungent lemon liquid. He waved at another waiter and took a brandy and soda, using the bitter liquid to scour his mouth of the sour taste of vomit.

'It is astonishing how quickly one becomes accustomed to so many servants.' Isabel made the remark as she scanned the room. The servants outnumbered the guests several times over, most simply standing impassively around the edge of the pavilion like so many bronze statues, waiting to answer any whim or command.

Her thoughtful comment hit the mark. Jack had barely stopped to consider his action. He had wanted a peg, so he had casually flicked his hand to get one. It was a sobering thought, and he wondered quite when he had begun to take the presence of so many servants for granted.

'Who was that girl?' He asked the question trying to sound uninterested.

'Oh, you noticed her, did you?' Isabel pouted as she replied.

'Only vaguely. I was pleased to see that you had begun to make some acquaintances here.'

'So the fact that she is stunningly beautiful passed you by. You are a terrible liar, Jack.'

'Come on, Izzy. I barely saw her.' Jack protested his innocence.

It was the first time he had used a shorter version of her name, and it brought a smile to her face just as he had hoped it would. It spoke of the growing intimacy between them and it mellowed her mood.

'Her name is Lakshmi.' She reached out and put her hand on Jack's thigh, pulling him closer so that she could rest her head on his shoulder.

'Pretty name.'

'She was named after the ruler of Jhansi.'

'So she has a name fit for a princess.'

'Well that is jolly handy, because she is a princess herself.'

'Truly? She is the Maharajah's daughter?' Jack sounded impressed, despite his attempt at appearing indifferent.

'Indeed she is. She told me that he has only two surviving children that he acknowledges. Their poor mother died giving birth to her brother, the Maharajah's son and heir.'

'His supposed heir. Did Proudfoot ever discuss that with you or your father?'

Isabel lifted her head from where she had rested it against him. 'No. What do you mean?'

Jack leant in so that he could speak in a whisper. 'Proudfoot told me that he would never acknowledge the Maharajah's son as his true heir. He is intent on annexation.'

Isabel gasped, earning her a glare of disapproval from Jack.

Fortunately, few people were paying any heed to the pair of white-faced strangers, and he continued quietly.

'He will apply Dalhousie's doctrine here. When the Maharajah dies, the kingdom of Sawadh will become part of the British Empire. At least, that is Proudfoot's plan.'

'It is preposterous! How can we dictate that his son is . . .' Isabel blushed before she spoke the next word, 'illegitimate.'

'Keep your voice down. I don't think we are safe here.'

Her concern was immediate. 'Why do you not think we are safe?'

'I was speaking to Count Piotr. It appears this court is a dangerous place. We will need to be careful.'

Isabel rallied well. 'Of course. Especially if what you say is true. If Major Proudfoot is truly intent on annexing the Maharajah's kingdom, then we will have to make sure we escape before it happens. Goodness, that man. He thinks he can dictate to a king! He has more ambition than I thought.'

'Of course. He is a political. They relish this sort of thing.'

'However unfair it may be?' Isabel looked genuinely flustered as she absorbed the news. Whether her reaction was caused by the potential threat to her life or the unfairness of Proudfoot's ambition, Jack was not sure.

'It's foreign policy.' He reached across and took Isabel's hand to reassure her. It looked small in his, her skin pale against his tanned flesh. 'I doubt fairness is high on their list of priorities.'

'But what of the boy? He will be cheated of his inheritance.'

'I'm sure the authorities will allow him to stay on and keep his title. Provided he keeps quiet and does not stir up any trouble, of course. But all power and authority will pass to the Governor. There will be no more of this halfway house of pretence and folly. Perhaps Proudfoot is correct. Perhaps it is better that we rule here.'

'Better for whom?' Isabel's whisper was icy. She withdrew her hand as her anger flared. 'Surely not better for the prince.'

'Better for the people, perhaps?' Jack was thinking aloud. He had not given much attention to the politics of British rule in India. He had arrived thinking only of commanding a company of redcoats. He was a soldier, not a politician, and the more he saw of the machinations of state, the less he liked them. 'We will build hospitals, roads, schools, universities even. The people will be better cared for under our laws and with all the benefits we can give them.'

Isabel became quiet as she listened to Jack's arguments. 'Yes. Perhaps that is better. It just feels wrong.'

'Is it wrong to want what's best for people? Even if they don't know it themselves?'

'You sound like a parent.' A mocking tone had returned to Isabel's voice.

'Do I?' Jack seemed appalled at the idea. 'Perhaps I'm getting old. I don't know. I just want to be a soldier. An officer if possible.'

'Only if you can keep finding people to impersonate.' Despite her best intentions, Isabel could not resist teasing him a little.

'Oh, it's not a perfect plan, I know that.' Jack became sombre as her comment made him think of his past. 'But it's all I have now.'

'Not all, Jack.' Isabel reached forward and took both his hands in her own. 'You have me.'

A gentle round of applause and the scraping of chairs being pushed back prevented Jack from replying. Around the pavilion people were getting to their feet, leaving the important business of eating and drinking to one side for a moment as they welcomed the Maharajah into their midst.

'You are here again, Englishman? We thought you would've had enough of crawling around on the ground for one day.'

The same young rider who had insulted Jack that morning greeted his arrival back with his fellow spears with a sneer of disdain.

'I'm pleased to be here.' Jack's voice was icy. He knew he should not let the youngster's insults irk him so, but he could not help responding. He found himself wondering how the boy would fare if he was ever thrown into battle. He would like to see how long his arrogance lasted under fire.

'We do not want you. Go back to the women and wait for the men to return.' The boy's two cronies laughed on cue, clearly understanding the insult.

Jack stayed silent but continued to look the group's proud leader straight in the eye. If he hoped to win a battle of wills or to gain a grudging respect, he was to be disappointed. The haughty young noble pulled hard on the reins of his horse, bringing it around in a tight circle as evidence of his superiority over Jack as a rider, as if any were needed. He spoke loudly in his own tongue, the sharp laughter that inevitably followed making it clear that Jack was the butt of yet another barbed comment, albeit this time one he could not understand.

Jack took firm hold of his new bamboo spear. This time, he promised himself, he would not fail to at least remain seated. He had endured enough laughter and scorn for one day.

The jungle rushed past just as before. Yet Jack was beginning to feel his senses coming to life, so that he was not completely overwhelmed by the experience. He no longer flinched from hazards; instead he kept his head up and tried to read the terrain ahead, adjusting his weight and his balance to naturally counter his horse's movements as it thrashed along at a terrific rate.

He could see the shadow of the boar in front of him, its huge, powerful body ripping through the thick undergrowth. His fellow riders were ahead of him, but this time only by a few lengths. His heavy bamboo spear was held tightly in his hand, his knuckles showing white as he grasped it in a vice-like grip. He was determined he would not suffer the shame of losing a second weapon.

The boar was twisting and turning as it charged headlong through the jungle, its loud snorts coming in fast rushes as it sought to escape the dreadful pursuit. Jack was close enough to catch an occasional glimpse of its heavy body, and every sight sent a primeval rush through his veins. He thrilled with the urge to hunt, the excitement of the wild ride spiced by sparks of fear every time he narrowly avoided another painful collision.

The young noble was in the lead, his horse moving with a lithe freedom as it bounded after its prey. The boy raked his spurs back hard, summoning a final surge from his willing mount, the hunt rushing to its conclusion. Jack saw his arm tense as he pulled back his spear, keeping the dreadful weapon still and level in a casual demonstration of exquisite skill. With a final loud yell he thrust the spear forward, ramming the wickedly sharp point into the boar's body with such force that the bamboo shaft splintered into matchwood. The point ripped through the boar's tough hide, taking the beast just behind the shoulder, the spear embedded deep in its flesh.

The boar grunted as the weapon was driven home, its legs still trying to power it forward despite the dreadful blow that sent it spinning to one side. The other riders flashed past, each man hauling on his reins to bring his mount around, their cries and shouts loud as they raced to turn back without colliding with one another.

Jack pulled on his own reins, ignoring the bright flash of pain in his arm. Somehow he managed to bring his horse to a halt, its body already bending to make the turn.

As the rearmost rider, he now had the advantage. He spurred hard, forcing his mount forward so that he led the charge back towards the wounded boar. His mind was racing. He remembered the count's warning that a wounded boar was a dangerous adversary. He had spotted the wickedly sharp tusks on the brute's head as they had raced past, and needed no one to tell him the damage they could do to anyone foolish enough to venture into their range. Yet still he charged back the way he had come, risking his life in a childish attempt to prove his courage after the shame of the morning's failure. He yelled at his mount, urging it on, desperate trying to stay ahead of his fellow spears.

He heard the roar of the wounded animal before he saw it, a deep, guttural shriek of pain and anger. He could see the patch of undergrowth where the boar had gone down, a dense tangle of thorny bush covered thickly with vines. He braced his arm, readying it to strike, aiming to bring his horse directly past the matted bushes so that he could thrust his spear down and take the wounded animal from the side as he rushed by.

A shadowy figure flashed past his left-hand side, followed quickly by another. Jack had the sense of movement all around him, dark outlines erupting from the undergrowth on both sides. All thoughts of the wounded pig disappeared in a heartbeat as the first screams rang out, the cries of men launched to the attack echoing around him.

Chapter Twenty-two

A figure burst out of the bush to Jack's left. He was dressed in a filthy robe that might once have been white but was now torn and stained to a muddy grey. Yet the flash of his talwar was bright as he rushed forward, his mouth open wide in a war cry.

Jack twisted in the saddle, yanking on the reins as he tried to turn to face the sudden threat. The ambusher was on him the moment his horse slowed. There was no time to react and he could only watch in horror as the bandit raised his weapon. The talwar slashed forward, the blade flashing once in a beam of sunlight before it thumped into the neck of Jack's horse.

The beast screamed in agony as the weapon ripped through its flesh, blood gushing from the dreadful wound. The stricken animal pumped its legs, still trying to obey its rider's command. Yet it was too badly wounded. Its forelegs buckled, its strength failing fast.

Jack pushed against the saddle as he felt the horse going down, kicking the poor beast mercilessly as he struggled to get free. For one dreadful moment his boot stuck in a stirrup, but he ripped it out and threw himself to one side, thumping painfully into the muddy ground. In an instant he had scrambled to his feet, ignoring the flash of agony that followed the jarring impact, knowing he had only moments before he would have to fight for his life. As soon as he found his footing, he brought the heavy shaft of his pig-sticking spear across his body, his hands locked liked claws into the thick wood. He had barely a moment to plant his feet on the slippery ground before the ambusher was on him.

The talwar slashed forward, a controlled swipe at Jack's neck that he parried with the shaft of his spear. The bandit leered as he attacked again, his mouth twisted with hate. The blows came fast now, attack following attack with such speed that Jack was denied any chance to counter, his bamboo spear hacked and splintered as he was forced to block blow after blow.

He was being driven steadily backwards, forced to give ground as the bandit came at him relentlessly. Somehow he kept his composure, an eerie calm descending on him as he fought. He read his opponent's intentions in his eyes and each time he was able to place the thick shaft of his spear in the right place to counter the vicious blows. He defended patiently. Waiting for the chance to strike back.

The bandit's foot came down on a patch of sodden earth layered with a slimy crust of brown mould. It took him no more than a heartbeat to feel himself beginning to slip, but it gave Jack the opening he had been waiting for. The instant he realised what had happened, he whipped the spear around so the point was at his assailant's stomach, then stamped his foot forward just as he had been taught in a hundred sessions on the grey, damp training grounds of England, using the spear as an improvised bayonet and musket.

An explosive grunt was torn from his mouth as he thrust the sharp point into the bandit's stomach. The heavy spear was designed to pierce the tough hide of a wild boar, and it punched into the man's body with ease. He tore the spearhead free from the wound and thrust again, mercilessly hammering it past the man's hands, which were desperately trying to wave it away. The tip tore through the man's throat, ripping a grotesque hole in his neck, the sudden eruption of blood bright red against the backdrop of matted jungle.

Jack felt no shame at his vicious assault. There was no time for remorse now that the ambush had been sprung. As the first bandit dropped to the ground, he was already turning to find where the rest of the shadowy figures had gone.

The sounds of combat came from no more than a dozen yards away, but the dense undergrowth prevented Jack from having a clear view of exactly who was fighting whom. He had no idea who had come to attack the hunters, but he did not care. There would be time for understanding later. Without a backward glance he charged towards the noise. It was time to see how the arrogant young man was faring against an opponent who fought back.

The shouts of anger and confusion grew louder as Jack ran. The thick swathe of jungle masked some of the sounds, the dense vegetation muffling even the harsh noise of combat. It made it unlikely that any of the other groups of hunters would be able to hear the fight. Jack knew then that he and his three fellow spears were on their own.

As he burst from the undergrowth, he realised that a desperate struggle was taking place. Two of the riders were still in the saddle. Their horses reared and plunged as a press of bodies circled around them, looking for an opportunity to attack. The third horse was down and Jack could see nothing of the rider beneath the hacking talwars of three bandits. A dozen bandits were attacking the three horsemen, each as filthy and dishevelled as the one Jack had already struck down. Only one wore black robes.

Jack felt nothing of the madness that had erupted from the blackest depths of his being at the Alma. In its place was coldness, his rational mind holding sway against the insanity of battle. He tasted the bitter tang of fear, the gut-churning horror that he could be about to die. Yet still he threw himself forward without hesitation, gambling on violence and speed to overwhelm the attackers.

He leapt over a fallen log and rammed his heavy spear into the back of one of the bandits circling the riders. A thin mail coat over heavy blue robes protected the man, but the vicious spear punched through it all as if it were silk. The force of the attack drove the spear clean through the man's body, the tip erupting in a gory explosion from his stomach, his anguished howl of horror the last sound he would ever make.

Jack was drawing his new talwar even before the man had hit the ground, abandoning the heavy spear now that it was inextricably embedded in the man's body. The bandits' heads whirled around at the unexpected assault from the darkness of the jungle, their eyes showing white under their tightly bound pagdis. His second target had no longer than a single heartbeat to glimpse his attacker. It was time enough for his mouth to gape open in shock before Jack's talwar slashed across his neck, ripping out his throat.

The proud young nobleman roared as Jack flew into the bandits like a berserker of old. The boy was brave, fighting hard. He spurred his horse forward, using the confusion that Jack's attack had caused to thrust his spear down into the breast of one of his assailants.

His companion was not so lucky. The black-robed Tiger sensed his men's fear at the sudden assault and pushed himself to the fore, striding into the vicious battle. His heavy talwar drove forward, cleaving the closest rider's spear in two, the raw power of the assault unstoppable. The terrified hunter dropped the ruined weapon and reached for his own talwar, but the Tiger was simply too fast. Recovering his sword from the blow, he brought it around in a glittering arc above his head before smashing it across the mounted hunter's breast. The talwar drove deep, tearing a wide gouge that gushed forth a torrent of blood. The man toppled silently from the saddle, two of the bandits pouncing before he had stopped moving, driving their own blades into his dying body.

Jack fought on, slashing his sword forward, only to scream in frustration as his next victim turned in time and parried the blow, driving both blades wide. Jack ignored the wild defence and stamped forward into the opening, slamming his head forward so it crashed viciously into his opponent's face. The bandit crumpled, his nose pulped, the blood smothering the hands that he clutched to his battered face. Jack was merciless and he immediately thrust his sword down, piercing the man's body as it fell, driving the tip through his back and into his heart.

A shriek of horror came from Jack's right and he twisted on the spot, his latest victim already forgotten. The young man who had thought nothing of insulting the white-faced stranger had finally been thrown from his horse, the brave beast succumbing at last to the dozen wounds it had taken. The youngster hit the ground, his sword knocked from his grasp as he crunched with bone-jarring force on to the jungle floor. Two bandits came at him the moment he fell, their teeth bared in delight, like a pair of wolves going for the kill, their swords thirsting to be buried in his flesh.

All trace of the boy's arrogance was gone. His face was ashen with fear as he looked up and saw the bandits charging towards him, death in their wild eyes, and he screamed in horror, his terror bright in the darkness of the jungle.

Jack threw himself at the boy's attackers, no time for anything other than a wild charge. Leaping over the body of the first man he had slain, he lowered his shoulder and hit one of the men with a force that knocked him sprawling to the floor. The impact nearly threw Jack off his feet, and he stumbled, lurching to one side, fighting to stay upright; it saved his life.

The second bandit had a moment to react to Jack's sudden arrival, and he used it to redirect his blow, turning his blade in mid-air so that it sliced across Jack's path. The blade keened as it stung the air before scoring a thin line across his fine new uniform coat, missing his stomach by no more than half an inch. Had he not slipped, he would have been sliced in two.

Jack threw himself forward despite the flash of fear as he saw the blade whisper past his stomach, and crashed into the man who had so nearly killed him, knocking him violently to the ground. He felt the man's body underneath his own, and immediately drove his elbow down, smashing it into the bandit's windpipe. It was a vicious blow, the kind so common in the gutter fights he had been brought up with, and it crushed the bandit's throat, choking him.

There was no time for pity. Jack sensed movement behind him and pushed himself to his knees, using the choking bandit's body for leverage. By some miracle he had managed to keep a firm grip on his talwar, and he slashed the blade around his waist, using its momentum to bring him face to face with the new threat.

The talwar rang with a violent impact that jarred Jack's already battered sword arm. His instinct had saved him. As he spun around on his knees, he saw that he had driven his sword into the side of the bandit he had knocked to the floor. The man had quickly scrambled to his feet thinking to bury his own sword in Jack's unprotected back. Instead he had been cut down, his intended victim turning with an astonishing speed. Jack saw the man's shock before he fell face first to the ground, his body giving a single violent shudder before it lay still.

Jack hurt. The twin collisions sent waves of pain scoring through his veins. Stabbing his talwar down into the ground, he forced himself to his feet. As he rose, he saw the look of astonishment on the young nobleman's face, terror alive in his wide-eyed stare. There was no time to spare the young man a word. Jack hauled the astonished boy upright. He might be young, but Jack would need all the help he could muster if he were to bring them both out alive.

For the fight was far from over. Jack had fought hard and saved one of his fellow spears from death. But he had spied the man in the black robes and he now knew who was attacking them. If he were to somehow save them both, he would have to face the man who had already bested him once in combat.

He would have to face the Tiger.

Chapter Twenty-three

———◆◈◆———

'Get ready, boy.' Jack spat a wad of phlegm to one side as he growled the words. 'Let's see if you can fight as well you can talk.'

He saw the boy swallow hard, his Adam's apple bobbing up and down as he pushed down his fear. The youngster raised his talwar. He held the blade low, ready to rip out the guts of the first man to charge him, handling the sword with obvious familiarity. Someone had trained him well. Jack nodded in encouragement as he saw the boy's weight move to the balls of his feet as he found his balance. His talwar was a thing of beauty, its long blade decorated with a fine tracery of swirling lines so that it seemed to pulse with life as the sun caught it. It was a fabulous weapon, the kind only the very wealthy could afford.

The surviving bandits faced the two hunters with obvious confidence. There was no haste in their movements, no sign of panic despite the sight of so many of their brethren struck to the ground. At their centre the black-robed leader walked calmly to the fore, bringing his enormous two-handed sword round as he readied himself to fight on.

'He cannot be killed.' The boy whispered the words, his voice cracking as he recognised the bandit leader.

'Bollocks.' Jack spat out the word. The pause in the fight was starting to stretch his nerves.

'He is the Tiger. He is a prince of the darkness. He cannot be killed.' The boy sounded close to panic.

Jack quickly counted off the bandits. The black-robed leader had five men left, less than half the number he had been able to command when he unleashed the ambush, but still too many for Jack to fight on his own. He looked across at the boy. He could see the youngster's terror, the point of his sword beginning to twitch as the fear took hold of him. He would not be able to fight.

'Fuck it!' Jack screamed the words, trying to summon the madness he knew he needed. He took a deliberate pace forward, lifting one bloodstained hand so that it pointed straight at the Tiger.

'You!' He shouted the word, jabbing his finger so there could be no doubt who he was addressing. 'You, you black-robed arsehole. Just you and me.'

He stalked forward, his talwar hanging casually at his side. The madness he craved stayed stubbornly distant, but there was something in the sheer folly of what he was trying to do that was intoxicating.

'Just me and you. You understand?' He lifted his talwar, taking a firm two-handed grip on the handle as he saw the black-robed man raise his hand and gesture for his men to hold. 'That's it, you bastard.'

Jack's heart hammered in his chest. His fear flared bright, the foolishness of his action screaming through his mind. Yet even as his emotions started to burn, a part of his mind remained calculated and calm, planning the fight he was summoning, seeking a path to victory despite the violent emotions that stirred in his soul.

He looked into the pitiless black eyes of the Tiger and he felt his confidence wane. He remembered the intensity of the bandit leader's attack, the speed of his sword and the dreadful power of his blows. He could feel fear beginning to win the battle for his soul, the madness he craved swamped by the icy rush of terror that was surging up from the pit of his belly.

'That's it. Just you and me.' The words calmed him, his own

voice reassuring. The Tiger kept coming, his men obeying his command to hang back.

'Time to dance, you bastard!' Jack screamed the words aloud and threw himself forward. He would have to banish his fear. This time he would not submit. He would kill the man who could not be killed.

Or he would die.

Jack's talwar scythed through the air. He kept the movement controlled, his muscles already braced for the Tiger's parry. The blades came together, the noise of metal grinding on metal loud in the enclosed space in which they fought. Jack recovered his blade just as he planned, twisting his wrist before slashing his sword backhanded, battering it against the huge talwar that flickered out to meet it.

Again and again the two men slashed and parried, their swords glittering in the dappled sunlight as they flashed back and forth. Jack fought with restraint, concentrating on his speed, never once trying to land a telling blow but flowing through the impacts, trying to find a gap in the Tiger's defence.

He grunted as the Tiger parried, the huge sword meeting every attack, the man matching his speed with ease. He could see the smile behind the mass of beard that covered so much of his enemy's face, the black eyes that gleamed with perverse enjoyment, as if the two men were contestants in a hard-fought sport rather than deadly foes fighting for their lives.

Jack took a half-step back, pretending to give ground. The Tiger came after him in a heartbeat, the talwar slashing hard at his guts. But Jack had planned the feint and he twisted past the fast-moving blade, driving off his heel and stabbing his own talwar forward with a lightning-quick jab. He yelled as he felt the tip of his sword tear into the black-robed man's flesh, the sweet roar of victory surging through him. But the Tiger was fast, quicker than any man Jack had ever fought. Before Jack could thrust his full weight behind the blow, the bandit leader brought his sword back in a frantic parry. The wild blow knocked Jack's talwar aside, the sharpened tip only able to score a deep gouge across the Tiger's front rather than the killing blow Jack had hoped for.

The tantalising glimpse of blood flecking the tip of his sword gave Jack hope. But the Tiger recovered quickly from the momentary lapse. His great sword rose to deflect Jack's next riposte before driving forward and forcing him to parry quickly lest he be caught himself.

Now the Tiger began to chant, his deep, melodic voice clear despite the animal grunts as the two men kept up the pace of the fight. It was just as Jack remembered, the rhythmic resonance of the words sending a shiver down his spine. There was no pause in the bandit leader's attack as he chanted; indeed, he began to push Jack backwards with a series of blows even faster than before. Jack parried one after another, his arm beginning to feel like lead as the onslaught continued. Again and again the Tiger attacked, the blows ringing down. Jack's defence began to falter, and twice the Tiger nearly had him, the tip of the talwar whispering past, his weakening parries only just doing enough to deflect the merciless assault.

The Tiger bellowed the last word of the chant, his voice rising in a crescendo loud enough to wake the dead. His sword flashed past Jack's face, a final mighty sweep of the blade before he lifted it above his head, readying the killing blow.

One Jack had seen before.

He dived forward, hitting the ground with his shoulder. He sensed the Tiger's sword scything down, the dreadful edge reaching for him, the heavy talwar cutting through the air where he had just been standing. He scrabbled on the ground, twisting around in the matted undergrowth before driving his boot forward and smashing the heavy heel into the huge man's groin.

The Tiger grunted in pain but his sword continued its descent, hunting for its prey. The blade cut into the undergrowth, missing Jack by no more than an inch, and stuck fast in the spongy ground. Jack rolled away and stabbed his own talwar upwards. It had been badly battered but the point was still sharp, and it punched into the Tiger's body, tearing through flesh and gristle as Jack drove it deep. Blood ran down the blade, washing over his wrist and arm and falling to stain the front of his blue uniform coat, yet still he twisted it, tearing the life from his foe.

With the blade still buried deep in his body, the black-robed bandit leader toppled to one side. He made no sound as he fell, his huge sword dropping to the ground as his nerveless hands lost their strength.

Jack scrambled to his feet, never once taking his eyes off the huge man he had just defeated. Unable to comprehend that he had won.

With their leader struck down, the bandits fled into the jungle, running for their lives despite the fact that Jack was battered and exhausted. At that moment a washerwoman with a kitchen knife could have defeated him, but the bandits clawed at each other in their haste to get away, the jungle hiding them from view as they scattered in every direction.

Jack walked to stand over the body of the black-robed Tiger. He looked down at the face of the man who could not be killed. He did not see a prince of the darkness. Nor did he see a man who had been feared and hated in equal measure. He simply saw the lonely face of someone moments from death. The Tiger's eyes were open, the vitality of life still alive in the blackness. They moved as Jack stood beside him, fixing him with a hard, flat stare of hatred.

The Tiger's lips began to move. At first the words were barely audible, but from deep in his soul he found the strength to speak louder. As he did so, he kept his eyes fixed on Jack. The words flowed from him, their pace and tone steady, with the same deep, melodic rhythm that had so unsettled Jack when they fought.

Jack sensed the presence of the nobleman he had saved. The youngster came to look down at the man who had so terrified him.

'He is cursing you.' The boy spoke in no more than a whisper, his fear still very real.

Jack felt a shiver run down his spine as he met the Tiger's merciless stare, the terror he had kept contained for so long once more writhing deep in his belly.

'What does he say?' He spoke firmly, wrestling with his emotions as if they were a demon to be fought and imprisoned. He felt the calmness begin to return as he regained control, the fear forced to the recesses of his mind, committed to the darkness in his soul.

'He is condemning you to a life without hope. A life alone.' The boy's voice trembled as he told Jack the meaning of the foreign words, translating them with reverence and no trace of vindictive pleasure.

The Tiger stopped abruptly. Jack never once let his eyes move from the bandit's unwavering stare, and he saw the glimmer of life flicker, then leave the pitiless black eyes for ever.

The man who could not be killed was dead.

The crowd jostled around him. Jack felt his exhaustion build, his body craving rest. The bewildering hubbub continued unabated, shouts and questions bellowed back and forth in the language of the Maharajah's court that Jack did not understand. The young noble he had saved stood at the centre of the melee, surrounded by a crowd of men who were all talking at once. Jack recognised the urgency of their words, the hurried interrogation of people desperate to find out what had happened so they could either claim some share in the victory or steer well clear of the blame.

The young noble's higher-pitched tones cut through the deeper voices of the men who challenged him, carrying an authority that silenced them. He spoke quickly and firmly and the crowd pressed forward as they listened to his hurried account, captivated by the drama.

Jack wanted no part of the inquest. He had done what he had felt to be his duty. Now that the vicious fight was over, he wanted nothing more than to fade back into the background.

The Maharajah and his entourage arrived, the ruler's huge white stallion flecked with mud and sweat; it had clearly been ridden hard to get here. Jack saw the distress on the Maharajah's face, the strained expression of someone seeking news they knew could change their life for ever.

The entrance of their king silenced the throng that had gathered at the site of the ambush. With an athletic bound the ruler of Sawadh leapt from the saddle and rushed towards the young noble who now owed his life to the white-faced foreigner he had treated with such disdain. Without stopping, the Maharajah reached forward and crushed the boy to his chest, enveloping him in a fierce embrace, the bright prick of tears in his eyes.

Finally Jack realised who the youngster was, and why his comrades had been so ready to laugh loudly at his quips. Jack had just done the British government a great disservice.

He had saved the life of the Maharajah's heir.

'There are no words to convey my thanks, Jack.'

Jack could not meet the Maharajah's intense stare. He looked to his boots but the Maharajah reached forward, lifting Jack's hands and enclosing them in both of his own. The touch was intimate, the Maharajah's hands warm and the feel of his flesh shocking. Jack felt intensely uncomfortable at the contact, his natural reaction to withdraw, but the Maharajah held him firm.

'You saved my son. I am in your debt.'

'I did what had to be done, sir.' Jack's reaction was stilted.

'You English. You are so bloody stuck up!' The Maharajah dropped Jack's hands, smiling at the obvious relief on his face. 'I thank you anyway. Whatever you say, I owe you a great deal. My son has told me what happened here.' He turned and looked at the dead bandits that his men were dragging unceremoniously into a grotesque heap. 'You certainly do know how to fight.'

'I'm a redcoat. It's what we are trained to do.'

'My son said he has never seen anyone quicker.' The Maharajah's voice was full of admiration. 'You killed that black-robed bastard. For that alone I owe you a reward.'

'I do not ask one, sir. You have already shown me favour by allowing me to stay in your court.'

'One of the best bloody decisions I ever made.' He turned and gestured for his son to come to him. 'I am forgetting my manners. I suspect you have not been properly introduced. Jack, this is my son, Abhishek. He will rule after I am dead and gone. Thanks now to you.'

Jack looked the boy in the eye. The earlier childlike arrogance was gone. Abhishek's privileged background had been no protection from the brutal reality that so many boys his age would already have experienced. Jack hoped the bitter knowledge would teach him well.

'Thank you.' The boy's voice was small, the moment clearly

embarrassing him. But he was also the rajkumar, and he pulled himself upright, standing with a stiff back in front of the man he had insulted so cruelly but who had saved his life. 'You have done our country a great service.'

The Maharajah whooped with delight at his son's pomposity. 'You see, Jack. I have bred a fine boy. He has the grace of a king. He is not like me at all.'

Jack inclined his head to acknowledge the boy's thanks. 'It was my pleasure to be of service, sir. I can only hope that my disgusting stench no longer offends you as once it did.' He could not resist the barbed comment. The boy might have been a prince, but that would not stop Jack twisting his tail.

Abhishek's mouth opened but no sound came out. He glanced across at his father before bowing his head.

The Maharajah clapped his hands with enjoyment. 'You are priceless, Jack, absolutely bloody priceless. Now then, let us speak of your reward.'

'Sir, there is no need for a reward.'

The Maharajah flapped his hands to silence Jack's protest. 'Enough of your bloody English modesty. I wish for you to become my adviser.'

Jack laughed at the notion. 'Sir, you most certainly do not need my advice.'

'That is my decision, not yours. You will also assume command of my lancers. As of this moment, you are my general.'

Jack shook his head in denial. The promotion was meteoric indeed but the idea that he could be a general was laughable. 'I cannot accept, sir. As your son here will attest, I cannot even ride a horse properly.'

'I will not be gainsaid. Not even by a hero. Abhishek will teach you to ride. It can be his punishment for not treating one of my guests with the right amount of courtesy.' The Maharajah was clearly delighted by the idea. 'Now we must leave this place.' His face twisted with distaste as he surveyed the scene where his son had come so close to death.

Jack stood back as the Maharajah left. Like most ambitious men, he had come to India to seek his fortune. He had never dreamt it would lead him here. It might only be in the service of a wilful maharajah, but Jack had been made a general.

It was quite a step up for an urchin from the East End of London.

Chapter Twenty-four

Jack belched as softly as he could. The lamb kidneys on sweet naan had been his favourite dish, but there had been so many that he was fast losing track. The feast arranged in his honour was only an hour old, but already his stomach felt fit to burst. Dish after dish had been placed before him by the hundreds of servants charged with seeing to every whim of the Maharajah's guests. As the principal guest, Jack was the first served, and he had felt compelled to take something from every dish offered. They had started to eat just after sunset, and he was now beginning to wonder how he would continue to cope should the feast go on all night.

'They were delicious.' Isabel dabbed at her mouth with a gold silk napkin. She reached across, using it to wipe clean a stain from Jack's mouth. 'How's the head?'

Jack instinctively raised a finger and poked carefully at the yellow and purple mark in the centre of his forehead. 'Not so bad.'

Isabel smiled. 'Well that's what happens if you are foolish enough to use it as a weapon.' As much as she tried to make light of the comment, he saw her distress. She had already witnessed one brutal battle, so she knew what it was for men to fight to the death. She would have some idea of how dangerous the ambush had been, how hard Jack would have had to fight to survive.

Jack did his best to return her smile. A servant bowed in front of him as the next dish arrived. He looked at it with caution. He had learnt to be circumspect. He could still taste the effect of the fish on wooden skewers. He had only taken a single mouthful, but it had been so hot that it had felt as if his brains had been blown out of his head. He dipped a small morsel of naan bread to taste what looked to be a quail stew. Reassured, he continued with more freedom, ramming home a few mouthfuls like a gunner double-shotting a cannon. As he ate, he noticed Isabel looking at him.

'What?' he asked, raising his own napkin, suspecting he had dribbled some of the stew across his chin.

Isabel blushed. 'You surprise me.'

'Surprise you?' Jack scowled. 'Do I eat that badly?'

'Don't be silly.' She smiled. 'When I first saw you in Proudfoot's bungalow, I had no idea of the kind of man you are.'

It was Jack's turn to blush. He sat back in his chair, wincing as the movement jarred his body. He knew he had been lucky to survive the fight with nothing more than bruises and a battered arm, but it still felt as if he had gone a dozen rounds with a back-street prizefighter.

'And now?'

Isabel arched her eyebrows. 'Now I think you're a fool! We came here to hide, yet you have already saved the life of the Maharajah's only son and been appointed a general in command of his lancers.'

Jack frowned, sensing mockery. 'I did not have much choice in the matter.'

Isabel laughed aloud. She placed her hand on his forearm. 'You keep surprising me, Jack. That is all.'

The sound of music interrupted their conversation and the room quietened as a small group of richly dressed men and women were ushered in, singing as they were escorted through the wide double doors. It was a lament, the soft blend of voices merging together in harmony to weave a spell over the hushed audience. Jack listened to the strange music, feeling it resonate deep in his soul. He did not understand the words, but the melody touched a place he had thought hidden, and for a reason he could not fathom, he felt the prick of tears at the corners of his eyes.

The gentle rhythm of the song faded to silence before the musicians, unseen behind a lattice screen, picked up the tempo. At once the doors to the dining hall were thrown open again and a troop of nautch girls bounded in. They raced across the room, moving into position in front of the tables, where the Maharajah's guests clapped and roared with delight as the entertainment took a more lively turn.

One girl spun to halt directly in front of Jack. She writhed on the ground, lithe as a panther, her hips thrusting forward, before springing to her feet to pirouette so that her back faced him. She gyrated, arching her spine like a cat, before shaking herself with the wanton rhythm of the music. The silk gauze she wore revealed much to his rapt gaze, the sheer fabric stretched tight over her dark body. No part of her was truly naked save a wide band around her taut midriff, but it was not difficult to imagine how she would look were the flimsy silks whipped away. And Jack had a fine imagination.

The hypnotic, pulsating rhythm stopped abruptly and the girl froze in her pose, every sinew stretched tight as she held the final position of her dance with dramatic poise. The insubstantial costume rose and fell around her chest as she panted with the exertion, a thin shimmer of sweat glistening above the veil that masked the lower half of her face.

Jack did his best to ignore the heaving chest inches in front of him and stared into the huge brown eyes that looked at him over the thin veil. The girl matched his appraisal, shameless in front of his scrutiny, her eyes mocking as she saw the man she had danced for transfixed by her supple beauty.

A hard wooden fan rapped sharply on Jack's arm, its intricately carved handle turned into an improvised weapon that was used with some force to attract his attention. He turned and saw Isabel arching her eyebrows in his direction.

'Do stop staring, Jack.' She was clapping her hands with an enthusiasm that was not mirrored in her eyes, which flashed venomously as Jack continued to gaze at the young dancer. 'You may also wish to return your tongue to its rightful place in your mouth.'

He belatedly joined the applause, looking around to see if anyone else had noticed the way the dancer had gripped his attention. The smiles on so many of the faces told him that it had been obvious to all, and he felt his cheeks sting as the inevitable blush spread quickly across them.

The girl bowed and trotted away, the dozens of bangles that adorned her wrists and elbows jingling together as she moved. Jack snatched one last look at her bouncing behind before turning to Isabel with as much nonchalance as he could muster.

'She was a fine dancer. Did you enjoy her routine?'

Isabel raised the fan threateningly. 'Don't make me use this again.'

'I was merely admiring her abilities.'

'Oh, I am sure,' Isabel said tartly, 'and from your avid inspection I am certain you found both of them much to your satisfaction.'

Jack was saved from a reply as the sound of the gong being rung silenced the room. A flurry of activity followed the last reverberation and an army of servants rushed into the room, arms full of empty platters and steaming bowls of water. They attacked the huge trestle tables with gusto, their practised hands deftly removing the remains of the feast and cleaning away the mess that the guests had created. In less than a minute the room was once again immaculate, every trace of the enormous banquet swept and wiped away.

The Maharajah got to his feet and everyone fell silent. In the glow of the thousand candles that lit the huge room, he looked like a king from a fairy tale. He was dressed in fabulous crimson robes, for once eschewing the practical garb of a soldier, and was covered in jewellery, some adorning his clothing, still more draped around his neck and smothering his fingers. His head was bound in a plain gold pagdi adorned with a single ruby that was at least the size of Isabel's hand. It was a vivid reminder of his power, and Jack felt the stirring of unease deep in his belly. He was a foreigner in a king's court, beholden to a whimsical ruler he barely knew.

The Maharajah began to speak. His voice was deep and he demonstrated obvious charm, clearly relishing being the lead actor on the stage. The audience hung on his every word, as rapt as Jack had been when he had stared so obviously at the young dancing girl. He addressed his court in their own language, but Jack did not have to be able to understand every word to hear the sparkle in his voice, his dramatic pauses and changes in tempo revealing his oratory skill even to a foreigner.

Jack stole a glimpse at Isabel as the Maharajah spoke. She was clearly enthralled. He saw her eyes moisten as the Maharajah dropped his voice to the hushed tones of a man in pain, caught in the emotion of his own words. She was clearly spellbound by the foreign king, and Jack found he could not tear his eyes away from her. He stared in fascination at the base of her throat, the soft white skin gently pulsating with each beat of her heart. Her wild hair had been tamed for the evening, and it shone in vivid contrast to the dark hair of all the other ladies. She was dressed in the same simple gold sari she had worn the evening before the hunt, and Jack did not think he had ever seen anyone look as beautiful.

The Maharajah's voice rose to a climax, his arms spread wide in a dramatic gesture as he brought his speech to a resounding finish, and Jack forced his gaze away before Isabel discovered his intense scrutiny.

On cue, two lancers strode purposefully into the room. As they marched forward, Jack noticed with mounting horror that every head in the room had turned to stare in his direction. To be the object of such examination was excruciating, his embarrassment surely clearly visible to all. The agonising sensation was not helped by the Maharajah, who walked towards where Jack sat, his arms spread wide in greeting. As he drew close, he turned and gestured to the audience, encouraging a round of applause.

'Stand up, Jack.' The Maharajah was close enough to give the order quietly.

Jack glanced imploringly in Isabel's direction, as if she could save him from the very public spectacle. But Isabel was little help; she too raised her hands and lifted them to clap in his direction.

'Come now, Jack.' The Maharajah beamed with happiness as he relished Jack's obvious discomfort. 'Enough of the reluctant hero. Try to enjoy the moment.'

With his face burning, Jack slowly got to his feet, grimacing as the movement encouraged the enthusiastic crowd to redouble their efforts.

'There, that wasn't too bad, now was it?' the Maharajah whispered softly, before reaching out to clasp Jack's hands across the table. Then he turned to address his beloved audience once again, keeping Jack's hands held fast in his own.

Jack was forced to stand in embarrassed silence as the Maharajah began another dramatic soliloquy. Several gestures were aimed in his direction and he forced his face into what he hoped was a good-natured smile. Despite not understanding a word of what was said, he did his best to join in, nodding and chuckling when the Maharajah made some quip or wry comment that had his audience guffawing with delight, and trying to look suitably sombre when the king's voice dropped into more emotional tones.

Finally the torture was over and Jack immediately tried to sit down. The Maharajah was having none of it. He continued to clasp Jack's hands in his own, keeping him on his feet whilst nodding to the pair of lancers to step forward.

For the first time Jack noticed that both carried a blue velvet cushion. On the first was a naked sword, which gleamed in the soft candlelight. The blade was decorated with an intricate swirling pattern of letters and designs that flickered and twisted along its length as they caught the light. The grip was wrapped in a beautiful deep red sharkskin; the craftsman who had made it had given it a practical, workmanlike finish that showed it was a weapon to be used rather than just worn for ceremony. The guard that would protect the hand was a thing of beauty and the gleam of a dozen precious stones flashed brightly as the Maharajah finally let go of Jack's sweating grip.

The audience hushed as they saw their king look in awe at the beautiful sword. He turned to face Jack before presenting it reverentially forward.

'This is for you.' The Maharajah had been watching Jack closely. He had read the younger man's emotions as he looked at the weapon, and now he willed him to accept the gift.

Jack was struck dumb. The sword alone must have been worth a lifetime of a captain's pay. Yet the second lancer bore a leather scabbard decorated with golden clasps that was also worth a small fortune. Now the Maharajah was offering them both to Jack, who up to that moment had owned nothing save for the clothes he had already been given.

Jack reached forward, his hand shaking, and caressed the tip of the sword, the metal cold under his touch. He could feel the tracery of the letters, the delicate script scrolling under his fingers as he ran them down the length of the blade. A spark of avarice suddenly surged unbidden into his heart. He took the red grip in his hand and felt the weight of the sword for the first time. The sour taste of greed dissipated in a heartbeat as he held his reward with all the care of a father holding his firstborn son.

He looked up into the Maharajah's eyes and saw the pleasure his taking the sword had given.

Jack held a king's ransom in his hands.

'No, no, no! How many times must I tell you the same things?'

Jack eased back on the reins, bringing his sweat-streaked horse to a stand. He stifled a belch, the spicy reminder of the previous night's feast nearly making him gag.

His instructor spurred hard across the dusty ground to stand at Jack's side, his exasperation clear. Jack used the momentary halt to look across to where Isabel sat on her own horse. To his chagrin, he saw the slow shake of her head as she despaired at his lack of progress. He tried to curb the flush of anger that stirred inside him, and lifted one hand from the reins to wipe away some of the sweat that ran down to sting his eyes. At his side, his new sword lay flat against his thigh, the long straps holding it firmly in place no matter how hard he worked his borrowed mount. He still could not believe his good fortune, and he reached down to touch its golden guard, the feel of the cool metal still sending a spark of excitement through his tired body.

His riding lesson was taking place in the wide area that separated the Maharajah's palace from the walls of the fortress. It had been designed as part of the fortress's defences, the open space a killing ground should any foe ever succeed in breaching the walls. It was also used as a parade square for the hundreds of men of the

Maharajah's army that were garrisoned in the fortress, which also meant it was the place where punishment drills were carried out. Jack was beginning to wonder if any unfortunate soul had ever been made to suffer more than he was, the long riding lesson a torture he would happily have forgone.

'Jack. You must listen to the prince. It really is not so difficult.' Isabel had ridden over to join in Jack's latest lambasting. His slow progress and lack of natural ability were clearly beyond the understanding of a girl who had learnt to ride as soon as she could walk. Isabel was proving to be a harsher critic than even the maddened prince.

'I'm doing my best,' Jack growled as he endured another tongue-lashing. He felt he was making fine progress, his confidence in the saddle growing with each long minute of this, the first of what would be many such sessions. But it was clear that his frustrated teachers were not so pleased.

'Well you must try harder!' Isabel snapped the words.

'You are savage. You pull too hard and you kick like an angry peasant. You yank when you should be gentle and you are gentle when you should be firm.' The prince shook his head, once again wondering at the punishment his father had given him.

'Feel the horse, Jack. Be sensitive to him. He should be an extension of you. He is not some tool to be used.' Isabel leant forward and teased the ears of her own horse, smiling as it flicked its ears at the touch. 'Treat him gently.'

Jack sighed. It was hard to remain calm in the face of such criticism. 'Perhaps that is enough for today.'

'No!' The prince snapped the words with all the authority of the heir to a kingdom. 'You will ride again until you get it right.'

Jack heard the pique in his voice. It was clear the boy wanted the lessons to come to an end quickly. If that meant Jack being ridden into the ground, then that was a small price to pay to end the harsh punishment his father had chosen to inflict.

'You are too hard on him.'

The unexpected voice came from behind Isabel. A rider with the slim body of a young boy rode to join them. 'You should not shout at the king's general so. He is a man of much importance.'

The owner of the voice turned a pair of enormous brown eyes on Jack. He had not expected to find a supporter so close at hand.

'Hush, sister. You are not the one instructed to teach this barbarian to ride.' The prince was quick to interrupt, yet he beamed with delight as his elder sister pouted at his rash choice of words. It was clear there was much affection shared between the Maharajah's two children.

'Barbarian, is it? Is that how you address the man who saved your precious hide?' Lakshmi matched her brother's hectoring tone.

The prince had the grace to blush. 'I am very grateful for his service, of course.'

Lakshmi turned the power of her presence on Jack. 'You have my brother's gratitude. Let us hope it will prove as useful as the talwar my father presented you with.'

Jack was lost as he returned the princess's frank and open expression. She was a rare beauty, her tiny features perfectly symmetrical. Her dusky skin shone with vitality, but it was her eyes that captivated him. They were large for her face, two deep, liquid pools, and they sparkled with life.

'You will find Jack is a man of few words, Your Highness.' Isabel spoke for Jack as he failed to reply. She was clearly comfortable in the princess's company, and from the warm smile Lakshmi shared with her, it was obvious that the two young women had already struck up a friendship.

'Enough!' snapped the prince. 'We are here to ride. Not to gossip like washerwomen.' He eased his horse forward so that he blocked Jack's view of the two females. 'Go round again. And this time do not kick so hard.'

Jack turned the head of his horse, reluctantly urging the recalcitrant beast into a trot. As he moved away, he twisted in the saddle to flash what he hoped was a dashing smile towards the female part of his audience, keen to show his growing competence. His borrowed mount chose that as the perfect moment to lurch itself into a fast canter, and Jack had to grab hard at the saddle lest he be sent sprawling to the ground.

With his ears ringing from the prince's tirade and his face burning with embarrassment, Jack forced his aching thigh muscles to grip the saddle whilst doing his best to ignore the mocking female laughter that found such delight in his ineptitude. He was a general being taught to ride by a prince under the gaze of a princess. If his breath had not been coming in laboured gasps, he would have laughed at the impossible twist his life had taken.

Chapter Twenty-five

———•◦•———

'They are beautiful, are they not?'

Jack started as the words interrupted his thoughts. He had not heard anyone approach as he studied the series of astonishing paintings that adorned the grand room outside the Maharajah's durbar. He had stolen an hour's solitude and had thought to explore more of the fabulous palace that had become his home. He was fascinated by the magnificent works that were scattered with vulgar abandon throughout the public rooms, the fantastic pieces of art demoted to the role of mere props to impress visitors with the Maharajah's phenomenal wealth.

There was something in the intricacy of so many of the objects that intrigued him. Each one had required exquisite skill to produce, and he wondered how their creators would feel to see their precious handiwork displayed on such a vast scale, the minutiae of their tantalising detail lost in the grand spectacle.

It appeared someone had noticed his fascination, and he turned to face the Maharajah's only daughter, his heart pounding.

'They are more beautiful than I could ever have imagined was possible.'

'I love these paintings. They are my favourites.' Lakshmi stood close enough that Jack could smell the delicate fragrance of her perfume. She was so small that she did not even reach his shoulder. She had all the delicacy of a small bird, but she possessed an aura of confidence that belied her tiny frame.

Jack did his best not to stare at her; instead he wrenched his eyes away and returned his gaze to the painting in front of him.

'Do you understand what it is that you see?' Lakshmi asked, lifting her finger so that it hovered close to the painting, tracing yet not touching the intricate artwork.

The many bangles she wore chimed as they slid down her bare arm, revealing the dusky skin beneath. To Jack's fascination, her wrists and hands were decorated with patterns of black henna, an intricate web of fine tracery that curled and twisted across her flesh. It would have been easy to wonder what other surprises lay beneath the pure white sari that was bound tightly around her slight figure, and Jack had to force his mind to study the painting rather than dwell on the fascinating creature at his side.

A tiny monkey perched on her shoulder, its wide eyes fixing Jack with a knowing stare as if reading his lustful thoughts. The creature was dressed in a miniature crimson coat and its ankles were tethered by a delicate golden chain that was held in place by golden rings. The odd little creature chattered incessantly, as if affronted by Jack's interest in its mistress, only hushing when Lakshmi lifted a slender finger and stroked it into gentle submission.

'Do they tell a story?' Jack felt his voice catch in his throat. He hoped Lakshmi could not tell how nervous she made him. 'They are by the same hand. That much I can tell.'

'They are of the Ramayana. They have been in my family for centuries. The Ramayana is a story, a poem, written by the great Valmiki long before the birth of the Christ that you Christians have chosen to worship.'

'And these depict scenes from the poem?' Jack was intrigued. He wanted to know more, to add to his meagre knowledge. And he wanted to prolong the encounter with the Maharajah's beguiling daughter.

Lakshmi nodded. She stared at the picture for some time before speaking again, as if it had been a long time since she had contemplated its fine artistry. 'This is from the Yuddha Kanda, one of seven books that make up the Ramayana. It tells us how Rama, the favourite son of the great king of Ayodhya, takes his army to fight Ravana, the king of Lanka.'

Jack wrestled with the strange foreign names that echoed in his head. Lakshmi's accent rolled the sounds around, their rich timbre warm and fascinating.

He peered at the picture. 'With an army of monkeys?'

Lakshmi laughed at his tone. 'Yes! With an army of monkeys.'

Jack liked the way her face flushed as she laughed. 'I wish I could remember all this.'

'I will teach you. If you like. My brother can teach you how we ride. I can teach you of our history. You will need both if you are to prosper as a general in my father's army.'

Jack watched Lakshmi as she spoke. He was mesmerised by her vitality. He did not think he had ever seen anyone so full of life.

'Do all Englishmen stare at women in such a way?' Lakshmi turned her head sharply, her eyes narrowing as she rebuked Jack for his intense scrutiny.

Jack blushed and hung his head at being so transparent. 'I am sorry, Your Highness. I didn't—'

Lakshmi reached forward and stopped his stuttering apology by placing a single, cool finger on his lips. The monkey chirruped and chattered for attention, jealous at seeing its mistress touch another.

Lakshmi smiled at the animal's fuss. 'What a silly creature. Getting all hot and bothered so very easily.'

Jack had a sneaking feeling the princess was talking about him, and not about the chattering monkey. He remained silent under her touch, every fibre of his being coming fully alive at the feel of her flesh pressed against his.

'Do not apologise, General Lark.' She withdrew her hand but continued to stare at Jack's face, a frank look of obvious humour on her face. 'I am quite used to such attention.'

Lakshmi laughed as she spoke. It was a soft sound that emanated from deep in her throat, and Jack immediately smiled in response.

'You are the rajkumari.' He stumbled over the recently learnt word, his clumsy attempt to use Lakshmi's correct title sounding lame even to his own ears. 'I am sure it is inevitable.'

Lakshmi pouted. 'So you stare because of the accident of my birth? Not because you consider me beautiful?'

Jack saw the sparkle in her eye as she replied. He sensed the danger of talking so freely to the Maharajah's only daughter. Yet he could not help his attraction. 'You are as beautiful as the morning sun, Your Highness. I cannot imagine a day without the radiance of your presence.'

Lakshmi snorted in a very unladylike manner at Jack's courtly tongue, causing her pet monkey to start and shriek. She stilled the startled creature with her hand before turning the full weight of her attention back on Jack. 'My father was quite wrong. You would make a wonderful ambassador. You are wasted as a general.'

'Your father does not truly know me, Your Highness.'

'Does anyone?' Lakshmi was suddenly serious. She reached forward and grazed the skin around his eyes with the tip of her finger. Her touch was as light as a feather, and Jack shivered. 'I see pain in the lines on your face, General Lark,' she continued, her finger sliding gently down his face so that it traced along his jawline. 'The stain of suffering that should not scar a face as young as yours.'

Jack could not speak. His face tingled where her finger had been, the gossamer lightness of her touch inflaming his soul.

Lakshmi stepped back, Jack's skin suddenly cold as she withdrew her touch. 'You are an interesting man, General Lark. You intrigue me.'

Jack had to clear his throat before he could speak. He was certain Lakshmi could see the desire on his face, the lust that had charged into his eyes when he felt her touch on his skin.

'I am pleased you find me so fascinating. But I am not a painting to be studied.' His shame made him harsh.

'Oh, I know that.' Lakshmi flushed crimson as she spoke, her eyes suddenly downcast as if she was ashamed of her own behaviour. 'No one will ever be able to own you.'

Without another word, she turned and walked quickly away, her small bare feet whispering across the marbled floor with barely a sound.

Jack watched her go, his emotions in turmoil. Lakshmi fascinated him. She was beautiful and exotic and he couldn't help but be attracted to her. She beguiled him in a way that Isabel never could. But he had made his choice the moment he agreed to go on an afternoon's picnic to visit a crumbling stone tower. His head might be turned but his heart could not be.

The sound of laughter echoed down the passageway, the hard marble floor and the wooden panels on the walls making the sound reverberate so that Jack heard it clearly even though he was still yards away from the source of the frivolity.

He turned the corner to see Prince Abhishek standing on one leg in front of a clearly delighted Isabel. The boy's antics were obviously the source of the warm sound of amusement, and Isabel was clapping her hands together with glee at his jests.

'What is going on here?' Jack snapped the question in the commanding tone of a British army officer.

The prince started, the sudden interruption nearly causing him to lose balance. A fleeting look of guilt flashed across his face, like a schoolboy who had been caught cheating at a game of cards. Jack understood the expression at once. He made a mental note to keep a close eye on the Maharajah's son.

'Jack!' Isabel bounced with girlish glee as Jack strode into view. 'Prince Abhishek was imitating his uncle's favourite pet monkey. The poor thing only has one leg and must hop everywhere!'

Jack had a pretty shrewd idea that the prince had been thinking of a different kind of antic, and the bright crimson flush on the boy's cheeks confirmed his suspicions. He was not the only one becoming infatuated with a foreign woman.

The prince held his hands together in front of his body as Jack approached, nervous to have been discovered cavorting with his father's guest. Jack made sure to look the younger man firmly in the eye, unconsciously straightening his spine to emphasis the difference in their heights.

'Your Highness is a fine comedian.' He spoke the words through gritted teeth. The boy recognised the tension in the words and dropped his eyes, suddenly fascinated by the intricate veins in the marbled floor beneath his feet.

Isabel laughed at Jack's heavy flattery. She saw nothing of the challenge in his posture or in the veiled menace of his tone. 'Prince Abhishek has been regaling me with so many stories! Why, Jack, you would not believe half of them.'

Jack smiled, keeping his eyes firmly on the top of the prince's head. 'I am certain the prince knows how to tell a story. All boys of his age have a fine imagination.'

The prince looked up and quailed as he saw the older man's heavy scrutiny. 'Please excuse me. I must attend on my father.' He quickly muttered the polite phrase before scuttling away, his tail tucked firmly between his legs.

Jack watched him leave, a wry, mocking smile on his face. For the first time Isabel noticed his mood.

'Have I done something wrong?' She moved forward, placing a hand on Jack's arm. He had unthinkingly taken a firm hold on the hilt of the sword at his hip.

'You? No? But you should keep an eye on that boy.'

'On Prince Abhishek? Why? He is charming. Why should I be concerned about him?'

'I have a notion he would like to be not so charming. And he is no boy. He has the emotions of a man, and I rather fancy you have stirred some passion in him.'

'Jack!' Isabel stepped back as if horrified at the base observation, her mouth open in amazement. But the look on her face told Jack she was not totally put out at the notion of being the object of a prince's desire. 'How can you say such a thing?'

Jack snorted at the veiled innocence. 'He is a young man. You are a blonde angel like no one he has ever seen. He cannot but be infatuated.'

Isabel stamped her foot. 'That is not so. You are just saying it to be spiteful.'

'Don't be so ridiculous. I'm letting you know so you don't encourage him.'

'Encourage him! Why on earth would I encourage him?' Isabel looked at Jack through hooded eyes. 'Why, I think you are jealous!'

'Jealous! Of a whippersnapper who has only just stopped having some nanny wipe his arse.' Jack chuckled as if amused by the notion. 'I'm not jealous. I'm simply concerned that you do not know what you are doing when you flutter your eyelashes at the poor boy.'

Isabel's temper was rising. 'How dare you! Why, it is at times like this that I am reminded of how coarse you really are.'

'I may be coarse, but at least I'm able to see what is staring me right in my damn face.'

'Oh, really.' Isabel moved forward, wagging her finger inches in front of Jack's nose. 'So what of the princess? Don't think I haven't seen how you moon over her.'

'Now who is jealous?' He raised his hand and used it to push Isabel's wagging finger to one side.

Isabel's mouth opened and closed several times, but she was unable to speak. With a final grunt of barely suppressed anger, she turned sharply on her heel and stamped away down the passageway.

Jack felt a pang of regret. He had no desire to hurt Isabel, but his building infatuation with the beguiling Lakshmi had made him feel guilty. Mixed with a little jealousy, it fermented a cocktail that he had been powerless to control.

'General Lark!'

A voice called his name, interrupting his train of thought. He pushed the difficult emotions away and forced a smile on to his face. It felt odd to be addressed as 'general' but he had a feeling he could get used to it.

'So, you have been given my lancers!'

Count Piotr strode jauntily across the marble, the spurs on his high black boots jangling with every step. There was no trace of animosity in his words.

'I have to learn to ride first.'

'Yes, you must!' The count laughed as he replied. 'I cannot have my men led by a damn infantryman.'

'I shall do my best.'

Count Piotr nodded in agreement. He was watching Jack closely, as if considering something.

'Whatever you have to say, just say it.' Jack was blunt. The confrontation with Isabel had worn his patience thin.

The count's eyes narrowed. 'Very well. You are an astute man, Jack, for all your attempts to portray yourself as nothing more than a humble soldier.' He paused, his brow furrowed. 'Did you stop to ask yourself why you have been given the command of the finest men in the Maharajah's army?'

Jack smelt trouble. 'No.' His answer was wary but honest.

The count snorted once before he replied. 'I thought so. It is a fitting reward for a man as brave as you, no?'

'Perhaps.'

'Did you think on what had happened to the man who had commanded them before you?'

'No.' Jack had been too wrapped up with his spectacular rise to give the matter serious thought. 'What happened to him?'

'He was deemed to be too old to continue in his command; past his usefulness. You have replaced him.'

Jack heard the bitterness in the revelation. 'I'm sorry. I did not intend to force you from your position.'

To Jack's surprise the count laughed again. 'You are a quick-witted fellow, Jack. Perhaps you will do well in your new role.' His face changed, his expression suddenly serious. 'I do not begrudge you commanding my men. But you would do well to think on your life here. Are you being rewarded for valour? Or are you a bauble? An adornment that satisfies the Maharajah's fancy.' He waved his arm, indicating the dozens of fabulous objects scattered around the corridor in which they talked. 'He has many trinkets. They interest him for a day, perhaps a week.' He fixed Jack with an intense stare. 'And then he tires of them.'

Jack understood immediately. The Polish count was warning him for a second time. 'So what happens to you now?'

Again the count laughed. 'You must not worry about an old man. I am still here. I shall still advise the great king although I am not so sure he will listen to me. But he has not fully tired of me. For the moment at least.'

He chuckled, as if amused at a joke only he had heard, before he turned on his heel and walked away.

Jack watched him go. He would heed the count's warning. He would take nothing for granted. As long as he served the Maharajah, he would be on his guard.

Chapter Twenty-six

---◆◈◆---

Jack stood in the white durbar room, trying to look composed and assured. The chamberlain had positioned him near the Maharajah's simple throne, in full view of anyone entering the room. The richly dressed noble to his left had taken a self-conscious step to one side as Jack arrived, leaving him to stand quite alone.

He was dressed in another new uniform, the tailored lancer's coat now adorned with the thick white epaulettes of a general in the Maharajah's service. Yet today the fine blue officer's jacket felt tight around his chest, and the waistband of the new white breeches cut deeply into the flesh around his stomach. Even the tall black boots he had worn for several weeks now pinched across the instep, the highly polished leather suddenly tight and unyielding. His discomfort was made worse as it dawned on him that he had been positioned with care. He was supposed to be seen, his presence in the durbar arranged with calculated design.

The last weeks had passed quickly. Jack had been made to work for his keep. He had spent countless hours under the uncompromising tutelage of the Maharajah's son, learning to ride and gaining the skills he would need to fight in battle from the back of a horse. As he progressed, he had begun to spend more time with the blue-coated lancers. At first he had been thrust into their ranks, trusted with nothing more than learning the complex mounted drill that Count Piotr had passed on to the Maharajah's favourite troops. He had accompanied them on long marches through the Maharajah's domains, hardening his muscles and broadening his knowledge of the lands and the people of Sawadh.

As he became more accomplished, he had begun to take his position at the head of the lancers, slowly starting to live up to the grandiose title that had been bestowed upon him. He was nearing the point where he would be able to influence his command, moving from student to teacher, passing on what he had learnt of battle, of what it took to translate the manoeuvres and drills from the parade ground to the battlefield.

The rest of his time had been spent with Lakshmi and Isabel, exploring the palace and learning more of the country that sheltered them from the righteous anger of the British authorities. The friendship that had developed between the two young women fascinated him. He would stare at them as they wandered the corridors and rooms of the fortress arm in arm, talking ten to the dozen, as if they had known each other all their lives. He did not understand how they had established such a strong bond, but somehow it made it easier for him, his fascination with Lakshmi neutered with Isabel present. Not that he had the energy to even think of anything untoward, the hours spent with the Maharajah's lancers sapping him of the necessary energy and strength.

He looked around the durbar room, trying to remember the names of all who were present, just one of the many things he was struggling to learn as he took his place as one of the Maharajah's inner circle of advisers. His heart was pounding in his chest as he waited for those who had come demanding an audience with the Maharajah. He sensed that his future hung on the events of the next hour. The calm of recent weeks had dulled his anxiety, the simple pleasure of life in the Maharajah's court allowing him to put his concerns for the future to one side. Now the urgent summons to the durbar room mocked such complacency.

The Maharajah lounged on his simple throne. He was dressed in the unassuming shirt and breeches of a soldier, only the fabulous golden silk cravat revealing any flamboyance. Every insouciant gesture reaffirmed his lack of concern, as if the meeting that was about to take place was as mundane as dealing with the trivial arguments solved by his junior ministers. Yet Jack had known him long enough to see the anxiety in his eyes. The Maharajah might have presented the calm facade of a man fully in control of his destiny, but Jack sensed the tension that was building within.

The Maharajah was right to be concerned. For the official delegates of the British government had arrived unannounced and demanded an immediate audience. He could not ignore the men who governed his land under the terms of the treaty signed by his father.

As for Jack, he would have to stand in full view as Major Proudfoot ventured into his enemy's lair. For good or for ill, he was about to come face to face with his former commanding officer.

The large doors swung open, the two guards standing rigidly to attention as the British deputation strode purposefully into the durbar. The sudden flash of their scarlet coats jolted Jack and he felt a tremor of shame deep within his belly. He was wearing the uniform of a foreign power, and for the first time he felt like a traitor.

Proudfoot marched towards the Maharajah's throne. Jack could see the major's face set into a purposeful scowl, the look of a schoolmaster before he administered the cane to an errant yet deserving boy. He walked with the air of a man in charge, as if he, not the man who lolled in the room's only chair, were the rightful ruler of Sawadh.

Lieutenant Fenris followed Proudfoot into the room. He caught Jack's eye, the sudden flare of recognition quickly replaced by a look of such loathing that it momentarily stunned Jack with its force. He had known that the junior officer had become his enemy, but he was still struck by the power of the hatred that emanated from the younger man. Proudfoot himself glanced across at Jack for no more than a single heartbeat before he bowed to the Maharajah and began to speak.

'Thank you for agreeing to see us at such short notice, sire.'

'The pleasure is all yours, I am sure.' The Maharajah still lounged on his throne, one leg thrown casually over its arm. He looked thoroughly bored, and Jack wondered what emotions were hidden behind the mask of supercilious disdain.

'Indeed it is, sire.' Proudfoot did not bat an eyelid at the rude remark. 'I trust we find Your Highness in the very best of health.'

'I am full of the joys of spring, Proudfoot. Much, I am sure, to your disappointment.'

'I am delighted to hear it, sire. I hope that the rest of your family is equally healthy.'

'If you have come all this way merely to ask after the health of every Tom, Dick and Harry who lives in this damn palace, then you have had a wasted trip.' Some of the Maharajah's tension escaped as he tired of Proudfoot's insincere enquiries. He twisted athletically in his chair, swinging his leg around so that he sat facing forward. 'I would ask you to say what you have come to say. I am a busy man.'

'Very well, sire. As you demand.' Proudfoot turned and gestured for Fenris to hand him a roll of cream parchment that the younger officer had carried into the durbar. 'I have come to deliver you this document.'

The Maharajah chuckled. 'You British set such stock by documents. What of a man's word? Is that not enough any more?'

'Such things must be done correctly, sire.'

'What things?' The Maharajah gestured impatiently for the parchment to be handed to him.

Proudfoot passed it over and then stood back, his face betraying an air of arrogant satisfaction. It was quickly replaced by irritation as the Maharajah casually tossed the rolled parchment over his shoulder.

'I would rather you simply told me what's in it, old boy,' he said, lounging back on his throne.

Proudfoot looked longingly at the discarded parchment. He took a moment to compose himself and still any outward sign of temper. 'Of course, sire. I am afraid I am the bearer of sad tidings. Have you heard of the Doctrine of Lapse?'

Jack's heart had been pounding ever since Proudfoot had begun to speak. The dry legal phrase stilled it in an instant.

The Maharajah sat forward in his chair, his attempt at nonchalance abandoned. 'I'm familiar with the term, though I do not understand why you would mention it.' His tone was icy. The court froze, as if every person drew in breath as one.

'That is why I am here, sire.' Proudfoot thrived on the attention, hostile as it was. 'The Governor has ordained that due to your lack of satisfactory evidence to the contrary, he must assume you to have no heir.'

Jack stared in fascination at the Maharajah. There was no trace of emotion on his face. Where a lesser man would have leapt to his feet, roaring in indignation, he sat still and composed, only the hard, flat stare an indication of the emotions that were raging inside.

'I see.' The Maharajah said nothing further; simply sat where he was, his attention fixed on the political officer standing in front of him.

No one dared speak. Jack watched as Proudfoot rode out the storm of silence, his own composure matching that of the Maharajah. Only Fenris seemed uncomfortable, visibly squirming as the uncomfortable hiatus went on.

'There has been a mistake,' said the Maharajah finally, in the quiet tones of a reasonable man, his delivery careful and deliberate. 'I am sure the Governor is very busy and is poorly guided in this matter. There has never been any doubt that I am blessed with two children, both of whom are more than able to rule here in my stead when I am gone. The Doctrine of Lapse cannot . . .' he paused before continuing, '*shall not* be applied here.'

Proudfoot smiled, without any trace of warmth in his expression. 'There has been no mistake, sire. We have been given no proof that the children you mention are indeed your own. If you were able to produce their mother . . .'

'She died in childbirth.' The Maharajah snapped the words. 'Not even a king can raise the dead.'

Proudfoot gave no sign of embarrassment. 'Then we have no choice, sire. In cases such as this, the doctrine must be applied. The Governor has been magnanimous in allowing you to be apprised of the situation so that you are able to make . . .' he paused, matching the Maharajah's style of delivery, 'suitable arrangements.'

The Maharajah contemplated Proudfoot's words. 'So I must provide proof that my children are indeed my own? Or should I simply sire more heirs? Perhaps you would like to nominate someone to bear witness as I perform the necessary act.'

Proudfoot shuddered with distaste at the notion. 'There is no need for such excess, sire.'

'So when I am dead, the British will rule the land that has been ours for centuries?'

Proudfoot spread his hands apologetically and shrugged. 'The Governor would deem that the best course of action, sire.'

'And if I resist?' The Maharajah spoke in no more than a whisper, yet every ear in the room heard his words.

'That would be . . .' again Proudfoot paused, as if sucking each word to check it was not too peppery, 'ill advised. As you will be aware, we have recently applied the doctrine successfully elsewhere, and it would really be better for everyone concerned if it were also to be applied here. Though only at the proper time, of course.'

'When I am conveniently dead, you mean.' The Maharajah gave a mocking smile. 'I admire boldness, Proudfoot. You are nothing if not bold.'

Proudfoot held out his hands in apology. 'We merely seek to do what is right, sire. What is best.'

For a moment Jack was certain the Maharajah would unleash his temper. He could see the rage flashing across his eyes, but it was nothing more than a fleeting glimpse of the man's true feelings. Somehow the emotion was contained.

'We will consider what you have said. I must thank you for taking the time to deliver this message to me personally.'

Proudfoot bowed at the waist. 'It was my pleasure.' He made no attempt to hide his satisfaction. Jack would have gained a great deal of pleasure from slamming his fist into the centre of the man's smug face and seeing how pleased he looked then.

Fenris leaned forward and whispered into Proudfoot's ear, shooting a venomous look in Jack's direction as he did so.

Proudfoot nodded, as if reminded of a minor item he had overlooked. 'There is one other small matter, Your Highness, if I may?'

The Maharajah fluttered his fingers to acknowledge the request.

'Thank you. I'm afraid this is a delicate matter and one that is somewhat . . .' again the annoying pause, 'embarrassing.'

'Go on.'

'It has come to our attention that there is a criminal at large. He is a man who is adept at the art of masquerade and he has been able to dupe a number of unfortunate souls with his evil cunning. To my shame I must admit that I myself was one of them.'

Proudfoot looked across at Jack before returning his gaze to the Maharajah. If he hoped to see any sign of encouragement, then he was to be disappointed.

'He has gone to great lengths to hide his deception and he will stoop to any depths to avoid being brought to justice. I am afraid to report that this has included deceiving an innocent young girl and encouraging her to accompany him on his foul mission.'

'I have no idea of what you speak.' The Maharajah's voice hardened. 'I shall have my men inform you should this miscreant make the mistake of trying to dupe me.' He looked at Jack and gave him a very obvious and unsubtle wink.

'Sire, I am not a fool.' Proudfoot spoke in little more than a whisper. 'The man stands in plain view.'

'He does?' The Maharajah made a show of looking around the durbar room. 'I see no one who does not belong here.' There was a warning in his tone that was quite lost on Lieutenant Fenris, who was unable to contain himself any longer.

'He stands right there! As bold as brass!' Fenris' anger made him quiver with indignation, his finger pointing directly at where Jack stood in silence.

The Maharajah turned the force of his attention on the young lieutenant. 'That man is my trusted general. You are mistaken, Lieutenant Fenris.' There was naked venom in his voice now, and Proudfoot stepped forward, placing himself between his errant subaltern and the ruler.

'Very well, sire. As you will. But I would beg you to enquire after the young girl. We believe this insidious man had inveigled her into his evil scheme. She should be returned to her father. I would hope you would understand that.'

For the first time the Maharajah seemed to accept the political officer's words. 'I shall see that the lady in question is asked for her opinion on the matter. Should the situation arise.'

Lieutenant Fenris opened his mouth to object, but Proudfoot pre-empted another outburst by placing a warning hand on the officer's arm. 'Thank you, sire. We can ask for nothing more.'

Jack had stood mute throughout the exchange. It would have been easy to remain silent, safe in the knowledge that the Maharajah was protecting him. But he could not stand back and say nothing. He would not hide.

He stepped forward, his spine tingling with discomfort as every eye turned towards him.

'Proudfoot.'

The major looked surprised that Jack had chosen to speak. He quickly glanced in the Maharajah's direction, checking for any sign of intervention. Seeing that none was forthcoming, he turned and faced his fellow countryman, lifting his chin in a supercilious gesture of disdain.

'I have nothing to say to a traitor.'

'I am no damned traitor.' Jack felt his emotions surge through him. He had not imagined how difficult it would be to speak to the British officer, to face his own side whilst wearing the uniform of another.

'I can call you nothing else. You should do the decent thing and turn yourself in, and allow Miss Youngsummers to be returned to the care of her father. It is the only chance you have of avoiding the noose.'

'I'm to be hanged?' Jack did not sound surprised. He had always known the penalty for this charade.

'It's what you deserve, you damned villain.' Fenris hissed the words, his anger naked.

'You should quieten your lapdog, Proudfoot. Before he bites off more than he can chew.'

Fenris stiffened, but Proudfoot once again placed a warning hand on his arm, silencing the furious younger officer.

'Did you have something you wanted to say?' Proudfoot was urbane in the face of his subaltern's righteous anger.

'You should tell Reverend Youngsummers that his daughter is safe and well. I would not want him to be unduly worried.'

'How magnanimous of you.' Proudfoot's sarcasm was obvious.

He turned as if about to leave before pausing, struck by a sudden thought. 'You know, it really is a pity I had not known of your true abilities when we first met. I would have found a use for a man of your resourcefulness.' He shook his head, clearly disappointed by the missed opportunity. 'Would you allow me to know your real name?' He asked the question with what appeared to be genuine interest. 'I should like to be able to address you properly.'

'Lark. My name is Jack Lark.' For a moment Jack was tempted to offer his hand, but he held back, still unsure of Proudfoot's motives.

But Proudfoot simply nodded. 'Lark. A good name for a man who commits his life to such wild escapades.' He looked up and gave Jack a mocking half-smile. 'Well met, Jack Lark.' Then he turned on his heel, ushering the still enraged Lieutenant Fenris out with him.

Jack watched him go. To his surprise, he felt a strong sense of regret.

Chapter Twenty-seven

'You must accept, Your Highness. To do anything else would be folly.' Count Piotr sat ramrod straight in his chair and offered his opinion in the flat, dry tone of someone who regarded any other course of action as simple madness.

'I shall never accept. Never!' The Maharajah slammed his fist down on to the thick mahogany table that had been painted a brilliant shade of white.

The count was unfazed at the display of temper. He sat back in his chair on the other side of the round table and stroked his thin moustache. 'You cannot fight them.'

'Why not?' The Maharajah leapt to his feet and stalked around the room. The small, intimate chamber was decorated with wooden panels painted dark crimson that stood in stark contrast to the plain marble floor and crisp white ceiling. Unlike so many of the rooms in the palace, there was little else in the way of decoration. The plain, workmanlike feeling was echoed in the placement of the many console tables around the room, their highly polished surfaces covered with paper, inkwells, quills and blotters.

But there was no clerk present that day to record what was said. The Maharajah had summoned his closest advisers to discuss the news delivered by Major Proudfoot, and their words were to remain closely guarded, known only to the participants in the secret durbar.

For they talked of war, the modest room bearing witness to a discussion that would decide the fate of a nation.

Jack watched closely as the Maharajah stalked around the chamber. With no strangers present, he was able to give vent to his feelings; it was a miracle that he had been able to contain the full force of his rage during the audience with the British officials.

Jack had seen the ruler of Sawadh many times before today. He had enjoyed their conversations but they had often been inconsequential, jokey affairs, the Maharajah revealing nothing of his opinions or his aspirations for his domain. For all his grandiose titles and fabulous uniforms, Jack was still the outsider, still the firangi. He had not forgotten Count Piotr's warning and he had done his best to remain wary, to not become too comfortable or complacent in his new life. Now, for the first time, he had been summoned to join the Maharajah's inner circle of advisers, his council of war. He did not know what role he would be expected to take, so he guarded his emotions, keeping his face neutral as he waited to discover if he would be asked for advice or whether he was there to offer information.

He recognised only three of the other men summoned to join the intimate council. One was Count Piotr, who had surprised everyone by being the first to offer the one piece of advice that was sure to set the touchpaper to the Maharajah's temper.

On the far side of the table sat the vizier, the man who had been so keen to see Jack executed when he had first arrived at the fortress. It was he who was next to speak, the rotund official beginning a long, passionless speech in his own language. To his left sat two other dark-faced advisers, who both nodded enthusiastically at the course of action that was being suggested by their colleague. The three men were clearly used to each other and they formed a cohort that would offer a single opinion even if it were delivered from three separate mouths.

It was obviously a forceful argument, and the pace of the Maharajah's angry tread slowed as he contemplated what was being said. Jack sincerely hoped that the vizier was advising the Maharajah to not contemplate open rebellion against the British; he knew that this would place him fully in the role of traitor. Yet it was not solely through a notion of self-preservation that he so desired the Maharajah to find a peaceful solution to Proudfoot's plans for his dynasty. For Jack was certain that if the Maharajah decided to fight the British, he was doomed to defeat.

Count Piotr spoke again. 'If you fight, sire, you will die, and your ambition, and your dynasty, will be so much dust.'

Jack envied his calm manner. It was a bold man who addressed a king so. He was intrigued to hear that the Polish count's opinion matched his own; glad that he was not the only one who saw the certainty of defeat.

'Why? Explain to me why I cannot defeat the British. My army is bigger than theirs. We have more horsemen and many more foot.' The Maharajah came to a stop next to the count, leaning forward to take his weight on his arms as he sought the answer to his earnest question. 'Why must I stay my hand when I could defeat these fools with ease?'

'Because the British do not understand defeat,' the count replied quietly. 'They refuse to be beaten. No matter how many times you fight them, they will always return, and each time they will be stronger. You can win a battle, maybe two. You cannot win a war.'

But the Maharajah did not agree. 'They will understand defeat soon enough. I will destroy them and their stupid little town. I will show them what happens when they treat the Maharajah of Sawadh with such disdain.'

'Then you would be a fool.' The count snapped the reply. The quiet room fell into deathly silence as one of their number dared to confront the passionate ruler. The only man who seemed uncon-cerned was the count himself, and he leant forward, taking firm hold of one of the Maharajah's forearms. 'If you fight them, you will bring down a retribution such as you cannot begin to contemplate. The British cannot allow you to strike at them for fear of the example it would set. Even if you win and destroy their station at Bhundapur, they will come at you with such power that you will be lucky if a single man in your army is left alive.'

Jack watched the faces around the room. The two dark-faced advisers were animated, their loud voices denying the Polish cavalryman's words. The vizier sat in silence, his eyes lifted to the heavens, as if he summoned divine intervention. Yet his expression remained guarded, and Jack got the sense that behind his calm facade his mind raced in calculation.

'We can call on at least a thousand cavalry and more than double that number of foot soldiers.' A grey-haired man who had so far remained silent consulted a piece of parchment on the table in front of him. 'The British have fewer than one hundred of their own men and around three hundred native soldiers, a squadron of cavalry and no cannon. I see no reason why we should be afraid of that force.' There was no judgement in his voice, merely the matter-of-fact tone of a man seeking orders. He was dressed in the same blue and red uniform that Jack had seen on the guards who had first granted him access to the palace, and the Maharajah listened intently as he spoke.

'That is but a fraction of their forces.' The count's respectful manner made it clear that he too valued the older man's opinion. 'Destroy those and more will come. They will bring cavalry and cannon. They will reduce this place to so much rubble. It has happened before and it will happen again. There is no hope of resistance.'

'We could call on our allies. Nathe Khan or the Maharajah of Orchha could double the size of our army if we so wished.' The old man looked at the Maharajah as he spoke, presenting the option with no hint of whether he agreed with it or not.

'Those jackals.' The Maharajah did not bother to hide his own opinion. 'They would only join us if they thought they would be able to pick over our carcass. I will not ask for help.' His voice betrayed his pride.

The old officer nodded, the first sign of his own feelings revealed. 'Your army will fight if you command us, Your Highness. I do not doubt we would succeed against this man Proudfoot and his troops.' He looked across at the count. 'But I cannot say if we can defeat this white-faced horde that Count Piotr describes.'

'We must fight.' The final voice in the room spoke. It belonged to the third man that Jack had recognised. Prince Abhishek joined the conversation for the first time, his young face flushed with passion. 'We cannot accede to this demand. My ancestors fought for this land. They took it by being strong and they kept it by being stronger. We cannot sit back like women and let these British just take it all away.'

The Maharajah smiled with pride. 'You speak from your heart, my son. It does you credit.' He turned and looked around the room, resting his unsettling gaze for a moment on every face. He came to Jack. 'General Lark. You have been uncharacteristically quiet. What is your opinion?'

Jack felt a lump form in his throat as the Maharajah's attention fell upon him. There was nowhere to hide in the small room. He was an impostor, yet now he was being asked to advise on the fate of a nation.

'The count is correct.' He had to clear his throat as he began to speak. 'You cannot defeat us. The men at Bhundapur are well trained and well armed. If you attack, then they will stand and they will fight harder than you can believe is possible.' Jack's confidence grew as he began to string his sentences together. 'I do not believe you will succeed in destroying the station at Bhundapur. I think you will commit many men to certain death if you try. When you are defeated, the British will annex your land and rule here in your place. There will be no place for your son, and you will both be hunted down like dogs until you are brought to heel or killed in the process. The count is right. To fight us is folly.'

The Maharajah's son rose to his feet, indignation clear on his young face. 'This man knows nothing. He is a charlatan. A trickster. He says these things to frighten us. To save his countrymen from facing death at our hands.' He pointed a finger at Jack as he spoke. 'We should not listen to his false words.'

'I hear you, my son.' The Maharajah smiled warmly at Abhishek's passion. 'Now sit and calm yourself.' He turned back to Jack. Once again every set of eyes fell on him. 'Why?' The question was simple, and asked in the voice of a man searching for understanding. 'Why can you British not just leave us alone?'

For the first time Jack heard the pain in the Maharajah's voice, and he felt a prick of shame. 'I do not know. Your son is correct. I'm an impostor. I'm not a politician.'

The Maharajah seemed disappointed by the meek answer. He

pulled back from the table and began to once again pace around the room. The men left at the table sat in silence, each contemplating their own thoughts, none willing to look at another as they waited.

'My father faced this same question when I was but a small boy.' The Maharajah began to speak as he paced, circling around the table, fixing each man with his firm gaze as he walked opposite their place. 'He signed the treaty with the British because he believed he could not stand against their power, just as many others did. Yet my father was old then. He had lost the fire in his belly. Now the British are back and they want more. They want me to hand over the lands of my forefathers to them.'

He stopped his pacing, coming to a halt on the opposite side of the table to where Jack sat. Jack looked up into the fierce gaze and saw the anger in the Maharajah's eyes. The indignation of a man faced with injustice. The fury of a ruler about to send his country to war. 'The British want me to do as I am told. To go quietly and to accept the fate they have chosen for me. How little do they know me.'

The Maharajah paused. For a moment his head hung, as if the discussion had exhausted him, the enormity of the decision he faced physically weighing him down. Then he looked up.

'I shall not go meekly.' He stared at Jack, his eyes suddenly hard. 'I shall fight for my kingdom. I shall make the British regret their decision. If nothing else, I shall live what time is left to me in honour.'

Jack met the uncompromising gaze. 'You are wrong. There is no honour in sending men to their deaths. There is just pain and suffering.'

The Maharajah coloured. 'Perhaps death is better than living in shame.'

'Perhaps, for you. But your men do not have that choice. You will send them to their deaths for what? For your honour? For glory? For it is they who will suffer. It is they who will die.' Jack felt his own temper rising. He had known what it was to be ordered into battle. He had known what it was like to be a pawn in the game of war.

'The men will fight for their king willingly.' The old officer spoke for his troops.

'They would die for their king!' Prince Abhishek was more forceful, his face flushed crimson with his righteous anger as he leapt to his feet, his temper forcing him into motion.

Jack refused to be cowed. 'They will fight because you order it. Do not be so quick to condemn men to death. Their lives mean more than that.'

'You speak well, General Lark.' The Maharajah waved Abhishek back into his seat. 'You are right to question these things. But my son is correct. My country would rather die than become another vassal of your Queen. You are still a stranger here, no matter what the colour of your uniform. You do not understand us. You British, you look at us and see our ignorance. You look down your noses and see squalor, hear laws that do not make sense. But you do not see our souls. You do not see the lives that have been lived here for centuries. Oh, I am sure you wish to improve us. You are certain that your roads and your universities and schools and even your great white God will improve our lives. But I tell you this. We do not want your improvements. We do not want your hands in our lives. We will live as we have chosen or we would rather die.'

The Maharajah vibrated with passion. Jack heard the raw emotion and it struck home. He truly did not know these people.

'I warned you that this day would come, General Lark.' The Maharajah wiped a hand over his bald scalp, as if smearing away his emotions. 'We will go to war. Your precious redcoats are now my enemy. You must decide which side you are on.'

Chapter Twenty-eight

---

*J*ack sat in the room of the Ramayana paintings, savouring the peace and the solitude. It had become one of his favourite places in the palace. It was tucked away, far from the bustle of the public areas. He could sit alone, setting his mind free, testing the darkness within, something in the tranquillity of the room allowing him to dare to venture into his memories. He could not resist picking at the scabs in his soul, the itch of what had been simply too strong to ignore.

Only the subtle tick of a fine gold clock broke the quiet, yet his mind reverberated to the sounds of battle, replaying the horror of marching into enemy fire, the icy rush of fear flushing through him as he remembered taking his sword forward into the vicious melee of combat.

The Maharajah had called for war. Jack felt that he alone knew what was coming; no one else was capable of recognising the monster that was being summoned so willingly. The knowledge shamed him, and he could not help chastising himself for not having spoken out more forcefully against the bloodshed that was sure to come. He knew he had not done enough to avoid the conflict that was now inevitable.

His hand dropped to the talwar at his side. The sharkskin grip was still clean, not yet sullied by his sweat or by the blood of other men. If war came, then the sword would be forced into service, its master given the opportunity to show his true worth. For in the darkest recess of Jack's mind lurked the pride of what he became when battle was joined. He was an impostor, a charlatan, but in battle he was able to show the steel that lived underneath the folds of his assumed roles. Only then could he reveal his bitter talent. He might have wished for a peaceful resolution to British ambition, but he knew he would not avoid the battle if it came.

He heard the chatter of the monkey and quickly got to his feet. Yet it was hard to shake off the world of canister and volley fire even as he listened to the sound of bare feet whispering across the marble floor, the gentle chink of a slim gold chain as the beast it tethered capered on the shoulder of its mistress.

'General Lark.' Lakshmi's dusky voice cut through the echo of gunfire in his mind, yet it sounded muffled, the cries of the dead deafening the voice of the living. Even the delicate fragrance of her perfume did nothing to shake off the feeling of dread that was coursing through him.

She reached for his arm. Her hand was cool on his skin and he tried to focus on the gentle touch, but the bitter memories were strong and he felt distant, lost in a world of death.

'Jack?' Lakshmi's voice was small. She stood on tiptoe, leaning forward so that the wide silk hood of her dress whispered across his face. She kissed him on the cheek, her lips barely brushing his skin.

Jack felt a frisson of desire spark in his heart. It drove away the haunting shadows, bringing him back to the present.

'Where were you, General Lark?' To Jack's regret, she had pulled back, but the chill was gone, banished by the warmth of her lips.

Jack smiled. 'I was far away. Thank you for rescuing me.'

'You seem to be making a habit of being rescued by the women in your life.' Lakshmi mocked him, yet her eyes remained guarded, doubtful that he had still not fully come back to the world of the living.

'I am a lucky man.' Jack reached for her hand. It was tiny, the delicate fingers fragile in his grip.

'You are a bold man, that much is certain.' Lakshmi gently chided

Jack for his forwardness, but she left her hand in his all the same.

'*Per aspera ad astra*.' Jack's tongue tripped over the Latin phrase, but he was pleased his attempt made her smile.

'Through difficulties to the stars.' Lakshmi translated with ease. 'You truly do have the tongue of a diplomat.'

'A madman I once knew said it. He was trying to inspire us before we went into battle.'

'Did it work?'

'We won. Maybe it did.'

'You won.' There was sarcasm in Lakshmi's voice now. She snatched her hand back. 'You men talk of winning and losing. But there is no victory in battle. There is just pain and suffering and death.'

'I don't want war.'

Lakshmi looked deep into his eyes. 'No. I sense the pride in you. You want this as much as my father does.'

Jack shivered as she read his soul. 'You are wrong.' He made the denial bitterly, unable to reveal how close she had come to understanding him.

'No.' Lakshmi's monkey chattered angrily as it sensed its mistress's distress. 'You want to show everyone that you are a warrior. Even though you saved my brother, that is not enough. You have to prove yourself again and again.'

Jack felt a spark of anger. 'You do not know.'

'I know you, Jack Lark. You think you have nothing to offer the world except your sword. That your bravery is the one honest thing about you.' Lakshmi nuzzled her pet, using its familiar touch to calm her. 'You are mistaken. You have so much more to give, but you hide your real self away, protecting it under the shell of a fine British officer.'

She smiled, yet she looked so sad that it took all of Jack's willpower not to gather her into his arms.

'So you must leave. You cannot stay here and fight for my father. You must go to your countrymen. Wrap yourself up in the red coat and become the killer we expect.'

Lakshmi shamed him by speaking the truth. He thought of the brutality of war. A part of him loved the madness that drove him into the fight. With it he was a killer, the kind of leader that men needed in the dreadful bloodletting of battle. Only there could he prove himself and demonstrate just what he could do. He could not do that as a courtier, or as a gentleman. When war came, Jack knew he would not shirk from the fight. It was the one thing he was good at.

'And if I don't go?' He tried to keep the longing from his voice.

'You cannot stay. You cannot betray your homeland. It is not in you. Even if some would wish it otherwise.'

Jack heard the subtle promise. 'Would you have me stay?'

'Would you wear a chain like a pet?' Lakshmi wrapped a finger around the tiny gold chain on her monkey's foot. 'For to some that is all you would be.'

'No.'

'Would you fight your own kind?'

'No.'

'Then you cannot stay.'

Jack nodded, accepting the truth in her words. They built a barrier between them. One that he knew he could now never cross.

'Fight your battle, Jack Lark. Kill more men.' Lakshmi gathered her silver sari around her slight body as if suddenly cold. 'Be what you must be.'

'No. I forbid it. You shall not leave my service. Not now. Not ever.'

Jack forced his spine straighter. 'With respect, sir, I am not asking for your permission.'

The Maharajah leapt to his feet. The durbar room was empty and the noise of his boots hitting the marbled floor echoed around the enormous chamber.

'How dare you! I have given you everything! Now you stand there, wearing the uniform of my general, and tell me that you are leaving like it is nothing more than a bloody house party!' The Maharajah's voice rose, his anger spewing forth.

Jack focused on a spot an inch above the Maharajah's eyes, which blazed with rage. He thought of the colour sergeant who had dominated his early life in the army. This rant paled in comparison.

'I gave you back your life when I could have ordered you killed.'

The Maharajah stalked forward, his face thrust into Jack's. 'Your body would be rotten now. You would be putrid, nothing more than fat maggots and bleached bones. You live because of me. You stand there because of me. Your life is mine. I decide what you do, where you go. You forfeited your right to choose when you came to me, begging to be taken in.'

Jack lowered his eyes and met the uncompromising stare of the Maharajah. He did not flinch from the confrontation.

'Sir—'

'Enough!' The Maharajah snapped the word, cutting Jack off. 'I have heard enough of your whining. You are in my service until either I or death release you. Do not make me choose the latter.' He spun on his heel, stomping away, heading for the small door at the rear of the durbar room that led to his private apartments.

'You owe me.'

Jack said the words softly, yet the Maharajah whirled around as if he had shouted the foulest abuse.

'I owe you nothing!' he screamed. His boots pounded on the floor as he strode towards Jack, his hands balling into fists.

Jack didn't flinch. 'I gave you your son's life. You gave me mine. We are even.' He spoke firmly as the Maharajah came close.

'Do not talk to me of debt. I am king. Do not think to stand there as my equal. You are nothing but a mewling worm. I can crush you under my boot without sparing you a second thought.'

'That's as may be. It will not stop me leaving.'

'You would turn your back on me? You would fight me?' The Maharajah sounded calmer. Jack looked him hard in the eye, searching his gaze for a softening in his stance.

'I have no choice.'

The Maharajah's head seemed to sag, as if his quick rage had exhausted him. He looked at Jack, his eyes full of bitter sadness, and then he sighed. 'No, none of us have a choice. Not even a king. You can no more stay and fight for me than I can sit behind these walls and let you British take my country.'

'I cannot fight my countrymen.' Jack thought of Lieutenant Fenris. 'As much as I may wish it otherwise.'

'You will warn them if you go. They will know I am coming.'

'They will know you are coming anyway. You cannot hide an army.'

'You can tell them of my forces. Our numbers. Our plans.'

'Does that matter? Will you fight any differently?'

The Maharajah sighed. 'I thought you no diplomat. Yet your bluntness seems more effective than I gave you credit for.'

'I am sorry, sir. For whatever that is worth, I am truly sorry. I did not want this.' Jack spoke earnestly. He meant every word.

The Maharajah sucked in a deep breath. He pulled himself up straight before fixing Jack with a firm stare. 'You can go. Take Miss Youngsummers and go back to your countrymen. But you will obey one last order for your king.'

Jack nodded. 'Yes, sir.'

'Warn them.' The Maharajah stood uncomfortably close. Jack could feel the warm touch of the king's breath wash over him as he was given his final order. 'Tell them I am coming with all my strength. Tell them to leave my land and save the bloodshed.'

Jack nodded. 'I will, sir.'

'Will it make a difference?' The question was asked sincerely.

Jack hung his head. He thought of Proudfoot and his ambition. 'No.'

The Maharajah's stare betrayed nothing. 'What will they do with you?'

'I don't know.'

'If they are wise, they will hang you.' The Maharajah snorted as he made the wry observation. For the first time a trace of a smile lit up his proud features. 'You willingly give up everything you have here so you can return to the people who will likely denounce you as a thief and an impostor and string you up like some common criminal.' He shook his head, as if unable to understand. 'I hope they do not. The world is a more interesting place with you in it, Jack Lark. Let us hope the information you bring will be enough to save you.'

He paused, looking around the fabulous durbar room as if seeking inspiration. When he faced Jack again, his expression had hardened. It was a transformation Jack had seen before. The warrior king was looking at his enemy.

'Go now. The debt is paid. The next time we meet, I will try to kill you.' The Maharajah spun on his heel and walked away.

Jack watched him go. He had done what he came for. Now he would return to his own people and deliver the Maharajah's warning. Only time would tell if it would be enough to save his neck.

Chapter Twenty-nine

---◆◆◆---

The army assembled at dawn. They formed up in the wide
maidan that separated the walls of the fortress from the
splendour of the palace. Hundreds of armed men brought
together by the Maharajah to carry out a lightning strike against
the British cantonment at Bhundapur.

The cavalry occupied nearly half of the available space. At the
front stood the famous blue lancers, as neat and ordered as any
British regiment. Behind them were the irregular horse that made up
the bulk of the Maharajah's cavalry. These were the hard men who
lived in the hills of the kingdom of Sawadh. They had arrived in
small groups, each local chieftain leading his men to meet his ruler's
summons, and were fearsomely armed with a bewildering array of
weaponry, from ancient silver jezzails to modern percussion muskets
and carbines. All wore at least one blade, either a curving talwar like
the one Jack himself carried, or a straight blade more similar to a
British heavy cavalry sword. They were a formidable force, a warlike
band that would clearly relish a fight.

The infantry formed up in the large blocks in which they would
march towards Bhundapur. At the fore stood the ordered and
regimented lines of the Maharajah's guards. They were dressed for
war with mail coats worn over their dark blue uniforms, their heavy

talwars hanging at their hips. The sun shone on their armour, glinting from the massed ranks, adding more grandeur to the spectacle of so many assembled in one place. They looked like soldiers of old, more suited to the wars of the past, where every man fought with the brutal weapons that could hack an opponent to pieces or hammer him into bloody submission. They were the Maharajah's finest warriors and they would fight to the death for their king.

Behind the precise ranks and files of the guard stood the massed bulk of the foot soldiers. They were armed and dressed in wildly different styles, yet all bore the same warlike expression. These were hard men from a hard country, and they would fight with as much devotion as any trained soldier. To a man they hoped for loot, for a reward more earthly than the more ethereal value of serving their overlord. They were bandits, landless men from the robber country, whose keen eyes looked for gain, their light fingers and quick wits ready to seize the opportunity to increase their store of wealth.

Guardsmen walked through the ranks, issuing a blue silk armband to every man. The Maharajah's pandit had blessed each one and now they would be worn to unite the disparate troops, adding a uniform touch to the wild men who had come to answer their Maharajah's call, forming them into a single army with a single purpose: to destroy the British cantonment at Bhundapur.

Jack felt cold as he sat in the saddle watching the thousands of men coming together. He was struck by the gaudy vibrancy of the scene, the lack of a single uniform creating a kaleidoscope of colour. Yet there was no doubting the unity of the men. The warlike horde knew they had been summoned to fight, and that purpose united them more forcefully than any uniform.

'We will truly have to fight them?' Isabel spoke in a voice laced with horror. She sat at Jack's side, her young mare quivering as it sensed its mistress's distress.

Jack reached across and squeezed her hand where it rested on the pommel of her saddle. He looked at her rare beauty, savouring the vitality of her youth, very aware that he had made two choices when he had asked the Maharajah for permission to leave.

At least he no longer dreaded being in the saddle, the long, difficult hours of drill with the Maharajah's lancers leaving his muscles hard and well used to the demands of controlling the powerful horse he had been given from the Maharajah's own stables. The uncompromising lessons had taught him well and he could now ride as hard as any lancer, a skill he was certain to need in the bitter fight that was surely to come.

'We will fight them if we have to. If they attack the cantonment at Bhundapur then we must do what we must.' Jack's voice was cold.

'They frighten me,' Isabel spoke softly, a child faced with the monster from a nightmare.

Jack's jaw was set firm as he ran a professional eye over the Maharajah's army. 'They have numbers on their side, but that is all. I'd still wager on our boys seeing them off. But we will need to stand firm and keep them out, butcher them with our volleys. God help us if they get close enough to fight hand to hand.'

Isabel shivered despite the rising heat of the morning. Sunrise was still a long way off, but already the day promised to be brutally hot. It would be an unpleasant day in the saddle, but Jack was determined they would ride for as long as they could, no matter what conditions they faced. They had been given permission to leave, but still he would take no chances. He would not rest until they were a long way away from the army that the Maharajah planned to unleash.

The noise of the gathering horde suddenly increased. The cacophony of sound was deafening. There were none of the martial tones used to inspire and control the British army. In place of the strident call of the bugle and the disciplined staccato of the drum, there was an ear-splitting medley of screech and bawl, an unholy frenzy that erupted in one spontaneous roar.

Jack grimaced as the sound swelled. Thousands of men were cheering, their coarse bellows underscoring the higher-pitched din. His heart pounding, he searched for the source of the unprompted raucous symphony, wondering what could have inspired such bedlam.

The gates to the fortress had been flung wide open, the passageway into the heart of the citadel lined with immaculately dressed guards who snapped to attention at the shouted commands that were barely audible against the frenzy of sound. From the darkness of the gatehouse the Maharajah emerged to address his army, and Jack watched in awe as the man he had begun to think of as a friend entered his domain with all the great panoply of a powerful ruler.

The Maharajah was seated on the back of an enormous elephant. The creature's grey hide was thickly covered in silver traces that shimmered and shone as the animal emerged into the early-morning sunlight that was just beginning to stream across the fortress. Its head was painted in fabulous patterns, bold crimson and scarlet swirls intertwined with gold and silver ornaments to create an intricate display. Its tiny eyes were surrounded with wide white bands, an extra pair of huge staring eyes making the beast appear like a monster from a fairy tale, a creature from another world summoned forth by the great power of the Maharajah.

The Maharajah sat high in a splendid golden howdah. He was dressed in the same crimson robes he had worn when presenting Jack with the sword that he still wore at his hip. He looked every bit the magisterial ruler, the very epitome of a foreign king. Everything about him appeared almost other-worldly, as if he were a creation of divine power imbued with earthly life, a child of the gods given leave to rule mortal men.

Jack heard Isabel draw in a sharp breath as she saw the cause of such frantic devotion. It was hard to equate the magnificent ruler in front of them with the man they had so often seen dressed in the simple garb of an ordinary soldier. The contrast was astonishing, and Jack could not truly believe he had once sat on the Maharajah's council, at the heart of his inner circle.

The elephant walked calmly into the sunlight, beginning a long procession that would bring the Maharajah into full view of his assembled army. This was grandeur on an impressive scale, and Jack wondered if he had been right to be so confident that the British at Bhundapur could withstand an assault by such a force as he was witnessing. Isabel was not the only one frightened by what they saw.

'Okay, laddie. Time to get you two out of here.'

Jack looked down and saw Subedar Khan glaring firmly back at him. This time he intended to do exactly as he was told.

The Maharajah was stirring his men into a frenzy. He stood high above them, haranguing them in their own tongue, exhorting them to be ready for battle, to take the fight to the white-faced invader who threatened to rip their land apart. Jack had never heard him talk with such powerful invective. He spoke like a man possessed, his wild gestures and bold oration in stark contrast to the mild, sophisticated man who had treated Jack and Isabel with such good humour. Jack knew then that he had made the right decision in asking to leave.

'Cover your faces. Quickly now.' Subedar Khan handed over two of the silk bands they had seen being given out to the assembling warriors. It was good advice. More than one swarthy face had started to stare in their direction. The Maharajah was urging his army to slay their new enemy, and it made no sense to present themselves as an easy target for the wrath that was building so quickly.

Jack could feel the strain in the air, like the tension that built before a summer's thunderstorm. He sensed the danger, as did Subedar Khan, who beckoned to a detachment of his guards to form a protective cordon around Jack and Isabel.

'Let's go.' Jack bowed low in the saddle, speaking into the ear of the subedar, who had remained close to his stirrup.

The blue-uniformed guards led them away, skulking around the edge of the inner wall, doing their best to ignore the building hatred. The army began to chant, the deep, rhythmic sound coming in pulsating waves as the men responded to the call to war. It hammered into the small party as they scurried away, the noise more terrifying than any Jack had heard before, even the sound of the huge Russian columns paling in comparison.

The dark gatehouse was cold after the warmth of the morning sun, the sudden chill shocking against their exposed flesh. Yet it was a relief to be away from the dreadful keening, the thick stone walls deadening the oppressive sound of the army's visceral chant.

'Ride quickly, laddie. Do not stop for anything.' Subedar Khan offered the final words of advice as they passed through the immense outer gates and on to the long, twisting ramp that led down to the wide plain surrounding the fortress.

Jack nodded his thanks before jabbing his spurs into the flanks of his horse. It was time to ride, to escape the refuge they had sought so willingly. The palace that had given him so much was now the heart of his enemy's strength.

He had made his choice. He could not betray his country, no matter what penalties he faced. He was a redcoat, and nothing could change that. War had come, and Jack had chosen his side.

The Maharajah of Sawadh had become his enemy.

Chapter Thirty

The sound of polite laughter and the chime of cut crystal were clearly audible over the chirp and buzz of the thousands of insects that had come alive as soon as the sun had set. The bungalow in front of them was ablaze with light, the shadowy forms of people flitting across the drawn curtains as they moved within.

Jack turned to look at Isabel, wanting to savour the moment. He knew it would be the last time he would be able to look at her so freely. The sense of impending doom was heavy upon him, but he strode towards Proudfoot's bungalow nonetheless. He had made his choice.

The journey had exhausted them. He had forced the pace, making them ride through all but the very hottest hours of the day. They had encountered no interference, and seen barely a sign of another living being. Jack sensed the Maharajah's hand in their eventless journey. Whether it was to preserve Isabel's skin or to ensure the delivery of his dire warning he was not sure, but he felt a sense of relief as they finally made it to the British cantonment at Bhundapur.

'Wait here, if you please, sir.' Colour Sergeant Hughes spoke respectfully yet firmly. The four redcoats he had brought with him stamped to a halt, the presence of their colour sergeant necessitating the utmost attention to their drill.

Jack noticed Hughes's furrowed brow. He did not know what reaction he would get from the men he had commanded for barely more than a day. He could read little in the colour sergeant's expression, the man's demeanour as calm as it had been the first time he had met his bogus captain.

He nodded his understanding, and watched as the 24th's senior non-commissioned officer marched up the steps to Proudfoot's home, his bearing erect and disciplined, as if the arrival of the most wanted felon in all of Sawadh was an everyday occurrence. He risked a surreptitious sniff at his armpit. He stank. The hard ride had left him reeking, his shirt and breeches stained and rank. He had decided against wearing his blue lancer's uniform. There was no sense in reminding Proudfoot of his role in the Maharajah's army; it would only add to the man's belief that he was a traitor. So he had hidden it, bundling it up and pushing it deep under some rocks a mile from the cantonment. He still wore his talwar, the curved blade hanging at his hip, and now he reached across, running his fingers over the coarse sharkskin hilt, seeking reassurance as he prepared to welcome his fate.

'Jack.' Isabel whispered his name. 'Everything will be all right. We are doing the right thing.'

Jack smiled at her reassurance. It was some indication of how much she had grown up that she now sought to support him despite her own misgivings. 'Whatever happens, I don't regret my choice,' he replied.

'Neither do I.' Isabel's face betrayed her own anxiety. He was not the only one meeting his fate that day. They had talked on the journey. He knew she faced little physical danger, her punishment likely to be nothing more than her father's ire followed by a rapid departure for the backwaters of an English county. But disgrace and ruin were no small punishment, and Jack thought he could understand just what it was costing her. Her duty to her kin and to her countrymen had come first, even though she would be forced to pay the price for her wanton behaviour for years to come, perhaps for the rest of her life.

In Proudfoot's bungalow, the sound of polite conversation froze, the shadowed room falling into silence as the tall colour sergeant interrupted the soirée to deliver his news. Jack could picture the faces as the first whiff of scandal whipped around the room. Like vultures spying a fresh corpse, the upper echelons of the cantonment's limited society would relish the occasion of Jack's disgrace. That the villain had returned to the scene of his crime was a juicy morsel that would only add to their enjoyment of the dish.

Proudfoot emerged to stand at the top of the steps. He was dressed in a crimson smoking jacket and he still held a crystal goblet of dark red wine the colour of old blood. If he was surprised to see Jack and Isabel, it did not show on his urbane features. He even managed a thin smile, the kind a gracious host reserved for an uninvited guest.

'Mr Lark, so very good of you to return. Miss Youngsummers, I am delighted to see you back safely.'

He stood straighter as his guests pushed to the door behind him, elbows and sharp heels working furiously to secure a better view of the entertainment. Jack saw Major Dutton, his florid face flushed from the heat and from the effects of the first of the evening's sharpeners. Kingsley was there too, but he hung back, as if unwilling to be seen, or perhaps simply bored with the evening's turn of events. Jack caught a glimpse of Fenris before his face disappeared from the throng. He could only wonder at how their first meeting would turn out, but he was certain it would not be pleasant, for him at any rate.

'I have sent a runner for your father, Miss Youngsummers. I am sure he will be as delighted to see you as I am,' Proudfoot continued, clearly relishing the chance to be the lead actor on the stage. 'However, I'm afraid I doubt there is anyone here pleased to see *your* return, Mr Lark.'

Colour Sergeant Hughes emerged from the crowd. Major Proudfoot nodded in Jack's direction, and Hughes came down the stairs to stand a yard away from him. Jack felt the shackles of his former life slip around him with all the iron-hard resolution of the manacles that he was sure awaited him. He said nothing in reply to Proudfoot, merely standing by as if he were a fascinated spectator to the events unfurling around him. The only emotion he felt was one of disappointment that his arrival had created precisely the reaction he had expected.

Proudfoot, however, was clearly delighted by the turn the evening had taken, and he puffed himself up so that he would not let his audience down. 'Colour Sergeant Hughes. Have that man arrested and taken to the guardroom. He is to be watched at all times.' The dramatic words had the desired effect, and Jack could see the pleasure on Proudfoot's face as his guests welcomed his order with a gasp of gleeful horror.

'Sir!' Hughes stiffened to attention. Whatever the non-commissioned officer thought was well hidden behind the dignified facade of a British sergeant, the twitch of his thick moustache the sole reaction to the command to arrest a fellow redcoat.

'No!' Isabel shouted the single word firmly. 'Major Proudfoot. Mr Lark saved my life. He is not a common criminal and you must not treat him so.'

Proudfoot appeared genuinely taken aback by Isabel's firm denial of his orders. He turned and handed his glass to Major Dutton, who had arrived to stand at his shoulder, before carefully walking down the steps.

'Miss Youngsummers. I cannot begin to imagine what you have gone through. It must have been a traumatic experience for someone of your tender years.' Proudfoot spoke in the oily tones of the professional diplomat. 'I can only hope that the love of your father and the opportunity to rest will allow you to recover your senses.'

'Damn you, Proudfoot.' Isabel stamped her foot, her mouth twisting in vexation as her oath drew a sharp intake of breath from the watching crowd. 'Jack came here of his own free will to warn you.'

Proudfoot winced at Isabel's language before turning to face Jack. 'It is clear you have had some significant effect on Miss Youngsummers.' He chuckled at the notion before continuing. 'So you have come to warn me? That really is very magnanimous of you, given your straitened circumstances. It must be something of grave importance to risk having your neck stretched for it.' He smiled at his own pun, turning to acknowledge the one or two men in the audience who chuckled at his wordplay.

Jack watched Proudfoot closely. He could see the delight in the major's sparkling eyes. It would feel good to puncture his conceit.

'The Maharajah of Sawadh has gathered his forces. He plans to attack Bhundapur. As of yesterday, you are at war.' Jack spoke softly, lowering his voice so his announcement did not carry to the watching crowd.

Proudfoot absorbed the news without a twitch. The silence drew out, the official not even deigning to reply. His guests had spilled out on to the wide veranda that surrounded his bungalow, and now they pressed forward, anxious to listen to the hushed exchange taking place between the cantonment's commander and the charlatan who had been the topic of nearly every whispered conversation for weeks in the news-starved community.

Then Proudfoot began to laugh. There was no shred of enjoyment in the dry, humourless sound. It was the noise of a man suddenly realising he had managed to carry off an outrageous bluff at cards.

'You are not surprised?' Jack managed to keep the disappointment from his voice. He had staked his life on the news, hoping that the warning would keep him from the scaffold.

'Surprised! Why on earth would I be surprised?' Proudfoot spun on the spot, suddenly unable to stand still as he savoured the news. 'Why, it is exactly as I planned.' He spoke quietly so the audience on the veranda could not hear his words, but the triumph in his voice was unmistakable.

Jack looked at Isabel. Her expression betrayed her distress at the official's reaction to the news they had ridden so hard and so far to deliver.

'You planned this?' Her face was white as he spoke.

'Of course.' Proudfoot was all scorn now. 'Why else would I give the damn man the news that his kingdom will lapse when he dies? I wanted him to react.'

'Why?' Jack asked the question, yet he already knew the answer. His stomach churned as the full scale of Proudfoot's ambition became clear, the sour taste of having been fooled bitter in his mouth.

'Because only then can I crush him.' Proudfoot's voice was dispassionate as he discussed the death of hundreds of men. 'How else was I to draw the sting of this damned viper? I have not long left here and I simply have to get this done before I go. One has to think of one's career. How can I compete with Nicolson and the rest if I fail to deliver this pathetic little place?'

'You bastard.' Jack hissed the words, stunned at the man's ruthlessness.

'I shall take that as a compliment, coming from you.' Proudfoot's voice was cold. He turned to the colour sergeant. 'Bring me this villain's sword and have him put in manacles.' He offered Jack a mocking bow. 'Welcome home, Mr Lark.'

There was nothing more to be said. Even Isabel was stunned to silence. Neither offered a word of protest as Jack was turned and led away by the four-man escort brought to ensure he did not escape for a second time.

Jack and Isabel had ridden hard to warn their countrymen of the impending attack. Yet it had been Proudfoot's plan all along to drive the Maharajah to war. Hundreds would now die, sacrificed to a single man's ambition.

Jack sat alone in the darkness. The guardroom had a single cell set aside for detaining errant redcoats. It was windowless and boasted nothing more than a simple cot with a straw mattress, a single thin blanket and a rusty piss-pot. The floorboards were stained and scuffed, whilst the once white walls were scarred with the markings of the dozens of men who had picked and scraped at them to leave some evidence of their passing.

It was hard not to notice the contrast with the gilded cage he and Isabel had been shown to when they threw themselves on the Maharajah's mercy, but at least there was no pretence here, and it was certainly an improvement on the storeroom prison used by the bandits. Jack grunted as he considered his fate. He was heartily sick of being held captive, but he was beginning to suspect he would be seeing the inside of many more prison cells in the coming months. For any hope of reprieve had been cruelly dashed, his naïve assumption that by delivering warning of the Maharajah's attack he might somehow be forgiven his crimes now proven to have been utterly false. He had been wrong to think that warning the British would save him, just as he had been wrong to think that serving the Maharajah would offer him a new life.

Yet as much as he regretted his fate, he could not see how he could have stayed with the Maharajah. He tried to picture riding at the head of the blue-coated lancers against the red-coated soldiers of the Queen. It was an impossible notion. Lakshmi had been right. For better or worse he was a redcoat. He had done what his conscience dictated, and now he would have to wait and see what penalty he would pay for staying loyal to the country of his birth.

He heard footsteps outside his cell, the heavy tread of more than one man loud on the hard wooden floor beyond the locked door. He couldn't make out what was said, the low voices speaking too quietly for their words to penetrate the thick door.

He rose to his feet as he heard the key turn in the lock, his heart pounding a little faster as the door opened, revealing the face of the man who had come to disturb his peace.

'Hello, Lark.' The voice was laced with derision, the haughty upper-class drawl relishing Jack's incarceration.

The door was closed quietly and the two burly redcoats who had followed the man into the room took up station either side of Jack. None of the men were armed, but Jack sensed that violence had crept in along with the three red-coated soldiers. The two at his sides took a firm grip on his arms, their fingers digging into his flesh, forcing him to stand facing the officer who had ordered them into position.

With his arms held he could not protect himself, and the fist came at him fast, driven by weeks of loathing. It smashed into his undefended face. The explosion of agony drove into his skull, the pain flashing white-hot across his vision. He felt the blood gush from his nose, the heat of it warm on his lips.

Lieutenant Arthur Fenris stood back, blood smeared thickly over the white of his knuckles, a sneer of satisfaction on his thin face.

'Welcome home, you bastard.' He spat the words as he lashed out again, both fists flailing hard at Jack's body. He kept on punching long after Jack had been beaten senseless, his hatred leaving no room for mercy.

Chapter Thirty-one

———◆•◆———

'Gentlemen. Your attention please.'

Major Proudfoot looked around the room. He had gathered his officers in his bungalow, seating them around the dining table, which had been hastily cleared of the detritus of that evening's entertainment. The cut-glass crystal and phalanxes of wine bottles had been replaced with charts and ledgers as the officers began to plan the defence of Bhundapur.

He looked at each officer in turn, fixing them with a piercing stare. Major Dutton's face might have been flushed scarlet from the bottle of claret that he had consumed to dull the boredom of another suffocating evening, but his eyes were sharp. The most senior of Dutton's three lieutenants, a garrulous Scotsman named Campbell, met Proudfoot's gaze with calm confidence. The youngest of the subalterns, Lieutenant Gartry, a ginger-haired nineteen-year-old whose clergyman father had still not forgiven his only son for refusing to join the church, looked nervous, his tongue flickering over his cherry-red lips in short, darting movements. He failed to meet Proudfoot's stare, his eyes downcast as if that would somehow save him from saying anything.

The last of Dutton's lieutenants, Lieutenant Spencer, a tall, grave man who looked more suited to the sombre trade of an undertaker than the violent world of being a soldier, gazed down on the preparations like an ancient vulture wondering if it could raise the strength to join in a squabble over a rotting carcass. Yet at least he appeared to be giving the discussion his full attention, unlike Captain Kingsley, who stood and walked away, preferring to concentrate on filling his glass with more of the major's port rather than contribute to whatever plan his fellow officers were concocting.

'As you now know, we face a perilous few days.' Proudfoot spoke in an earnest tone, only the slightest furrow in his brow revealing his annoyance at Kingsley's lack of attention. 'It is time to show that blackguard of a maharajah that he cannot stand against Her Majesty's authority. He must be brought to heel and I am relying on you to do it. Dutton, what say you?'

'A fortress.' Major Dutton began to outline his proposal in the clipped, controlled tones of a man sure of his strategy. 'We build a defensive wall here. The 24th's barracks can form the right flank, with the storerooms as a strong point on the south-east corner.' He thrust a podgy finger at the corner of his scribbled pencil drawing, smudging the thin line that denoted the western wall of his fortress in the process. 'That gives us a field of fire here and here' – again the thick finger poked at the paper, leaving behind more sweaty fingerprints – 'and strong points here and here.'

The look on his fellow officers' faces revealed both their understanding and their approval of the plan. Dutton commanded three companies of the 12th Bengal Native Infantry, each led by one of his lieutenants. All were young, ambitious men who had purchased a commission in the East India Company as a means of securing what they hoped would be a glittering and financially rewarding future. Each was the sole white officer in their company. Their subalterns were all native men of long experience who had worked their way through the ranks, earning each promotion through long and blemish-free service. None had been asked to attend the officers' conference.

'Write it up, Gartry, there's a good fellow.' Dutton gave the order as he finished explaining his outline for the defence of the cantonment.

The younger officer looked relieved to have been given such an undemanding role, and he pulled over some blank paper so he could begin a neater version of Dutton's plan.

Dutton nodded in approval. He looked at his third subaltern, who had so far remained silent. 'Lieutenant Spencer, begin listing the provisions we will need to bring into the fortress.'

'Very good, sir.' The grey-faced lieutenant picked up a bottle of ink and a steel pen, his face still as neutral as it had been when Dutton first announced that the cantonment was about to be attacked.

'Kingsley?' Dutton sought to bring the commander of the 24th's single company into the discussion. 'How would you suggest we dispose our forces?'

Kingsley walked slowly towards the table, contemplating the last remnants of port in his tiny glass. 'What's that you say, Dutton?'

'Our forces.' Dutton made little effort to contain the tetchy note in his reply. As ever, Kingsley's supercilious demeanour nettled the major. He had only been in the cantonment for a short time, but he had made it clear from the start that he looked down on the four officers who held commissions granted by the East India Company rather than by the Queen. Dutton had done his best to be open and welcoming, but his patience was wearing thin. 'How would you suggest we deploy the men?'

Kingsley drained his glass and moved forward to peer at Dutton's scribbled map. 'The 24th will hold the barracks. I suggest your men hold the rest of the perimeter. If you can.'

Dutton spluttered at the captain's choice of words. 'What the devil do you mean, if we can?'

Kingsley sneered disdainfully. 'I doubt your damn sepoys will stand. My men will hold the strong points and I would suggest you stay close enough to make a dash for our ranks when your fellows bolt. You, Spencer or whatever your damn name is,' Kingsley fluttered a finger in the lieutenant's direction, 'make sure the ammunition and spare muskets are in my men's barracks. The last thing we need is to be left without enough damn cartridges.'

Dutton snapped his pencil as he struggled to contain his rage. 'How dare you, Kingsley! My men will stand and fight, goddammit. I bet my very life on it.'

'Well then.' Kingsley didn't bat an eyelid at the major's angry display. 'I rather fancy you'll get your chance to do just that pretty soon, don't you?'

'Gentlemen, please.' Major Proudfoot had left his officers, moving to sit in a fine leather wing-backed armchair facing away from the table. He spoke in the mild tones of a gentleman in his club ordering a peg and soda. 'We cannot waste time arguing amongst ourselves.'

Dutton looked like he was about to explode. 'That damned man made a very serious accusation. I'll not stand by and let him insult my command.'

'Dutton, please.' Proudfoot crossed his legs as he spoke, folding his hands into his lap. 'Your idea of establishing a fortress is a fine one. But do you not think it a little tame?'

'Tame?'

'Well, I rather think it looks as though we are skulking away, don't you agree?'

'Do you have a better idea?' Dutton threw the remnants of his snapped pencil on to the table, his temper threatening to bubble over.

Proudfoot formed his fingers into a steeple, holding them to his lips as if mulling over the problem. The officers waited with growing impatience for his answer, his enigmatic silence picking at their already thinly stretched nerves.

The door opened, breaking the silence. Lieutenant Fenris walked into the room. His right hand was heavily bandaged, the dull red stain of blood a dark shadow against the clean white of the dressing.

'I say, sorry I'm late. I had a little business to attend to. Did I miss anything?'

Proudfoot smiled indulgently at the junior officer's nonchalant confidence. 'The Maharajah is going to attack us, Arthur. We are planning our defence.'

Fenris smiled at the announcement, clearly not shocked by the revelation. 'Well that's a jolly good show. It's about time we brought the bugger to his knees. So what's the plan?'

The officers looked at each other, the tension obvious in the glare Dutton shot towards Captain Kingsley.

'There is some debate on the matter.' Proudfoot offered the bland explanation with a humourless smile. 'Would you care to venture an opinion?'

'Well it's damn simple, isn't it?' Fenris helped himself to a glass of port from the opened bottle left on a side table. 'Beat the buggers black and blue and send them scurrying away with their tail between their bloody legs.'

'In open battle or in a defensive stand here at the cantonment?' Proudfoot enquired reasonably.

'What? In the open, of course.' Fenris held his hand to his head in a dramatic gesture of understanding. 'Dutton wants to stay here, don't you, old boy?'

'I think that would be the sensible course of action, yes.' Dutton bristled at the young officer's theatricals.

'Of course you do. Much safer.' Fenris smiled thinly. 'But that's all a bit dull. Sitting here blasting away from behind a wall won't make great reading, will it? I say we fight them properly. Like the old duke would have done. Engage them in battle and beat the living daylights out of the impudent buggers.'

Kingsley walked to his subaltern's side, snatching away the bottle of port that the younger officer was threatening to empty all on his own. 'Fenris is right. We should fight them in the open. There is no need to hide away from a bunch of bloody bandits. We find them, we fire a few volleys and they run for their sorry lives. It really is awfully simple.'

Proudfoot smiled wolfishly at the advice. 'You are a man after my own heart, Kingsley. Indeed you are.' He rose athletically to his feet as if suddenly revitalised by the new plan. 'That does sound somewhat grander, don't you think, Dutton?'

Dutton opened his mouth to snap back an answer before thinking better of it, biting off his angry words before they were said. He looked down and studied the table, using the distraction to compose himself. When he turned to face Proudfoot once again, his expression was calmer.

'The Maharajah has more than two thousand men.' He spoke quietly. 'Most of those are mounted cavalry, but even his infantry outnumber us many times over. If we venture into open country,

we will make their task easier and ours a damn sight more difficult. We have neither cavalry to protect our flanks nor cannon to
engage them at a distance. It would be a close-run affair.'

Kingsley snorted, his opinion of Dutton's analysis clear. He
walked across the room taking the port with him, refilling his glass
as he walked and downing the heavy fortified wine in a single
mouthful.

Proudfoot was more vocal in his condemnation. 'Major Dutton.
I have lost count of the times you have told anyone who cared to
listen that the Maharajah's forces amount to nothing. Why such
timidity now?'

Dutton cleared his throat before dodging the question. 'It is my
professional opinion that we must fight a defensive action. To
engage such superior numbers in the open is foolhardy.'

Proudfoot nodded wisely before adopting a more formal tone.
'Thank you for your advice, Major.' He turned and addressed the
captain of the 24th Foot, who had refilled his glass and now sipped
more cautiously at the contents. 'Captain Kingsley. You have heard
Major's Dutton's conclusion. What say you?'

'My opinion hasn't changed. Fight them in the open and get the
damn thing over with. That rabble will soon run when the lead starts
to fly.' He turned and sneered sarcastically at Dutton. 'I bet my life
on it.'

Proudfoot nodded again. 'I'm of a mind to agree with you,
Captain Kingsley.' His grave expression did not sit well with the
gleam of triumph in his eyes. 'My decision is made. We will fight
the Maharajah in the open. Build your fortress, Dutton, if it makes
you feel any better. We will need somewhere to corral the women
and the sick. You can leave half a company here as a reserve. But we
shall fight like British soldiers, not some bloody Frenchmen.' He
glared at Dutton, daring him to continue to argue.

Dutton swallowed hard as he was overruled. 'Very well, sir. I
shall see that my men are ready to march.'

Proudfoot was clearly delighted to have won the battle of wills so
easily. 'Thank you.'

Yet the commander of the 12th was not quite finished. 'What of
the impostor, Lark?'

Proudfoot's face creased into a scowl. 'What of him?'

'Where is he to be during the action?'

'Move him into the storerooms. He can rot there for all I care.'

Dutton reached forward, taking the two halves of the broken pencil, holding them carefully together as if trying to repair the damage. 'I would have thought that was a waste.'

'A waste!' Fenris interrupted before Proudfoot could reply. 'The man will hang. Who cares where the bastard goes.'

'I do.' Dutton's eyes flashed in anger as he sought to enforce his will over his superior. 'He is the only man here to have seen the Maharajah's forces up close, and the only man who has actually been involved in some action.'

'Only if you believe that cock-and-bull story he concocted.' Fenris snapped his reply.

Proudfoot lifted a hand, silencing the junior officer. 'Hush, Arthur. Go on, Dutton.'

'Whether or not you believe his story, he is still the only man to have seen the enemy. He is too valuable to be ignored.'

Proudfoot scowled as he thought on Dutton's words. 'You are right. Speak to him, Dutton. See what he knows.'

'And what can I offer him?' Dutton smiled, but with no warmth. 'Why should he help us? He knows he is to hang.'

Proudfoot nodded. He paced across the room, clearly deep in thought, before slumping back into his favourite armchair.

'You are quite right, Dutton. Lark could be a valuable asset. It would be foolish of us to dismiss him out of hand.' He pondered the matter further before smiling as he found a solution to his liking. 'Offer to let him fight. The man is supposed to be a redcoat, after all. Let him ply his trade in his true rank. Who knows, if he proves himself in battle, perhaps it will go well for him. If he falls, well, no one is going to lament the passing of a damned villain.' Proudfoot arched his eyebrow at Lieutenant Fenris to make sure he had got the message before picking up the most recently arrived copy of *The Times*, which had been neatly folded and left on the small drum table near his chair. 'If he agrees to provide the information, then he can join the 24th.'

Dutton nodded, glad to have secured one victory, albeit a small one. He returned to the sketch of his fortress, oblivious to the look of delight on Fenris' face, as he understood his commander's pointed comment.

The commander of the British forces had made his decision.

Chapter Thirty-two

'Up you get, sir.'

Jack obeyed the corporal's order as quickly as his abused body would allow. He had been lying on the lumpy mattress in misery, battling with the pain and wondering how long he would be left there. The interruption had come as something of a relief.

'What's going on?' He sucked air through his teeth as his body protested at being moved. He recognised Corporal Jones from his one day spent with the company, the soldier's Welsh accent a welcome touch of something familiar.

'Sorry, sir. I ain't allowed to talk to you.' Jones offered a smile before he ignored his orders and gave Jack some explanation. 'The ruperts want you, sir. I don't know any more than that. I am to let you clean yourself up and then take you to Major Dutton's office.' Jones clearly felt safer calling him 'sir', and Jack did not have the strength to tell him that the title no longer applied.

'Do you know why?' He was curious despite his pain.

'No idea, sir. But then who knows what goes on in the head of a bloody officer?' The corporal chuckled as if struck by an odd notion. 'Except you might, I reckon.'

Jack tried to smile. He felt the stirring of hope. He might be a villain, but if the corporal was indicative of his fellows, it appeared the redcoats bore him no ill will. Now he had been summoned, and anything was preferable to lying alone in the gloom, so he let himself be led out of the room and into the darkness that had smothered the cantonment now that the sun had long set.

'Mr Lark. Sit down.'

Dutton rose to his feet as Jack was ushered into the room. It was close to one in the morning, but the major was still keen-eyed and looked workmanlike in his shirtsleeves. Jack took the chair opposite, wincing as he lowered himself carefully down, and waited to see why he had been summoned in the middle of the night.

The major chewed on his lip as he considered him. 'Good God, what happened to you?'

'I fell down some stairs.'

Dutton snorted. 'What bloody stairs?' He shook his head. 'Fenris?'

Jack nodded.

'The blackguard. Well, it won't happen again. I'll see to that.'

Jack didn't care to acknowledge the promise. He eased himself into as comfortable a position as he could and waited for Dutton to speak.

Dutton returned his attention to his paperwork, leaving Jack to sit in uncomfortable silence. Several minutes passed before the major finally shoved the papers to one side and looked at him.

'It doesn't feel right. Calling you Lark.' Dutton's manner was bluff. It was clear he was uncomfortable, as though he was not sure how he should deal with an impostor.

Jack was in no mood to make the major's life easier, so he simply sat in silence, returning the scrutinising glare with calm indifference. Dutton's office was cramped, and Jack's head bumped against the wall behind him. The narrow desk had plainly been in use for decades, its pockmarked surface betraying its long service to the East India Company. The contrast with the magisterial splendour of Proudfoot's rooms was not lost on him.

Dutton frowned at Jack's silence. 'You look damn composed for a man facing a dance on the bloody scaffold.'

'I'm not on it yet.'

Dutton guffawed at the glib reply. 'You are a brave fellow, Jack. I knew it as soon as I clapped eyes on you. But this impostor business, took me by surprise, that did. I would never have thought you were a damned charlatan.'

'None of you did. Not even Proudfoot.'

'Indeed.' Dutton shook his head as if clearing away an unpleasant memory. 'It's nice to see that damned man make a mistake. He may turn out to be human after all.' He looked at Jack warily under a furrowed brow, suddenly cautious about revealing his true feelings towards his superior officer. Jack didn't bat an eyelid. It was no surprise that Dutton and Proudfoot did not see eye to eye.

'Why am I here, Dutton?'

'To business, then.' Dutton seemed relieved. 'I want to know everything about the Maharajah and his army. Numbers. Weapons. Everything.'

'So now I am to be treated as a spy?' Jack sensed the irony of his new role. The Maharajah's vizier may have been right after all.

'Yes, if you like. The Maharajah is going to attack. You told us that much already. Now I need details. I want to know who I am going to meet in battle.'

'No.' Jack spoke the denial quietly, yet there was no mistaking the force in the word. He had hoped that the warning about the Maharajah's impending attack would save him. Proudfoot's reaction had made it clear he had been wrong. He saw no point in offering what little information he possessed without receiving anything in return. Dutton plainly wanted it, so Jack would wait to see what bargain could be struck.

Dutton chewed on his moustache for a moment before he spoke. 'I knew you would say that. I told Proudfoot the very same. He has allowed me to offer you a deal.'

'A deal?'

'Tell us all you know and you'll be rewarded.'

Jack snorted. 'Bollocks.'

Dutton grinned at Jack's forthright phrase. 'You'll be allowed to fight.'

'I can't see Proudfoot trusting me with a bandook. What's to stop me shooting the bastard between the eyes the moment I get the chance?'

'You will be given a weapon, Jack. You'll be allowed to fight with the 24th. You can help us beat the Maharajah.'

'How the hell is that supposed to work?'

'You would be a redcoat. You'd fight in the ranks.'

Jack understood immediately. 'And likely spare you all the shame of a court-martial. It would be more convenient if I died in the battle, wouldn't it just. No messy trial. No unpleasantness. Just an unmarked grave and bang, there you go. No impostor. No scandal.'

'If I were in your shoes, I'd jump at the offer. I'd rather take my chances in battle than face being strung up like a common thief.'

'So you're doing me a favour? Like I already said, bollocks.'

Dutton sat back in his chair. 'Help us, Jack.'

'Help you? I'm a bloody villain. Why would you need my help?'

Dutton rubbed a hand across his face, as if trying to wipe away the exhaustion. 'Because we need you.' He sounded drained as he confessed the true situation. 'Proudfoot and his lapdog Fenris have decided we are to fight the Maharajah in the open. That damn fool Kingsley agrees. They want some grand battle.'

'The fucking fools.' Jack shook his head in disbelief.

'Proudfoot is already composing the dispatch he'll be able to send the Governor. He wants a glorious victory.'

'And it's up to us to give it to them.'

'They think it will be easy. Kingsley believes the Maharajah and his men will take one look at us standing in line and run for the bloody hills.'

'Never. He's coming for blood. He won't run.'

'I know. Which is why I need your help. We need every mother's son who is fit to fight if we are to stand a chance. My lieutenants are already arming every bloody cook and bottle-washer in this damn place. Help me, Jack.'

Jack heard the pleading tone. He had given up his place in the Maharajah's court to return to his countrymen. Could he really sit by and watch them be destroyed?

'What happens to me after the battle?'

'After the battle?' Dutton snorted. 'Who knows what will happen to any of us. The Maharajah has over two thousand men. I'm not so bloody sure we can think about after the battle.'

Jack nodded at the honest reply. It was clear what he had to do.

He had chosen his side. He would tell Dutton everything he knew and then take his place in the battle line and fight as an ordinary soldier in an effort to snatch victory from the face of certain defeat.

He was a redcoat. It was all he knew.

They marched well before dawn. The four companies formed one long column that snaked through the cantonment before turning east. The 24th Foot led the way, with Dutton's three companies from the 12th Bengal Native Infantry forced to march in the cloud of dust kicked up by their heavy boots.

There was no fanfare to announce their departure, only the martial call of the bugle and the rhythmic beat of the drum driving them forward. The redcoats sang as they marched, their deep voices lifting as they bellowed out the 24th's regimental march, 'The Warwickshire Lad'. They might not have been as good a choir as Reverend Youngsummers would have hoped for, but they sang with vigour, if not with harmony.

> Ye Warwickshire lads and ye lasses,
> See what at our Jubilee passes;
> Come revel away, rejoice and be glad,
> For the lad of all lads was a Warwickshire lad,
> And the lad was a Warwickshire lad.
> Warwickshire lad! All be glad,
> For the lad of all lads was a Warwickshire lad.

They had no colours to lead them; the pride of the battalion was back with the bulk of the regiment far away in the Punjab. They had only their officers to inspire them, their sergeants and corporals to rally to.

Fewer than four hundred redcoats marched to do battle with the Maharajah's army of more than two thousand.

Chapter Thirty-three

The redcoats waited patiently in line, standing at ease now that they had been ordered to a halt. Colour Sergeant Hughes was on the far left of the line, so the redcoats who stood in the centre files could mutter to one another in low voices without being detected. The march had been short, but it had become increasingly wearing as the column marched and counter-marched, often retracing its own tracks as the commanders fussed about the position of their troops. They had finally settled on the current position just after the sun had begun to rise, the redcoats belatedly ordered into the two-man-deep line in which they would be expected to fight.

Jack approved of the officers' choice of battlefield. The redcoats' line stretched across a valley, its flanks securely tethered against sharply rising ground to either side. The ground to the front was open, with the well-worn path that led to Bhundapur meandering through the centre. It gave the thin red line a good field of fire, the Maharajah's army forced to advance along the narrowing valley if they wanted to bring the smaller British force to battle. The steep sides acted like a funnel, compressing any attacking force whilst denying the opportunity for enemy cavalry to manoeuvre around the redcoats' flanks. Dutton and Kingsley might not have agreed on how to fight, but they had at least chosen good ground.

The cantonment was only around half a mile to the south-west, with the walls of the city of Bhundapur a similar distance to the west. Once out of the valley, the ground opened to a wide plain, and Jack offered a silent prayer that the redcoats would be able to turn back the enemy tide without the need to retreat. Any withdrawal into the open ground would be fraught with danger. If the redcoats were forced to retreat, they faced destruction, the wide-open space the perfect killing ground for the vast numbers of enemy cavalry.

Dutton had got his wish. A makeshift company had been formed from the many supernumeraries in the cantonment. These rough-and-ready soldiers stood guard behind the walls of the temporary fortress Dutton's sepoys had constructed around the 24th's barracks. The storerooms had been packed with ammunition and the cantonment's few women and children were safe in the barrack buildings. Dutton had planned for disaster with the same meticulous care that Proudfoot was putting into the preparation of his victory dispatch.

Jack wondered how Isabel would be coping with being confined. He knew she would rather have been allowed to ride with the fighting column, and it brought a smile to his face as he imagined her arguing with Proudfoot when she had been ordered to remain behind.

The thought of Isabel sent a spark of anger through Jack's soul. They had both paid a high price for remaining loyal to the country of their birth. He pushed the rage down, storing it deep inside, searching for the patience he would need. He had witnessed the destructive power of battle before. Nothing was certain once the violent struggle began, and anything was possible in the chaos that would follow. He would have to bide his time and wait.

'My eye, would you look at that? Kingsley looks like he needs a good shit.'

Jack kept his expression neutral as the man in the file next to him offered his judgement on the company's new commander. Unaware of the acidic remark, Captain Kingsley slid from the saddle of his grey mare and took up the proper position for a company commander on the right of the redcoats' line.

'I'm sure Fenris would offer to wipe his fucking arse for him.' Corporal Jones, in charge of that section of redcoats, added his own ribald observation.

Jack smiled. He found nothing odd in the men being so vocal in their criticism of their officer. Redcoats would always grumble the moment they got the chance. Just as they would fight with vicious determination when their officers removed the leash and sent them at the enemy.

'So what do we call you now we aren't supposed to call you "sir"?' The soldier to Jack's left nudged his arm, interrupting his thoughts. His sing-song accent reminded Jack of a Welshman who had fought in his company at the Alma.

'Jack. My name's Jack.'

The Welsh soldier clicked his tongue. 'We can't call you that, boyo. There's already a Jack in the company. That bloody Englishman over there.' He nodded in the direction of a ferret-faced man on the far right of the company.

'There's too many bloody Englishmen around here, if you ask me.' Corporal Jones chuckled as he offered the barbed comment. Jack smiled, enjoying the banter. The transformation in Jones was fascinating. Around officers he had been ill at ease. Now, back in the ranks, he was clearly one of the company's most popular non-commissioned officers, enjoying a warm rapport with the men under his command.

'Corporal Jones never forgave his sister for marrying a boy from Bath.' Jack's new friend winked as he spoke confidingly. 'Isn't that right, Corp?'

'You talk too much, Jenkins.'

The redcoat was not put out by his corporal's instruction to be quiet. 'So what did your mates call you before you went and started impersonating a bloody rupert?' He was several inches shorter than Jack, as were most of the men in the company, with the pinched face that came from a childhood of hard work and not enough food, yet he had an open smile, and Jack was drawn to his good humour.

'Mud. They called me Mud.' It felt like a lifetime since he had heard the nickname, an obvious reference to the mudlarks who tried to eke out a living picking at the detritus that flowed down the River Thames.

Jenkins chuckled. 'So you're a bleeding Londoner!' He leant forward so he could peer along the line. 'Heh, Brown! We got one of your lot here.'

Jack saw another redcoat lean forward to join the conversation, his face creased into a scowl.

'Keep your voice down, you dozy Welshman.' Brown shook his head at the foolishness of his fellow redcoat. He fixed Jack with a rueful grin. 'Most of this bloody company is from up north, apart from those two Welsh chumps. Us Londoners need to stick together. So where you from?'

'Whitechapel. You?'

'Bow. Right shit-hole it was.'

'Private Brown! Silence in the ranks or you'll be on a charge.' Colour Sergeant Hughes stamped down on the idle conversation, his fierce glare settling on the last redcoat to speak.

Brown pulled his head back, but not before flashing Jenkins a filthy look.

Jack smiled at the exchange. It felt good to be back in the company of other soldiers. The red coat he had been given might not have been tailored to fit, nor was it made of the same fine scarlet weave as an officer's uniform. But it didn't come weighted with responsibility, the burden of command that accompanied the golden buttons and bullion epaulettes. For once, it was a relief to simply march in the ranks, following the directions of the officers and the sergeants.

'Company! Company attention!'

Colour Sergeant Hughes called his men to readiness. A handful of Proudfoot's vedettes were returning to the thin red line, their horses lathered in sweat from being ridden hard in the early-morning heat. They made straight for the gaggle of officers in the centre. The 24th were the right-most company in the line, with the three companies from the 12th Bengal Native Infantry arranged in order to their left. Dutton and Major Proudfoot stood in the middle of the four companies, with a handful of mounted native troopers waiting

patiently behind them, ready to act as scouts or to deliver orders
to the company commanders. Proudfoot had insisted that Lieutenant
Fenris also remain mounted, and he had been ordered to stay at
the political officer's side. His subaltern's abrupt promotion to
aide-de-camp went some way to explain Captain Kingsley's peevish
expression.

'Company! Company prepare to load!' Colour Sergeant Hughes
delivered the order with the clipped precision learnt in two decades
of soldiering. 'Load!'

The redcoats had stiffened to attention the moment they had
heard their senior non-commissioned officer draw breath. With the
final bellowed command still echoing around the confined valley,
they began the process of loading their muskets.

Jack followed their lead without hesitation, his movements
instinctive. In unison with the rest of the company he extracted a
fresh cartridge from the pouch at his waist, lifting it to his lips. He
bit off the bullet, the bitter, acrid taste of gunpowder just as he
remembered, then spat the heavy metal ball into the barrel of his
musket, following the procedure he had learnt through hours of
repetitive practice. It had been many months since he had loaded a
musket, but the memory came back without conscious thought, the
drill buried into his very being.

With their weapons loaded and primed, the redcoats were ready
to fight. They stared down the valley, looking away to the south.
Waiting for the first sight of the enemy. Waiting for battle.

Around Jack the men fidgeted and worried, fiddling with their kit
or picking at their uniforms. It was the time for fear to build and for
nerves to be stretched thin. Jack remembered the feelings he had
endured the night before the battle at the Alma River, the tension
that had gnawed deep in his guts, the terror that had built so that
when the redcoats stormed the Russians' redoubt, he had been
screaming his horror aloud.

Somehow he had contained his fear. In its place had been the
dreadful rage that had driven him in a mad assault on the Russian
columns. After the battle, he had been terrified by what he had done,
yet alongside that emotion he felt pride at what had been unleashed,
a sordid joy that he buried deep in his corroded soul. Only the

Maharajah's daughter had spied his rotten core. Lakshmi had told Jack that he hid his real self away, and she had been quite correct. To reveal his true nature would be to inspire repugnance. For only in the horror of battle could Jack show his true worth.

Chapter Thirty-four

The redcoats heard the enemy long before they could be seen. The Maharajah's army advanced with raucous grandeur, the loud trumpeting and the crash of drums reaching the straining ears of the four hundred soldiers who waited in silence for them to arrive.

Then the horde appeared.

The redcoats stared at the enemy force as it swarmed into view, the dust kicked up by the hooves of the horses billowing down the valley to sting their eyes. There was no fanfare, the British drummers and buglers remaining silent, greeting the Maharajah's host in the timeless manner of the redcoats: silent and stoical no matter what the provocation.

Horseman after horseman arrived, smothering the far end of the valley. Rank followed rank, the mounted warriors gathering, easing their tired horses to a stop as they spied the thin red line across their path. The sun flashed from thousands of pieces of armour and naked steel as the enemy pulled talwars from scabbards and prepared for the battle that was sure to come.

The redcoats watched wide-eyed as the enemy kept growing.

'Fuck me.' Jenkins spoke in an awestruck tone. 'There's hundreds of 'em.'

Jack saw the ghostly white pallor on the man's face. 'That's just their cavalry. We haven't seen their infantry yet.'

'Well that's just lovely, isn't it now. I'm glad you're with us, Mud. I wouldn't want to have fought those buggers without knowing how many more of them are to come.'

The men around Jack chuckled, seizing on the weak jest to help force down their emotions. For fear fluttered in every man's belly as the enemy horde swelled. The minutes stretched on, the redcoats forced to stand in impotent silence as the enemy gathered its strength. The leading horsemen were the warriors from the hills, the irregular troops that had assembled at their overlord's command. There was no sign of the blue-coated lancers or any of the beautifully uniformed guardsmen that formed the elite of the Maharajah's forces. Yet there were still enough men to outnumber the British by over two to one.

As the red-coated ranks stood baking in the increasing heat, the enemy cavalry studied the British line with wolfish fascination, sensing its fragility, the puny number of foot soldiers surely unable to withstand the power of the massed horsemen. They imagined an easy victory. If the thin red line were broken, then the way to the cantonment would be open. The bravest riders would have first pickings, the right to ransack the homes of the white-faced foreigners falling to those daring to be in the leading ranks of the attack.

The horsemen looked at the British line and thought of plunder.

'Look, you! Look at that.' Corporal Jones called for his mates' attention as a lone horseman left the throng and rode steadily towards them.

Jack, like most of the redcoats around him, had been lost in his own thoughts. It had been a long night with little sleep as he provided Major Dutton with all the details of the Maharajah's army. His body still ached from the beating Fenris had delivered, but the long wait in the harsh sun had dulled his senses so that he stood as if in a trance, awake yet far away. Lost in a world of painful memories.

The lone rider pulled up a hundred yards clear of the massed ranks of horsemen. He stood tall in his stirrups and raised his arms. In his left hand he held his naked talwar, the blade flashing bright in the sun. In this right he held a carbine that he shook in the air as he began to shout.

The redcoats were too far away to make out the words, but the message was clear. The rider was taunting the British soldiers, insulting their manhood and rousing his fellow warriors to action. He punched his weapons into the air as he challenged the British, daring them to react.

'Steady in the ranks.' Colour Sergeant Hughes began to prowl behind the 24th's part of the line. His voice was calm, a balm to the fears of his soldiers, who were forced to endure the enemy soldier's display in silence. Still the tension rippled through the tight ranks, the pressure building round them as they tasted the threat of violence in the dry, arid air.

More horsemen rode forward to join the first, pulling up alongside him and raising their own voices in a deep, visceral chant. The sound echoed down the valley, building steadily as other men came to join them, washing over the thin red line. Yet more riders made their way forward, swelling the lead rank, filling the width of the valley.

Along the line, the redcoats felt fear surge into their bellies, the icy rush of terror as they realised that the enemy was preparing to attack.

Major Dutton spurred his horse forward, then turned it around carefully, as if aligning himself on a marker.

'Men!' His voice was firm as he called for attention. 'The enemy is near. It is time for us to defend our homes and the honour of our Queen. I expect you all to do your duty. Stand firm and shoot straight. Together we will be victorious. Together we will make our country proud.'

He looked along the line, his florid face flushed crimson with exertion. Satisfied with his speech, he nudged his horse back into the line, easing it around so that he once again stood alongside Major Proudfoot.

'What a fucking idiot.' Jenkins gave his judgement on the call to arms. 'Together, my arse. First sign of trouble and I bet that fathead will be galloping back to the cantonment. I know I would if only those bastards would let me have a bloody horse.'

Jack chuckled at the damning verdict. He was glad he was not Jenkins' officer.

Then the chanting stopped, and with a final deep-throated cheer, the mass of cavalry lurched into motion.

The battle for Bhundapur had begun.

'At one hundred yards. Volley fire.' Major Dutton shouted the command that was immediately picked up by the officers along the line.

The effects of the volley would be dreadful. Four hundred balls of lead would be spat at the charging horsemen. The leading riders and their mounts would be gutted, the massed volley capable of butchering the head of the enemy attack. Those struck down would immediately create a bloody obstacle that would disrupt anyone still trying to press home the charge. The single massive blow would spread chaos amongst the attackers with the same wanton cruelty as it would spread death.

The volley had to be timed to perfection. Fired too soon and it would lose most of its effect. The muskets were useless at much over one hundred yards. Dutton would have to let the enemy close on the line if he wanted the volley to destroy the leading ranks and ignore what would certainly be a burning desire to fire early. If he left it too late, then he would commit an even more fatal error. The volley would still smash the head of the charge to smithereens, the muskets capable of horrific damage at close range, yet the enemy's momentum would drive them forward, man and horse turned into a projectile that would slam into the thin line and tear huge holes in its ordered ranks. The horsemen left intact would pour into the gaps, their naked talwars and sharpened spears capable of spreading havoc if they broke into the line. The redcoats would be easy targets and Dutton's small command would be torn apart in a heartbeat.

It would take only one volley for the charge to be bludgeoned to a bloody halt. But it had to be timed to perfection.

'Company! Prepare to fire!'

Kingsley had left the orders to his colour sergeant, deeming the act of shouting himself hoarse beneath the dignity of his rank.

The redcoats pulled their muskets to their shoulders, settling the heavy stocks so that they rested snugly. They peered down the simple sights, aiming the barrels so that they pointed at the throng that was speeding towards them. The staccato drumming of so many horses made the ground shudder under their feet. Along the line the muskets wavered, the redcoats feeling the weight pull at their arms as they waited for the command to fire.

The horsemen were covering the ground fast, the riders leaning forward in the saddle to urge their mounts to even greater efforts. This was no ordered attack, and some riders pulled ahead of their fellows so that the front of the charge bulged. With dreadful speed they tore over the dusty scrub, every heartbeat bringing them closer to the steady double line of men that stood silently in their path.

The enemy was close enough that the redcoats could see the snarls and twisted grimaces of hate on the faces of the wild horsemen thundering towards them. Every man felt the knot of terror deep in his gut, the fear twisting through his veins. The charge seemed unstoppable, its dreadful momentum sure to rip the frail line into bloody ruin.

At one hundred and fifty yards, Jack forced his aching muscles to harden, stilling the slight movement in the barrel of his musket, tensing his sinews as he prepared to fire. The horsemen were moving with mesmerising speed now, and his finger tightened on the trigger as he anticipated the order. The horsemen gouged their vicious spurs into the flanks of their tiring mounts, their soul-searing bellows of hate intensifying as they hurtled forward, the inevitable collision with the red-coated line coming closer with every bound.

Jack's mind screamed the command to fire, sensing the moment for the deadly volley to be unleashed. Yet Dutton remained silent. Jack tore his eye from his musket. In desperation he looked across to where Dutton sat in the centre of the British line, staring rapt at the enemy charge that was bearing down on his small command with such dreadful purpose. Jack was close enough to see the throb of a vein in the major's forehead, the tension in the man obvious even from fifty yards away.

A surge of horror seared through his body. Dutton was leaving the volley too late, the inexperienced officer failing to judge the distance correctly.

It was the worst mistake he could make.

Chapter Thirty-five

'ire!'

Jack screamed the command. He did not care that he stood in the line of redcoats as a private soldier. He had to rectify Dutton's dreadful error if they were to stand any chance of survival.

The men of the 24th looked up in surprise as the strange voice shouted the order.

'Fire! Now!' Jack twisted on the spot, bellowing the command for all he was worth.

He was roundly ignored.

He saw Dutton's head snap around, a look of shocked surprise on his face as he heard Jack's desperate order. For a fleeting moment he caught Jack's eye, before turning back, his bottom lip reaching up to chew on his thick moustache.

Jack felt a hand clap hard on to his shoulder.

'Shut your mouth.' Corporal Jones had been ordered to stand watch over the charlatan in the ranks of the 24th. But there was little force in his warning to be silent. He too was staring in horror at the enemy horde racing towards them. Jack was not the only one sensing that the officers were about to commit a terrible mistake.

Jack shook off the warning hand. He pulled his musket back into his shoulder and squinted down the sight. The enemy horsemen were dreadfully close, surely no more than fifty yards away from the redcoats' fragile formation, and closing fast.

There was no time left.

He pulled the trigger. He felt the kick of the musket as it fired, the stock punching hard into his shoulder.

'Fire!' He screamed the command as the crisp cough of his shot died away.

For a single, dreadful heartbeat there was silence.

'Fuck it!' Corporal Jones muttered the oath under his breath before sucking in a lungful of the scorching air. 'Twenty-fourth! Fire!'

This time the redcoats responded. Jack caught a glimpse of the shock on Kingsley's face as his command opened fire without orders, before the cloud of foul-smelling powder smoke rolled back over the line and hid him from view.

At such close range, the effect of the volley was terrible. Those enemy horsemen charging the 24th were scythed down, the head of the charge gutted by the deadly accurate musket fire. The heavy balls punched through the flesh of man and beast, killing and maiming indiscriminately. Men shrieked as they were torn apart, adding to the inhuman cries of the horses. More riders and horses went down as they collided with those struck by the close-range fire, the front half of the charging horde reduced to chaos in a heartbeat.

'Reload!' Colour Sergeant Hughes bellowed the command, taking over the orders that Kingsley should have been delivering. The 24th had taken the bit between the teeth, fighting and killing without command, saving themselves as their officers looked on.

Dutton nearly fell from the saddle when the 24th's volley roared out.

'Damn you! Not yet!' The major pulled hard on his reins, wheeling his horse around as he shouted in anger.

Proudfoot kicked his own horse forward, his face twisted into a snarl of recrimination.

'You fool! That was Lark!' He snapped the words with anger.

But Dutton was no longer looking towards the 24th. Instead he was staring in horror at the horde of enemy horsemen thundering towards them.

'Oh God!' The colour fled from his florid face as the full weight of his error struck him.

Proudfoot looked aghast at the commander of his native troops before turning to see just what had caused the major such utter dismay.

The horde of horsemen was no more than twenty yards away. The speed of their advance was mesmerising. They were tearing across the ground, covering the dusty soil far faster than either man would have believed possible.

'Fire!' Dutton screamed the command to his own troops, his terror given voice.

The roar of the sepoys' volley thundered out, the three hundred muskets firing in unison. The wave of sound slammed down the valley an instant after the storm of musket balls drove into the enemy horde.

The volley ripped the leading ranks apart. The riders at the front of the charging cavalry were butchered, the bodies of both man and horse torn apart at such close range. Yet the momentum of the charge was irresistible. Even as they died, the leading riders slammed into the sepoys' ranks in the thin red line, tearing huge gaps all along its length.

Sepoys went down, limbs twisted and broken by the weight of the dead horses and riders, their terrified shouts cut off as they were struck to the ground. Behind the gutted ranks, dozens of the Maharajah's irregular cavalry thundered into the dead and dying, their shouts of warning replacing the dreadful keening for blood. Many were thrown to the ground, unable to stop in time, adding to the chaos. Other riders, untouched by the volley, plunged into the maelstrom, forcing their terrified horses through the blood and the confusion. Free from the melee, they gouged their spurs back, throwing their mounts into the gaps that had been torn in the sepoys' ranks, their talwars flashing bright in the harsh sunlight as they slashed at the heads of the stunned redcoats, who suddenly found themselves easy targets for the surviving horsemen.

* * *

Major Proudfoot watched in growing horror as he saw Dutton's men reduced to a broken rabble in no more than a dozen heartbeats.

'Arthur! With me!' he shouted across to Lieutenant Fenris, who was staring in amazement as the British line was torn to shreds before his eyes. 'Ride, man!' He didn't wait to see if his new aide-de-camp heard him. He put his spurs to his horse's flanks, turning its head and urging it into a gallop.

He would not wait to bear witness to the destruction of his redcoats.

Jack flinched as the sepoys' volley roared out. Ahead of him, the 24th's own volley had bludgeoned the enemy horsemen to a halt, the power of their musket fire smashing the charge into bloody confusion. He could see riders trying to pick their way through the carnage, but it would take time for them to get past the gruesome obstacle. Around him the redcoats reloaded their weapons, their hands moving in haste as they strove to be ready before enough of the enemy riders could break free and once again threaten the frail line.

It had only been a matter of seconds between the 24th's volley and that of the native soldiers in the 12th, but already the sepoys were broken. Those left standing huddled together, desperate to find safety with their fellows. The merciless horsemen swarmed around these small islands, leaning down from their saddles, slashing and thrusting their vicious sabres.

With their flank no longer protected, the 24th was in dreadful danger. They had butchered the riders who had sought to charge them, but if they stayed in line, they stood no hope.

'Colour Sergeant Hughes!' Jack's voice was huge. 'Form square!'

The tall colour sergeant heard the command. He glanced around for his captain, but Kingsley still stood mute on the company's right flank, staring in rapt horror at the destruction Jack had ordered.

'Now, dammit. Form square!' Jack repeated his command.

This time the colour sergeant did not hesitate. 'Company! Form square!'

The redcoats knew their business. The company would reform into square, each flank three ranks deep. The formation would bristle with bayonets, a wall of steel that no horse would be able to penetrate. If they could form it in time and if they remained steady, then they would be safe from the marauding cavalry.

Colour Sergeant Hughes's command was still echoing around the confined valley when the men of the 24th started to move. With their corporals acting as marshals on the pivot points, the flanks of the square quickly started to form. Ignoring the chaos to their left, the 24th manoeuvred to save itself from destruction.

'What the devil do you think you are doing?' Jack's shoulder was yanked backwards and he spun round on the spot to face a furious Captain Kingsley.

'Saving your bloody command!' Jack snapped back, his anger flaring. Around them the square was nearly fully formed, the sergeants and corporals bustling round, positioning their charges to ensure that each of the four flanks was properly aligned.

'Fix bayonets!' Colour Sergeant Hughes had moved to the centre of the square, taking command as his officer chose to confront the man who had just saved them from certain destruction.

'You bastard.' Spittle was flung from Kingsley's lips as he damned Jack. 'These are my men. Mine, do you hear me?'

Jack glanced through the side of the square nearest the slaughtered horsemen. Already many of the enemy had picked their way through the grotesque barrier and in moments the 24th would be under attack. There was no time to waste.

Jack did the only thing he could think of. He snapped his fist forward, punching Kingsley square on the point of his chin. The captain's jaw shut with an audible snap, his head slammed back by the force of the blow. He fell to the ground with all the grace of a sack of horse shit.

Jack was turning away even before Kingsley's body had stopped moving.

'Corporal Jones. Make sure you drag this fool with us. Don't leave him behind, however tempted you may be.' Jack nodded as the one corporal he could name doubled over and took a firm grip on Kingsley's collar.

'Colour Sergeant Hughes!'

'Sir!' Hughes's reaction was instinctive. Jack might have been dressed as a common redcoat, but there was no doubting who was in command.

'We will make a fighting retreat to the cantonment.'

'Sir.' A flicker of concern appeared on the colour sergeant's weather-beaten face. It was a daunting order. The 24th would have to make its way over half a mile of open terrain whilst remaining in square. To keep the ranks tight would have been a hard task even on the parade ground. To accomplish it whilst being harassed by hundreds of horsemen was going to take a Herculean effort.

'Have the NCOs watch the files at all times.' Jack gave his orders calmly, despite the peril of the situation. 'If we leave a gap, you can bet those bastards will be in here in a flash. If that happens, then we are all dead men.'

'Very good, sir!' Hughes nodded his understanding.

The 24th were about to attempt the near impossible. If they failed, they faced being butchered by the merciless horsemen who would soon swarm around them.

Jack had saved them from the first dreadful moments of the enemy's charge. Now he had to bring them to safety.

Chapter Thirty-six

———◆———

The sepoys never stood a chance.

Here and there a subedar managed to gather together enough men to force the Maharajah's irregular cavalry to veer away, but most of the native soldiers were simply cut down where they stood, butchered by the horsemen who rode them down with cruel precision.

Some tried to run, throwing away their muskets as they made a desperate bid for safety, but there were simply too many horsemen for them to stand a chance. The sepoys were slaughtered, their heads and shoulders sliced open by the sharpened talwars. Dozens were killed in the first few minutes of the attack, flung to the ground to lie like discarded rag dolls, their precious lifeblood soaking into the parched soil beneath their ruined bodies.

'Form on me!' Major Dutton screamed in desperation as he tried to rally the remains of the three shattered companies. 'On me! On me!'

A horseman rode close, his talwar aimed at Dutton's heart. Before he could get close, Dutton lifted his arm, aiming his revolver with bloodshot eyes. The bullet took the rider in the throat, snatching his body backwards, throwing him from the saddle.

'On me! Spencer, here!' Dutton saw a hatless Lieutenant Spencer stagger from the melee. The tall officer looked up, and Dutton was given just enough time to see the look of anguish on his face before the young lieutenant was ridden down, a thick pig-sticking spear punched through his stomach from behind.

Dutton bellowed in rage. He emptied his revolver, killing another pair of fast-moving horsemen. He spied one of Gartry's subedars holding a small group of sepoys together and rode towards them, dodging around the wild hooves of a fallen horse that thrashed the ground in agony, a sepoy's bayonet driven full length into its chest.

'Reload!' Dutton snapped the command as he forced his horse in among the sepoys. 'Form two ranks. Front rank, kneel and present bayonets!'

The orders came fast as he sought to bring order from the chaos. More men ran to join them, adding weight to the frail formation. Dozens more tried but failed, the Maharajah's horsemen circling through the valley, cutting down the slowest, spilling still more blood on the arid soil.

'Ready!' Dutton's hands worked furiously to reload the five chambers on his revolver. 'Fire!'

Fewer than a dozen muskets answered the order, a desultory volley that still managed to knock over a couple of the circling riders. Dutton glanced up quickly before returning his attention to his revolver.

'Reload! Front rank, prepare to receive cavalry.' He snapped his revolver shut and looked around, trying to begin to make sense of the disorder. He heard the ordered commands of a British officer and through a gap in the cloud of powder smoke that billowed across the battlefield he saw the 24th's square. The redcoats were firing when ready, a stream of musket fire rippling around the tight formation. Their steady fire was exacting a toll on the circling horsemen, who were already backing off, seeking easier targets amongst the scattered ranks of Dutton's own soldiers, the men he had failed, rather than face the disciplined bayonet walls of the 24th.

Dutton sucked down his shame and his despair. The redcoats were still fighting. All was not lost.

* * *

Jack stood in the centre of the square that inched slowly away from the carnage. Even with only twenty men on each face it was an ungainly manoeuvre, many of the men forced to march either sideways or backwards as they tried to make progress towards the cantonment. The sergeants and corporals were screaming themselves hoarse as they constantly dressed the ranks to ensure they kept a wall of bayonets presented outwards. The redcoats were still firing on the enemy, but there were long gaps between shots, the sheer difficulty of reloading whilst constantly moving slowing their rate. Yet there were still enough muskets to fire on any rider who ventured close, and the irregular cavalry were becoming wary of the white-faced redcoats and their accuracy.

Step but weary step, the 24th were dragging themselves clear.

'Company! Company halt!' Jack's voice cracked as he shouted the order, the foul-smelling powder smoke sucking every last drop of moisture from his parched mouth. He pushed himself into one of the flanks of the square so he could get a better view. The 24th had stopped barely two hundred yards from where they had waited so patiently for the enemy to arrive. Two hundred yards that were now covered with the fallen bodies of the enemy cavalry, the company's passage marked in blood and spent cartridge wrappers.

He took another faltering step away from the safety of the square, unable to fully comprehend what he was seeing.

The enemy riders had gone.

'They've gone to loot the cantonment.' Captain Kingsley elbowed his way out of the square. 'And you are going to hang.'

Jack was too tired to argue. 'Form the men into column, Kingsley. Let's get them back whilst we can.'

He looked anxiously down the valley, expecting to see the rest of the Maharajah's force arrive at any moment. He offered a silent prayer of thanks to whichever God had been looking over the redcoats. If they had been facing the Maharajah's elite troops, then the battle would still be raging. Thankfully, the wild men from the hills were driven as much by the lust for plunder as they were by achieving the military aims of the Maharajah's lightning strike against Bhundapur. They had fought hard, winning a fabulous victory by destroying the redcoats' frail line, but when faced with the choice of continuing the fight or being first into the cantonment, they had raked back their spurs and raced for the bungalows and barracks of the British camp, leaving their dead and dying comrades to bleed and suffer in the dust.

'Damn you!' Kingsley spat the words into Jack's face.

Jack was certain a raised fist would follow the oath, and he instinctively twisted on the spot, his arms rising to defend himself. Yet Kingsley was no fighter, and he took a step backwards, as if he too had expected to see a blow aimed squarely in his direction.

'Corporal Jones. Disarm this bastard and guard him. I want him in irons the moment we are back in the barracks.' Kingsley snarled the order, hiding his fear under a thin veil of anger.

Corporal Jones eased his way through the ranks of men, who stood and stared at the captain. 'Sir?'

Kingsley's anger flared. 'Damn you, Corporal. Arrest this man.'

Corporal Jones stamped to attention. 'Sir!'

Satisfied, Kingsley turned his back on Jack and stomped angrily into the safety of the square, bawling for Colour Sergeant Hughes to form a company column for the march back to the hastily erected fort that Dutton had insisted on building, and which now offered the redcoats their only hope of sanctuary.

'Sorry, sir.' Corporal Jones was apologetic as he reached for Jack's musket.

Jack handed over the weapon. 'Looks like you can drop the "sir" again, Corporal.'

Jones offered a thin-lipped smile. 'The man's a cock.'

'He's an officer.' Jack returned the grin. 'What else do you expect?'

'Captain Kingsley! Well done. Well done indeed!'

Major Proudfoot stood just outside the temporary wall that had been built from mealie bags and storage crates. He had begun to clap as the weary company from the 24th trudged back, and now he shouted his approval to welcome their return.

Kingsley strode forward, his chin lifting as he accepted the applause. He shook Proudfoot's hand before turning back to face his command. If either officer saw the scathing looks on the grimy faces of the redcoats, then neither made any remark of it. The two officers stood back and watched as the exhausted soldiers clambered over the three-foot-high defensive wall.

'I had to have that bounder Lark arrested. He tried to run.' Kingsley's smug expression betrayed his satisfaction at delivering the accusation as Corporal Jones reluctantly brought Jack to stand in front of the two officers.

'That's a bare-faced lie.' Jack delivered his reply calmly. 'I saved this fool's company, although I had to knock him down so I could do it without his damn interference. But his men fought well. They are good soldiers.' He raised his voice so that the tired redcoats could hear his praise.

Proudfoot turned to face Captain Kingsley as if Jack had never spoken. 'Well done, Kingsley. You have delivered your men safely. That is highly commendable under the circumstances, highly commendable indeed.'

Corporal Jones cleared his throat noisily.

'Corporal. You wish to speak?' Major Proudfoot lifted an eyebrow as the corporal dared to interrupt.

Jones's face glowed as scarlet as his jacket. It was likely the first time he had ever spoken to anyone as senior as a major. 'Yes, sir. If you please, sir.'

'Well, out with it.' Proudfoot was all warmth. He glanced over his shoulder and saw dozens of the 24th watching him, the whites of their eyes bright against the thick caking of dust and sweat that smothered their young faces. 'Do not be afraid to speak.'

'Mr Lark didn't run, sir.'

'Shut your mouth, Corporal,' Kingsley interrupted. He stepped forward so that he stood chest to chest with Jones. 'This is not the time for your damn lies.'

'Captain Kingsley. Let the man speak.' Proudfoot's voice was quiet, but there was no mistaking the authority in his tone.

Kingsley opened his mouth to argue further. 'I shall not stand here and—'

'Let him speak.' Proudfoot screamed the words. The sudden rage was astonishing, and Kingsley quailed. 'Please carry on, Corporal.' Proudfoot was all polite reason again, the sudden flash of bright anger hidden once more.

'Sir!' Corporal Jones stood to attention, seeking some familiar security as he dared to speak out. 'Mr Lark saved us, sir. Not Captain Kingsley. Without Mr Lark I reckon we would all be dead'uns.'

'Thank you, Corporal.' Proudfoot turned and smiled warmly at the watching redcoats. 'I am glad you felt you could speak out. I thank you for your words.'

Jack was close enough to see that none of the warmth reached Proudfoot's eyes. He met the major's stare, sensing the anger that simmered just below the surface.

'Corporal, please carry on.' Proudfoot gave the order and a relieved Jones stamped his foot once before scurrying away. 'Captain Kingsley. Mr Lark. Please come with me. We have much to do.'

Proudfoot turned on his heel and walked away.

Behind them, the remnants of Dutton's command were limping towards the temporary fortress. Less than half of his men were still standing, and the watching redcoats of the 24th saw the horror in the native soldiers' eyes as they staggered towards the barracks.

Dutton rode in alone. None of his three lieutenants had survived the massacre, and so he returned at the head of his battered command as the sole surviving white officer. Not one of the watching redcoats could meet his eye as he clambered wearily from the saddle, the bitterness of defeat hanging around him like a cloud.

Chapter Thirty-seven

'He's gone?' Jack was astonished.

'Fenris left an hour ago with the last of Proudfoot's cavalry. Gone to summon assistance.' Dutton sounded bone-weary as he replied.

Jack looked hard at the British major. For a reason he could not fully fathom, Proudfoot had let him go free, despite Kingsley's loud protest for him to be locked away. With no other responsibilities to tend to he had sought the major out, bringing with him a bottle of Proudfoot's brandy to loosen Dutton's tongue and allow him some solace. Jack had seen the man's shame. He himself could well remember the heavy burden of having failed when faced with the enemy for the first time. They sat on the defensive wall barricading the small area where the tired sepoys and redcoats huddled together, sharing the harsh spirit and watching in silence as the cantonment burnt. The sounds of the looters were loud in the darkness, the wild, cackling laughter and shrieks of delight reaching the ears of the exhausted redcoats who had been dispersed around the short perimeter.

Occasional gunshots rang out, but whether they were fired in anger or in celebration Jack could not tell. Dutton's fortress had good fields of fire on three sides, the wide sweep of the parade ground wrapping around the 24th's barracks, which formed the eastern wall of the defensive line. On the far side of the barracks a series of administrative buildings lined a neat pathway that had been edged with whitewashed rocks. It was the one weak spot in the fortress, and all the men knew it.

The 24th had spent the last hours making their barracks as impregnable as possible, gouging dozens of loopholes in the side facing the east and barricading the wide windows that had once been so coveted but which were now the building's biggest weakness. There was nothing else they could do. They all knew the barracks would be the scene of the heaviest fighting when the Maharajah's army arrived to attack the survivors of Proudfoot's forces.

'Wanted to keep his special chum safe, I expect.' Dutton's voice was slurred, and he took another large mouthful of the brandy. 'Good riddance, if you ask me.'

Jack reached out for the bottle, wiping the neck on the sleeve of his red coat before taking a more circumspect sip. He was surprised at Proudfoot's decision to send Fenris away. 'Where will he go?'

'Fort St John. There is a column based there. Mainly cavalry, too.' Dutton looked longingly at the brandy as Jack drained a fair quantity of the precious liquid. 'Because of me, we need help.' His head hung in shame as he admitted his error.

'You wanted to fight. That's what it's like.'

Dutton looked up at Jack's harsh words, pain etched into the lines on his face. 'I was a fool. I wish I had died with my men.'

Jack scowled. 'Then you truly are a fool. You are alive. Be thankful for that.'

Dutton snatched the brandy back, lifting the bottle to his lips but keeping his eyes on Jack as he drank, careless of the fiery liquid that spilled from his mouth to run into his beard. When he finally lowered the bottle, he turned to stare outwards again, the light of the burning cantonment reflecting in his moist eyes.

'I killed them, Jack. I killed my own men.'

'No. Those bastard horsemen killed them.'

Dutton shook his head slowly. 'I fired too late. If I had given the order earlier, we would have stopped them. As you did.'

'You did your best'

'And I failed.' Dutton's head hung so that his chin rested on his chest, as if his neck was no longer capable of supporting its weight.

'I know.' Jack waited for Dutton to look at him. It took a while, but eventually the major raised his head. 'It was your first battle.' Jack spoke softly. 'It's not some bloody parade. It's vicious and it's violent.' He held Dutton's stare as he spoke, delivering his biting judgement with bitter honesty. 'Either you live or you die, and there is bugger all you can do about which of those it is. You and your men fought hard and you brought as many of them here as you could. That's all that matters.'

Dutton looked at Jack for some time, as if trying to come to terms with what the younger man had said. Eventually his face softened, whether from finding some peace of mind or simply from the large amount of brandy he had consumed Jack could not tell.

'So what happens tomorrow?' Dutton asked, his voice calm once again.

'They attack. Those horsemen today were his irregular cavalry. The main body of his army has only just arrived. I expect we will have to face his infantry first, and believe me, there are a lot of those bastards. They'll hit us on all sides, and if we break, he'll send in his bloody lancers.'

Dutton listened to Jack's prediction before sucking in a deep breath. 'So tomorrow we die.'

Jack snorted at the melodramatic phrase. 'No. Tomorrow we fight.'

He turned as he heard the soft tread of footsteps behind them, wary of anyone coming to interrupt his conversation.

'Good evening, General.'

'Isabel.' Jack could not hide the pleasure in his voice. 'Does your father know you're here?' He smiled as he helped her on to the fire step behind the barricade, offering her his hand so that she could sit beside him.

'Father is drunk.' The corners of Isabel's mouth twitched in disapproval.

'Sensible fellow.' Dutton took another slug of brandy, already too drunk himself to be concerned about his behaviour in front of a lady.

'Perhaps. May I?' Isabel held out her hand questioningly towards the brandy, which Dutton passed over, as if sharing hard spirits with young women was an everyday occurrence.

She took a demure sip, grimacing at the harsh taste. 'Your wife is asking after you, Major Dutton. She seems most concerned.'

Dutton shook his head ruefully. 'Poor Hilary. She is not cut out for any of this.'

Jack felt Isabel's body pressing against his side as she sat beside him. She smelt wonderful, the delicate fragrance of her fresh perfume a balm to his soul, its subtle aroma driving away the smell of burning and of death.

'She is made of sterner stuff than you give her credit for,' she replied evenly, brushing at her dress. 'She is with the wounded. Doing what she can to help.'

'She is a fine woman. She deserves better.'

'None of us chooses our fate.' Isabel looked at Jack as she offered her advice to Dutton. 'It chooses us. All we decide is how we face it.'

The three sat in silence as they contemplated Isabel's words. The cantonment was well ablaze, the heat of the flames warm on their faces as the chill of the night set in. Shadowy figures flitted into view amidst the burning buildings, but none ventured close to the temporary refuge the British had erected. It seemed the survivors were to be left in peace for the night.

Isabel slipped her hand forward so that it rested on Jack's thigh. 'Perhaps we didn't do the right thing after all.' She broke the silence with a whisper, her mouth close enough to Jack's ear that he could feel the warmth of her breath on the side of his face. Her fingers were like red-hot coals on his leg and he wished they were alone.

'And miss all this. How can you even think that?'

Isabel rapped his leg. 'So what happens now?'

'We fight.' An unexpected voice answered her question.

None of the three had heard the footsteps of Major Proudfoot as he approached. 'We hold here until the flying column from Fort St John arrives. Isn't that right, Lark?'

Proudfoot bounded on to the fire step, the jet-black cloak draped over his shoulders billowing around him as he leapt athletically over

the wall of mealie bags, landing on the balls of his feet before turning
to face his meagre audience.

Jack looked at the odd creature that had capered across the wall
like a demented goat. 'I reckon that's right.' His voice was guarded.

'Major Dutton.' Proudfoot lifted a quizzical eyebrow in his
subordinate's direction. 'Can we hold?'

'Maybe, maybe not.'

Proudfoot nodded his head as if Dutton had offered wise advice
rather than such a bitter statement. He spun on his heel and studied
the burning cantonment for some time.

'Do *you* think we can hold?' Isabel asked the question to the back
of Proudfoot's head when she could stand the silence no longer.

'Of course,' the major answered without turning round. 'But
perhaps you should ask the commander of the 24th?'

'He's not here.' Jack answered the odd question. 'Kingsley
appears to have disappeared.'

'Captain Kingsley is indisposed.' Proudfoot steadfastly refused to
turn around and remained facing the fires. 'He is with the sick. He
will stay there until after the battle. He took a nasty blow to the head
and it has quite addled his wits.'

'Then ask your lapdog when he gets back.' Jack's opinion of the
lieutenant was clear in his derisory tone.

Proudfoot wheeled round suddenly and Jack felt Isabel start at
the dramatic posturing. 'Fenris does not command the 24th.'

'Then who will?' Jack's tone was belligerent. He had endured
enough of the major's games.

'You. You will command them.'

'Me!' Jack was genuinely astonished.

'As of this moment I am promoting you. You are to be Captain
Lark. The 24th are yours.'

Jack blinked hard. 'I thought I was to hang?'

Proudfoot smiled. For the first time Jack saw some warmth make
its way into the major's eyes. 'That was before. This is now. I want
you to command the 24th. You are the best man for the job. You
proved that today.'

Jack laughed. He threw back his head and guffawed, careless of
the men who turned to stare at the madman hooting so loudly.

'Do you accept?' Proudfoot chuckled, joining in Jack's mirth.

'Oh yes. I accept.' Jack slipped from the wall and walked to stand in front of the major.

'Then you will be wanting this.' Proudfoot pulled open his cloak. For the first time Jack saw that he was wearing a sword.

His sword.

He watched, his heart hammering in his mouth, as Proudfoot undid the buckles that held the scabbard around his waist. It was only when the major handed him the fabulous weapon that he realised how much he had missed it since it had been taken from him when he had first been arrested. He had never owned anything of such extraordinary value, yet it was not the wealth it gave him that he had missed.

He had been awarded the sword for his bravery. He had not bought it. He had not taken it. He had earned it.

Jack took a step backwards and carefully, reverentially, buckled the slings of the scabbard to the belt around his waist.

He was a captain. This time he hadn't stolen the rank. It had been granted freely. He was an officer. It might only be temporary and out of convenience, but it did not matter. He had been a maharajah's general, then a British redcoat. Now, for the first time, he was Captain Jack Lark. Perhaps it would only be for a matter of hours, but Jack did not care. He would lead the 24th into battle, and he vowed he would not let them down.

Chapter Thirty-eight

―•◆•―

The noise started just before dawn. The impenetrable blackness of the night still wrapped its heavy arms around the tired redcoats in Dutton's temporary fortress when the wild blare of trumpets split the quietness asunder.

The sounds rose in a crescendo, the chaotic medley denying the defenders the sanctuary of sleep. Underscoring the frenzied orchestra was the deep, visceral chanting of hundreds of voices, which came and went in waves of sound, throbbing and pulsating with a nerve-jangling tremor.

The violence in the air was palpable, and every redcoat shivered as they listened to the mob that had arrived and was now preparing for the battle to come.

The defenders greeted the dreadful cacophony in silence. Each man was left alone with his fears, forced to endure the last of the night wrestling with his demons unaided. It was the time for silent prayer and superstitious ritual. For each redcoat to find a way to face the peril they knew would come with the dawn.

'Stand to!' The two surviving buglers sounded the rising notes as the first enemy troops were sighted. The defenders took their places in the bayonet-tipped perimeter, which would have to stand firm if they were to survive the day.

Dutton's sepoys manned the outer wall. Just under one hundred and fifty men had answered the roll call in the cold air before sunrise, less than half of the three companies left after the previous day's massacre. Their ranks had been swelled by a number of servants who had stayed loyal to their masters and who had been given hasty lessons in how to reload a musket. The extra bodies and the shortness of the perimeter allowed Dutton to keep back fifty men, whom he organised into a flying column, ready to pounce on any part of the wall that started to give way.

The 24th were left to defend their barracks and the storerooms that formed the easternmost wall. The long, airy barrack block had been transformed into a stronghold, allowing the redcoats to bring as many guns as possible to bear on the narrow pathway that made straight for the pair of wide double doors facing the east. Any attack on this side of the fortress could be made under cover, the attackers only having to break into the open when they were no more than fifteen to twenty yards away. The 24th would have to fight the Maharajah's men in bloody hand-to-hand combat, the power of their muskets diminished by the lack of an open field of fire.

The rest of the cantonment's population was crammed into the largest room in the 24th's barracks that did not have a wall or window facing to the east. There the wives, children and clerks would have to endure the battle, sweltering in the heat as they willed the defenders to hold out.

It was a time for prayers, for the faithful to beseech their God with pleas for deliverance. It was a time for hopes to dwindle and for men to place their faith in seventeen inches of cold steel.

Jack peered out of the window. The fresh breeze was cool against his skin, the layer of grime and sweat congealing to leave his face feeling as stiff as dried parchment. The bugles were calling for the defenders to be ready, the first sighting of the enemy stirring Dutton's men into action. The proud notes sounded defiant, the clear rising call a challenge to the bewildering hubbub that summoned the Maharajah's men to readiness.

'Hold your fire.' Jack pulled back from the window and walked down the centre of the barracks. He had over half his men at the eastern wall, their bayonet-tipped muskets pointing out of the windows or loopholes, ready to fire as soon as the first enemy soldier dared to show his face. He had stationed another fifteen on the roof to act as sharpshooters under the command of Colour Sergeant Hughes; he hoped they would be able to fire down on to the heads of any enemy troops milling around outside the barracks. The final dozen waited as a reserve, ready to plug the inevitable gaps, Jack's final throw of the dice should the Maharajah's men force a breach in his defences.

'Shoot the bastards in the guts.' Jack stalked behind the men pressed to the wall. 'Make them bleed.' He offered his advice in the even tones of an instructor on the firing range, as if they faced stuffed woollen dummies rather than men bent on their destruction. 'The more you kill, the fewer you will have to fight.'

He caught the eye of Corporal Jones. The Welshman stood at the head of Jack's flying squad, looking as composed as if the 24th faced nothing more than a routine drill.

'Be ready for my signal, Corporal.'

'We'll be ready, sir.' Jones risked a smile. 'Feels right to call you "sir" again, sir.'

Jack paused in his pacing. 'Thank you, Corporal. I'll do my best not to be a cock.'

Corporal Jones coloured as the other redcoats smiled at Jack's choice of language. Jack looked into the eyes of the men now under his command. He saw their fear, the waiting pulling at their courage. But he recognised their determination to get the job done. His hand fell to the talwar at his hip. He ran his fingers over the coarse shark-skin grip, the knowledge that he would soon draw the blade in anger for the first time adding to his own anxiety. On his other hip he could feel the reassuring weight of his revolver. He had borrowed the gun from Major Dutton, unwilling to fight without one. He was still dressed in the red coat of a private soldier but now he at least carried the weapons of an officer. Like his men, he was prepared to fight.

'Sir! Here they come!'

Jack whirled on the spot. 'Company! Ready!'

He shouted the needless order, his men already bracing themselves for the attack. Those stationed at the windows and loopholes pulled their muskets into their shoulders, aiming the weapons outside. The men in the flying squad hefted their muskets, or reached for their bayonets, reassuring themselves that the seventeen inches of steel was attached securely.

The tramp of footsteps rolled down the pathway that led away from the barracks. It was the rhythmic thump of men marching in formation, the regular tempo of disciplined troops manoeuvring into position.

'Prepare to fire!' Jack peered anxiously into the bright sunlight. The path was empty but he knew the enemy was close. He let his hand fall to his hip, undoing the flap of his holster so he could withdraw the heavy revolver. The solid lump of metal was cold to his touch, but it felt good to have the weapon in his hand.

The pounding stopped. The ears of every man stationed in the barracks strained to hear the sound of the attack beginning. The red-coated soldiers waited anxiously, their nerves screwed to fever pitch as they endured the last moments of peace. Loud voices echoed around the remains of the cantonment, the last shouted orders as the defenders prepared for the assault.

Yet not one enemy soldier was in sight.

Jack could barely breathe as he stared out of the barracks window. He could sense the enemy soldiers were close by, but they remained stubbornly out of view.

'Come on now. This ain't bleeding fair.' The redcoat to Jack's right muttered the words under his breath as he continued to peer down the barrel of his musket.

'They're coming.' Jack reached out and patted the redcoat on the shoulder. He pulled back and quickly moved to a window near the centre of the barracks, seeing if the new viewpoint would reveal the enemy.

Nothing.

And then they appeared.

They came in a rush. One moment the pathway was empty; a heartbeat later, the enemy infantry rushed forward, erupting around the corner in a wild mob.

'Company!' Jack's voice was steady despite his heart hammering in his chest. He had a moment to realise that the men swarming towards the 24th's barracks were dressed in the splendid red and blue uniform of the Maharajah's guards, the familiar sight sending a tremor of guilt through his soul. 'Fire!'

The muskets fired in unison. The enemy were close enough for Jack to hear the grotesque sound of the balls slapping into living flesh, followed by the screams of those struck down.

There was no time for the men to reload before the enemy reached the walls, and for a dreadful second there was silence as the appalled redcoats witnessed the destructive power of their volley at such close range. The musket balls had cut a bloody swathe through the leading ranks. Many guardsmen had been struck by more than one bullet, their bodies shredded by the disciplined fire. Dozens of the enemy had been cut down, the storm of musket fire gutting the attack.

Jack nearly choked on the foul-smelling powder smoke that filled the room, his eyes watering as the rotten egg stench filled his mouth and nose.

'Kill them!' He screamed the order, breaking the spell that the sudden lull had cast over the redcoats. Through the smoke he could see the enemy charging at the walls, the Maharajah's best soldiers clambering over the dead and the dying, callous in their desire to reach the hated redcoats.

The men Jack had stationed on the roof opened fire as the enemy stormed forward. He could hear Hughes marking the targets for his sharpshooters. Half a dozen of the blue-coated guardsmen fell to the well-directed fire, their bodies tumbling to the ground, trampled underneath the boots of their fellows.

The first enemy soldier reached the wall. His talwar keened as it sliced through the air, the man behind the blade screaming like a fiend as he tried to strike at the redcoats who waited behind the window.

The killing began.

More and more of the enemy pressed up to the windows. Blade after blade was thrust forward, reaching for the flesh of the defiant redcoats. A dozen or more guardsmen packed against each of the openings. Each rammed his weapon forward, striving to be the first to break into the heart of the foreigners' stronghold.

The redcoats held their ground. Time and time again they punched their bayonets forward, using the point of the vicious seventeen-inch blade just as they had been taught on the drill square. They plied their trade with dreadful effect, taking advantage of the height of their position to hack down at the faces of the enemy horde. The men at the loopholes loaded as quickly as they could before thrusting their weapons out once more, the cough of their muskets cracking out every few moments.

'Hold them! Hold them!' Jack screamed his encouragement, his voice straining with the effort.

More of the enemy were falling to the shots coming from the roof. Hughes was controlling his sharpshooters well, directing an effective fire that was striking man after man from the Maharajah's ranks. Still they pressed forward, ignoring the dead and the dying underneath their boots, the ruined bodies trodden thoughtlessly into the dust as the guardsmen strove to batter their way into the barracks.

The redcoats were fighting hard but the enemy were relentless. Each redcoat faced a dozen blades. As quickly as they struck one man down, another two took his place. Sharp talwars were thrust forward from every direction and the redcoats were reduced to a desperate defence as they were forced to block again and again, the enemy blades reaching for them with dreadful persistence.

'Hold them!' Jack threw himself forward as the first redcoat fell to the ground, his hands clutched to the ruin of his throat, ripped open by a fast-moving sword edge. He snapped his left hand forward, thrusting the barrel of his revolver into the thickly bearded face of the first enemy soldier to reach up and try to scramble through the window.

'Fuck off!' he screamed as he pulled the trigger.

The man's face disappeared as the heavy bullet punched through skin and bone, a nauseating explosion of blood and offal splattering both Jack and the two redcoats who were still desperately defending the window.

Jack pushed into the gap the fallen redcoat had left. The

blue-coated infantry were pressed tight against the window, and now they were reaching up to haul themselves into the opening. Jack got a blurred impression of the hatred in the bright eyes of the dark, bearded faces as he raised his revolver once more and fired into the pulsating mass that screamed its horrifying war cry in the faces of the defenders. The four bullets left in the revolver punched into the closest bodies. Jack steadied his aim after each shot, making sure each one counted. The dreadful salvo cleared a space, each bullet striking a man to the floor, easing the pressure on the route into the barracks.

Jack saw the opening and reacted without thought. The madness was irresistible. As soon as he had pulled the trigger for the first time it had overwhelmed him. Nothing mattered save the dreadful urge to fight, to hack at the enemy.

He put one arm on the ledge and leapt through the window.

Chapter Thirty-nine

He landed on the balls of his feet, the small drop down from the window barely registering in his mind. His beautiful sword whispered from the scabbard, the bright gems encrusted on the hilt flashing in the bright sunlight. The wild call of battle surged through him, the same soul-searing madness that had driven him into the Russian ranks at the Alma coursing through his veins.

He flailed the sword forward, sweeping its sharpened edge in an upward arc, slashing it into the astonished face of the closest enemy soldier. The talwar scoured through the man's heavy beard, gashing a wide channel that immediately filled with blood before the man fell to the floor, his hand clasped to the dreadful wound.

Jack recovered the blade, punching the hilt forward, driving the heavy guard into his next target. He screamed as he fought, a terrible snarl of animal anger. He moved fast and the blade sang as he threw himself at the enemy. He thrust the point hard into a man's guts before recovering the blow and flashing the blade away, using the sharpened rear blade to slash the throat of another blue-coated soldier who took the first pace towards his left side.

'Come on!' He challenged the enemy to attack him. He twisted on the spot, sliding his hips to one side to let an enemy talwar whistle past his body before countering with his own blade, skewering the man who had tried to kill him with a single thrust to the heart.

He stamped forward, moving away from the window and into the space he had cleared. He did not feel the bodies under his boots, the flesh that slipped and pulsed under his callous tread. He felt nothing save the urge to fight.

'Forward the 24th!'

The loud cry barely registered in Jack's mind. He saw the eyes of the man to his front widen as more redcoats threw themselves from the window, Corporal Jones leading his flying squad in a wild charge after their captain.

The dozen redcoats drove into the packed ranks of blue-coated soldiers, firing the shots saved for this moment. The close-range volley butchered the nearest enemy soldiers, knocking them over like skittles at the fair. The redcoats did not hesitate. They stormed forward, thrusting their bayonets at any stunned guardsmen left standing. They forced their way through the men who milled around the window in an onslaught of bloody violence that had the enemy soldiers backing away in horror.

In the face of the counterattack the enemy ranks broke. The press of bodies eased as the Maharajah's men turned and ran, pushing and pulling at each other in their eagerness to get away from the red-coated devils who had charged with such madness. The men from the 24th that Jack had stationed on the roof kept up their fire as the enemy fled, picking at the retreating mob, adding impetus to the rout.

Jack's lungs heaved as he tried to suck in mouthfuls of the scorching air. He sank to his haunches, suddenly exhausted, his battle rage vanishing as quickly as it had appeared.

'Sir.' Corporal Jones appeared at his side, his gory, blood-splattered bayonet held inches from Jack's nose. 'Time to get back inside.'

Jack wiped his face with the dark green facing of his jacket. 'Thank you for coming after me, Corporal.'

'My pleasure, bach. We couldn't lose our only officer, now could we? Right careless that would be.'

Jack nodded his thanks. A sea of blood surrounded him, the

twisted and torn bodies of the men the redcoats had struck down littering the ground. Some still moved, living on despite the dreadful wounds they had taken, their pitiful groans and whimpers loud in the sudden lull.

A fresh round of musket fire broke out. Jack sheathed his sword, ignoring the blood that was smeared on the beautifully decorated steel. The 24th had driven off the Maharajah's first assault, but the rest of the tiny fortress was still under attack.

'Corporal Jones, leave half the men here. Give me the rest. We'd better see if we are needed outside.' Jack snapped off the order within moments of climbing back into the smoke-filled barracks. There was no time to take stock or to rest on their laurels. Dutton and his sepoys were still heavily engaged, and Jack would not let them fight on alone.

'Very good, sir.'

'And well done.' Jack raised his voice so that the watching redcoats could hear his words. Three of their number lay stretched out on the ground, whilst many others nursed cuts and wounds caused by the sharp sabres that had tried so hard to strike them down. They had been lucky.

'Sergeant.' Jack called to one of the company's sergeants, whose name he still did not know. 'Stay here. Make sure the men are loaded and that they all have a full pouch of caps and cartridges.'

'Sir.'

Jack turned to the hastily formed platoon that Corporal Jones had put together. 'Stay with me. Let's go.'

They set off at a fast trot. The sounds of muskets firing had ceased but they could all hear the clash of blade on blade. The perimeter was hard pressed on all sides. Dutton had already been forced to commit his own flying squad to reinforce the north wall, where the Maharajah's men had nearly broken through. Everywhere the sepoys were fighting hard, Dutton's command fully engaged as the swarm of men pressed along the length of the makeshift barricade.

Jack flinched as a volley of musket fire cracked out from overhead. The resourceful Colour Sergeant Hughes had turned his men around, bringing the muskets under his command to bear on the closest enemy troopers attacking the rest of the perimeter, and Jack made a mental note to thank him later.

He turned to his men. 'Follow me! Whatever happens, stay together.' He scanned the grimy faces, which looked back at him with intensity. He could see the determination in their eyes. His new command would not let him down.

They went off at double-time, their equipment clattering as it bounced off their bodies. Jack led them fast across the parade ground and towards the western wall, where he saw at least a dozen sepoys on the ground.

'Forward the 24th!' His sword rasped as he pulled it from the scabbard.

The dusty ground passed quickly under their fast-moving boots, the last yards rushing by. Jack saw a tall blue-coated guardsmen pull himself on to the barricade. The huge man kicked out, smashing his foot into the face of a sepoy who had been raising his bayonet to cut him down. The attacker threw his head back, screaming his challenge to the gods before he leapt down on the sepoys' side of the barricade. Men poured over the makeshift wall behind him, a dozen of the Maharajah's best troops finally forcing their way into Dutton's fortress.

'At them!' Jack screamed the command to his half-company.

The giant guardsman saw him coming and took a double-handed grip on his huge talwar. Jack recognised him instantly. Subedar Khan was serving his master well by leading his men from the front.

'He's mine!' Jack roared the challenge, rushing towards the man he had come to know during his time in Maharajah's palace. He could not let any of his men face the huge man in combat. That responsibility was his and his alone.

He slashed his own sword forward as he skidded to a halt, flashing the blade at Khan's body. He sensed his men pushing past, wielding their own weapons as they fought to drive the enemy back over the barricade, leaving him to fight alone.

'Come on then, laddie! Let's fucking dance!' Khan parried the first attack, swatting Jack's fast-moving blade aside with ease. His counter-stroke lashed out, but Jack had been ready for it and he ducked low, letting the talwar swipe through the air over his head. He recovered his balance and attacked again, battering his sword at the target in front of him.

Khan snarled in anger as the speed of Jack's blows forced him to give ground before he scythed his own talwar back, the growl turning to a roar of frustration as Jack parried the attack.

Jack was astonished by the calmness running through him. There was none of the battle madness that had taken charge when he flung himself through the barrack-room window. Instead he fought with icy detachment, his fear banished and replaced by composed confidence.

He thrust his talwar forward, aiming it directly at Khan's heart, picking the spot with ruthless precision. He felt nothing as the subedar parried the blow, driving his blade wide. He waited for the inevitable counterattack, snapping his neck backwards so that Khan's wild slash whispered past his face.

'Damn you laddie!' Khan roared before he attacked again, flailing his sword at Jack's body, his words drowned out as the two swords clashed together.

Jack stayed silent, his emotions banished. He felt no remorse. He stamped his foot forward, attacking with a series of blows that used all of his speed. Again and again Khan parried the flashing talwar, each time only just catching Jack's blade an instant before it ripped into his flesh.

Around him the 24th drove the enemy soldiers backwards, forcing the Maharajah's men back over the wall. They were not having it all their own way. Two redcoats were down, their bodies torn open by the sabres of the blue-coated soldiers, who fought on even as they were driven backwards, refusing to give up the hard-won foothold on the redcoats' side of the barricade.

Khan came at Jack, releasing a blow driven by a wild fury. Jack stepped backwards quickly, letting the talwar pass in front of his body. As the blade went wide he saw the opportunity. He snapped his wrist forward, ramming the point of his sword into the giant man's chest, the force of the blow driving it deep into the man's body.

Khan grunted as the blade pierced his flesh. Yet still he fought on, slashing his talwar at Jack in a final gesture of defiance.

Jack twisted as he suddenly saw the fast-moving blade in the corner of his vision. He flung his arm up into the sword's path, the reaction uncontrolled and instinctive. The sharpened blade sliced into his left forearm. He felt the edge bounce off the bone before the burning agony seared into his skull. Then Khan fell. Jack's talwar was ripped from his grip, the beautiful blade trapped, buried nearly to the hilt in his adversary's body.

Jack clasped his right hand over the deep gouge that was already slick with blood. He barely heard the cheer as the last of the blue-coated infantry were forced back over the wall, his exhausted redcoats driving off the enemy soldiers who had come so close to breaking their dogged resistance. He stared down into the face of Subedar Khan, who lay in the dust no more than a foot from his boot. The Maharajah's officer was dead, his eyes glazed, his life torn away. Jack gripped his arm, feeling the blood pulse over his fingers as it pumped out with every beat of his racing heart. He forced the coldness into his soul, denying the emotion that was trying to take control.

The shouts of victory sounded distant as he nursed his wound, the defenders roaring in triumph as the Maharajah's finest troops pulled back, beaten by the resolute defiance of the redcoats.

The defenders of Bhundapur had survived the first attack.

Chapter Forty

───◆◆◆───

'Hold still.'

'It bloody hurts!'

'Don't be such a baby.' Isabel stuck the tip of her tongue out as she concentrated on tying off the bandage she had used to cover Jack's wound.

'Sweet Jesus!' Jack hissed the oath as the tight binding sent a spasm of pain running up his arm.

'Listen to you.' Isabel shook her head in resignation, busying herself gathering up the cloths she had used to clean the wound. 'I've never heard such fuss.'

'My apologies, ma'am.' Jack opened and closed his hand, testing its mobility. The pain was like a red-hot poker buried deep in his flesh, but his arm was usable. He had been lucky. Khan's strength had been failing when the blow landed. Had it been driven with full force, Jack knew he could have lost his arm.

'You should take better care of yourself.' Isabel tried to sound light-hearted, but Jack could hear the strain in her voice. A smear of blood had dried on her cheek, the grotesque rouge dark against her pale skin.

For the first time, Jack understood her father's longing for her to live a normal life. She did not deserve to be surrounded by death. A girl her age should be worrying about what dress to wear to the ball, which young gentleman would receive the honour of being the first name on her dance card. She should not be forced to wallow in blood, bearing witness to the basest emotions of man.

'You should go home, Izzy.' He spoke softly.

Isabel bit her lip. He saw the pain in the green eyes that had so captivated him, from the first moment he had seen her at Proudfoot's gathering the night he had arrived in Bhundapur. She didn't speak, but Jack caught the slightest nod of her head as she acknowledged his words.

He reached across with his good arm, entwining his fingers around hers. 'You deserve so much more than this.'

Isabel shook her head, forcing down the shudder that ran through her body. 'There, that's your arm done.' Her voice was cool. She slid her hand from his, gathering up the remnants of bandage before wiping clean the bloodstained scissors that she then slipped back into the front pocket of her smock. 'How does it feel?'

Jack lifted his arm, flexing the fingers to demonstrate the successful dressing of his wound. 'It hurts, but it's fine.'

'It won't stop you fighting?'

Jack looked up sharply as he heard the ice in her voice. 'No. It won't stop me. It can't.'

'So you can do your duty. You can go on killing.'

Jack closed his eyes. Her bitterness hurt. When he opened them once more, she was staring at him. 'Yes.' He acknowledged her condemning words. 'I'll fight.'

'You frighten me, Jack.' Isabel's voice cracked. 'And I am so tired of being scared.'

The words were like barbs.

She sniffed once before rising to her feet, brushing away the dirt that had stuck to her simple dress. The heavy tread of army boots prevented Jack from saying anything further, and he too eased himself upright, cradling his arm gingerly as he moved.

'Begging your pardon, sir. I'm sorry to interrupt, but Major Proudfoot would like you both to join him.' Colour Sergeant Hughes stood ramrod straight in the doorway, his eyes elevated as if embarrassed at spoiling the moment.

Jack smiled at the sergeant's sensibilities. He couldn't help thinking how he could have used a man like Hughes in the Crimea. 'Thank you, Colour Sergeant.'

'How's the arm, sir?'

'Bearable. It could've been worse.'

'Indeed, sir. I was watching you.' The colour sergeant spoke plainly. 'You fought like the very devil.'

'Mr Lark is a fool, Colour Sergeant,' Isabel interrupted. 'He throws himself around like a schoolboy, thinking he cannot come to harm.'

'He's an officer, ma'am. It's what they do.' Hughes offered the explanation as if it was all the answer that was needed. 'The best of them, anyhow.'

Yet Jack heard the censure in Isabel's words. The enemy were at the walls and he would have to fight again if he was to do his duty. But he knew he was losing the girl who had saved him. Doing his duty came with a price.

Jack helped Isabel across the barricade, cherishing the thin smile she gave him in thanks. They had been ordered by Major Proudfoot to join the deputation that would answer the enemy's summons to a parley.

A party of exhausted sepoys were checking the enemy bodies that littered the ground outside the barricade, doing their best to separate the living from the dead. There was no time for anything more; the dead would simply have to be left where they lay. They had at least cleared a path, so that Isabel and the cantonment's officers would not have to walk on a carpet of bodies, although the ground under their feet was still soaked in blood, the pale dusty soil stained dark mulberry.

Proudfoot was dressed in uniform, the first time Jack had seen him in the scarlet coat of a British officer. Ever the dandy, he had eschewed the regulation shako, preferring to wear in its place an old-fashioned bicorn topped with an enormous ostrich feather.

'I hope the bastards are asking for permission to bugger off,' Dutton growled as he walked at Jack's side. 'Beg your pardon, of course, Miss Youngsummers.'

Isabel looked across Jack and smiled sweetly. 'I have spent too long with Jack to be shocked or offended by such words, Major Dutton. Have no fear for my sensibilities.'

Major Proudfoot heard the words and laughed aloud. 'You have a great deal to answer for, Jack.' There was no trace of nervousness on his face. Clearly being summoned to a flag of truce on a bloodstained battlefield did not daunt the British political officer.

'As do you.' Jack's arm was hurting like the very devil, and his reply was belligerent.

Proudfoot simply shrugged the barbed comment away. 'I am glad the Maharajah demanded that you and Miss Youngsummers join our jolly gathering. It would have been so dull with just Dutton for company.'

They picked their way over the bloodstained ground beyond the north wall in silence. Jack wondered at the Maharajah's summons. He felt the twist of nerves deep in his gut as he walked towards the man he had abandoned. Isabel's presence only added to his disquiet, and he wondered what strange design the quixotic ruler of Sawadh was trying to conjure.

As the two parties came together just fifty yards away from the defenders' perimeter, Jack studied the three men who had called for the truce. He was not surprised to see the Maharajah; he could not imagine the ruler of Sawadh leaving the negotiations to anyone else. He was flanked by his son and by the grey-haired general Jack had met for the first time at the conference of war shortly before he and Isabel had fled.

'Sire.' Proudfoot opened the conversation. 'I truly regret it has come to this.'

The Maharajah's face creased as he tried to contain his temper. 'No. I don't think you do. I think this suits you very well.'

Proudfoot looked suitably shocked at the accusation. 'I cannot fathom why you would say that, sire. No man can wish for war.'

The Maharajah snorted before focusing on Jack. 'So, my general now fights against me?'

Jack had forgotten the force of the Maharajah's personality. It was only as the man's hard brown eyes fixed his own that he felt the first stirring of remorse. Until then, he had simply been carrying out his duty, doing what he knew best. Coming face to face with the Maharajah once again made him doubt the wisdom of his choice. 'I had no option, sir.'

To his surprise, the Maharajah smiled. 'I would not have expected anything else from you, Jack. You would have disappointed me had you betrayed the country of your birth. As much as I might wish you had chosen differently. I want you to know that I forgive you. I bear you no ill will.'

Jack found it hard to swallow, and remained silent as the Maharajah turned to Isabel. 'You should not be here on the field of battle, Miss Youngsummers.'

'Where else would I be, Your Highness?' Isabel lifted her chin as she answered the Maharajah.

'I would wish you were somewhere safe. I would ask you to consider coming back with me. I will personally vouch for your safety.'

Jack saw the look of longing in Prince Abhishek's eyes. Clearly the heir to the throne had his own desire for Isabel's company.

'I will not go.' Isabel's voice quavered as she replied, but her face betrayed her resolution.

The Maharajah smiled at her conviction. 'I did not expect a different answer, but I could not have lived with myself if I had not made the offer. Perhaps after this is over you will consider once again being my guest?'

Major Dutton had endured enough of the opening flattery and gave Isabel no opportunity to reply. 'Let us dispense with the pleasantries. What do you want?'

The Maharajah's eyes were cold as he turned them on the English major. 'What I want, Major Dutton, is for you to leave my land. I will stand by the terms of the treaty my father signed, but I will no longer tolerate your presence in my kingdom.'

'I'm afraid that really isn't possible, sire.' Proudfoot's oiled tones reclaimed the conversation. 'You must become accustomed to the idea that we will rule here when you are gone.'

'And if I refuse?'

'Then we will rule here now.' The oil was gone from Proudfoot's voice. There was just steel.

'In that case we have nothing more to discuss.' The Maharajah's face betrayed his anger. 'I will allow an hour's truce for removal of the wounded.'

'Four hours.' Proudfoot smiled with false charm as he countered.

'One hour. My men will understand.' The Maharajah's voice was as hard as the rock that littered his land.

Proudfoot pouted and opened his mouth to carry on the negotiation, but the Maharajah raised a hand to silence him.

'There is nothing more to say. You have one hour and then you will die.'

Jack saw the hard glare in the Maharajah's eyes. He had seen this transformation before, the sudden switch from urbane gentleman to wolfish ruler.

The Maharajah turned, showing his back to the British party. There was no more to be said.

They had one hour. One hour to see to the wounded and prepare for the next assault. An assault they would have to repel.

One hour until they would have to fight or die.

Chapter Forty-one

T he defenders sat in an uneasy silence. The hour had passed swiftly, the time spent in rushed preparations, the tired men harried as they prepared to fight again. Ammunition had to be distributed, weapons cleaned and reloaded and water had to be drawn from the well just outside the 24th's barracks. Wounds had to be dressed and the dying cared for, whilst all the while watching for the enemy to reappear.

Jack had been forced to reduce the number of men stationed on the roof of the barracks to just five, under the command of a corporal. It was not ideal, but the 24th had lost nine men in the first assault and there would be too few to defend the barracks if he left the original number to act as sharpshooters. He had retained his small flying squad, although this time he had vowed not to do anything as reckless as throw himself out of the window and into the middle of the enemy.

'Why don't the buggers come, and get it over with?' Private Jenkins asked the question that was on every redcoat's mind. The waiting played at their nerves, the fear scratching at them, an itch that could not be ignored.

'Are you off somewhere special then, Private?' Jack had been peering out of the same window as the anxious redcoat.

'I just want it over with, Mud. I mean, sir.'

'We all do.' Jack unbuttoned his holster and made sure his sword was loose in its scabbard. The rest of his men were doing the same, fiddling with their kit as they went through the superstitious rituals that they believed might be the difference between life and death, each fearing the dreadful lottery they would soon have to face.

'They are brave, aren't they now, those blue-coated buggers? They nearly got in here last time. For a moment I thought it was going to be like Chillianwala all over again.'

'You were there?'

'I was, bach. Bloody slaughtered, we were. There were only five of us left standing in my company when it was over. Those Sikh boys fight damn hard.'

'Well we stopped this lot once. We'll just have to do it again.'

'That we will, boyo.' Jenkins had clearly forgotten he should be addressing Jack as an officer. They were just two redcoats standing waiting for the enemy to appear. 'No bloody heroics this time, though.' Jenkins had been in the flying squad that had followed Jack on his foolish charge. 'We are all getting too old for that kind of nonsense.'

'I can't promise.'

Jenkins shook his head despairingly. 'Officers. They always know best, isn't that right, bach? No matter how bloody foolish it may be.'

The crack of a musket firing prevented Jack from replying. A salvo struck the side of the barracks, each bullet smacking into the stone with an ear-splitting crack. The redcoats came to life, flinching instinctively as the fusillade gouged thick crevices in the heavy stone.

'Bloody hell!' Jenkins lost his shako as he ducked down behind the protective wall of mealie bags that blocked off the lower half of the window. 'It's going to be like that now, is it?'

Another salvo of musket fire cracked out. The second assault in the battle for Bhundapur was about to begin.

'Mark your targets!' Colour Sergeant Hughes snapped the order as the redcoats cowered from the steady fire. 'Aim at the smoke.'

The Maharajah's men had learnt from their first assault. This time there would be no wild charge. The musket fire coming from the windows and doorways of the buildings that lined the pathway leading away from the 24th's barracks drove the redcoats down behind their walls and barricades.

Yet there was no precision to the enemy fire. There were no massed volleys, the gunmen shooting as they were ready, forcing the defenders to endure a constant barrage that sometimes died away before rising to a climax as half a dozen men fired at once. The cough of each gun sounded different, the redcoats under fire from a collection of weaponry ranging from ancient silver jezzails to Brown Bess muskets that would have been at home on the field at Waterloo. As varied as the guns were, each was still capable of killing if its bullet found its mark, and the redcoats kept as low as they could behind the windows, or stayed carefully to the side of the loopholes that dotted the wall closest to the enemy.

'Commence firing!'

Jack was taking a risk. He had been tempted to hold back, waiting for a charge. But he had seen the anxiety on the faces of the redcoats as he made them endure the withering fire. He had to let them reply, trusting them to be able to reload in time if an assault looked to be building.

The muskets rang out almost in unison as the men's tense trigger fingers were finally released. The deeper cough of their percussion muskets drowned out the enemy fire, the effect of nearly sixty guns firing together creating a thunderclap of sound that echoed loudly in the confined barracks.

'Reload! Look lively.' Jack urged. He peered through the window, screwing up his eyes at the inevitable cloud of powder smoke that billowed back to flood the room. He saw a couple of bodies slump to the ground as the 24th's fire found its target, but it was difficult to tell how effective it had been.

Another smattering of bullets crashed into the barracks, gouging more holes in the already heavily pockmarked walls. It appeared the Maharajah's men were happy to stay out of sight and engage the 24th in a duel of musketry. It would be a long, tedious war of attrition, but it would pin the redcoats in place, the idea of abandoning the barracks simply unthinkable.

A huge cheer sounded from outside. It was a feral roar, the sound of the mob screaming its hatred. The terrifying noise of warriors released to the charge.

'Sir!' Corporal Jones summoned his officer.

Jack bounded across the room, cursing aloud as an enemy bullet scorched past his ear and knocked a fist-sized lump of plaster from the scarred wall.

'Sir! Hundreds of the bastards!'

Jack followed the corporal's pointing finger. The Maharajah had altered his plan of attack, using the hour-long truce to gather together all his remaining foot soldiers. They had been formed into a huge phalanx that was aimed like an enormous fist at the north wall. The Maharajah was gambling everything on a single, massive assault, a sledgehammer blow that would smash a hole in the defenders' frail perimeter and create an opening for his precious lancers.

Jack stared at the enemy's massed ranks and saw certain defeat.

'Half the company with me. Colour Sergeant Hughes, keep the rest of the men at the windows and return fire.' He snapped off his orders. His men responded calmly.

Jack ran his eye over the Maharajah's assault, which was already charging towards the north wall. They seemed unstoppable, and the tips of the sepoys' muskets were wavering as they stared down the barrels of their weapons at the immense horde tearing towards them.

'Fire!'

Jack clearly heard Dutton's order before the roar of a massed volley crashed out. The major had timed it to perfection. The enemy horde was no more than fifty yards from the barricade when the horror was unleashed. At such close range the sepoys' muskets couldn't miss. The men leading the rush were struck down as if someone had suddenly lifted a rope to trip dozens of them at once. The musket balls tore into the packed formation, flaying the front ranks, the blood bright as bodies were torn and shredded.

'Hold them!' Dutton's voice was huge in the shocked silence after the volley. His sepoys heard the cry, bracing to meet the wave of hatred that was coming for them. Every inch of the barricade was blocked, the sepoys standing shoulder to shoulder, their wicked bayonets reaching forward and presenting an unbroken front towards the enemy.

Then the screaming began.

The enemy wounded screamed, their voices rising in horror as their bodies were mangled and shredded by the well-timed volley. The living screamed as the shadow of death passed them by, the delight of living turned into a visceral shriek of hatred as they bounded past the ruined bodies of their fellows and used their sabres to hack at the men who had so nearly killed them.

There was no time for the sepoys to reload.

The enemy stepped past the dead and the dying, ignoring the cries for aid as they pressed home their attack. They came at the barricade in a rush, filling every part of the wall, the deep ranks of the mob driving those at the front forward, the power of the charge relentless.

The sepoys stood their ground. They stabbed across the barricade, punching their bayonets into the bodies of their enemies. Time after time they rammed the weapons forward, twisting and recovering the blades before thrusting again, trying to hold back the tide of shrieking devils that swarmed around them.

But there were simply too many men fighting against them. Sharpened spears reached across the barricade. The Maharajah had packed the leading ranks with the weapons, the longer reach of the spears allowing the attackers to stab at the sepoys whilst keeping away from the bayonets that the red-coated soldiers were using with such professionalism.

All along the barricade the redcoats fell. The long spears found their way past even the most determined defence, the vicious weapons driven deep into the sepoys' flesh. The enemy leapt forward as soon as a gap in the line appeared, swarming over the barricade before turning and unleashing their talwars at the nearest defenders.

It was chaos.

Dutton's men fought on, using the butts of their muskets as clubs, striking back at the enemy that now swarmed around them. They refused to be beaten, and here and there the enemy was driven back over the wall, the desperate defiance of the defenders sealing the gaps.

Dutton charged at the head of his flying squad. They tore into the largest gap, the cough of the major's revolver loud enough to be heard even above the noise of the violent struggle. The charge drove deep into a pack of the Maharajah's soldiers that had breached the wall, the sepoys flowing past their commander to ram their bayonets forward, the disciplined charge sending a shudder through the enemy ranks.

Yet too many holes had been torn in the defenders' perimeter. Even as Dutton's charge thrust a path into one gap, so another breach was made further down the line. The melee descended into swirling chaos, men fighting in desperation as they sought to kill or be killed. The shrieks of the living added to the screams of the dying to create a cacophony that belonged in hell itself.

A trumpet blared, its rising call clear even over the shrieks of the men fighting for their lives.

The Maharajah had waited for this moment.

His lancers rode forward, their ranks ordered and precise.

The trumpet called again, and the two lines of cavalry halted, dressing the ranks so that every spacing was in perfect order. The lances were lowered, each man crouching with the dreadful weapon tight under his right armpit, the vicious blade held still.

The trumpet blared for the last time. The lancers kicked their mounts in unison, ordering them forward whilst keeping the line straight, the precision drilled into them by the countless hours of instruction they had endured in preparation for this moment.

The horses lifted their heads, sensing the building excitement. Their riders were forced to pull hard on the reins to keep their mounts in check as they maintained the pace of the walk. The slow, steady movement would soon build into a trot, then a canter, before they were finally released to the madness of the gallop that would see them committed to the attack.

The Maharajah rode at the lancers' head, leading his beloved cavalry forward, taking the power of his own sword to fight against those who would strip his descendants of their right to rule.

Chapter Forty-two

'Front rank! Kneel!'

Jack had formed his half-company into a double rank facing towards the north wall. He saw the desperate struggle around the perimeter but he held his men back, certain that to commit them now would be to throw their lives away. Their barrack block was behind them, a final refuge should they be forced to retreat.

The drumming vibrated through the ground. He had felt the dreadful noise before and he knew what was coming.

The trumpets sounded again. He had recognised the call. His body still reacted, the thrill of the rising notes setting his nerves on edge. This time he was the target of the charge.

'Stand firm, men.'

He saw the look of horror on his men's faces, their eyes wide as they watched the confused melee in front of them, their knuckles showing white as they held their weapons tight.

The lancers were moving fast now. Jack could see glimpses of their beautiful blue jackets and he felt a pang of pride at the disciplined order of their charge. The sepoys saw them too. In desperation, they ran, fleeing the dreadful weapons that were held so still despite the wild motion of the galloping horses. The Maharajah's foot soldiers cut them down as they tried to escape, slashing their weapons forward before they too fled, scrambling away to the flanks lest their own cavalry ride them down.

Jack watched as the surviving sepoys broke. They had fought hard, defying the terrible odds, holding the line when lesser men would have run.

Yet none could stand in the face of the lancers.

Dutton roared as he fought. He stamped his right foot forward, driving his sword into the guts of one of the wild hill men who had broken through the line. He twisted the blade, stepping backwards before backhanding it and beating aside the spear that had been thrust at his side. He punched the sword forward once more, snatching away the throat of the man who had tried to kill him, the whisper of blood flung wide by the blow.

The press of men around him eased, the nearest enemy soldiers backing away before turning to run.

'Thank God.' Dutton felt the surge of relief course through him. They had held. They had done the impossible.

'Back to the barricade! Well done, men! Well done ...' The major's voice died away. His men were running. The enemy were clearing to the flanks, their faces twisted in fear as they fled.

Dutton didn't understand. He looked at the remains of the wall he had ordered made. There was little of it left, the mealie bags and crates pushed aside or lying crushed and splintered where the enemy had broken through. Along its length was a carpet of bodies, the bright red of the sepoys' jackets spread thickly amidst the corpses of the enemy.

The ground vibrated under his feet, a deep, resonant thunder that reverberated through his exhausted body. Dutton looked up, and for the first time he saw the blue line that surged towards him.

The lancers charged the barricade. The horses leapt over the remains of the obstacle, their riders swaying in the saddle as they adjusted their weight to absorb the landing. They swept on without a pause, their lances twitching as they calmly picked their first targets.

They hit the running men with an audible slap. The screams of the dying were shut off as their bodies fell under the galloping horses, the heavy hooves crushing away any last vestige of life. The lancers' line broke as they charged into the fleeing sepoys, the riders yanking at the reins as they sought more targets for their blood-splattered lances. The sepoys were slaughtered as they ran, the merciless lancers spurring hard to ride down any that survived.

'Front rank. Fire!' Jack roared the order as soon as he saw the left flank of the lancers' line break through the thin screen of scattered sepoys. 'Reload!'

He watched in grim satisfaction as the nearest lancers fell to the first volley, the musket balls slamming cruelly into the flesh of horse and rider, the fire indiscriminate.

'Rear rank, present!'

He counted the seconds in his head. He knew it would take his men around twenty seconds to reload, and he had to hold back the rear rank's volley to make sure the redcoats kept up a regular fire on the swarming lancers. He waited, his icy calm reassuring his command, who watched in horror as the enemy lancers butchered the remains of Dutton's fortress.

The seconds crawled by. The front rank rushed to reload their muskets, but to Jack it seemed as if time had frozen. He saw an unseated lancer scramble to his feet, his hands reaching for the sabre belted around his waist. He stared at the man, recognising him from the long hours spent drilling with the lancers. He saw sadness on the man's face as he watched his mount drumming its hooves into the ground in agony, its body swathed in a sheet of red blood from the dreadful wound in its chest. The lancer turned, his face twisted in hatred, his sword lifting as he charged towards the 24th, determined to carry on the fight, to take his sabre against the men who had killed the horse he had loved.

'Fire!'

The second rank's volley crashed out. Jack gripped and re-gripped the handle of his sword as he began the long, slow count for a second time. The unseated lancer was gone, his remains lying no more than ten paces from the thrashing body of his mount, his rage and desire for revenge obliterated by the musket ball that had torn his body apart.

'Dutton!' Through the powder smoke Jack saw the major staggering backwards. His hat was gone and a river of blood ran from a dreadful wound to his scalp. Jack was close enough to see the blood that stained the sabre in Dutton's hand. The major turned, his face twisted into a grimace of horror.

Jack held his stare. He could see the pain in the older officer's face, the dreadful shock at the lancers' charge clear in his wide, vacant eyes.

A lancer rode Dutton down. The long lance was driven through the major's back with such force that the tip emerged from his chest in a gory fountain of blood. Dutton fell instantly, his body thrown like a rag doll to lie face down in the dirt.

'Front rank! Fire!' Jack ordered the next volley despite the shudder that ran through him as he watched his fellow officer die. He was acting like an automaton, the commands coming unbidden to his lips as he handled the power of the 24th's brutal volleys with familiarity, a craftsman using his tools.

The lancer who had struck Dutton down turned as the volley thundered out. He didn't flinch as the bullets whispered past, but pulled hard at his horse's reins, his free right hand reaching for the jewel-encrusted sabre at his waist now that his lance was stuck fast in Dutton's body, the need to fight driving him, the urge to kill all-consuming. Jack recognised the rider. The Maharajah of Sawadh had not shirked the fight.

Jack stared as the Maharajah rammed his spurs hard into his mount's side, the enemy leader's mouth wide open as he summoned his riders to greater efforts. Jack tore his eyes away. There was no time for regret. He stalked along his thin line, walking from flank to flank, prowling behind his men, counting off the seconds until the next volley, the steady rate of fire the only thing that could save them from the same bloody fate as Dutton and his men.

The lancers ploughed across the parade square. The open area that had seemed such a boon to the defenders was now transformed into a killing ground.

A handful of sepoys still ran for their lives, the terrified fugitives scattering to the wind as they tried to escape the dreadful lances.

None made it more than fifty yards. Red-coated bodies lay dotted in every direction. A few still lived, twisting and writhing on the ground in agony, the wounds inflicted by the razor-sharp lance tips horrific. Most lay still, in the unnatural, twisted poses of death, victims of the dreadful skill of the disciplined lancers.

Jack heard the trumpet blare. The Maharajah's voice roared as he ordered his men to re-form, reasserting control over the lancers who had ridden to such bloody success. For the battle was not yet finished.

The Maharajah reined in, coming to a halt directly opposite the 24th's thin line. The lancers began to assemble around him, the ordered lines rebuilding after the careering gallop in pursuit of the fleeing sepoys.

Jack pushed through his men. 'Reload.' He gave the order quietly as he walked to stand in front of the line, directly in the Maharajah's path. As he did so, he watched the Maharajah. He saw the rueful smile on the man's face, the slow shake of the head as the ruler realised that the Englishman he had allowed to live was standing in his way. Yet there was coldness in the brown eyes now, a despair that Jack had not seen before.

He withdrew his revolver, taking it in his left hand, his talwar ready in his right. As he watched, the smile left the Maharajah's face. It was replaced by the dispassionate expression of a killer.

Behind him, the outnumbered redcoats stood in silence. In front of them, the lancers aligned their ranks so that their charge would bear down on their red-coated opponents who waited so patiently to meet them. The defiant British soldiers were the final obstacle between the Maharajah and success. It would take one last charge, one last bloodletting, and he would claim the victory that could save his kingdom.

The trumpet blared. The three notes were clear, the even call echoing in the silence that had fallen over the blood-soaked battlefield.

It was the call to charge, the challenge to the cavalry to rake back their spurs and commit to the final madness.

And it came from the British.

* * *

The 1st Bengal Irregular Cavalry responded to the call to charge, the tide of bright yellow jackets flowing quickly into the wide expanse of open ground. With teeth bared, the dark faces beneath the golden headgear opened their mouths to scream their challenge aloud, the thrill of combat driving them forward.

A red-coated officer led the charge. Even from a distance, Jack could recognise the man who had become his enemy. Fenris held his sabre raised above his head as he thundered towards the Maharajah's cavalry.

The British tore into the flank of the stationary lancers. They scythed through the ordered ranks, cutting the blue-coated men down before they could react. The right-hand side of the Maharajah's formation was gutted in moments, the British irregular cavalrymen ripping it to shreds.

The lancers broke. The easy victory was snatched away, the final charge against the stubborn redcoats forgotten as they pulled at their reins and urged their tired mounts to turn and make a dash for safety.

The Bengal Cavalry went after them, cutting down any too slow to escape their brutal assault. Some lancers broke free from the vicious melee; Jack saw the Maharajah bent low over his saddle, surrounded by a group of his men who were thrusting their lances at the yellow-coated cavalrymen, selling their own lives in a desperate bid to give their ruler the chance to escape.

'Stay here!' He shouted the order as he ran, leaving his astonished command to watch as he dashed towards the heart of the melee. It was time to find a horse.

The animal pulled away from Jack's approach. Its nostrils flared wide in distress, but it had been trained well and it only shied away before again standing still close to the torn body of its fallen master.

Jack murmured as he approached, using the words he had learnt under Prince Abhishek's tutelage, holding out his hand to the nervous animal. He trod carefully around the ruined body of the lancer. The poor man had been hit full in the face by a musket ball, and there was nothing but a nauseating, pulsating mass where his head had once been.

The animal whinnied, something in Jack's manner reassuring, the soft words soothing its fear. It shivered as the unfamiliar touch ran over its flanks, but it stayed still long enough for Jack to launch himself into the saddle.

He slipped his feet into the stirrups, the familiar feeling of being astride a horse rushing through him. He pulled gently on the reins, turning the animal's head around before kicking it into motion.

He rode after the Maharajah.

Chapter Forty-three

━━━◆━━━

$\mathcal{P}$rince Abhishek cursed. He stayed at his father's side, urging his tired horse to keep pace with the Maharajah's escort even as the British cavalry tore through the men behind him. He dropped his bloodied lance and tugged his talwar from its scabbard, knowing the long reach of the lance would count against him in the vicious melee of hand-to-hand fighting.

The small group broke free and rode for the sharply sided valley that still bore the churned-up, bloodstained soil of the previous day's fighting. They rode for their lives, staying close to one another as they raced away. Yet their horses were already tired, the long ride from the citadel followed by the charge against Dutton's sepoys draining much of their strength. There would be no easy escape.

Abhishek glanced over his shoulder and saw the throng of horsemen riding after them. They were led by one of the red-coated devils who had plagued his father's land for decades. Abhishek knew then what he had to do. His father had to escape. He was the only man capable of binding the kingdom's wounds and finding a way to secure some sort of future under the oppressive authority of the foreign queen.

He reined in hard, slowing his mount and yanking its head round so that he faced his pursuers. The Maharajah and his remaining lancers did not notice his sudden manoeuvre and raced on, their horses labouring to keep them from the relentless pursuit.

Abhishek threw his head back, calling to his gods, daring them to bear witness to his death. He thrust his spurs into his mount's sides, making it rear on its haunches before it gathered its last strength and once again strained its aching sinews as it accelerated. Prince Abhishek, heir to the kingdom of Sawadh, was riding to meet his death.

He screamed as he charged, roaring his challenge to the gods he had summoned. He closed on the pursuing riders, urging his tired mount into the gallop, feeling the joy of the charge for the second time that day.

But this time he knew he would die.

He roared as he slashed his blade at the first figure that rushed past him, his arm jarring as the sharp edge caught the man's ribcage. The blow knocked the rider from the saddle, his chest sliced open by the single strike, the red stain of blood bright against the gaudy yellow of his jacket.

Abhishek was turning even before the man had hit the ground. He backhanded his weapon, using the sharpened rear to strike at a second rider, slicing across the man's face to leave a nauseating flap of skin hanging as he scored a deep wound through his features.

The pursuers were turning now, wheeling round to counter the madman who had charged into their midst.

'He's mine!'

Abhishek heard the red-coated officer bellow at his men, but he was in no mood to listen. He rose high in the stirrups, urging his horse to leap forward, timing the movement perfectly, punching the tip of his talwar into the spine of the nearest enemy rider. He twisted the blade as soon as he felt it catch the man's backbone, releasing the weapon from the clutches of his flesh. He had enough time to recover the blade before the red-coated officer came at him.

Their blades met, the vicious contact jarring both men's arms. Neither flinched. They hacked at each other, using their knees to control their mounts as they twisted round. Their swords slashed and parried, yet neither could penetrate the other man's defences. They bellowed as they fought, grunting with the force of the blows, howling in frustration as they failed to land the telling attack. Parry followed parry, the strikes coming in quick succession, both men fighting with desperate skill as they battled to cut the other down.

Jack heard the sound of fighting before he could see what has happening. He had urged his mount on, feeling the tremors in the horse's body as he drove it past the point of exhaustion, cruel in his mastery. He saw Prince Abhishek engaging Lieutenant Fenris, unable to do anything but spur the flagging animal onwards as the two men fought their desperate duel.

He was still a hundred yards away when he heard Fenris shriek in victory.

The British officer deflected the prince's sword wide, finally beating aside the man's defences. He rammed his sabre forward, punching the tip into the prince's body, and bellowed in victory as he felt the sword slide into the younger man's guts, the resistance of the flesh giving way against the vicious blow.

Fenris leant forward, pushing all his weight behind his sword, twisting the blade so that it churned in his opponent's stomach, the blood pumping from the dreadful wound to run hot and sticky over his hand. He saw the shock on the prince's face, the searing agony reaching the young man's eyes.

'Die, you bastard.' Fenris eased his weight forward so his face was inches from the dying prince's. Vicious in his victory, he spat out the words, his spittle flung to fleck his enemy's face. 'I won.' Abhishek's eyes glazed over, the prince's face betraying his youth as he approached death. 'You lost.' Fenris gave his blade a final twist before he pulled the sword out, swaying backwards to avoid the body that toppled from the saddle.

The boy hit the ground face first. The Maharajah's son and heir, the rajkumar, was dead.

'Ride them down!' Fenris snarled the order.

The men from the 1st Bengal Cavalry had watched in horror as the British officer cursed the Maharajah's son. Now they gathered their reins, exchanging looks with their fellows, disgust mirrored on every face.

'Ride, damn you!' Fenris turned his horse in a tight circle, sneering into the faces of the men who surrounded him. 'Ride!'

The habit of obedience ran deep. The rissaldar who led the riders barked his own orders, throwing his reins forward and spurring his horse away. His men followed, happy to be away from the vicious officer who fought with such disdain.

'Fenris!'

Lieutenant Fenris started at hearing his name. He had thought to take the body of the young prince back to Proudfoot, claiming the reward he knew would be his for removing the only male heir to the throne of Sawadh. He saw a rider hurtling towards him and he felt the hatred flare deep in his veins. It appeared he was being given the chance to bring back two bodies. He smiled as he recognised the opportunity that was being presented to him.

He would add the body of the charlatan to that of the foreign prince.

'Hello, Arthur,' Jack called out in greeting before slipping from the saddle as his horse came to a halt.

Fenris turned, a twisted smile on his face. 'Good timing. You can help me with this corpse.'

Jack looked down at the body of the prince. He thought of the times he had cursed the Maharajah's son, damning the prince for the long, hard hours he had endured as he learnt to ride. He recalled too, the jealousy he had felt when he understood the young man's desire for Isabel. Now, he studied the bloodstained corpse lying face down in the dust and tried to feel nothing, to deny the emotion that surged through him.

'Put the dirty beggar back on his horse, would you, old chap?' Fenris stood still as he gave the order, using his sabre to point to the pathetic remains of the Rajkumar of Sawadh.

Jack saw the calculating look on Fenris' face. He noticed the sword still held low in his right hand, dripping with Abhishek's blood. He looked into Fenris' eyes and saw death.

'You killed him. You do it.' He turned his back on the lieutenant, making as if to walk back to his own horse.

He heard the scrabble of feet on the dusty soil and turned just as

Fenris launched himself forward, his sword flung in a wide arc, the blow aimed at Jack's head. At the last moment, Fenris twisted his wrist, angling the sword down so that it was aimed at the joint of neck and shoulder, the sudden change in direction almost quicker than the eye could detect.

But Jack was faster. His talwar cut through the air as he lifted it into position to parry the attack he had sensed was coming. He flicked his wrist as the weapons came together, turning his rising blade so that Fenris' sword sliced along its edge, the cowardly attack blocked and battered away.

In a heartbeat, he went after Fenris. He punched the talwar forward, ready for the inevitable parry, already switching his weight so that he could bring his blade round, slicing it at the red-coated officer's side. He followed the attack with another, flowing through the movements, his mind watching from afar as Fenris was forced to back away, his sword only just managing to beat aside the series of blows. They came so fast that the lieutenant was given no time to counterattack, and Jack smiled as he fought, feeling the speed coursing through him.

Fenris was panting with exertion, sweat slicking his dark hair to his forehead. For the first time, Jack saw panic reach his opponent's eyes, the terror building as he felt the presence of death looming at his shoulder.

In desperation, Fenris gambled. He stumbled backwards, moving quickly away from the dreadful talwar that came at him at such speed. The tip of the blade scored across his chest, splitting open the fabric of his scarlet coat. Yet it failed to touch his skin, and the manoeuvre gave him space, his gambit leaving Jack's defences open.

The moment Jack's sword went wide, Fenris flung himself forward, driving the tip of his sabre at his opponent's guts. He had risked his life to launch the attack, and he howled in joy as he saw the blade slip into Jack's stomach.

Jack felt the prick of steel against his flesh. He flung his sword at Fenris' blade, his calm detachment disappearing in a moment of wild panic. The talwar keened as it whipped through the air, driven by every ounce of strength that Jack possessed.

Fenris' howl of victory turned into a bitter shriek of frustration as Jack's sword punched his blade to one side before he had time to drive it home.

Jack sensed the madness blazing through him. He could feel the ooze of blood on his stomach, the bright pain of the wound flashing across his skull. A feral roar escaped his lips as the wild emotion wrestled away the last of his self-control, the delirium of battle filling every fibre of his being.

He threw himself forward, battering his talwar at the red-coated officer who had come so close to killing him. He let the madness have its head, hacking at Fenris, who was forced to scramble backwards, his sword trying desperately to beat aside the dreadful series of attacks.

Fenris screamed as the first blow pierced his defences. The talwar sliced into his side, gouging a thick crevasse in his flesh. Blood poured from the wound, flowing down his body to stain his white breeches. Another attack followed, knocking his sabre from his hand, the last of his defences torn away. As the fight ebbed from his body, he lifted his arms, shielding his face in a pathetic gesture of utter defeat.

'Don't kill me! Please! I beg you.' The strength left his legs and he fell heavily on to his backside. 'Don't kill me!' He sobbed the words, waving his arms in from of his face as if he could ward off the killing blow he knew was coming. He tried to shuffle backwards, his arms scrabbling at the rocky ground in a desperate bid to flee, the blood pulsing from his wound leaving a gory smear on the ground.

Jack advanced after the man he had defeated. The madness of the battle still roared in his ears, and he braced his arm, ready to thrust the talwar forward, any thought of mercy driven from his mind.

'Stop!'

The command came from behind him. It was a voice of authority but it would not stay his hand. He took a pace forward, ready to kill the pathetic creature begging for his life at his feet.

The crack of a revolver echoed loudly in the confines of the valley. The heavy ball crashed into the rock in front of Jack, the whine of the ricochet whistling past his ears.

'I said stop.'

The sound of the revolver's chamber rotating reached Jack's

ringing ears. He considered ramming home his sword regardless, the bitter desire to finish the worm that crawled on the ground in front of him almost too strong to resist.

'Jack Lark. I order you to stop.'

Jack felt the rage leave him. He lowered his sword and turned his back on Fenris, leaving the beaten man to sob in relief as he realised he had been spared.

Major Proudfoot smiled, smug satisfaction writ large on his face.

'Thank you, Jack.' The revolver was still in his hand, a thin trail of smoke leaving the barrel. 'I am genuinely sorry that I have to do this, but it really is for the best.'

He smiled at Jack before he pulled the trigger.

Chapter Forty-four

---

*J*ack flinched as the revolver fired, every muscle tensing as he anticipated the impact of the bullet. The sound of the shot echoed in his head but he felt nothing. He glanced over his shoulder and saw Fenris' body lying on the ground, blood pooling around his twisted corpse. The man who had come to hate Jack was dead, shot through the heart by a single bullet.

Proudfoot laughed. 'Not you, Jack.' He threw his head back and laughed at the sky. 'You should see your face.'

Jack tried to swallow and found he couldn't. He felt his body trembling, the shadow of death walking across his soul.

'Why?' His voice cracked as he forced out the question.

'Because he was a party to all this. I wanted to finish it.'

Jack spat out a thick wad of phlegm. 'Making everything neater.'

'Something akin to that.' Proudfoot was urbane in his reply.

'So you are executioner as well as judge and jury.'

Proudfoot laughed at Jack's bitterness. He plucked at the sleeve of his scarlet uniform. 'I'm a redcoat. Isn't that what we do? Besides, had I not interrupted you, I rather fancy you might have killed him yourself. I wanted that honour.'

'So you got your war.' Jack spat again, the words souring his mouth. 'And we gave you your victory. I hope you think it was worth the cost.'

'The cost?' There was a trace of fire in Proudfoot's voice now. 'I would say that for bringing a whole kingdom under the Company's control, it was a veritable bargain.'

'You bastard.'

Proudfoot frowned, as if chewing on something unpalatable. 'I wouldn't quite put it like that.' His face cleared, the joy of his success still too fresh to be soured by Jack's condemnation. 'But I have to thank you. I rather think we might have lost had it not been for you.'

Jack shuddered. It was akin to being thanked by the devil. He had done what he had believed to be his duty. The notion that he had been nothing more than Proudfoot's pawn shamed him.

Proudfoot saw the look on his face. 'Now, now. There is no need to be so modest. You are a killer, Jack. That is what you do. I saw you fight. You have a talent for it. Besides, I suspect you enjoy it.'

The words hit home. Jack shivered as he remembered the thrill of the battle, the soul-rending madness that had overwhelmed him. A part of him savoured the memory. Proudfoot had summed it up best. He wore a red coat. Killing was his trade.

'I must ask you to do one last thing for me.' Proudfoot absent-mindedly toyed with his revolver. Jack heard the gentle grind as the chamber moved around to bring a fresh cartridge under the hammer.

'What?' Jack felt the chill of fear.

'Run.' Proudfoot chuckled at the look of surprise on Jack's face. 'Come now, Jack. With Dutton and Fenris dead, you are the last man alive who knows all that has happened. Besides, you are a murderer. Didn't I just witness you kill Lieutenant Fenris in cold blood? Added to your other crimes, there really is no other option. But I owe you a debt for what you did today, so I will allow you to try to escape.' He lifted his arm, aiming the revolver at Jack's heart. 'Run, Jack, run.'

Jack's mind raced. He was tempted to stand his ground, to let Proudfoot administer a solution to his despair. He thought of Isabel, of the dreams he had foolishly allowed to grow. Her words before the final battle haunted him. She did not deserve to live with the constant fear of discovery, with only a killer to turn to for love. She deserved much more than he could give her. He thought too of Lakshmi, sensing the emotions she had awakened. Despite everything he had endured, he felt the will to live like a knot in his belly. He was a charlatan, an impostor, a thief and a killer. He would never submit meekly to his fate.

Proudfoot barked with laughter as he read the play of emotions on Jack's face. 'You are a fool, man. Did you ever truly imagine a future with that girl? Would she really give up everything for you? You are cursed, Jack Lark. I believe you will come to a very sorry end.'

Jack shivered, the echo of the Tiger's curse in Proudfoot's verdict. He looked up into the major's eyes. He saw nothing but death.

So he ran.

The ground was treacherous, the scree slope uneven and scattered with rocks lying ready to trip the unwary. Jack lurched into motion, his movements clumsy. He made it no more than half a dozen paces before he stumbled, his ankle twisting on the uncertain footing. He went sprawling, any last shred of dignity gone.

Proudfoot cackled wildly. 'Run!' He screamed the single command, his voice rising in pitch as he laughed at the sight of the proud charlatan scrabbling on the ground in his desperation to get away. Proudfoot feared the impostor. He had watched in awe as the man fought, terrified by the brutality as he hacked at the enemy. To reduce such a man, such a killer, to nothing more than a floundering fool desperate for life was as great a victory as the one he had won over the Maharajah of Sawadh.

He raised his revolver, aiming squarely at the back of the man who was trying so frantically to escape. He had had his amusement.

It was time to end the charade.

Jack sucked in a last breath, filling his lungs with the scorching air. He nearly choked on the dust his fall had kicked up, but he forced himself to still his quivering muscles. He slipped his hand across the front of his body, hiding the movement from Proudfoot. He heard the man's laughter but ignored it, refusing to let the flare of anger overwhelm him. He had to be in control. He closed his eyes, summoning the calm he would need.

The holster was unbuckled and Jack slipped his revolver free.

In one motion he scrambled to his feet and brought his arm around. He saw the look of surprise on Proudfoot's face as the barrel of the revolver appeared, heard his laughter cut off abruptly as the man he had believed to be fleeing for his life turned to fight.

Jack felt the tension of the trigger underneath his finger. He had seen too much death that day, enough to stain his soul for a lifetime. Yet he did not hesitate as Proudfoot's terror-stricken face filled the simple sight at the end of the barrel.

He pulled the trigger.

The blast of the revolver was loud. Jack walked forward, emerging from the inevitable cloud of powder smoke, keeping the weapon pointed at the man who had been the cause of so much death. He fired again, the action instinctive, the second bullet following within a heartbeat of the first.

The echo of the twin shots reverberated around the high ground before silence once again reclaimed the deserted, lonely hillside.

Jack's aim had been true. Proudfoot lay spread-eagled on the ground, striking as dramatic a pose in death as he had in life. Blood pooled around his body, which twitched as the last vestige of life escaped. Jack watched until at last Proudfoot lay still. The devil had taken another soul.

Jack stood over Proudfoot's body. The first bullet had hit the major in the chest, killing him instantly. The second had taken off the political officer's shoulder, the heavy bullet tearing a grotesque hole in what had been living flesh. The grey pallor of death had already laid claim to Proudfoot's face, his last, dreadful look of horror now fixed for ever.

Jack felt no remorse at having killed a fellow countryman. The man had deserved to die. He turned and savoured the peace. He was quite alone, only dead men for company.

Proudfoot's words settled in his heart, the echo of the Tiger's curse hardening like lead in his soul. He knew then he was destined to be alone. To be the killer everyone expected him to be.

It was time to leave.

He worked quickly. It did not take long to drag the two corpses to the horse that would carry them. Lifting them took more effort, but the lancer's horse was well trained and stood still, even as its nostrils flared at the sweet tang of the blood that still poured from the dead bodies. With an effort, Jack draped the bloody corpses across the saddle, using the long stirrups to bind them in place.

He pulled himself into the saddle of Proudfoot's sable mare, keeping a firm grip on the lead rope of the horse he had taken from the field of battle. He did not look at the body of the man he had just killed and that he now left behind for the vultures and the dozens of other animals that would relish a feast on such fresh flesh. He eased the mare's head round, turning his back on Bhundapur. With a click of his tongue and a gentle nudge of his heels, he eased the horse into motion, settling down into the slow walk that would take him up the steep side of the valley and away from the scene of so much death.

The tower stood silently as Jack approached, watching his progress with serene indifference. The last moments of the long ride brought back memories. He saw again the place where the Tiger and his men had ambushed the picnic party. He recognised the spot where he had fought the black-robed bandit leader, a shiver running down his spine as he felt again the presence of death at his shoulder.

The village was empty. The few who had survived the Tiger's ravaging horde had abandoned the place that had become a graveyard for their greed and their futile ambition. Jack rode along the dusty paths alone, only breaking the silence to click his tongue to urge on the pair of tiring horses, which strove to do his bidding despite their exhaustion.

The white-robed priest watched him approach. The man was old, his dark face creased and wrinkled with the passage of time. At his side was a boy. The youngster could not have been more than seven years old, the body under the simple langoti just sinew and bone. The priest laid a protective hand on the shoulder of his new apprentice before ushering him forward to help the white-faced stranger who had brought his dead to the tower.

Jack helped the boy with Fenris' body, his nose wrinkling in distaste at the stench of dead flesh. Together they dragged the corpse to the door of the tower, the officer's heels leaving twin trails in the sandy soil.

The white-robed priest did not say a word as the man walked away. Yet he stared for a long time at the back of the tall, lean officer with the hard grey eyes before he turned to the orphaned boy he had found hiding in the rubble of his grandfather's house, his days of goat-herding ended with the slaughter of his meagre herd and the massacre of his family.

The British officer did not turn back.

Chapter Forty-five

Jack had seen the lancers long before they spotted him. They rode towards him slowly. He waited for them patiently. He knew there was every chance that they would take one look at the white-faced man in the blue lancer's uniform and kill him out of hand, but still he sat and waited, the bloodstained talwar left in its scabbard.

The lancers came close. There were eight of them. All were old men whom he did not know from his time in the fortress. But he recognised the man who led them.

'He should've listened.' Jack spoke loudly as the lancers approached, his bitter words the only greeting he would give.

Count Piotr Wysocki said nothing. He halted his escort and contemplated the weary rider in front of him.

He finally broke the silence. 'He is a proud man. He did what he thought was right. We cannot judge him.'

Jack clenched his jaw, biting off his anger. 'Were you there?'

The count shook his head. 'I was left behind.'

Jack heard the acid in the words. The former commander of the Maharajah's lancers had remained in the fortress with the rest of the old men and the boys too young to fight. The only ones not trusted in battle. Now the party of decrepit lancers was the sole force the beaten Maharajah could muster, the ancient warriors forced back in the saddle to do their master's bidding once more.

'Yet you stayed.'

Count Piotr nodded, his face grave. 'Yes. I stayed. I had started to think my time here was done. Now, I think, it has just begun.' He looked Jack hard in the eyes. 'It is a strange thing, loyalty, is it not, Jack? It binds us to our fate, no matter how much we like to think we can choose.'

Jack thought on the count's words. His own notion of loyalty had bound him to the British. It had led him to forsake the Maharajah, to fight against the man who had saved him. In the aftermath of the battle, Proudfoot had claimed that he had made the difference, that his actions had been decisive in handing the British their victory. The notion shamed him.

'He will listen to you now.' Jack forced himself to speak, to not dwell on the emotions the count was stirring. He was no longer certain where his loyalty lay, what path his future would take.

'He will. He has no one else. The rest have forsaken him. They have abandoned the palace, taking anything of value. Only Lakshmi remains. He has lost everything.'

Jack turned in the saddle. He looked at the pathetic corpse draped over the saddle of the horse he had taken from the field of battle. The Maharajah had paid a high price for his ambition.

'I would take him his son.'

The count kept his eyes on Jack's. Then he nodded, acquiescing to the request.

Nothing more was said as the lancers formed up behind their former general, taking position around the body that Jack had brought out of the bloody carnage. Their brooding silence wrapped around him. He gave no command, but walked his horse forward, knowing they would follow.

The Taragarh looked deserted. Jack led his escort up the long sloping ramp towards the heavily protected gates. This time there was no traffic, no carts jostling and pushing as they were forced to wait for entry. The gates were open and unguarded. The mighty fortress of the maharajahs of Sawadh had finally been overcome.

Not through siege or escalade, but by the complete defeat of the army that defended the walls and guarded its gates.

A single rider rode to greet them. At first Jack thought it was a boy, the only one left to greet the remnants of the lancers who had ridden from the same fortress with such hope and pride just days before.

He halted the lancers, letting the rider approach. It was only as it got closer that Jack recognised the slim figure, the face that had once beguiled him now grey and stricken with grief and fear. Lakshmi's eyes searched his face, as if trying to find something she had lost.

Jack watched as she looked past him and saw the body he had come to deliver. Her eyes betrayed nothing, yet he saw the tears as she pulled at the reins, turning away from the man who had come to destroy any lingering hope in her heart.

He followed her, entering the Star Fort for the last time.

'You are a brave man, General Lark. Or a foolish one.'

Jack turned as he recognised the voice. He had been standing in the room of the Ramayana paintings. He had walked the familiar corridors of the palace, the memories of his life there haunting him. The place was deserted, the fabulous decorations intact but somehow now faded, as if life itself had fled. He had found himself in his favourite place, his feet taking him there without conscious thought. He had thought to rest, his battered body begging for some respite. He was still wrapped in the grime of the battlefield, the blood of his enemies mixed with that he himself had shed. He had hidden the filth under the dusty blue uniform he had retrieved from its hiding place, and now he faced the Maharajah dressed in the trappings of the life he had forsaken.

'It was my duty.' Jack's own voice was cold.

The Maharajah said nothing. He stared at Jack for a long time. Neither flinched from the scrutiny of the other. Jack saw the pain etched into the king's face, the grey pallor of grief stealing the vibrancy from his face. He looked as empty as his palace, his vitality swamped by the bitterness of defeat.

'Thank you.' When the Maharajah spoke, it was barely even in a whisper. 'Thank you for returning my son to me.'

'He needed to be brought home. I was honoured to escort him.' There was little sympathy in Jack's voice. There had been too much death for him to feel pity.

The Maharajah cupped his hand over his eyes. Jack could see the shudders that racked his body. When the hand fell away, he saw an old man.

'You and the Count were right. You English do not accept defeat.' The words were spoken without emotion, the Maharajah's eyes blank.

'You must do as they tell you now. You will be treated well.'

The Maharajah waved the words away. 'Nothing matters any more.'

'Of course it matters.' Jack's voice was brittle, but it was sharp too. 'Your people need you more than ever. You led them to this place. You cannot forsake them now.'

The Maharajah looked as if he had been slapped. 'Do not dare to tell me my duty.' He was vibrating with emotion, his face stricken with a mixture of grief and despair.

'I dare tell you, for it must be said.' Jack spoke without hesitation, the voice of an officer to a subordinate. 'You chose to go to war. Now you must deal with the peace you have forced on your people.'

He let his hand fall to the hilt of his sword. His fingers brushed the sharkskin grip. It was mottled now, stained with blood and with sweat. It was no longer the pristine weapon of a prince. It was the bloody tool of a killer.

The blade rasped as he pulled it from the scabbard, the noise loud in the quiet of the room. The balance of the weapon was still perfect, and Jack held it in his hand, feeling the power of the beautiful steel.

He reached across with his left hand and took hold of the blade. The edge was notched and pitted, the marks of combat etched deep. He had done his best to clean it, but flecks of blood were still stuck in the swirling script that decorated the talwar's faces, the residue of men's lives embedded in the steel.

He hefted the sword, then turned the blade, offering it hilt first to the Maharajah. 'This is yours.'

The Maharajah said nothing. He looked at the sword. His hand twitched, the fingers reaching instinctively to take the grip, then went still. He looked at Jack, fixing him with a stare that contained a spark of his former power.

'No. I have no need of a sword any more. The days of fighting are done. It is yours and yours alone.' He stood back, taking a step away from the man he had once sheltered. 'You are right to chastise me.' He looked at Jack for a long time without speaking. 'I think perhaps I underestimated you, Jack Lark.'

'Perhaps.' Jack had endured enough of kings. He felt the urge to leave, to get away from men with ambition. He suddenly felt foolish, standing holding out his sword in some theatrical gesture. He reversed the blade and thrust it back into its scabbard, a flicker of anger forcing away the sadness that had engulfed him since he had first seen Lakshmi riding towards him.

'Perhaps.' The Maharajah repeated the word softly. Then his face hardened. 'I will do as you say. I must lead my people, even though my heart is broken and my country will be swallowed by you monstrous British.'

'You must. The time for resistance is over. A new agent will come. He will treat you better than Proudfoot. He will ask you to sign another treaty, one that will let us rule here. Your time is done.'

Jack had nothing more to say. Too many men had died for him to feel sympathy, their lives sacrificed at the altar of the Maharajah's pride and Proudfoot's ambition. He took a step back, preparing to leave the Maharajah for the last time.

'Where will you go?' The Maharajah stopped him before turning and sitting heavily in a gilded chair that faced the window.

'I don't know.'

'What of Miss Youngsummers?'

Jack bridled at the sudden flurry of questions. 'She has no need of me. She needs a good man, not a killer.' He remembered Isabel's face as she had dressed the wound to his arm. He had seen her fear, her tiredness. He could not stay in her life. She deserved more.

'Perhaps you are both.' The Maharajah looked past Jack. He was staring at the small courtyard outside the window. The ornate fountain at its heart was silent, the water that gave it life gone.

Jack looked at the man who had once been king. 'No. I am one and one alone.'

He said nothing more. He left the Maharajah to stare into nothingness and walked away.

Epilogue

———◆·◆·◆———

The loud voices of the hawkers and the boldest stallholders called to the tall sahib who rode through the packed streets, each begging for his attention with their fantastical promises and unsubtle suggestions. The rider studiously ignored the entreaties, pushing away the bewildering array of objects that were thrust towards him. It made for slow progress along the narrow paved streets that wound their way through the city like a maze, but the rider did not care. He was in no hurry.

He watched a group of small boys playing at marbles as he rode by, their playground a gutter full of filth. The boys were naked save for golden cords around their necks and the gold and silver bangles on their wrists and ankles. One gleeful boy was clapping another hard on the back, the downcast expression on the second boy's face telling all who had won and who had lost. The crowd of at least thirty other boys were cheering at the tops of their lungs, the loud shouts of 'khoob! khoob!' drowning out even the most enthusiastic merchants.

The rider edged his horse around a filthy fakeer who sat plum in the middle of the narrow street, holding his palm aloft to display the scruffy tree growing through the centre of his hand. The manoeuvre took him close to the next stalls, and he was immediately besieged by eager merchants keen to have him part with his money. Yet something in the white-faced rider's face deterred even the most avaricious stallholder from pressing too close, the beautifully decorated talwar that hung at his hip too well used to be worn solely for decoration.

Authoritarian voices bellowed for attention and the rider edged his horse into a gap between the stalls as a palki pushed through the crowd. The curtains were pulled together, but there was enough of a gap for the rider to snatch a glimpse of a doe-eyed beauty reclining on scarlet cushions, the vision of loveliness disappearing quickly as her bearers jogged past.

He eased his horse back into the throng, taking care to steer a wide path around a group of hard-faced men mounted on sturdy mountain ponies, doing his best to ignore the appraising gazes that ran over him. This was no place for a fight, but still his hand crept to the holstered revolver at his hip, his fingers deftly undoing the buckle that held the flap in place. The gesture did not go unnoticed by the men from the hills. They saw too the anger in the eyes that flashed over them, and they let the stranger past.

The crowd thinned out as the loud calls from the minarets echoed through the tightly packed streets, the faithful called away to prayer. The rider hesitated, as if suddenly unsure of where he was headed, before he pulled off the street and passed through an intricately carved doorway and into an empty courtyard.

The place was an oasis after the jostling crowds of the thoroughfare. A marble fountain tinkled gently, the sound of moving water calming and cooling after the bedlam of the street.

The syces leapt to their feet as the rider eased himself wearily from the saddle, the young boys undoing the straps that held his belongings on his horse's back before his feet had even hit the ground.

'Welcome, sahib, welcome.' The owner of the hotel came bustling out from a room that overlooked the courtyard, hastily brushing the flakes of pastry from his white robes as he advanced on the tired rider. 'You have chosen a fine establishment for your stay.'

Something in the rider's flat stare made the owner pause. But he was too eager for the coins in the man's saddlebags to remain silent for long.

'Yes, sahib, this is a fine hotel. I shall give you the best room, yes, the very best room.' He clapped his hands, shooing the young boys into the whitewashed corridor that led into the interior of the hotel.

'Now, sahib, let me prepare you some refreshment! I have the very best Bass's beer, just what you need to clear the dust from your throat. Yes that's the very thing.'

More servants were sent running from the courtyard as the owner bowed at the waist and ushered the tall visitor into the shady interior of the hotel. 'This way, sahib. This way.'

The grey-eyed rider let himself be shown inside, the marble floors and white walls beautifully cool after the heat of the late-morning sun.

'May I ask your name, sahib?'

The tall man stopped and turned to face the owner, fixing him with a penetrating gaze. He let the silence stretch out, causing much hand-wringing from the anxious hotel owner, who wondered what offence the simple enquiry had caused. At last he spoke.

'My name is Fenris.' The man was curt, his voice clipped. 'Lieutenant Arthur Fenris.'

Historical Note

———◆•◆———

I must start my historical note with an apology. The kingdom of Sawadh did not exist, and the story of Proudfoot and his bloody plans for annexation is nothing more than the product of my imagination. However, I wanted to write about the last days of the East India Company's rule in India, and so the wonderful Maharajah and his colourful land came into being.

It now seems preposterous that a commercial company whose sole motivation was the creation of profit should be allowed to govern an entire country. Yet for one hundred years that is what happened in India. Jack arrives as the British East India Company's great power is at its peak, its unfettered management (some would say mismanagement) of the jewel in the British Crown shortly to come to an end in the ferocious storm of the Indian Mutiny.

In such an environment, men like Proudfoot thrived. These political officers were entrusted with enormous responsibility and pretty much left alone to run whole countries, some bigger than England itself. With few resources they were expected to govern in Britain's name, responsible for everything from taxation to the dispensation of justice. It is no wonder that so many became the splendid characters that make the history of the Victorian British Empire so fascinating.

The Doctrine of Lapse, instigated by the Governor General, Lord Dalhousie, in 1848, is all too real, as is the fate of Jhansi, Satara and Nagpur, all of which were annexed under the doctrine. Annexation was also the fate of Oudh in 1856, and many historians have pointed to Dalhousie's heavy-handed approach to diplomacy as one of the contributory factors that led to the wholesale slaughter of the Indian Mutiny. It is hard to look back on the policies instigated by the East India Company and feel much pride, but as a storyteller I have to be thankful for the events that created such a vibrant world against which to set Jack's story.

Anyone wanting to learn about the astonishing men of this time would do well to start with *Shooting Leave* by John Ure, or *Soldier Sahibs* by Charles Allen. For more on the lives of the men sent to fight in Britain's most successful colony, I can heartily recommend the superlative *Sahib*, by Richard Holmes. I am forever in debt to this peerless historian.

My apology must also extend to the men of the 24th Foot and the 12th Bengal Native Infantry. Both are regiments who served in India at the time; however, I must admit to stealing the four companies away from their historical duties so I could use them in my story.

The 24th would go on to become one of the best known of all British infantry regiments for their disastrous defeat by the Zulus at Isandlwana, followed by the extraordinary efforts of their B Company on 22 January 1879 at Rorke's Drift. Both events live on, especially in the minds of impressionable young boys like me who sit riveted by the films *Zulu* and *Zulu Dawn*. It is worth noting that the regiment's famous 'Welshness' is something of a myth. They did not become the South Wales Borderers until 1 July 1881, and so for both the time of my story and that of the fight against the Zulus, they were still very much the 2nd Warwickshires and as English as any other regiment of the time.

The 12th Bengal Native Infantry would also find fame, although for much more sinister reasons. In the dreadful bloodletting of the Indian Mutiny, they would turn against their British masters, and a wing of the regiment was present when the garrison of Jhansi mutinied on 5 June 1857. The subsequent massacre of the fifty-six Christian inhabitants of the city is just another in a long list of atrocities committed by both sides in the brutal fight between the rebels and their British rulers.

Jack's time with the British army is now done, for the moment at least, and he faces having to rebuild his life after the cataclysm of battle. Yet he is a survivor and he will march again, no matter how many obstacles appear in his path. He has now enjoyed a meteoric rise to the rank of general, followed by an equally spectacular fall to being nothing more than a humble redcoat. The experience will only serve to galvanise his desire to better himself and to prove just how far an urchin from the rookeries of London can go.

Acknowledgments

Second novels are supposed to be torrid affairs, written with great angst and with much gnashing of teeth. I am happy to say that was not the case for me, and the second instalment in Jack's adventures was written with great relish and barely a moment of hesitation or anxiety.

Without doubt, the fact that there is a second book at all is down to the tireless efforts of my wonder-agent, David Headley, who never fails to greet my endless barrage of questions and fanciful ideas with anything other than a patient smile and perceptive advice. He is the one who made all this happen and I owe him a great deal indeed.

My editor at Headline, Flora Rees, has worked incredibly hard to make this story so much better than I could on my own. I am exceptionally fortunate to have been granted the help and the insight of such a professional and understanding editor for my work. Headline is a great organisation to write for and I am deeply indebted to the efforts of Flora, Ben, Emma, Tom and the rest of the team who have worked so very hard to make this book what it is today.

My family are what makes everything worthwhile. My three fabulous children, Lily, William and Emily, keep my feet firmly on the ground, no matter how grand my plans or ambitions and they have my love and my thanks for always. My mum and dad never fail to offer every support and my friends and family are a constant source of encouragement. To Dan, Mandy, Harry and Kayla all I can say is thank you for everything and roll on the next trip to Florida or France. It cannot come soon enough for me.

I would also like to take this opportunity to thank my father-in-law, Alan, for his support and friendship over the last twenty something years. I often bore him with rambling plot summaries and half-baked ideas but no matter how much I witter on he is always encouraging and supportive.

My work colleagues continue to keep me sane and I am forever grateful for their companionship. The camaraderie at work is the best thing about coming into the office every day and I would like to publically thank them for their backing. I must also thank my counterparts in the repo market for their supportive reaction to my attempts to become a writer. I am proud to know them all and to call so many friends.

As a debut novelist I was amazed at the warm welcome I received from fellow authors as well as from the many bloggers and reviewers who give up their time to read, and more importantly to review, new books coming to the market. They are a wonderful collection of individuals and I look forward to getting to know them better. Without doubt I owe them a large thank you.

Finally, to Debbie, thank you. Enough said.